Ask
for Nothing
More

Ask
for Nothing
More

JAMES ELWARD

HARPER & ROW, PUBLISHERS, New York
Cambridge, Philadelphia, San Francisco, London
Mexico City, São Paulo, Sydney
1817

FIRST EDITION

Designer: Jane Weinberger

Library of Congress Cataloging in Publication Data

Elward, James.
   Ask for nothing more.

   I. Title.
PS3555.L84A9   1984   813'.54   83-48344
ISBN 0-06-015137-4

84 85 86 87 88 10 9 8 7 6 5 4 3 2 1

For
Paul and Eileen Elward
and
Joseph
William
John
Thomas
Patrick James

Prologue

You can see them in public places, if you know where to look. A middle-aged couple, quietly dressed, usually seated at an excellent table: the one with the view or the corner banquette. If you are busy with your own concerns you would consider them just another man and wife and forget about them. But if you study them carefully you would notice little things that might puzzle you. The man is older than the woman, perhaps by ten years. They also talk together throughout their meal, with none of the bored or contented silences of couples who have been married for a long time, but more like people who have a great deal to catch up on.

The sharp-eyed would notice that while they both wear wedding rings, the rings do not match. Brother and sister, you might say, or perhaps business partners, but there is an atmosphere of intimacy about them that is too personal for those relationships. He orders her drink without having to ask her choice. There is nothing secretive about their appearance together; the waiters know them and the captain, clearly certain of a good tip, is most solicitous. There is nothing improper in their behavior, no holding of hands, no subtle whispers followed by quiet smiles, no signs that they have been in love for a long, long time.

However, time is an important part of their meetings. When the coffee is served, both of them check their watches. Sometimes one or the other will leave the table to make a phone call. If the man is left waiting, he will call for the check and study it quietly. If the woman is left at the table, she will examine her appearance in her compact, more from a sense of neatness than vanity. Her hair has gray in it, not the fashionable streaks of an expensive hairdresser but a soft powdering as if she had just come in from the snow. When the one who went to the telephone returns, there is a quick look between them. Usually it means they will make their departure, the woman pulling on her gloves as she rises, the man holding her chair and then her coat, perhaps holding it a second or two longer than needed. But sometimes the call has given them a reprieve; they order another pot of coffee and a brandy and settle back to enjoy the precious extra minutes they will have together.

If there are young people in the restaurants, which is unlikely, as these places are expensive and exclusive, they would be amazed and, perhaps more than their parents, shocked to discover these two are lovers and have been for a long time. Not lovers who will leave to go to some nearby motel for an hour of satisfaction, not givers and takers of expensive presents, not romantics who grow starry-eyed at the sound of "our favorite song." These are lovers of memories, of experiences shared, both of pain and happiness, and most of all of the years in each other's lives.

He is, of course, the Married Man. And she is the Other Woman.

One

The Sunday after the Thanksgiving of 1964 when Mary Conroy realized her marriage was finally over was the first time she saw Dan Martin.

She had been sitting in the apartment alone ever since she had returned from Sunday mass. She went to church seldom these days, but she knew it wasn't fair this week to leave Patsy to face the neighborhood alone. So she had sat with her sister-in-law and the three children. As they stood on the front walk later, Patsy invited her once more to come down for dinner.

"Mary, it's no good sitting by yourself," she said, shooing the three children up the front steps to their apartment. She hoped Tim was awake and in a good mood, but she doubted it. Ever since Mary had knocked on their door the previous Sunday, her face blank and drained, Jack's letter in her hand, Tim had been ready to throw a fist at anyone who so much as spoke above a whisper. "I've got a roast," she added hopefully. "Not just leftover turkey."

"Thanks, Patsy. But the lawyer wants me to get all Jack's bills together. Figure out the total. Not that I expect in just one week we'll have heard from everybody."

Patsy shivered in the cold. Thank heaven the sun was out and the last of the snowstorm of the week before had been neatly shoveled to each side of the concrete walk. They must look crazy standing out there in the cold, she thought, pulling her coat tighter around her bulky body. If the Monahans across the way or old Mrs. Cranick were snooping from their windows they'd wonder what the two of them had to say that couldn't have been handled better indoors. Not that the whole neighborhood didn't already guess what had happened; she had seen the curious eyes in church as she and Mary took their places, Patsy's three squirming children placed for control between them. But she wasn't about to go into the house until she heard the worst. Tim would be wanting to know, although he'd bite off his tongue before he'd ask her directly. And she knew she wasn't smart enough to find out subtly with the children racing around her, banging their toy cars and asking more questions than she suspected Mary could answer.

"Does the lawyer really want you to do that . . . other thing? I mean . . . right away?"

"He says divorce is the only way I can protect myself—and the house. File the papers. He warned me Friday. Do it as quick as possible. Before we discover how many other people Jack owed money to. Something about maybe the house being seized for his debts."

Patsy shivered, and this time it wasn't from the cold. Their two-flat building on the West Side of Chicago was the only solid thing she could count on in life. Tim was a good worker, but jobs were scarce, and with his short temper, having a job this week was no guarantee he would have it next. Without a place to live, where could she and the children go? She looked up at the neat front window of the sunporch of her apartment as if to reassure herself it was still there. The African violets were lined up along the windowsill behind the clean curtains she had washed just this past week. This was *home*. She couldn't bear to think what they'd do without it.

"They couldn't do that, could they? Take the house?" she asked her sister-in-law. She'd always found it hard to talk to Mary, especially about anything intimate like money or love. Mary Scanlon had never been like the other girls who had grown up in the neighborhood, going to the same schools and movies, walking the same dull straight streets. Of course, Patsy was four years older, almost another generation when you were young, but today, when they were both grown women and "family," it wasn't any easier.

"I don't know, Patsy. I don't know what can happen."

"But Jack . . . wouldn't he have to sign something? You can't just get a divorce all by yourself, can you?" Just saying the word *divorce* came hard to Patsy. Nobody she had ever known, or her family either, had ever done such a thing. Divorce was for people who lived in the rich suburbs like Glencoe and Wilmette, with big houses along the lakefront and servants and cocktails before every dinner. It wasn't something for Irish Catholics on the West Side of Chicago who needed their jobs to pay the gas and electric bills. Even the actresses who played nice women in the movies weren't divorced. They were always widowed or something had happened to their fiancés during the war. Or if they did get a divorce, they were always reunited in the end. Only that wouldn't be happening here. Not in real life.

"Fred Reiner says Jack's letter will be enough. At least to file the papers. That way we'll all be protected."

Oh, God, Mary thought, please let this be over! Patsy's scared about her home and I know she wants to help, but I don't think I can take any more. Not today. All week long her sister-in-law had been trying to get close, hovering in the hall doorway when Mary came back from work at the hospital, tapping gently on her door to ask her if she wanted a cup of tea, inventing excuses to climb the stairs to Mary's quiet apartment, expecting to find Mary in tears with a long litany of Jack's sins to relate. The way every other woman in the neighborhood would have done if her husband had walked out. Only every other woman would feel she had been the injured party. And Mary knew she couldn't feel that way; it wouldn't be fair.

Mary forced herself to smile, putting her arm around the older woman. "I'll be all right, Patsy. Honest. And thanks for asking me for dinner. I'm just not very hungry, and I do want to get this all finished so I can drop the papers off at Reiner's office before I go back to work tomorrow morning." She slipped her arm through Patsy's, and together they walked up the stone steps to the entrance of the building. That would give the neighbors something new to talk about, she thought. Standoffish Mary Scanlon—no, Mary Scanlon Conroy—arm in arm with her sister-in-law. She wondered idly if she was still Mary Conroy, or would be after the divorce. She'd have to ask Fred about that if she saw him in the morning. But not his secretary, if he hadn't come in yet. Maggie Feeney had a mouth big enough to be in proportion to her wide hips and sagging bosom; with her living just down the street, it would be all over the parish by sunset that Mary Scanlon was grieving for Jack Conroy, who had walked out on her, grieving enough to want to hang on to his name.

Only I'm not grieving, Mary thought as she started up the hall stairs to her own apartment. I'm not crying or tossing in the wide bed at night in sorrow and loss. They'd really be curious if they knew what she actually felt, had felt since the previous Sunday afternoon when he'd left.

She felt guilty.

It had started as an ordinary Sunday, that day the week before. She begged off church with Patsy with the excuse that she wanted to do some ironing on her one free day from the hospital. Church hadn't mattered so much since her mother died. She did not take the easy release of blaming God as so many people could and did when they lost someone they loved. She knew her mother was at peace, had known it since the morning she had found her still and quiet in the big bed she had shared so many years with Mary and Tim's father. The bed had haunted Mary the last years of her mother's life; each morning when she brought in a breakfast tray, the bed had seemed a little bigger than the night before. A trick, of course. She'd felt it often enough in the hospital, watching the terminally ill, knowing it wasn't the bed that changed in size but the person in it, growing thinner and weaker and paler, day by day, as her mother had. The first thing after the funeral she had offered the bed to Patsy and Tim, knowing from their hastily exchanged glances it was not the sort of thing a woman engaged to be married should be suggesting. But whatever it cost, she wasn't going to start her marriage with Jack Conroy in that bed. Although most of her savings had disappeared in the three years of her mother's illness, she had gone down to Marshall Field's and ordered a new bed, one that had no memories of the past.

Not that the bed had changed anything between her and Jack, she had thought to herself as she folded the comforter and put it back on the silk spread that Sunday afternoon seven days ago. No, be honest, she thought to herself. It wasn't Jack's fault their marriage had become a lonely silence. He was neat and quiet in his ways, always thanking her for any little thing she did for him. Warm and loving in the new bed, respectful of her wishes on the nights when she couldn't force herself to respond. Even today when he left he had given her that shy smile that had always touched her heart and then, impulsively for him, had come back up the stairs to kiss her passionately as she stood in the doorway.

Later she was to remember that kiss, wondering whether things might have been different if she had reacted with the same urgency to his love. If she had pulled him back into the apartment, back to their dark bedroom, held him and comforted him and pressed her body close to his, would he have stayed? Would they have been able to talk this time, instead of living in the arid silence they had shared for most of their married life, along with their mutual guilts and problems?

For she *was* guilty. It had haunted her all this past week. She had cheated him from the beginning. To be fair, she had never told him she was in love, and Jack, patient and tactful, had never asked her to say it, not even in their marriage bed, his naked body tight against her, his strong hands moving across her skin. He'd seemed content with things as they were.

Except of course for the gambling. That, too, she could see was her fault, must have been, or she would have heard rumors before they were engaged. Rumors that would have reached her ears or at least her mother's before she started urging Mary into the marriage.

They had been sitting together quietly, Mary and her mother. This was before the pain had become so terrible, sweeping with great waves over her frail body to disappear just as quickly, leaving her white and shaken. The real pain came only in the last weeks, when she would switch in one minute from clutching Mary's hand in a grip that seemed to use up all of her strength to planning quietly where they would go together on Mary's next vacation. Those were the last days when the doctors had said there was nothing more they could do and allowed Mary to bring her mother home, home to the large bed and the last hours of her life.

No, the afternoon Mary remembered was the one in October two years before her mother died. The window was open, and Tim was burning leaves in the back yard. The smell was toasty, drifting in through the open window. Mary had been reading the newspaper to her mother; that and the radio were all she had to take her out of this room. It would be too dark soon to read without putting a light on, and as she read, Mary was already planning in her mind the supper tray she would start at six.

"Mary, don't read any more. Let's talk." Ellen Scanlon's voice was still strong in those days.

Mary put down the paper. "I'd think you'd be tired of the sound of my voice by now. Don't you want a little rest before supper?"

"I'll rest soon enough." Ellen reached across the bed and took her daughter's hand. "You've been a wonderful daughter, Mary. Even before this terrible thing. Now, don't go making shushing motions as if I didn't know what's the matter with me. You may be the nurse, but I'm not a fool either. And that's what I want to talk about."

"Ma, there's nothing to be worried about. You know what the doctors said. Once you get your strength up, they're going to try a whole new set of treatments, maybe another operation—"

"Mary, don't lie to me or to yourself. This thing is all through me, and nothing's going to cure it. It's not me I'm worried about. It's you."

"Me? I'm fine."

"No, you're not." Ellen sighed, loosening her grip on Mary's hand a little. "I don't know why there's always one in a family that makes the sacrifices and the others just let it happen and don't do anything about it. You had so many bright dreams in your head when you were a child. Not that you'd ever talk about them much. You always were the close-mouthed one. You must have got that from my side of the family; the Scanlons never had a thought in their heads that wasn't out their mouths the next minute. But I'd watch you, your head always buried in a book, reading."

There was silence between them for a moment. The years go by so quickly, Mary thought. She tried to remember the books she would have read in those days, the dreams she must have had. It all seemed so long ago.

"You should have gone on to college," Ellen said with unexpected firmness. "I should have made your father let you go."

"Don't fret about it." What chance would there have been? With her father laid off most of the time after the accident, and the compensation money so small when it finally came, somebody had to bring money into the house. Mary settled back against the headboard next to her mother. "College wouldn't have changed anything. I'd still have to earn a living."

"Not as a nurse! Tidying up after sick people for the rest of your life, that's no way for you. You could have been a teacher, or a secretary for one of the big law firms downtown. You could have traveled, seen something more of the world than what's left of the Chicago stockyards."

"Mother, I'm satisfied. I like my work; I've liked having you to come home to; I wouldn't change a thing."

"And marriage?"

This had been a touchy subject between them for a number of years, and for Ellen, always so tactful, deliberately to bring it up now meant there was no way Mary could avoid hearing what she wanted to say.

Still, she tried once more to change the subject. "Not everybody has to get married. And there are very good reasons why this particular woman shouldn't."

"So you can't have children. That was just one doctor saying that, and you were—what, nineteen? Bodies change."

Mary made no answer. She knew enough about medicine now to know the reason why the doctor had said she was barren, and she knew it was not a condition that years could alter.

Ellen broke the silence between them. "There are men that don't want children. Not all of them are breeders like Tim and his fat Patsy downstairs." Mary didn't have to move to know the look on her mother's face. Patsy had never been what Ellen would have chosen for her one son. Pudgy as a child, plump as a girl, each year she had grown heavier, settling as rapidly as she could into looking like a middle-aged matron. Mary had often wondered if Patsy had done it deliberately as a way of discouraging Tim from desire, but this one subject she could not discuss with Ellen. Sexual relations were barely mentioned, except when Ellen used the old-fashioned phrase "submitting to your husband." It was a burden to be endured the same as the next nine months of carrying the inevitable child.

"Mary, I want you happy." Ellen's voice was softer. "I want you happy and *safe*. That's not easy for a woman alone in this world. Oh, I suppose some can handle it, but it's not right for you. You've got so much to give, so much kindness and warmth and love. I don't want you spending your whole life parceling it out to patients who'll forget you as soon as they leave that hospital downtown, if they ever do leave it on their own two feet.

"I'm not saying marriage is all golden even with a good man, and with all his faults, your father was one of the best. But it's better than being a dried-up old maid, Aunt Mary for Tim's monsters, clinging to the edges of their family parties the rest of your life. I'd rest a lot easier when the time came if I knew you had a man and a home of your own. The home I've already taken care of through Fred Reiner; the man is something you'll have to do on your own."

Mary found herself smiling. "And what am I supposed to do? Go out and lasso one on the streets? Ma, you know I've never been much for the boys."

"Because you never had a chance!" There was anger in Ellen's voice, but Mary knew it wasn't directed at her. "With me to look after and before that your father. Working all hours at the hospital so anyone who did catch your eye could never make any plans." Her anger faded as quickly as it had come. "Mary, you've been cheated of life—you, who had so much to offer. You're thirty. When was the last time you ever had a day without everybody's problems on your shoulders?"

"You haven't heard me complaining, have you? There are all kinds of lives. I'd say what most of the world has is a lot worse than mine."

"Don't go noble on me, Mary Scanlon," her mother retorted with a trace of her old bite. "I want you married before I'm in my grave, and I'm not going to let up on it either."

She hadn't. Almost her last words to Tim two years later as she drifted off into her final sleep were, "Don't you let anything delay Mary's wedding, Tim. No excuses about mourning or funerals or any of that nonsense. I want that as a promise from you."

Tim made the promise almost sheepishly. Neither he nor his mother thought to ask Mary.

Tim was the one who brought Jack Conroy into her life. Five years younger than Mary's brother, Jack had met Tim at a veterans' get-together formed by the parish, though by then it was over fifteen years since the peace had been signed. Most of the men looked as if they had spent their time eating, Tim thought sourly, proud of his flat stomach. And it looked as if all of them had a gold ring on their left hands. Nothing for Mary here, Tim thought, wondering how soon he could duck out and head for home. But then the oldest Monahan boy introduced him to Jack Conroy, new to the neighborhood, and over a pitcher of beer (the only spirits the Monsignor would allow on the premises) the two men found they had a lot in common. Not a drinker, Tim noticed during the next hour, as Jack nursed a single glass of beer. Tim had taught himself to stay away from the stuff, mostly because he always had a suspicion in the back of his mind that if his father had been totally sober the accident that had cost him his leg might never have happened. No wedding ring on Conroy's finger either. Nice-enough looking fellow, Tim thought to himself as he watched Jack carefully. Tall enough for Mary and older too, he found out, with a steady job as assistant manager of that new hardware store over on Western.

By the time the meeting was over it seemed perfectly natural to ask Jack for family dinner the following Sunday.

From the beginning Mary knew Jack was attracted to her. Shyly at first, but with growing persistence, he asked her out, never grumbling when the hospital shifted its schedule and made her cancel one of their dates, never bad-tempered, but always making sure they set another time on another day before he let her off the phone. A decent, honest, respectable man, satisfied with a kiss (or sometimes two) in the hallway before she went up to her mother's apartment, with none of the restless grabbing and pawing the other boys she had gone out with felt was the necessary end to an evening. Perhaps it was because Jack wasn't a boy any more but a grown, lonely man.

By their tenth date he was already talking of marriage. Painfully, Mary tried to explain she would never be able to give him the family he so clearly wanted, but by that time it was too late; he was too much in love.

"If it turns out that's the way it is, Mary, we'll adopt them. God knows I spent enough time being an orphan to know how much it would mean to give one a home." He smiled and smoothed away the half frown on her face. "Or maybe two or three orphans. We'll see how it works out."

So Mary allowed herself to drift into the engagement, finding it peaceful to be loved by him. He coaxed her with patience, much as he might have trained a wild animal to come out of the woods and into a garden. There was only one specific thing that worried her about him: his extravagant way with money. Her diamond ring, when he finally presented it to her, was bigger than any the other girls she knew had received. Clearly expensive, it had come from Peacock's downtown, the best jewelry store in Chicago. When she protested, Jack merely laughed and said he'd been lucky in a poker game. Ellen laughed too, when she heard the story from Jack. She had taken to him at their first meeting, and Mary, grateful for anyone who could bring a smile to her mother's face those last months, had forced back her doubts and said nothing.

They were married two weeks after her mother's funeral. It was a quiet wedding with only Tim and Patsy as witnesses and one of Patsy's soggy cakes afterward at the reception at home. Mary knew the eyes of the parish would be on her waistline for the next months, wondering if the wedding had to be that soon because a baby was expected. How furious and disappointed they'd all be by next summer, she thought, as she closed her overnight bag that afternoon. Jack had planned a honeymoon in Florida, and Mary had even managed to get a week from the hospital for it, although the younger nurses usually had to take what time was left after the registered nurses and the supervisors made their choices.

Only two days before the wedding, Jack had told her they would have to cancel the trip. "Something at the store," he'd said, and for once his face was closed, shutting her out. Their wedding night was spent at an expensive hotel downtown, with dinner in the main dining room and dancing afterward. It made a better beginning for their marriage, Mary thought later. Better than flying for hours to someplace without enough conversation between them to last more than ten minutes. Jack was a good dancer, and Mary, who always thought of herself as awkward, found her happiest moments were when he put his arms around her and twirled her lightly around the floor.

Reality didn't arrive until nearly a month after the wedding, with the bills that came the first of January. Jack had been lavish at Christmas—too lavish, Mary realized, as she opened the windowed envelopes. The silver toilet articles could go back. But she had already worn the full thick wool coat ("a real French design," Jack had said Christmas morning), and that would have to be paid for by installments. Even if they put five dollars a month aside for it, it would still be a couple of years before it was completely hers. Unless of course they used the mortgage money, which Mary kept under her slips in the bottom drawer of the dresser. She added to the envelope every payday. She never told Jack about that money, not knowing for sure why she kept it a secret but feeling it was her responsibility, not his. Only on the day the bills came in there was twenty-five dollars less in the brown envelope than there had been the week before.

They didn't fight that evening when Jack came home. When he saw the envelope on the dining-room table and Mary's face, he didn't even try to deny what she had already guessed.

"It's just that I want the best for you, Mary," he said over and over as they talked. "I'm usually lucky gambling, always have been." His eyes were tired, and there was a new edge of bitterness in his voice. "It's one of the few good things you learn in an orphanage or the army. Only lately . . . maybe I'm trying too hard."

"Jack, I don't ask for things. Have I ever? I'm happy with you, we have our home, our jobs—"

"We've got nothing, Mary!" He didn't say it with anger, but she could hear the fury inside him. "We have a home because your mother had the sense to leave this place to you instead of Tim. As for jobs, you're cleaning up other people's messes and I'm measuring out a pound of nails. That isn't what I want in life! That isn't what I want for you."

She pointed to the unpaid bills spread out on the kitchen table between them. "Is this any better?"

"Mary, there are times when you have to take a chance. I don't think I could stand living if I thought all we'd ever get was fifty years of me standing behind the counter of another man's store and watching you come home, tired to the bone, not living, not having anything, just watching the years go by with nothing to look forward to."

Children, she had thought numbly. If he had children, even the hope of them, he wouldn't be feeling this bleakness; there'd be no silences between them.

"Jack, I'm happy with you," she said finally. "I am, really. I never expected life to be glamorous or exciting. Just steady. That would be enough for me." She put her hand flat on the bills. "But I can't even have that if I have to worry about this all the time."

He promised never to gamble again. She didn't know it, but it was the first of the same promises he would make in the next two years, make and break whenever he had a hunch or got a racetrack tip, and make all over again. The last of her savings went first, then the money she had put aside toward the principal of the mortgage of the two-story building.

Next it was her diamond ring, over Jack's protests. Finally it was the finance companies, so friendly when you first walked in and so cold when a payment was missed. There were attachments made on Jack's salary, and the owner of the store, who had always seemed so cheerful to Mary in the beginning, began to look at her with hard eyes when she came by. Jack wasn't doing the store's accounts any more, and the owner had the only key to the cash register.

"As if I'd steal from him," Jack said with bitterness that last year.

He tried to reform, she had to give him that. They had taken all their bills to Fred Reiner, the lawyer, and the three of them had worked out a series of payments to be made from Mary's salary. She'd tried to be happy that day, but she knew in the back of her mind that this wasn't all that Jack owed. How many friends must have slipped him a ten or more when they thought he had a good tip?

It was the flowers that hurt her most. Such a silly thing, she knew, but it had been one of the bright things of their courtship and the first months of their married life. Every time he came in the house he had brought a flower for her. Sometimes a single rose or a little bunch of daisies, sometimes something more. He couldn't bring them now because they would be bought with her money, and his pride wouldn't let that happen. If she could only have held him in her arms and said, "A few more pennies wouldn't matter, and I miss them so." Only they both knew a few pennies *did* matter, and since she had been the one to be so hard about money, he never brought flowers again.

It was snowing lightly that Sunday a week ago. After Jack left and Mary made the bed, the bed they slept in silently now, as far apart from each other as they could, she had gone directly to the new hiding place she had for the mortgage money. She changed the location every week now, resorting to tricks she had read about in books about spies: the single hair placed between the lid of the coffee can that would show if it had been disturbed, the tape on the envelope. Cheap tricks that made her angry and bitter even as she did them, but if she didn't, she knew that each time she went out of the apartment she'd be afraid. She knew the money should go in a bank, but she'd heard enough grim stories of accounts being attached for debts not to trust either the institutions or her husband.

She knew before she opened the envelope that the dollar bills wouldn't be there. There was a piece of paper instead, neatly folded, with Jack's careful handwriting on it.

Dear Mary,

Yes, I found the money. There was supposed to be an absolute, positive winner in the first race yesterday. He won all right, but I got greedy or dumb or something, and your money and what I'd won went the way it always goes.

Mary, I'm heading out. I made that promise to myself if I didn't come home a winner last night. This is one promise I'm going to try and keep. I met a friend of mine with a trucking company. He's leaving Chicago this afternoon for—well, I guess I'd better not tell you where in case anybody comes after me. And they might. Don't worry, I didn't take anything from the store, and don't let the boss try to say I did. I'm not a criminal. Not yet, at least.

But I don't know what I might become if I don't get away. It isn't you. Please believe that. You've been the one good thing I've had in my life, and the fact I've messed up that shows there isn't much to me and probably never will be. I guess if I'm meant to be a bum I can do that on my own, but I'm not going to drag you down with me. So I'm leaving before you get to hate me. Or before I get to hate myself even more. Because I do hate myself, Mary, for making you unhappy, for putting you through these past two years. I can't take watching you so thin and nervous, jumping every time the phone rings, wondering who it is wanting his money. It'll just get worse if I stay, Mary. I know that.

So I'm breaking off. I don't know what the law says about a husband's debts; you'd better talk to Fred Reiner about that. He'll probably suggest you file for divorce, and if he does, I want you to do it. I couldn't take you losing the apartment building your dad worked so hard for because of me.

Someday I'll pay you back—and with honest money, don't worry. In the meantime, I just wish I could leave you a dozen red roses in this envelope to tell you I think you're the most wonderful woman in the whole world.

Love,
Jack.

She had cried then, the tears spilling down her face, one of them making a small bubble on the paper in front of her. She blotted it quickly; the paper would have to be seen by a lot of eyes before she could put it safely away, and she wouldn't have them think it was Jack's tears.

After a while, she washed her face with cold water and went down the hall stairs to tell Tim and Patsy.

The next week was more of a hell than she could have imagined. She hadn't planned on taking off from work, but after she'd talked to the lawyer on Monday it seemed like the phone at the hospital nurses' station never stopped ringing. Maggie Feeney must have had her ear pressed against the door that morning, for Mary had barely got to work when the calls started. It happened all day long, until her supervisor told her she might as well go home, she wasn't doing any good for the patients. All sorts of people were on the phone: neighbors and men she barely knew from the stores where they'd bought their groceries and strange persons whose names she didn't recognize. The worst had been Thursday when Tim Junior came home from school, his face dirty and streaked with dried tears, saying someone had called his Uncle Jack a thief.

Mary tried to keep a list of the amounts people said Jack owed, but after a while the amount got too high for her to think about. She'd known Jack was well liked, and God knows he had charm, but she had had no idea that so many people, people she didn't even know, would lend him a ten- or a twenty-dollar bill with no more than his promise that someday they'd get it back. Even Tim finally admitted to her, somewhat embarrassed, that he'd lent Jack over a hundred dollars. Oddly, it was at her Tim seemed to be angry, not Jack, as if she had led her husband into extravagance.

The phone was still ringing on and off all this Sunday afternoon, but she couldn't answer it. As far as she had figured through the week, there was close to fifteen thousand dollars she would have to pay back somehow, whether she was legally responsible or not. Or every time she bought a pair of shoes or a loaf of bread there'd be the hostile eyes of her neighbors on her, wondering when she was going to return what she owed. She couldn't help thinking that. It was her debt, not Jack's. I shouldn't have married him, she thought dully. He never would be in this trouble if she had been stronger, if she had stood up to her mother, turned down his invitations, faced that she was a woman with nothing to give. Now he was off in some strange place with only the clothes on his back. Someplace warm, she hoped. Where his luck would change.

Patsy knocked on the door. "Mary? I don't want to disturb you," she called through the closed door, "but the hospital called. They've been trying all afternoon to reach you. Please, would you call them? Tim's ready to pull the phone right out of the wall if it rings again."

"Thanks, Patsy. Tell Tim I'll call right now." She went to the kitchen and dialed the familiar number. Selena answered at the nurses' station.

"Mary, can you get down here tonight?" she said, without even saying hello. "I know you weren't supposed to come back to work until tomorrow, but we've got a real problem. Mr. Martin—he's on the Board of Directors—he's here throwing his weight around. His wife was in some kind of a skiing accident in Vermont. He flew her back today, private plane no less, and he's insisting on private nurses around the clock. On a Sunday! I can't get anybody." She added, before Mary could answer, "He's willing to pay extra."

Extra. That would come in handy, Mary thought. . . .

It was dark outside the windows of the twelfth floor when Mary finally arrived, crisp in a freshly starched uniform. Mary always hated the short days of winter; they made the night duty so much longer. At the end of the hall by the nurses' station, she could see Selena talking to an angry man.

He was wearing ski clothes, very out of place on Twelve, and apparently had been chain-smoking cigarettes, strictly against the rules even on this floor. Twelve was the floor of private rooms and special attention. But if he was a member of the Board of Directors of Midwestern Hospital she suspected he would be given the best of attention if he had stood there stark naked.

If Mary had known that evening this was the man who would teach her how to love and be loved, she would have turned around at once and gone back down the elevator to the empty winter streets outside.

But you never know the future, she realized later. That was perhaps the greatest blessing you got in life.

Two

Joan Martin couldn't feel the pain any more. She knew it was still there, waiting at the outer edges of her body. She imagined it at the ends of her fingers or toes, waiting for whatever they had given her to wear off before attacking again. But for this moment she was still safe, protected from the sharpness that had made her cry since the accident. She would be asleep again soon, and all this would be part of the past.

There were voices somewhere in the room, but it was impossible for her to open her eyes.

"'Can't you do something?" That would be Dan; even with her eyes closed she knew the expression that he would have on his handsome face: worried, thick eyebrows crowding together in a frown.

"We'll give her another injection, Mr. Martin. She'll sleep through the night."

An injection. That would be good. They were touching her, only she couldn't seem to feel them. Perhaps that was the medicine.

"Mr. Martin? Why don't you go home and get some sleep?"

"I'm not leaving her alone." Joan could hear the firmness in his voice. It had always been there, even when he was a skinny boy in her father's office, working his way through school. Strong, definite, so sure of himself.

"She won't be alone, I promise. I'll stay with your wife all night, right here in the room." That would be the nurse, Joan thought, as she drifted away from them. Another woman charmed by his concern, by his looks and strength. Not that Joan ever had to worry about him. She knew her husband. Thirteen years of marriage and he'd never strayed. She made sure of that.

That was the last Joan heard that night. Whatever they had given her was working swiftly. The pain was over; it wouldn't come back. Not with Dan to protect her. Dan and Daddy. They would see that nothing really bad happened. She was Joan Martin. Joan Paige Martin. That nice Mrs. Martin with the handsome husband, who had kept her figure even after two children. Joan Martin, who had dozens of friends and a beautiful Lake Shore Drive apartment that was photographed in magazines and a husband who adored her and brought her wild presents and took her on trips and taught her to ski. But she wouldn't think about skiing. She'd think about everything being perfect again. Surely by tomorrow . . .

Only it wasn't perfect the next day, or the days that followed.

Mary soon realized the major problem with having Joan Martin as a patient was not going to be Joan but the world that surrounded her. By the end of the first week Joan had requested Mary be moved to the four in the afternoon to midnight shift. "I'll sleep from then until morning anyway," she explained to Mary practically. "Surely there has to be one nurse with insomnia who wouldn't mind those hours. After only one week you're beginning to look like you should be in this bed instead of me."

Mary laughed, but there was a certain amount of truth in what Mrs. Martin said. She still had to go to Fred Reiner's office nearly every day, and trying to fit that in with a regular schedule made sleep almost impossible.

"Besides, you'd really be doing me a favor," added Joan. She smiled slightly. It was a charming smile, even with the scratches on her face, making her look pretty and much younger than her age. "Miss Wishy-Washy who's on in the afternoons is so scared of Dan and my father that she turns beet red the minute they come into the room. Anything they want changed she instantly says 'Yes.' I think if they said they wanted the whole floor roped off she'd be down in Maintenance trying to get string. Now you," she added, watching Mary as she straightened the covers at the foot of her bed, "you look as if you could tell off both of them—and get away with it."

"Are you sure you want someone tough around?"

"Absolutely! If being tough is going to get me out of this place any faster, I give you full permission to chew my head off. Or anything else that's hanging loose." Her eyes looked at Mary imploringly. Not for the first time Mary understood how her patient managed to twist the men in her life around her finger. Who could resist that look? "Please, Mary? Would you make the switch? For my sake?" Mary was happy to agree.

No, Joan was not the problem. The problem was who and what she was: the wife of the very demanding Daniel Martin, member of the Board of Directors of the hospital, and the daughter of real estate magnate Evan Paige, former Chairman of the Board. Between the two of them they had upset practically every rule governing the indulged patients on the twelfth floor, and after two or three encounters Mary would have been perfectly happy never to have seen either of them again.

"Why hasn't the specialist been in to see her? Her arm's still hurting her, and those scratches on her face—shouldn't there be bandages or something?" This was Dan on one of his daily visits.

"Now, Dan," Joan would say gently, putting out her left hand. Her good hand, Mary noticed, not the other one. Not the hand that had been x-rayed and shown to have no visible signs of damage. That hand lay quietly on the bed, graceful, beautiful, but more or less motionless.

"Mr. Martin, Dr. Osborne said there was no point in returning until a few more days have passed and the superficial injuries have had a chance to heal."

"You mean, Nurse, when he comes back from his winter holiday in Palm Beach. My God, is this any way to look after someone as badly hurt as my wife?"

"Dan, all I'm here for is a broken leg, and there isn't much they can do about that except let it heal. I could probably go home with that now if you'd let me. Couldn't I, Mary?" Joan had started calling her by her first name after that first dawn when she had washed her and changed her nightgown. Hospital rules or not, Joan was not going to be seen by anyone in the limp white open-at-the-back apron that was standard. "Not a chance," she had stated firmly. "I may be part of the wounded, but I don't intend to look like it."

"You are staying here, my sweet baby," Dan announced. "Until every part of you is healthy and beautiful and in sound working condition again. And that is an order."

"Yes, Massa," Joan replied in what Mary privately called her "little girl voice." Afterward, she apologized to Mary. "He just worries about me."

"We all do."

After the first week, Mary began to question that. Joan's right leg seemed to be responding normally, although it was hard to get any reaction with the cast covering all of it down to her toes. But no one seemed to notice how seldom she moved her right arm, now out of its bandages.

Privately, Mary examined Joan's records, having ones brought up from the files of her physical condition in the past. There was no sign in any of the charts that there had been any previous injury to her right side, not until this dreadful skiing accident. After returning the files Mary had tried to rationalize her suspicions. After all, she had never met the girl before.

She should call Mrs. Martin a woman, she realized. After all, she was four years older than Mary herself and the mother of two children. Hard to think of her that way, though; she looked so fragile and young lying there in bed. Since Mary had not seen her before the accident, how could she possibly know what she had been like? Only . . . certain things bothered her. That Joan would reach across her body for the water glass, using her left hand, if a nurse had placed the tray on the wrong bedside table. That she would prop up the mirror on her good leg when she arranged her hair before Mr. Martin's visits, rather than holding it with her presumably now-healed right arm. Once she even had the courage to question Joan about this, but her patient dismissed it with a light laugh. "Nothing wrong, Florence Nightingale. My arm just aches a little bit. Probably arthritis or bursitis or one of those awful signs of my increasing old age."

Mary smiled obligingly at the remark and forgot her doubts. For the moment.

But she wondered if Joan had the same doubts. For example, Mrs. Martin would not allow her friends to visit her. "Ugh," she'd said, making a small frown. "Not when I look like this. It'll be all over Chicago that I've turned into Scarface." Nor had her children been allowed admittance, although the boy at ten and the girl with the brisk name of Paige at twelve were old enough to visit patients. "Let's not scare them either," Joan had said sensibly. She made a point of calling home each day when the children would have returned from school and talking to them and the housekeeper, but Mary felt Joan made the calls more from duty than a need to be part of her children's lives.

No, Mary realized as the days went past, it was only Dan who mattered to Joan. Sometimes during his brief visits Dan would ask Mary to leave the room. When she returned she found that whatever intimacies they had exchanged had left both of them unsatisfied and vaguely puzzled. Gradually Dan stopped asking for privacy, content to have Mary as a starched-white chaperone as he sat beside his wife's bed and talked to her of his day, interrupting himself only to ask how she felt and then, not waiting for an answer, plunging back into the thread of his conversation. After his visits the rest of the evening would be quiet, a peaceful time in which the two women could talk, Joan more than Mary, and always about her husband.

"He's brilliant, you know," Joan remarked one night after he'd left. "I don't mean just bright and hard-working and ambitious. I mean really brilliant."

"And how do you define that?" Mary was working on Joan's back, rubbing the warm perfumed alcohol in carefully, trying to find a reaction from the muscles near her right shoulder.

"Oh . . . the way he looks at things. You should hear him talk about this city, its future, how it's going to grow. It's almost as if he were standing above Chicago, seeing the whole pattern of the streets and highways, knowing just how it'll change; this generation, the next one." She moved a little under Mary's strong hands. "I think that's what attracted me, right from the beginning."

"I didn't know city planning could be that seductive."

"You think I'm joking? Besides, it wasn't seduction then. I was—what, thirteen? And he was almost twenty. I was Daddy's spoiled brat. Mother had died so many years before. I was so afraid some other girl would trap Dan before I was old enough."

"He doesn't look the kind of man who could be trapped."

"He wasn't. I had to make him fall in love with me to get him to propose. And believe me, that wasn't easy."

"Sure. You're obviously one of my more repulsive patients." The night nurse would be coming in soon and would expect Joan ready to sleep through her shift. But Joan was in a mood to talk and would not be hurried. For the first time Mary found herself wanting her to continue, almost as if it were a story she had started reading in the middle and had no idea how it began or ended.

"I'm serious, Mary. Oh, I knew all the tricks of how a girl is supposed to get a man interested: the low-cut dresses, the perfume, the lean-a-little-closer-when-he-lights-your-cigarette routine. My God, women my age knew all those gimmicks before we had our second teeth.

"But Dan was different. Being the boss's daughter didn't help. Not that Daddy could do much. Paige Properties needs Dan a lot more than he needs us."

She took a sip from the cup of tea Mary handed her.

"Maybe that was part of it. The challenge. Everything I'd been trained to believe was important had been made easy for me. I was attractive enough, bright enough, and although Daddy gambles on land it's not the kind of problems you and your husband faced, so I've always been rich enough."

"Well, whatever it was that you did or have, it seems to have worked. Nobody could be more devoted than Mr. Martin."

"Do you think so? Really?" Joan lay back in her bed, her face puzzled. "I've been wondering about that, lying here in the hospital. Maybe I never had time before, to think." She smiled a little. "It's very time-consuming, being married to Dan. He's so full of energy, so hungry for things I guess I'd always taken for granted: money and power . . . and what I guess you'd call success. It hasn't always been easy for a West Side Martin to be married to a Lake Forest debutante."

"He loves you. He married you. Happy ending."

"Is it? I've been thinking about that too. Oh, I love him. In every possible way there is. But that wasn't the only reason I married him." She hesitated for a moment, and Mary could see in her face a cool determination she would have been willing to swear no man—not Joan's husband or her father or even her doctors—had ever seen. "You see, Mary, I think everyone, sooner or later in life, has to face a challenge you can't be sure of winning. Not with all the advantages of looks or education or being the boss's daughter. Maybe we all need that challenge. Maybe that's what makes us fall in love. . . . You meet a man you feel you aren't good enough for, even with all the fancy makeup and carefully straightened teeth and exercise classes. And he falls in love too. But it isn't the happy ending. That's the scary part. It's just the beginning. You wonder how long the spell will last, when the day will come that he'll look at you like a stranger. When he'll realize he's given the major part of his life to an ordinary woman who isn't his equal at all, just a moderately pretty, moderately intelligent woman who will be middle-aged soon."

Mary took the teacup from her patient's hand and set it firmly on the tray. "You listen to me, Joan Martin. You're an absolutely gorgeous knockout whose husband is damn lucky to have you, broken leg and all. And before you dissolve into a mass of self-pity, let me get you your bedpan and your sleeping pill. We'll worry about the problems of middle age another time."

Joan had laughed at that, and their evening together had ended cheerfully. But later, traveling home on the bus, Mary found herself thinking of what her patient had said. Was that what love was, the challenge that Joan had talked about? Was that what had been missing between her and Jack? She shook her head in disbelief. Whatever marriage was, it shouldn't be that, an edgy competition, an endless race to keep up with the man you loved.

Still, she'd feel a lot more relaxed about Joan's future if there hadn't been those unexplained signs that none of the doctors seemed to notice.

The signs were finally noticed the day after Christmas. Christmas was almost a forgotten holiday for Mary that year. She gave money to Tim and Patsy, emphasizing this was not part of repaying Jack's debts but for presents for the children. The few Christmas cards she received she opened and, after glancing at the name, dropped in the wastebasket; this was not a year when she would feel pressured into answering. It was a year for Christmas to be concentrated on the Martins.

The pleasant Negro housekeeper Mary had talked to on the phone arrived at the hospital on Christmas afternoon with the Martin children. Joey, the boy, was mischievous, full of questions, never still. His sister sat primly on the edge of a straight-backed chair; even opening the presents their mother had saved for them, the little girl was coolly polite. It was the boy who crawled onto his mother's bed and asked pointedly, "Why can't you put both arms around me?" Joan looked over his small shoulders at Mary anxiously but before Mary could move the housekeeper had the children bustling into their outer coats. Dan made no response to the question, but Mary caught a look at his face and it was grimmer than she had ever seen it, even more serious than that first night when his wife had been brought to the hospital.

The following day the truth finally came out. Late in the afternoon a Miss Wallis had arrived from the Paige Properties office with papers for Joan to sign. Mary gathered that for some sort of tax reason (quite obviously to lower the amount to be paid) Joan had a part interest in her father's firm. The secretary was a brisk, efficient woman in her middle thirties, not particularly attractive, but part of that may have been a deliberate effort to look as businesslike as possible. Mary would have stayed out of the room during the meeting, but her presence was needed as a witness to the signing of certain papers. When the necessary details had been settled, Joan's doctor came in and Miss Wallis used this as an opportunity to ask Mary to see her to the elevator. Once outside, with the door to Joan's room firmly closed, she stood in front of the nurse.

"What's the matter with her?" Miss Wallis asked Mary, the conventional smile gone from her face.

Mary found herself stumbling for words. "A broken leg—"

"I'm not talking about that," said the other woman briskly. "What's the matter with her face? Her right arm? Is that whole side of her body paralyzed or something?"

"We've found no signs of it," said Mary. She found herself becoming defensive at this direct attack from an outsider.

"Then I suggest you'd better start looking," said Miss Wallis. "This isn't like Mrs. Martin. Maybe she can fool her husband and her father and even you people here at the hospital, but she doesn't fool me. What else happened to her during that ski accident? Did she have a stroke?"

"I . . . I don't know. Nothing has shown up on any of the tests."

"You'd better take some new tests, then. I'm not kidding. I know Mr. Martin. He won't interfere with your little world of medicine until you say his wife is perfectly well. Then, if she isn't, all hell is going to break loose. And since you're apparently the one constant nurse here, you're going to get it in the neck. Believe me," she added for emphasis. "I've been working for Mr. Martin for the last ten years and I know him, inside out."

Know him and love him, Mary thought to herself. She wasn't usually that quick at spotting other people's emotions, but it was clear the plain woman standing in front of her was far more concerned about her boss than his wife.

"Thank you for the suggestion, Miss Wallis," Mary said quietly. Now that someone had finally said it out loud she could face her own suspicions. "I've been worried myself, but since I didn't know Mrs. Martin before—well, it seemed a little presumptuous to say anything." She tried to smile reassuringly. "Nurses don't rank very high around here, as you may have gathered."

"Then you'd better find somebody who does rank high enough. And fast." Kay Wallis nodded toward the room they had just left. "That lady in there is in big trouble, and somebody had better do something about it."

Mary spent the afternoon wondering whom she should approach. Joan's own physician, Dr. Osborne, was a highly social, very busy man who, summoned back from his vacation, contented himself with brief, brisk visits, concentrating solely on what he could discover about the progress of the broken leg. Various interns were available, of course, but while they might be interested, even anxious, to be called in to look at the wife of a member of the Board of Directors, it would not sit well with their superiors, a fact Mary suspected they knew. Finally Mary settled on Dr. MacCauley, a specialist who had, she knew, concentrated on nervous disorders since medical school. Without too many questions he agreed to check on her patient, Mary tactfully staying out of the room during the interview. When MacCauley reappeared, his usually pleasant face was serious.

"What the hell is the matter with that old poop Osborne? Your patient has suffered severe nerve damage down her whole right side. Somebody should have spotted it before this. I'll talk to her doctor today. When her husband comes, tell him I want to see him in my office."

Mary nodded and opened the door to her patient's room. Joan was sitting up in bed, her eyes fastened on Mary, and the nurse could tell Joan was finally facing the reality of her problem. There were no tears in her eyes. Only, when she looked at Mary, it was almost a look of accusation.

Generally the days between Christmas and New Year's were wasted time in a hospital. Labs were closed; specialists and technicians came in late and left early or made simple excuses for not appearing at all. It was understood that nothing of a practical nature was going to be done to any of the patients until after New Year's Day. With the influence of Dan Martin and his father-in-law, this was completely changed at Midwestern. A new specialist was flown in from Johns Hopkins, and a day later another one from New York. Over the disapproving Osborne's protests, Joan's cast was replaced with another one, shorter and lighter, and in the interim before the new cast was added every part of her body was subjected to new tests, x-rays, and injections.

By New Year's Eve a final analysis had been made of Joan's condition. Dan Martin arrived late in the evening, faultlessly dressed in dinner clothes, but Mary could tell from his flushed face he had primed himself with several drinks before the visit. He carried champagne and caviar.

Mary left them alone, ignoring a pleading look in Joan's eyes. When she heard the buzzer at the nurses' station it was nearly eleven, long past the time Mr. Martin or any other visitor should have left. He was seated on the bed as she came in, holding his wife tightly. Joan had her good arm around his neck, but like the pale reminder of the pain that surrounded them both, her right arm lay quietly at her side. She had been crying, Mary noticed, and while her hair was rumpled and the last of her makeup had long since disappeared, Mary thought she had never looked more beautiful.

"Dan, I'm going to be all right. Honest. Now you go home." He nodded, almost as if he didn't trust himself to speak. "But it's New Year's Eve. I don't want Mary to have to fight the crowds on the buses, if they're still running. Couldn't you drop her off first?"

The idea clearly wasn't anything that gave Dan pleasure, but he agreed somewhat brusquely.

Mary would have protested, but Joan shooed her off. "I'm going to sleep like a baby. And I suspect Dan has a few things to talk to you about." With that she turned away from them, settling into the pillows. Mary put out the lights and followed Joan's husband into the hall.

"I'll just check with the nurse at the station. The midnight-to-eight nurse might be a little late tonight because of the holiday," she said.

He made no answer. When she had picked up her coat, not bothering to change from her uniform, he was still standing where she had left him, for once not even smoking.

In the elevator on the way down he remained silent. It wasn't until they were outside that he said anything.

"Look, do you mind if we get a drink first?" Without waiting for an answer he took her arm firmly and led her across the street to a small bar. Whatever holiday festivities were being held throughout Chicago that night, they had not touched this place. It was small and quiet, and they were practically the only customers. When he had placed Mary in a booth and got them two drinks, he sat down opposite her.

"This thing with my wife, it's pretty bad, isn't it?"

"I haven't seen all the reports. . . ." She was lying badly and she knew it.

"I have. So don't try and soften it up. Is she paralyzed? Permanently?"

"All they know is the nerves in some parts of the right side of her body have been severely damaged."

"A stroke?"

"No, that's a shock from the brain. This is different." She leaned forward, trying to make him understand. "I'm not a doctor, but—well, can you imagine the nerves as something like an electric cord, the kind you have on a lamp or a radio?" He was staring at her intently, expressionless, not moving, not even lighting the fresh cigarette in his hands. "All right. The important part of the wire is covered with rubber or some kind of insulation. Nerves have the same protection, as well as being shielded by muscles and ligaments. Some of that protection on the right-hand side is badly torn, and they don't know yet how severe the damage is."

"Is she going to be crippled? Forever?"

"Nothing as dramatic as that. The body has a remarkable way of healing itself, if left alone." Mary leaned back and took a swallow of her drink. She wasn't used to whiskey, but she barely noticed the bitter taste, facing the man opposite her. "Maybe an electric cord wasn't a very good image. A wire can't heal itself, but a nerve can. There are things that can be done. We're not back in the Middle Ages. Massage, rest, heat treatments, eventually a plan of exercise—"

"Joan talked about that. She wants to go home, to get started doing whatever she's supposed to do until she's well."

"Her leg . . ."

"She says that can mend just as well at her home as in a hospital bed."

"Probably."

"The hospital gets on her nerves—" He grimaced. "Bad choice of words. Or is it? Anyway, she wants out."

Beneath that fragile exterior is a strong woman, Mary thought. What Joan wants, Joan will get.

"She needs help," her husband went on. "She knows that. She wants you to come with her. There's plenty of room at the apartment if you could arrange to stay over."

"But I'm not a registered nurse, Mr. Martin. Or a therapist. I'm just a floor nurse, a hospital employee." So this was what Joan had meant about "things to talk over"!

"And an underpaid one too, I'll bet. Look, don't worry about your job at the hospital. I can fix it so you'll be assigned to Joan. Leave of absence or something. I'll double your pay."

How she would have liked to tell this arrogant man that wouldn't be necessary. As if he had sensed her rejection of his use of money, his face softened. He took a deep breath and looked down at his glass quickly. "I ask for things badly. I apologize. I guess I'm not in the habit of asking. It's just, if Joan wants you . . ." He twisted the glass in his powerful hands around and around, making a wet circle on the cardboard coaster under it. "The whole damn skiing thing was my fault. I knew she wasn't up to that slope. But she always wants to try and go farther, do a little bit more. . . ."

Keeping up with you, Mary thought to herself. Not holding you back.

"And I've never said no to her. She's always had so much spirit. She's always been so perfect at everything she did. Sometimes it almost frightens me." He looked directly at Mary. "You can't help wondering what a girl like that ever saw in a guy like me."

Two secrets, Mary thought. Two people both thinking they weren't good enough for each other. Obviously in love, obviously attracted, with wealth and children and success and years of living together behind them, and they neither of them knew each other at all. She thought of her own marriage to Jack, of her father and her mother, Tim and Patsy. Was this what was behind the facade of all marriages, happy or not? Two people sharing a life . . . only it's really four. You as he sees you and you as you know yourself to be; he as he is and as he wants you to see him. It frightened her.

"Will you think about it at least? I mean, nothing could be done for another couple of weeks, anyway, Mrs. Conroy." He hesitated, frowning a little. "It *is* Mrs. Conroy?"

"Yes."

"Would Mr. Conroy object?"

"We're divorced. Practically." She could see him almost relax with relief. One less obstacle to worry about. As if he had guessed her reaction, he had the grace to look embarrassed.

"I'm . . . sorry. Still, it means you might be free to take the job." He got out of the booth without asking if she were ready to leave. "I won't press you now." He put some money on the bar and, almost as an afterthought, held the door open for her. As they started for his car, a long Cadillac parked in front of the hospital entrance, he spotted a lone cab coming along the empty street.

"There's an empty taxi . . . would you mind taking that home?" Without waiting for her answer he flagged the cab down, fishing for bills from his wallet. It was starting to snow again, Mary noticed as she got into the cab. The wind was already sliding a light film of it across the pavements.

Before he closed the door Dan Martin shoved a couple of twenty-dollar bills in her hand. That look was back on his face again, that desperately unhappy look she had seen so often when he left his wife's room, when there was no more reason to pretend. Tonight it frightened her enough to speak.

"Are you all right?" she asked.

"Don't be an idiot," he said gruffly. "Of course I'm not all right. And if you'll kindly get started, I'm going back to that bar and do something I've never done before in my whole life. I'm going to get blind roaring drunk." With that he slammed the cab door shut and strode back across the street.

For a change the cab driver was neither curious nor talkative, and Mary had a chance to think during the long trip west, away from the lakefront and the tall apartment houses of the wealthy. Without noticing it, she kept smoothing the bills he had given her. She should be angry, she knew. Not that she wanted him to drive her home; getting the taxi had been a lucky break. Otherwise he would have attacked her with more questions about his wife's condition during the whole ride, and, having no answers, she was glad to avoid that. Even his arrogance was almost forgivable. And the extra money would be a help, no denying that. She knew she could help Joan, she liked her, and certainly Joan would need someone with her.

Only something kept bothering her, something she couldn't explain that made her feel almost guilty, the way she had when Jack had left. She found herself comparing the two men as the driver headed slowly, carefully west on the nearly empty streets. In a strange way, they were alike. Both of them ambitious, both full of dreams of a better life, and both of them loving their wives and not really knowing anything about them. It's as if we live in two different countries, Mary thought as the cab made its way off the main avenues into the small blocks where she lived. With one exception, she thought wryly. Mr. Martin married the boss's daughter, and Jack had had the misfortune to pick a dried-up old maid with nothing to give. I shouldn't get involved with the Martins, she thought. Even for the money.

Unexpectedly, Tim was waiting for her there in the hall as she came in, his worn bathrobe pulled tightly, disapprovingly around his thin body.

"You had a phone call," he said, without any greeting. "From Jack. He wouldn't say where he was, but he wanted to tell you he had a job and to wish you a happy New Year. I told him you were at the hospital working for the rich people, but he said he'd already tried there." Tim stepped closer to Mary in the narrow hallway, suspicion clear in his eyes, and sniffed at the air between them. "I didn't know you were out on the town drinking." Without another word he closed the door in her face.

Half a highball, Mary thought as she climbed up the stairs to her apartment. She was putting her key in the lock when she heard in the distance the sounds of church bells and noisemakers. Happy New Year, Mary Conroy, she said to herself as she stepped inside.

Three

It was February before Joan Martin left the hospital. By then there was no question that Mary would accompany her. One talk about the unpaid bills on her lawyer's desk had taken care of that. In a way, Mary was as anxious for the moving day as her patient. The faces of her neighbors remained hostile, and Tim complained so much and so loudly about her changed position it would be a relief to be away from him during the week.

"I thought the Scanlons had risen enough in life that they didn't have to wait on the rich any more," he had grumbled through the last Sunday dinner they spent together.

"I'm nobody's maid, Tim. It's just that Joan—Mrs. Martin feels more comfortable with me to help her. Somebody has to. It's no different from working in the hospital." Somehow she got through the meal, and when the dishes were washed, she went up to her own apartment to pack, Patsy trailing behind her.

"What's it like, Mary?" she asked, folding the clean underclothes Mary had laid out for her open suitcase. "The Martins' apartment, I mean. You've seen it, haven't you?" She could barely keep the curiosity out of her voice. No one from the neighborhood had ever known anyone who had lived in the towering new apartments that were beginning to change the skyline of the city, stretching from the end of the newly named Magnificent Mile, Chicago's answer to Fifth Avenue, up toward the north and the once quietly sedate areas of Rogers Park. They were fabulous buildings, designed by some of the most famous architects in the world, symbols of the city's pride and ever-growing wealth. The Martins had the top floor of one of the newest buildings, two already large apartments pulled together. As Dan had said, there was more than enough room.

Dan. Mary stopped for a minute, not answering Patsy's questions. Just when had she started thinking of him as that, instead of Mr. Martin? Not that he was ever formal, any more than his wife, but still all these weeks at the hospital she had been Mrs. Conroy to him and he had been Mr. Martin. Only somehow since New Year's Eve the situation had changed; not changed exactly, but wavered, as if the thin line of formality between two strangers had been broken, and while hardly anything barely resembling friendship had begun between them he treated her in a different way. Not personal, there was none of the easy companionship she had with Joan, but more as if he regarded her with respect. Twice she had found him waiting in the lobby when she had come off duty, once when it was clear that Joan had had a bad day and he was anxious to know what had caused it. The second time was during a heavy snowstorm and, without having mentioned it to Joan, he took it upon himself to drive Mary home. Through the long drive he was silent for the most part; all the medical questions had been answered, at least for the time being. The only remark she remembered as they turned into the quiet street where she lived was, "I came from a neighborhood like this." From the tone of his voice she knew those years had not been happy ones. . . .

"The apartment, Mary. What's it like?" Patsy asked again.

"Beautiful. Big, of course. And no, my room's not back of the kitchen like Tim seems to think, it's in the other wing. With its own bath. Close enough that if Mrs. Martin needs me during the night I can get to her. They've fixed up the guest suite for her."

"They don't sleep together?" There was a slight edge of salaciousness in her sister-in-law's voice that irritated Mary more than it should have. So that's what interests you, Mary thought, not how it's decorated.

"She's a very sick woman, Patsy. That's why I'm there. For the present, Mr. Martin will have their room. But she needs a hospital bed, medical equipment; it's just simpler this way."

Patsy was clearly disappointed with her answer, but if the private arrangements of Mary's patient were not to be discussed, she was satisfied to return to her second area of interest. "How have they done the place, Mary? All satins and fancy antiques?"

"Modern." Very modern, Mary thought. Clean-lined and stunning with its views of the lake and the city. But cold and sterile, she had thought when the housekeeper had shown her the apartment. Lila Franklin had her own room, although it was only once a week she could be persuaded to stay over; she had children of her own on the South Side that were being raised by her mother and her husband in the daytime and by Lila only when dinner at the Martins was over.

"I'd love to see it sometime," Patsy said, the not-very-subtle request for an invitation clear between the two of them.

"I doubt if I'll be there all that long," Mary answered quietly. "Mrs. Martin is determined to get well as quickly as possible."

Mary had enough experience with patients to know the schedules they set for themselves were seldom, if ever, successfully put into practice. Joan Martin was an exception. Almost as if she were willing her body to get better, her improvement was more rapid than either her doctors or her nurse had expected.

Joan was a new breed of woman for her nurse. Mary had taken care of wealthy women before, coddled, protected women who could be charming to their husbands and friends and yet treated their nurses like slaves. Joan was different. She was as wealthy as any of the rest and not that much younger, but with much more vitality and determination.

The "postwar" woman was not written about at that time. The sixties were a decade almost exclusively given over to the changes that were happening to the young, the children born in the carefully demure world of the late forties and early fifties, born into a world of American colonial split-level houses and mothers in starched aprons who still wore little white gloves when they went out during the day. As the sixties progressed, the focus had moved to the children these women had produced: rebellious, indignant over the Vietnam War, long-haired, often sullen, making untidiness a personal manifesto. To their shocked parents and grandparents who had struggled so hard to move out of the blue-collar world and into the American Dream of middle-class conventions, these children adopted the denims and rough shirts of the working class, although many of them found the simple request to clean up their rooms labor beyond their energies.

But behind the furor over the length of hair on teenagers, the protest marches, and the flower children, a new breed of women was quietly emerging of whom Joan was almost typical. Carefully educated, these women still knew the proper way to serve tea, still stood when their elders entered the room, laughed with only slight embarrassment over the fact that they had had debutante seasons before their marriages. But with no warning, the world in which they were making their homes and their lives disappeared with World War II, a world of lazy afternoons playing bridge and lavish homes cared for by expert servants. "A lot of good a course on Medieval French poetry did me," Joan remarked to Mary once in the hospital. "They should have taught me how to repair a vacuum cleaner instead."

Not that this new woman bore any relationship to the women Mary had grown up with on the West Side. The Patsys of her world had sunk into their marriages with the same dreams of limited security and a lifetime ahead of balancing a meager budget just as their mothers and grandmothers had. Neither the upper- nor the lower-class wife was expected to work at that time. To do so if one's husband was wealthy was to mark one as "eccentric," unless it involved some occasion where the proceeds went to charity. If one's husband was not rich and the woman worked, it was not a "career choice" but a matter of necessity and a source of some embarrassment to her and her family.

Still, behind the clamor and noise the young were making and the constant coverage they received and often demanded of the press and television, Joan and the women of her age and class were slowly stirring, waking as if from a dream. Sometimes it was a reluctant move as they realized their families no longer needed them and the man they had promised to love forever could walk out any morning and marry someone else. Sometimes they moved their emotional and intellectual muscles as eagerly as Joan exercised her physical ones, anxious to discover if there was more to life than they had been trained to expect. Phrases like Women's Liberation or Equality of the Sexes had not yet been heard, except in small avant-garde intellectual groups, but all over the country the changes young people demanded as their due were beginning to penetrate the consciousness of their parents, especially their mothers.

Not that Joan had any desire for a career of her own. Dan was her career. And as a wife of her time, she expected whatever honors and successes that came her way would come through his achievements. To keep him happy was her career and occupation. If she could not make him happy, her job was at least to keep him. This meant she deliberately embarked on the course other women her age and educational level were also starting. It meant a healthy body, not soft flesh contained in girdles. It meant (especially after the young Kennedys entered the White House) an interest in sports, not as an observer but as a participant. That was what had led Joan to the disastrous ski slope. But she was still young, for all her protestations, and she had no intention of dwindling into a semi-Victorian, semi-invalid stage. She was bright and strong and, although she would have denied the word, spoiled. Not in the sense most people used the word, Mary reflected that first night as she lay in her new bed next to Joan's room. Joan had not been pampered with luxuries, did not expect instant service or the bowing and scraping wealthy matrons of an earlier period took as their right, the sort of manners that led women to spend a whole afternoon in one store and, having examined everything, sweep out without a purchase.

What had spoiled Joan was that, somewhat like her husband, she expected all of life to go *right*. Her children would be bright and attractive, her sexual life with her husband would be, if not always satisfying for her, at least more than sufficient for him. She would have the respect of her friends and her community. She and the other women of her age had been trained to be perfect in every way; that was supposed to be sufficient reward for their egos. Twenty years later they would be out in the marketplace competing with men and enjoying or suffering from it, depending on their success. Twenty years earlier, they would have taken their frustrations out in shopping, redecorating their houses every other year, and possibly, but very rarely, having a small discreet flirtation with one of their friend's husbands. The flirtations would never, or only rarely, actually lead them to a strange bed and a new sexual partner. The women of that generation knew the men of their world very well, and while one might dance better than the man they married and another would always compliment her on the new way she wore her hair, once in bed they would be the same simple, rather unsophisticated, and swiftly satisfied lovers as their husbands.

It was a world of high standards the Martins lived in, more demanding than that of their parents, less tolerant to alternative ways of living than their children were to know. Glossy magazines commanded their lives, telling them how to live, how to dress, what music they should like, and what art to put on their walls. Never was the pressure more intense than in cities like Chicago. Californians and Texans might spend their new money on wild extravagance; to a Chicago matron that was as vulgar as she imagined her East Coast sisters regarded it. But the East Coast, which had held control of the standards of taste for so long, was beginning to look a little tired and faded to the wealthy women of the cities growing west of the Hudson. It was a period of sliding transition for women. And because there was nothing that could be relied on totally, it created inside even the most outwardly happy of wives a small knot of fear that never quite disappeared.

The day after Joan's return from the hospital, she began her regime to become herself again. The exercises were designed to bring feeling and, with it, movement and control back to the right side of her body. After two months in the hospital, the muscles and torn ligaments resulting from the accident had not been fully repaired. Instead of leaving her nerves raw, as Mary had tried to explain to Joan's husband New Year's Eve, it had deadened them, closing off feelings and responses necessary to make her well again. Over and over Joan would insist on trying the exercises Dr. MacCauley had devised "just one more time, Mary," although her face and body would be glistening with perspiration. Once she was allowed to use the swimming pool (an innovation for an apartment building at this time), with the cast on her leg carefully wrapped in plastic, Joan progressed more easily. Held up by the water, she could force her legs to move, and even the right arm, which had so far resisted all attempts at recovery, began to show signs of progress.

That was not enough for Joan, at least not enough for her to emerge from her room and join in the life of her family. The children were admitted after her nap. For an hour Joan gave the impression of being the perfect mother—asking her serious daughter, Paige, about school, reading stories to the wriggling little boy, Joey—but neither seemed to give her any pleasure, a fact Mary hoped only she had noticed. It was a duty Joan performed precisely, and as with everything she attempted, she did it smoothly and easily. Still, there was a distance between her and her children. Her eyes would stray often to the clock on her bedside table to check if the hour was up. Paige, Mary knew, was aware of this, although she never said anything. Still, it was Paige who would get up dutifully a few minutes before the end of the hour, saying she had homework to do, and it was Joey who would squirm and demand "just one more story." Mary suspected Joey was his mother's favorite. He looked so much like a miniature version of Dan that a woman so deeply committed to her husband could hardly resist him. Between Paige and her mother, although neither would admit it and perhaps had not yet considered it, there was that age-old rivalry of two females both loving the same man and both determined to be the more important to him. Paige was always polite to her mother and Lila and Mary, but it was only when her father entered the room that her face lit up with genuine joy, the facade broken for a moment to let her look like the young girl she was.

Mary and Lila tried to arrange the dinner hour during the time Dan spent with his wife, but the children, missing one parent already, would have none of that. By dawdling, complaining, delays in "washing up," they managed to wait for their father to complete his evening visit with Joan. The time he spent with his wife was obviously the highpoint of both their days. Whether any sexual intimacies occurred between them at that time Mary didn't know, although she suspected not, and found herself blushing to think she had even considered it. The Martins had drinks together, and Joan was at her physical best for him, perfumed and gowned and carefully made up, lying on the long chaise, the hospital bed covered with a spread of bright Thailand silk. Mary was sometimes present, at least at the beginning of their hour together, bringing ice and glasses, placing the flowers Dan brought nightly in a new vase. There was never a night she took the flowers he brought to be arranged that she didn't think of Jack. There'd been no further word since that call she had missed New Year's Eve. She wondered if he, like Dan Martin, was sleeping alone these nights.

If Mary had somehow presumed that the cocktail hour the Martins spent together would be a daily "hour of charm," she was surprised at the changes that took place once Joan returned from the hospital. Obviously she was better, in mind and body, stronger and less frightened. But Joan was clever enough to know that merely being charming to her husband once a day was not enough to keep him interested, and often Dan would emerge from her room considerably less placid and soothed than when he had entered it. It was almost as if Joan, knowing her husband, deliberately decided to alternate his visits, one day giving him sugar and the next day turning salty or tart. Whatever he had discussed, if his wife had disagreed with him, he generally brought it to the dining table afterward.

"What were you and Mom yelling about?" Joey asked after one such session, heard throughout the large apartment.

"We weren't yelling, and take your elbows off the table." Still, before he raised his fork to his mouth he faced the table at large. "Your mother has this wild idea that Paige Properties should be buying up the land around O'Hare Airport."

"Oh, business!" said Paige with disdain. If her mother was interested in it, she was clearly determined not to be.

"Don't sniff at it, young lady," replied her father. "It's what's paying for your clothes, your very expensive schooling, and those braces on your teeth—which, from the dentist's last bill, must be made of platinum."

"Do we have to talk about money?" This was Paige at her grandest, but Mary, listening, knew her attitude was less because of a disdain for finances than being reminded of the metal bands she found so ugly to wear.

"The land out near the airport . . . that's not too far from where I live," Mary added, tactfully bringing the subject back to what had started Dan off. "I can't quite see it as a high-priced real estate area."

Dan instantly took his wife's side. "No, it wouldn't be for luxury housing. Joan wasn't thinking of that. Just the fact that O'Hare is fast on its way to becoming the biggest airport in the world. If they have to expand, and they will before the century's over, they're going to need more room for runways, hangars, offices. Hotels for travelers will be going up for people who haven't the time to get into the city. Homes for people working there." From a certain belligerence to his wife's ideas that had clung to him when he came into the dining room, Mary could see a growing admiration already appearing for her thinking. "Do you think she might be up to seeing me again after dinner? Just for a little? I want to show her a map, get her opinion on a couple of lots."

"I'll pick up her tray now. I'm sure she'll want to see you." Mary started for the kitchen. Dan was obviously not in a mood to wait for dessert.

"Dad! You said you were going to play Monopoly with us after dinner."

"We'll do it another time, Paige. Or maybe Mary will play with you." Was this the first time he had called her by her first name? Mary found herself wondering as she came back into the room, carrying the silver tray with the two delicate china cups. "Up to a game of Monopoly with these brats?"

"I'd love it." Mary could understand Paige's resentment. It would have been fun for them to have had the evening with Dan. She forced the thought back. "Time we women learned about the world of finance, right, Paige?"

Paige nodded sullenly.

"First thing to learn is don't sell any family property there." With that, Dan attacked his half-finished meal, eager for it to be over.

"I don't see why he has to spend all his time with *her*." Paige was still sulking, although Mary had deliberately let her win. Joey had long since disappeared, ostensibly to do his homework but actually, Mary suspected, to watch his own tiny television set. His report card since his mother's accident had been increasingly poor, the housekeeper had informed Mary, and Mary suspected Joey knew it was only a matter of time before all television would be forbidden by Dan. Joey could wait; it was Paige who needed listening to this evening. She's going to be a beauty, Mary thought as they put away the pieces of the game. Only tonight she doesn't know it, and it wouldn't give her much comfort if she did.

"I mean it." Paige's voice was sulky, rebellious. The grown-up facade of indifference had cracked, at least for a moment, and she was simply an unhappy, frustrated child. "We never seem to see Dad any more."

"He's concerned about your mother. He wants to spend time with her."

"And he doesn't like to spend it with us?"

"It's not a question of that, Paige. After all, he only has a certain amount of time. Once your mother's back on her feet, you'll be a family again. Then there won't be any question of his having to divide up his life, so much for each person." She smiled at the young girl in front of her, knowing Paige wasn't really listening, surrounding herself in her bad mood like a wall. "You probably won't like it very much when he does pay more attention."

As she expected, this startled Paige to the point of reacting openly. "What are you talking about?"

"The phone calls from young Mickey Harris you seem to get every night, helping you with your algebra."

"You've been spying!"

"I can hardly help knowing when Lila has to come in every evening to call you to the phone halfway through dessert." Mary smiled again, hoping to win over the child in front of her. It would help them all if she could relax and exchange confidences. Life in this household would be much easier if Paige didn't constantly wear a chip on her shoulder. "You might at least explain to young Mr. Harris the dining hours of this family or you'll never get to finish your ice cream."

"I don't care. I'm too fat anyway. And I absolutely hate and deplore Mickey Harris."

"He sounds like a very nice boy on the phone. As for being fat, you're practically a skeleton." Paige was at the age when she was all long legs and arms. "And I certainly wouldn't turn down anybody who could help me with algebra. I never could make head or tails out of it myself in school."

Paige was not to be won so easily. "If Dad wasn't so tied up with Mom he could help me. All because she had to ski down some dumb hill. I don't see why the rest of us should suffer."

"Paige, listen for a minute. I know you miss your father . . . and your mother. Try to understand this is a special time in their lives, in all your lives. It won't last forever, but it has to be lived through. Just like—well, you had measles, didn't you? That seemed endless, I suspect. I'll bet you can hardly remember it now."

"I remember." The young girl hesitated, and for once she allowed Mary to see the unhappiness behind her carefully controlled facade.

"It's just—everything's so mixed up. You here and Mom sick and nobody seems to care what we do."

"I care."

"That's different. Anyway, you're here for Mom, not for the rest of us."

"I'm here to help." Mary took the game from Paige's hands. How pretty the girl would be, even with her braces, if she allowed herself to smile!

"Nobody wants to help me," Paige said wistfully.

"Is there something special you need? Something you'd like to ask me about?"

Paige made a face. "You mean, 'women's problems'? We had all that in school. It hasn't happened, and I hope it never does. Anyway, that isn't it. They're having the auditions for the Choral Group day after tomorrow, and everybody has to bring their own music and I don't have any and Daddy won't let me go to the Loop by myself, so I won't be able to audition and I'll bet I would have made it if I had! And I can't ask anybody to go and I'll just have to get up and sing the National Anthem or some dumb thing like that."

"I've got an hour free tomorrow. And I know where Lyon and Healy's is." As she mentioned the name of Chicago's largest music store, Paige's face lit up. "What do you want me to get?"

"It's a Schubert *Lied*! I've been practicing from the record, but nobody can play it without the sheet music. Oh, Mary, would you—could you get it? I've got the name all written down in my room and I've got the money from my allowance. I was going to ask Daddy, but he went back to *her* and he'd probably get it wrong anyway or send that Miss Wallis at his office. And she'd probably think it was too complicated and get me "Over the Rainbow" or something dopey. Oh, Mary, if you'll get it for me, I'll love you forever!" She flung her arms around Mary and gave her a quick hug before dashing off to her room.

For a long moment Mary stood there, the game still in her hands. How long had it been since anybody had held her? she thought. Tim and his family were not demonstrative that way, never had been. Jack had been the last person to touch her, and not often in those last months before his sudden departure. Just that last time, when he said goodbye.

Suddenly she found herself remembering the way Dan's arms had held Joan when he visited her in the hospital. It had not been as if he were trying to pass his strength on to her, but as if in their closeness he was touching some part of himself. Mary was thankful there was no one else in the room, for thinking about them was making her blush.

You're getting to be a maudlin old maid, Mary Conroy, she told herself firmly and glanced at her wristwatch. Almost nine. After Paige came back she had better knock on Joey's door and start him for bed. She suspected his school books would still be sitting untouched on his small desk. She'd have to look into that tomorrow. It would keep her busy these evenings in Dan Martin's home. Give her something to think about.

Something safe.

Four

As the weeks moved slowly toward a late spring, other people were growing concerned about Joan's progress. On a rainy Tuesday at the end of April, Kay Wallis put the cover on her typewriter. Although it was after six, she knew she wouldn't leave the office until Dan Martin did. Mr. Paige had gone long ago for a drink at the Van Buren Club, plus whatever else he had planned for the evening. Probably dinner with one of his "ladies." Ten years at Paige Properties had taught Kay a great deal about the private life of her boss, or at least the man who considered himself the head of the firm. Although Evan openly admitted Dan was the one who actually ran things.

Evan Paige was very discreet about his affairs, but before the office had expanded Kay had also been his personal secretary, taking his phone calls and supervising his checkbook. She knew about the women in Evan's life. There were not many of them, and they generally lasted about two years before the calls were no longer placed and their names disappeared from the canceled checks that were forwarded by the bank each month.

Kay tended to call them the Wilson Avenue ladies, condemning a perfectly respectable part of middle-class Chicago as a sort of vaguely erotic extramarital zone. But after World War II there seemed to be a large number of apartment buildings on or near Wilson Avenue that were divided into studio apartments for the sort of women Joan's father picked. Never silly young girls or anyone really improper, she would remind herself. They never came to the office, they were all of "a certain age" (usually over thirty-five), and certainly Evan as a widower was entitled to his own choice of companionship. Not that he kept any of these women, exactly. Kay had only seen one or two of them, usually by accident, at a store or in a restaurant. They were generally divorced, Kay could recite the litany of names without hesitating: Mrs. Gerson, Mrs. Fenwick, Mrs. Lester. The checks Evan made out to them were never for any of whatever private activities they enjoyed together. The checks would be birthday presents or Christmas presents or for a little trip to New York or Florida, or a gift certificate at one of the better department stores.

Certainly Evan, in his sixties, wasn't hurting anybody. If any of the ladies had illusions of becoming his second wife, Kay suspected he swiftly discouraged them or else moved on to someone less demanding. His Wilson Avenue ladies were not supported by him; they all seemed to have careers or sizable alimony: women he had met in the course of helping them find or dispose of an apartment, women he could take to good restaurants or for an evening of dancing at the Pump Room in the Ambassador East Hotel. They were not invited to family gatherings of the Paiges or the Martins, that Kay knew. In many cases they had children of their own, now grown or conveniently away at school, or with their own homes and family festivities at which Evan's ladies would naturally spend their holidays. Each of the ladies had a good fur coat, often more than one, and excellent if somewhat flashy pieces of jewelry, not always gifts from the same man. They were handsome women with stylish wardrobes, whose makeup and hair were always perfect, who could match Evan drink for drink and hold their liquor as well as he did. As Kay tidied up the outer office that April afternoon, she found to her surprise that she envied them very much.

Not because of Evan. She shuddered a little at the thought of Mr. Paige putting his arm around her or touching her with his long hands. (She made a memo on her pad to remind him he had an appointment tomorrow for a manicure). No, it wasn't Evan she desired, it was the freedom of the women he knew and the ease with which they handled their lives.

If she could have that with Dan . . .

Don't be foolish, she told herself. Dan Martin wouldn't look at someone like her, Dan had never looked at her like that, wouldn't tonight when he finally left his office, except to wonder aloud why she was working so late. He would forget her as soon as he reached the elevator.

It had been like that from the beginning. She had known it the first day she had come to work for Paige Properties. She had been in his office taking dictation when Joan had phoned, and the sparkle in his eyes when he talked to his wife was enough to convince her he would never think of Kay with that same glow of happiness and desire. She should have quit that first week, of course. She had read enough novels and seen enough movies to know how fruitless it could be for a secretary to fall in love with her boss. There would be no moment of her taking off eyeglasses (which she didn't wear anyway) and his saying in a choked voice, "Why, Miss Wallis, you're beautiful!" the way it seemed to happen in bad romances. He was a married man in love with his wife, and when Kay finally saw Joan she understood and accepted it instantly. Kay was twenty-six then, and although it would have surprised some of her gossipy friends in the small town in downstate Illinois where she had grown up, she was still a virgin when she moved to Chicago. How they had all talked, her fat married sisters especially, when she left town and came to Chicago to live on her own, to shorten her unmanageable Ukranian name to Wallis, to get a job that paid better than anything her brothers-in-law made. To make her own life.

She wasn't a virgin after that first time Joan Martin came to the office. It seemed silly now, when she thought back to it. It had been a Friday afternoon, and when she had closed the office after Dan and Joan had left, she had called one of the other secretaries who worked in the office building, Kitty Sedgewick, with whom she had become friendly at the lunch counter downstairs. Kitty was always talking about her dates and, while a little on the plump side, gave the impression of having a busier social life than anyone else Kay knew. Kitty urged Kay to join her and some friends for a drink that evening, and Kay had gone along. She had worn a dress she had pushed to the back of her closet for being too tight and had put on more makeup than she usually allowed herself and some of the perfume that Kitty recommended and proceeded with the help of Kitty's boyfriends to get pleasantly intoxicated. And when one of the men, Stan—what was his name?—offered to see her home, she had accepted. It was only polite to ask him in for a drink, and rather more quickly than she expected she lost the virginity she had guarded all her life. Stan was a nice man, she realized later, although not quite understanding why she would not let him stay over, considering the lateness of the hour. He had called several times after that, and once or twice they had even gone back to bed together, but the experience never became anything that Kay felt was worth the inevitable hangover or the worry until her next period arrived.

Since then, there had been other men; not many, for Kay was not the type to be promiscuous, and certainly Stan had done nothing to make her sexually curious or even sexually satisfied. When she turned thirty she didn't spend her vacation at some glamorous resort that promised two weeks of adventure, but in moving to a new apartment, one not managed by Paige Properties. Furnishing it with careful attention to every detail down to the ashtrays on the end tables had given her more pleasure than any date she had ever had. It was also the most important two weeks of her life, she realized later, as much a turning point as the new decade she had entered. She did a lot of thinking those two weeks, hard thinking, and emerged secure in the fact that she had done something very few people attempt to do. She had faced reality and the choices reality gave her. She was not unattractive. She was not frigid, even though the men she had known had not touched any part of her emotions. She was good friends with other women. Quite coldly, she considered whether she might have some latent lesbianism in her nature. But her attempts at solitary sexual release using the image of women she knew or had seen on movie screens were unsuccessful. The only image that could give her the release she needed was Dan Martin.

That left her two choices. Either she could leave her job and start again somewhere else, or she could stay with Paige Properties for the rest of her life, knowing the limit of her pleasure would be to see him every working day.

Making that decision had taken a great deal of thought. On the sensible side, she knew she should find another job while there were still good opportunities open to her. But some last vestige of sentiment (or "softness," as she called it) remained in her, and she knew she would never leave him. If all she could have was the sight and company of Dan during business hours each day, that would have to be enough. And as the years went past, she had come to realize that, even if by some fantastic miracle he had proposed to her, it would still not have been what she wanted. Marriage, with all its inevitability, the attempts to keep him romantically interested the way his wife did, the careful attention to detail on which Joan expended so much effort, was not for Kay. No, the most she would have asked for was the freedom to be a Wilson Avenue lady for Dan from time to time. But she also knew that even if that were possible, it would be the end of the better half of her life, the important life they shared together in the office, where she knew she was valued and needed.

So, through the years, that was the side of Dan she concentrated on. She kept her appearance neat and attractive by carefully ignoring the fads and fashions that were making so many women in their thirties look foolish: the short and shorter skirts, the bizarre makeup, the free-swinging hair. Instead she had the crisp appearance of a woman executive, and with that look she gradually became aware she had alternative ambitions. What passion she might have brought to the bedroom, she began to give to finance, investing in properties that Dan was developing, sometimes with his knowledge, sometimes through a broker. Whereas other women her own age might be making increasingly desperate attempts to find companionship or love affairs with varying possibilities of permanency, she concentrated on money. By this time she was well on her way to becoming a financially secure woman. Her growing bank account, her perfect apartment, and her daily work with Dan were more than enough to fill her life. With careful planning she fully expected it to be enough forever.

Until his wife's accident. That had been something Kay was not prepared to handle. Somehow after that hasty flight back from the ski resort, the business days of Paige Properties began to unravel. Dan was on the phone more than before, but talking to doctors, planning the arrival of new specialists, delaying the return of business calls or sometimes forgetting them completely. Kay was once more called upon to handle personal checkbooks, and she watched with something close to shock the amount that was being spent on Joan Martin. It gave her a small chill to realize how expensive a serious illness could be, and she redoubled her own efforts to increase her savings. God forbid anything like that should happen to her. The checks for the nurses alone seemed incredibly high, especially the ones for this Mrs. Conroy, to whom Joan had apparently taken a fancy. She dimly remembered talking to Mrs. Conroy during her only visit to the hospital. She was one of those quiet women who never seemed to reveal what they were really thinking. Kay had never liked the type.

Only now this woman was established in the Martins' apartment. Kay didn't like that either, and she was wise enough about herself to understand why. She knew Dan Martin's moods better than anybody, probably better than his wife did. Over the years she could tell within minutes after his arrival in the office if the night before had been a happy one, and by "happy" she meant sexually fulfilling, although she would erase that thought from her head as quickly as possible. She could also tell if something was wrong, some small argument or unsatisfied restlessness. For the first weeks Joan was in the hospital, his deep fear and worry for his wife precluded any predictions Kay might make about his moods. But it was over two months since Joan had returned from the hospital, and Dan's moods should have been once more easy to read.

Only they weren't.

Whatever was happening between him and Joan, Kay doubted if it was sexual. Yet Dan was a vital, healthy, alive man in his forties. Kay could tolerate his bursts of irritation, knowing the cause. But now things were different somehow, different in a way Kay couldn't quite put her finger on. She didn't like that. She was accustomed to being the one who knew the secrets, usually before the people involved knew them. Dan was quieter these days, preoccupied. Not the way he had been at first after the accident, when Kay suspected he had spent most of his evenings drinking too heavily, simply to put himself to sleep. No, it was as if something new was beginning to occupy his thoughts to the exclusion of everything else. It wasn't business. Neither Evan nor Dan had started any new projects. Kay knew that even before the periodic examination of the office books she and Dan held the first of every month. That meant a couple of late nights for Kay next week. She wondered idly if she should make an appointment to have her hair done. There was supposed to be a good man in the Stevens Building, and it had been a long time since she had changed her appearance in any way. Not that she was contemplating anything . . .

"Still here, Kay?" He had come out of his office while she was thinking about him, and for a moment she had the guilty feeling that he could read her thoughts. But he had that look on his face as if he weren't really there, and she knew as always what she had been thinking was safe from his eyes.

"Just finishing up. Next week we'll have to get at the monthly statement. Do you want to schedule a night now?"

"No. I'll let you know the beginning of the week."

He was almost out the door before she remembered to say what she had deliberately been holding back from telling him all afternoon. "Oh, I meant to tell you. The florist shop downstairs is closed today, repainting or something. You'll have to go someplace else to pick up flowers for Joan."

"I'll get some candy instead. The kids'll like that too. Besides, Joan was saying her room was getting to look like an undertaker's parlor." He closed the door without looking back at his secretary.

Kay watched the door for what seemed like several minutes. Long enough for the elevator to come and for him to leave. So it's the end of the era of flowers, she thought. Of course it would have had to happen someday. But she had a feeling it wasn't because Joan had made some sudden remarkable leap back into health. Kay reached for the phone. That hairdresser kept late hours. Might just as well set an appointment for the weekend now, while she thought about it.

Joan lay quietly on her bed. It was only ten o'clock, but the apartment seemed a quiet, deserted ocean around her, outside her closed door. She had told Mary she was tired from the day's exercises and wanted to get to sleep early. Mary, she suspected, would be in the kitchen, making a last cup of tea and putting away the dishes. She knew Mary had been doing that for some time, although Lila had protested, but the two women had become friends and it gave Lila the chance to leave a half hour earlier if Mary emptied the dishwasher and set the table for breakfast. Dan would be in his study, or maybe in what had been their bedroom.

Joan thought for a moment of their large bed. She wondered if Dan was lonely there, although she could remember how he would sprawl out in his sleep, occupying nearly all of it, crowding her to the edge if she didn't nudge him back. Suddenly she could feel the warmth of desire coming over her body, starting at her toes, moving up to where he used to touch her so intimately. She held her breath for a moment. Had it really happened? Had she felt something in the nerves on her right side, actually felt it as she thought of Dan, or just imagined it?

Since the cast had come off the week before, she had forced her stiff muscles to exercise, doubling the amount of time she spent each day in the building's pool. There she felt herself free as she had been before, free to move and turn and bend. Even her right arm had seemed stronger in the water. As she lay in the darkness her mouth twisted into a wry smile. Care to be married to a mermaid, Dan? I could satisfy you that way. For she knew she would soon have to find a way to satisfy him. Dan was no monk, no pallid near-capon who would put up with weeks of "I have a headache," like the husbands of her other friends. They'd had a vigorous, active sex life before the accident, and if she hadn't enjoyed it quite as much as he had, preferring the warmth of his embrace and his gentle kisses before and after to the actual activity itself, she had found satisfaction in that as well. Once or twice, in the early weeks in the hospital she had tried to satisfy him other ways, ways they had learned in the months of her bulky pregnancies, but he had not responded, even with the door carefully locked, almost as if he was embarrassed or afraid of hurting her, and she had stopped trying.

Was it that? Or that she repulsed him? Like most healthy people, he hated hospitals and the sick, and she had been associated with both for far too long. She stretched her right leg tentatively. It moved and responded without pain; slowly, but still it *did* move. And she could raise her right arm up to the top of her head if she was rested.

She went back through the evening in her mind. No flowers tonight, but that had happened before—not often, but once or twice when a meeting had run late. She had teased him about bringing them just last week, so it wasn't his fault. Not really. Even after all these years of marriage she couldn't expect him to sense when she didn't really mean what she said.

Still, maybe it *was* time that she faced the fact that she had recovered, or recovered as much as she was going to at this point in her life. Because Dan was different lately. Warm and affectionate but *different,* another person, someone who knew her and was fond of her, loved her, but in an abstracted way, like a sister. She shuddered a little as she lay there in the darkness. That mustn't ever happen, not to them. Tomorrow. If she swam five lengths of the pool without stopping, as she had done today, she'd find some excuse to be alone with him. She knew she could walk to their bedroom without a cane; she had practiced it the Sunday before when everyone was out, leaning on the back of a living-room chair or the edge of the mantel when she became dizzy.

Tomorrow night then. She couldn't delay any longer. Something touched her bare shoulder, where the lace of her nightgown ended. She knew it was a petal from one of the flowers on her bedside table as she brushed it off in the darkness. The flowers he had brought her yesterday, not today.

For some strange reason she found there were tears in her eyes. Not sentimental tears, angry ones. Tomorrow, she promised herself. Tomorrow she would come back to life.

Dan wasn't in the bedroom that had been designed for his wife and only incidentally for himself. He found the room too feminine these nights when he slept alone to use it for anything but sleep. He went to it late, turning on only the light in the adjoining bathroom, not allowing himself to read in the enormous bed. He preferred to spend his evenings in his den, especially those first horrible weeks, sleeping there on the couch after the liquor had done its work and he could finally count on some oblivion from his thoughts. Thank God that period was over! Shows you can adjust to everything, he thought to himself. Given time. And he'd had enough of that, nearly half a year by now. Not that it took any great self-control to stop the heavy drinking that had soothed those first bad weeks. No, it was the look on the kids' faces when he brought a stiff martini to the table, although he had always kept his serious drinking until after dinner when they had gone to bed. Nor had anybody said anything to him; Evan was silent about his bad temper in the mornings, putting it down to strain and worry over Joan instead of a hangover. Lila hadn't made any comment, although she must have noticed the empty bottles he would carefully stash late at night in the garbage. Still, after Joan had come home from the hospital, he noticed there was always a fresh pot of black coffee on the stove, already brewed, just waiting to be reheated.

He wondered, and not for the first time, if that had been the work of Mrs. Franklin or if it was Mary's idea. Mary. He leaned back in his office chair and thought about her. It was happening more often than he liked, this thinking about her. Not that it was romantic, or sexual. There was nothing between them that he couldn't tell Joan, but when a stranger moves into your home, into your life—well, you can't help being curious. Not that his curiosity had got him very far. The evenings he had found himself stopping in the kitchen, sitting at the plain table while she had her last cup of tea, the coffeepot ready for him, he had tried to draw her out about her life, but she had a way of turning the conversation away from herself, toward him or the children. Divorced and Irish and probably a former Catholic, that was about all he knew. A brother and his family in that quiet little street on the West Side. He couldn't even guess her age. She was the kind of woman who had a serenity about her that he had always associated with older people, yet how much of that was due to her quiet ways? No children, he did know that. He wondered whose decision that had been, the absent husband or hers? He suspected the man; she was born to have children. Look what she had done with Paige and Joey just in the few weeks she had been here. He could hear her, from the den, evening after evening, working with Joey on his homework; certainly the boy's marks had improved. What was more important, Joey didn't seem to mind his schoolwork if he did it with her. Once or twice in what Dan thought of as the "old days" he had tried to help the boy, but he didn't have the patience and he knew it. Answers, especially in math, seemed so obvious to him he couldn't believe Joey wasn't faking when he stuttered that he didn't understand. Mary seemed to take that in her stride, saying something to make Joey laugh and then starting all over again until the boy got it right.

And Paige. Anybody could see the change in her. She didn't seem to resent her mother's illness any more; she was volunteering to do things for her: brushing her hair and helping Lila change the sheets, fresh every day. Mary, tall herself, had encouraged the young girl to stand straight, and there were even smiles now from the mouth with the hated braces. Paige would be a beauty like her mother; he could see it now that she had turned thirteen.

God, the years went by so fast! Paige thirteen! It seemed only last month he was that age himself, and now he was in his forties. It was a cold thought; as if he could move away from it, he got up and went over to look at the rain streaming down the window. Below was the wide Outer Drive, carrying Chicagoans north to their homes, Chicagoans who had dined well and gone to the theater or a concert and at midnight were heading back to their beds before starting another day. Married, most of them, as he was, he thought. Secure. Settled. With wives to sleep with. . . .

He felt the old familiar reactions and found himself grinning. Middle-aged or not, he wasn't that far from a teenager in the suddenness of his sexual urges. That hadn't made these last months any easier. Joan had tried, he had to admit, in the hospital, a handkerchief ready as they had done when release was desperately needed in the old days when pregnancy made the usual joining impractical. But it seemed wrong somehow, the noise in the corridors outside, that damn cast on her leg. . . .

The accident. It all came back to that. Dan didn't claim to be a saint, and of course he had looked at other women in appreciation and speculation on occasion. Nothing more, though. Joan was enough. Not that he didn't have chances. On quick trips to other cities he would sometimes be seated next to a single woman on the plane, obviously as devoted to her career as Dan was to his, their briefcases nudging each other until the inevitable "I'm sorry, is that in your way?" led to a conversation. They were attractive women, and if there was a wedding ring on their finger, it was usually on the right hand, showing the stranger's past had included a divorce. Dan was quick to spot that. Often they would be going to the same hotel, sharing a taxi to get there. Dan was sophisticated enough to know if he invited his companion to dinner she would probably accept, happy not to have to spend an evening with a room service meal and whatever the local television had to offer. After dinner, it would not have been hard to go a step further: a brandy, say, in one of their rooms. . . .

He had never done that. Not in all the years of his marriage to Joan. He would say a polite goodbye to the lady in the hotel lobby and disappear, usually not even eating in the hotel dining room that evening just in case she was secure enough to come down alone for her dinner.

No, he'd been faithful and he had hoped to stay that way always, but it was five months since the accident and he was honest enough with himself to know he needed a woman in his life. The adolescent releases he had been forced to return to on very rare nights had embarrassed him. That was something for kids. He made a mental note that he probably ought to talk to Joey about it one of these days. Only he knew he wouldn't; he would be too embarrassed and would put it off, hoping Joey would learn all he needed in school biology classes or else from boys his own age, the way the men of Dan's generation had learned.

But it wasn't just sex he missed, he thought, as he stood there, staring out at the rain and darkness. He missed being married. He knew that was a strange reaction for a man of his age. Many of his contemporaries were only too willing to spend long hours leaning on the bar at the Van Buren Club after office hours rather than going to their homes. Most of them had placed their wives firmly in the suburbs ("It'll be good for the children") with the conscious or subconscious thought that this gave them an excuse on the nights they worked late, or pretended to, to call home and say they would stay over downtown. They might consider themselves married, but they weren't working at it very hard. More than one had an involvement on the side, not so much out of desire (very often the "involvement" wasn't anywhere near as attractive as the wife) but simply because they seemed to need "adventure" as they moved into middle age.

That had never tempted Dan. Though he had been lonely these past months and sexually unsatisfied, it had never occurred to him to start something like that, even if it were available. He grinned at the sudden thought of the old cliché: the married man and his secretary. Prim Kay would probably faint if he so much as touched her. Faint, scream, and quit, and he didn't want that. Life was disorganized enough as it was.

Now, since Joan was home, life had become almost . . . settled again. He worried the thought over in his mind. Mary made the difference, of course. Someone to talk to late in the evenings. Someone who cared about Joan and the kids. Kind and thoughtful, attractive once she'd stopped wearing those frozen white nurse's uniforms. He had Mac-Cauley to thank for that; the doctor had suggested that Joan might find it easier if Mary didn't dress as a nurse, a constant reminder of illness and hospitals. It certainly had helped Dan. Since she had given up her uniform, it was easier to think of her just as a friend, a handsome woman in fresh blouses and plain skirts. Nothing glamorous. Not like Joan. Just someone peaceful and easy to be with at the end of the long day, now that he didn't want liquor to make him relax. Attractive too, not in a way that caught your eye at first, but in the evenings they had talked together. . . .

He looked at his watch. It was nearly ten. Mary would be heading for bed soon. But they'd have time for one cup of coffee together at least.

Five

It had started with the coffee, the night they had brought Joan home from the hospital.

After dinner Dan had come into the kitchen instead of going directly to his den. Lila, aware of how he had spent his other evenings, offered him another cup of coffee. He was clearly anxious about Joan—already asleep in her room—and her condition, and he questioned Mary persistently. When he finally left the two women he went to his bedroom, and Lila as she went home later said a silent prayer that the "bad nights," as she had privately labeled Dan's attempts to wipe out his memories with liquor, were over.

Although Lila said nothing to Mary of what Dan had been doing to himself during the weeks Joan had been in the hospital, Mary had sensed since New Year's Eve the loneliness and guilt Dan Martin was still suffering. From then on she and Lila kept coffee ready for Dan in the kitchen after dinner. But it only became routine for him to stop in the kitchen when Mary volunteered to clean up after the meal, allowing Lila to leave the Martin apartment early.

At first Mary had no reasons to question her motives for offering to help the housekeeper. She had grown fond of Lila and it had seemed only practical to offer to help. The housekeeper had a long trip to make each night home to the South Side, and with the large efficient dishwasher, it was easy for Mary to put the kitchen in order each evening. Joan would be reading or asleep, the children were struggling with their homework, it gave her something to do.

But as the weeks went by she had to realize she was looking forward more and more to the end of the day, or specifically, to talking with Dan. They soon exhausted any questions about Joan's progress. Joan herself had told Mary flatly that she didn't want her husband to know of the exercises or the therapy. "Let's surprise him," she had said to Mary. "When and if I can emerge from all the medical equipment." Privately, Mary suspected Joan didn't want Dan carrying an image in his mind of a perspiring wife, straining each muscle over and over again as she willed herself to improve. Mary had agreed and so her conversations in the evenings with Dan moved into other areas.

He talked to her as an equal now, not as his wife's nurse but as a friend, and as the days became weeks, Mary began to realize how few confidantes he truly had. And for that matter, how few people there were in her own life whom she could talk to honestly. With Dan, the doubts and worries he might have brought to Joan in the healthy years of their marriage he could no longer share; she still needed to be pro- tected from any external stress. And Mary suspected even in the best of their times there were things he had never allowed himself to discuss with his wife. For in Dan's struggle to be a success, he had learned to be careful of revealing all of himself to anyone. He had few personal friends; the men he knew socially or as golf partners were all part of his business world, friendly enough but still rivals who could not be trusted with his dreams of expanding the firm, with his struggles for financial security, and especially with the private doubts of his own worth. These were things men of Dan's age did not, could not, allow themselves to share with their male contemporaries. Dan's children were too young to share his concerns, and his father-in-law, already conservative, would not have hesitated to use Dan's confidences as weapons to curb his ambitions. The women he knew were wives, friends of Joan's and not to be treated as receivers of his secrets.

But Mary, coming from the same impoverished background as he, made an understanding and sympathetic companion these long winter nights. It was a new experience for Mary. Her life had been more shel- tered than she had realized, at least from the world of men. Her father and brother were never ones to voice insecurities or to ask for other people's opinions, especially not those of women. They had both been raised believing that such exposure of themselves was a sign of weak- ness. In time, Mary realized, she and Jack might have grown to share their problems, except for the sudden discovery of his gambling. That had kept them during most of their marriage uneasy and silent, hugging their separate secrets and troubles to themselves. At the hospital Mary had cared for as many male patients as she had female, the bodies of men were no particular mystery to her, but she realized during her evenings with Dan that he was probably the first man who could and did reveal to her the secrets of his mind.

They were just friends, she told herself firmly when they would both go to their own bedrooms each night. Friends who could confide in each other. There was no flirtatiousness in their conversations, no suggestions that he was interested in her as a woman. And of course she could never allow herself to think of him as an attractive man: he was Joan's husband, the father of Paige and Joey, her employer. Still, she found herself making sure her hair was neatly combed each evening and her blouses fresh. She bought a new lipstick and then, uneasy and embarrassed at the thoughts she refused to let stay in her mind, put it away untried.

Lila, she knew, suspected something. One afternoon in March the housekeeper even suggested that perhaps they should return to the previous routine. Mary, Lila said, had more than enough to do taking care of Joan and the children. Mary had rejected the offer and Lila had not pressed it. How much the housekeeper knew of the conversations Dan and she had each night Mary could not guess. She had always made sure the kitchen was spotless before she went to her own room. But Lila was wise enough to realize that even if she did stay after dinnertime, it would merely delay the evening meetings, not end them. She simply contented herself by saying, with her voice free from any hint of warning or disapproval, "My sister Martha is a great one for the old sayings, has one for every occasion. . . ."

Mary, she knew would pick up on that, and did. "What would she have to say now?" she asked the housekeeper, half afraid of the answer.

"Oh, I suspect something like, 'What the eye don't see, the heart don't hunger for,'" Lila replied, being careful to keep her back to Mary as she set out the silverware for dinner. She said nothing further that evening or later, suspecting she didn't need to and, worse, that it would do no good.

But that night it was Mary's turn to go home and Lila's to stay over and all the way west to her apartment Mary examined what Lila had said, what she'd meant and what Mary was beginning to face was the truth.

I can't be in love with Dan, her mind stated over and over again as if it were trying to build a wall thick enough to withstand all the niggling little questions that suddenly seemed to be attacking her from all sides.

Joan's my friend; naturally I want to help her any way I can, help her and her family. Love was something different, at least the kind of love people meant by the word. Phrases like "falling in love" . . . that had nothing to do with what she felt for Dan! Of course he was attractive, anyone, male or female, would have to agree to that. And he was lonely and she enjoyed talking with a healthy adult, someone who liked her, whom she could make laugh. But all the old clichés about love didn't fit here. She never dreamed of him at night, for instance. But the practical part of her defeated that objection instantly. Of all the myths about love, that was the weakest—you dreamed of people you hadn't thought about enough in the daytime and the thoughts of her days were fully occupied with all of the Martin family. It was Jack who had begun to appear in her dreams, his face vague, only his eyes staring at her silently.

I'm doing nothing wrong, Mary told herself during the long train ride west. Anyway, it's just for a little time, she thought, knowing she was contradicting herself. Just a little time to pretend that I matter to . . . *all* of them. It will be over soon. When Joan's cast is taken off. When she can come to the dinner table again. Surely it couldn't be wrong, just for this little while, especially since Dan had never thought of her as anything more than a friend. He wouldn't even miss her when she finally left. So it wasn't as if she were doing something that could hurt Joan or the children or any of them, just letting herself have a few days more. She would make herself work even harder when she returned to the hospital, she would spend more time with Patsy and her children. Make herself go to bed early . . .

But the winter held and the nightly conversations continued and each morning she woke to find herself happy that she would be seeing Dan again that evening.

Just one more time . . .

Go to bed, Mary told herself. There's nothing left to do here in the kitchen and you know it. The plates are all dry and put away, you set the breakfast table half an hour ago. There's fresh coffee made, and you've had two cups of tea already.

But she knew she wouldn't move. Not as long as she heard Dan pacing restlessly in his den down the hall. She knew she would wait until she heard the door to his bedroom close, and she was finally honest enough with herself to know she was hoping she *would* hear it, that tonight he wouldn't come into the kitchen. For if he did, she would have to tell him. She had promised herself that every night this past week, and every night she had failed. Tell him that it was time for her to leave. Joan was as well as she could be at this period of her life, with the cast finally off her leg. She could swim the length of the pool five times without stopping. There was no real reason for Mary to be here any longer. And so many reasons why she must go.

Because now she knew that for the first time in a long, long time she was really afraid. The other bad things in her life—the discovery that there would be no cure for her mother's illness, the sickening realization of how deeply Jack had got them into debt—these had been outside things, things she could not control. But Dan and what had happened to her feelings, that was her doing. And if she allowed it to continue, it would be her fault. He was another woman's husband, this was another woman's home, and she had no right to either. And she did want him, in a way she had never felt before, certainly not for poor Jack, who all the time, she realized, must have known he had been cheated of more than children.

She'd tried so hard to hide her feelings, even from herself, until finally these past nights as she lay in bed in the room next to Joan's, she had forced herself to question what it was she wanted. Not just an affair, his body next to hers, although there were times when he smiled or lit another of his endless cigarettes that she sometimes felt weak with the physical desire to reach out and touch him. Still, the sexual side, coming so late to her, after so many years of denial, was not the major temptation she feared. No, she had known for weeks the terrible sin she had allowed herself to commit was to make herself part of his life, each day sinking further into the impossible delusion that she actually was.

Joan had charmed her first, making her feel protective. Next had been the children, frightened and lonely with their mother an invalid, turning to her so gratefully. Now, finally, Dan.

He wasn't in love with her, whatever that meant for people their age. She knew enough about life and men to realize that. But he had grown to like her, to feel comfortable with her, their conversations late at night stretched longer and longer. And her guilt was that she had allowed him to begin to depend upon her for all the things Joan had given him so freely and naturally before the accident. All but the physical side of life. Instead, he had a cocktail hour with his wife, bright and vivacious and stimulating, in a room he went to after showering and changing into clean clothes, the smell of his after-shave lingering in the halls. Like visiting a shrine. And later with Mary he would relax, lean back with his tie loosened and tell her the wry stories of his struggle to reach the "beautiful life."

And you can put Joan and me together and he still doesn't have one real woman, thought Mary with unexpected bitterness.

"And what worries of the world would you be considering tonight, Mary Conroy?"

He had come after all, so quietly she hadn't even heard his footsteps. She would have to say it tonight. "Thinking of something I have to tell you," she said, surprised at the calmness in her own voice. She poured him a cup of coffee, pushing the sugar bowl near him as he stared at her. She had a feeling he knew what she was going to say. If she had any doubts, the sudden look of caution on his face banished them completely.

"Sounds serious."

"I think the time has come for me to leave."

"Why?" The word was blunt, hard, his cheerful laughter gone. It made her swiftly alert; surely he couldn't have grown to feel what she had?

"Joan is doing very well," she said carefully. "She's made enormous progress. We haven't talked about it, but I think she knows she's made as much of a recovery as she can at this stage of her life."

"She's still badly damaged."

"Not as much as she thinks. That's another reason for me to leave." She got up and poured more hot water into her teacup. Don't let him see my eyes, she prayed. Don't let him guess. Let me keep some part of my self-respect. "I think she's starting to use my staying on as an emotional cane. And that's not good. Besides," she said, trying to lie convincingly, "I've got my own life to get back to, and the salary you're paying me is ruinously expensive."

"Let me worry about the money." His voice was cold. When she finally trusted herself to look at him, she could see his eyes were fastened on her with an intensity she had never seen before. "What's brought this on so suddenly?" He was trying to relax, to treat this like one of their other conversations; but they both knew he wasn't succeeding. Oh, my dear Dan, she thought, don't let me fool myself that I'm important to you!

"Did something happen today? The kids say something? Joan get cranky?"

"It isn't sudden. I mean, we've both known sooner or later I would have to go." She forced herself to smile, hoping it would hide what she knew he would see in her eyes. Only now, for this one moment she was reckless enough not to want to hide what she felt: that she loved him and was afraid.

For one long moment they looked at each other, unspoken words heavy in the air between them; questions never asked but suddenly answered, doubts and desires neither of them had ever allowed to exist before, suddenly free to erupt into the reality that only silence could allow them.

Finally he looked away, as if he had come in out of sunlight into a darkened room. "I wish you could leave later," he said. "We'll miss you," he added awkwardly. "All of us."

"I'll still be here in Chicago," she said, trying to cover the embarrassment she felt. It's all been a dream, Mary Conroy, she thought to herself. And now it's over. Please let me manage it with dignity. "I'll be at the hospital if you need me."

"When will you go?" His voice was quiet, controlled. The closeness that had held them for that one moment was disappearing, they were two civilized adults again, an employer and an employee, discussing terms.

"When?" Tonight, her mind screamed. Before I walk over to you and put my arms around you and rest my head against yours. "I hadn't thought. Tomorrow, I suppose."

"No!" He knew he had said the word too quickly, too sharply, for she winced a little. But it was all so damn sudden! That look that had been in her eyes, he'd wondered how she would look if she ever showed her feelings, the deepest part of herself that somehow he suspected she had never shown to any of them in the months she had been in the apartment. Only now she had allowed him to see it, just for a moment, open and honest and as free of deception as if she had removed all her clothes. Naked and loving and decent. Shown what she felt for him, only to say goodbye.

"I . . . I think tomorrow would be a little . . . hard. On everybody. The kids . . . and Joan. . . . It means a whole new routine." He was lying badly, he who had always been so quick-witted. "Maybe we could cut back a little, gradually. Have you come a couple of days a week. . . ."

"It wouldn't work, Dan." She dared to say his name, the way she had whispered it to herself so often. "For any of us." She got up from the table and took her cup over to the sink. It's over, she thought. Whatever little there was, it's over. If I can just finish this without looking at him again.

"Will you . . . could you wait until the end of the week at least?" My God, he thought, I'm pleading! For a woman I haven't honestly thought of as anything but a friend. He knew, as he thought that, he was deceiving himself and had been for weeks.

With her back to him, she nodded and he knew she was as afraid of words tonight as he was. He pushed back his chair. The noise startled her, and she looked at him for the first time with something close to fear in her eyes. Don't touch her, he thought, as he took a step nearer. It isn't anything either of you can have and you both know it. Leave things as they are.

Her hands clutched the lip of the sink as if she, not Joan, were the one who needed support. He reached out slowly, turning his hand over, letting the back of it touch the back of hers. In an odd way, it felt more intimate than if he had taken hold of her and kissed her. And he couldn't do that; they could never do that.

"I've got a lot to thank you for, Mary Conroy," he said softly. He lifted his hand from hers. For a moment she moved as if she were about to reach out for him only to drop her arms back to her sides. He saw then what she would look like as an old, old lady: lean and beautiful and strong, facing whatever pains and losses life dealt her with a control she would not let be broken.

Without speaking, he turned and left the room.

Six

M ary did not leave at the end of the week, she left the next day. All the way back to the West Side in the taxi Joan had insisted on calling and paying for, she found herself wondering if in some way Dan's wife could have heard their conversation the night before, or even seen them in the kitchen. Not that there had been anything improper to see or hear. It would be impossible to hear anything less than an argument in the kitchen from Joan's bedroom. But certainly Joan could have walked that far. Still, when she had checked her one last time after Dan had gone and before she went to her own room, Joan's breathing had been soft and even, her eyes closed.

But after their swim in the health club that afternoon, Joan had called Mary into her room. Her face was thoughtful, and for once she was not trying to hide the still somewhat inert muscles on the right side of her face. They had never been a deformity; her face had barely been injured or else she had always been careful about controlling her muscles, the way many beautiful women learn to do early to prevent wrinkles. Now a slight frown had formed, giving her face a faintly quizzical look. She sat on the straight-back chair in front of her desk, and Mary noticed she was finally using her right hand, turning a pencil over and over with it, awkwardly, but persisting.

"Mary, my good, good friend," she began. "Would you hate me very much if I said I think it's time I fired you?"

She heard us, was Mary's first reaction, and the one that would come back to trouble her the rest of that day. She's known all along about Dan's visits to the kitchen, so innocent and so important. But the look on Joan's face was tentative, concerned, the am-I-being-cruel-or-rude? look Mary had seen so often when Joan thought she might be opposed in something she wanted.

"I think it would be an excellent idea," Mary managed. There was nothing in her voice to give her away; you learn that handling seriously ill patients over the years. "I've been hoping you'd have the courage to say it to me."

"Courage?" This was not a word Joan expected to hear and Mary knew her well enough to know it would make her angry. Good. Let it be that way.

"You can walk. You can move. And . . ." Mary hesitated for a second before going on boldly. "It's time you came back into your world. I've felt it for a couple of weeks. I've been afraid you were getting too dependent on me."

"We've all depended on you, Mary. More than any of us can ever thank you for."

How much did she know or guess with that strong pride of possession a married woman feels subconsciously? There was no trace of it on her beautiful face.

"You've nothing to thank me for, Joan. You've been a perfect patient." Keep this professional, Mary thought, now that it's over. "This is a comfortable apartment, the kids have been fun, and I've liked being here." Too close to the truth, Mary told herself. She went on quickly, for the first time shamelessly using the facts of her own life before Joan could start guessing. "You know about my husband leaving. It's been a relief to get away from my brother and that whole neighborhood for a while."

Instantly Joan's eyes were filled with concern. "Will going back now hurt you? I mean, the debts you're paying off. I could make out a check. . . ."

How like her, Mary thought. Kind. Yet some rebellious part of Mary's mind dragged up a remark she had heard or read somewhere: Nothing is easier for the rich to give than money. It was a mean thought and unworthy of Joan, or of her for thinking it. "Joan, I'll be fine. You and your husband"—put it that way, she thought; put them together as a couple and keep thinking of them that way—"have been very generous. The biggest debts are almost paid. The rest I can do regularly on my hospital salary. It will be no problem for me to leave." She added hastily, "And leave now. Could you manage if I went today?" The words were coming out quicker than she wanted, but the relief on Joan's face was so obvious she knew the other woman wasn't noticing. "I hate goodbyes. And the sooner you get back to a normal routine, the better."

For a moment she could see uncertainty in Joan's eyes. "Can I do it, Mary?" she asked. "Can I make it? MacCauley said last week after his examination that I might stay on this plateau for some time, not getting better, not getting worse. Is it good enough? Can I . . . manage?"

"Of course you can!" Mary made herself sound enthusiastic, knowing it was false and overdone, the way well-meaning hospital visitors try to be encouraging. Fortunately, Joan wasn't noticing; she was too involved in her own worries. "You're going to be just fine. Use the cane if you get tired." The cane had been a source of some contention when Evan had brought it that first week after Joan had come home. It was thin and elegant, dark mahogany with an antique silver head, and after he had left, Joan had flung it across the room in a rare burst of rage."Damn him!" she had shouted. "I could take one of those awful aluminum things, but something like this . . . it's like he's announcing I'm going to need it forever." Mary had calmed her about that, but the cane was brought out rarely and it was still a touchy subject. "Or if you don't like the cane, there are thousands of chic umbrellas; you can get one for each dress. Not that you're going to need them," Mary added hastily. "You already can walk around the block without stopping."

"Slowly." The word came out grudgingly.

"That will change. Come summer, the warm weather, and you'll continue the swimming."

"You really think I'll be all right?" A child, Mary thought. Pleading for reassurance that Christmas will come and the party dress will be perfect and the right boy will ask her to dance—all the insecurities every woman faces. "Be the way I was? Before the accident?"

"Sure! A gorgeous, healthy creature like you?" Mary forced herself to smile. "However, if you want my opinion, I'd give the skis away . . . and I wouldn't enter any polka contests—not just yet."

Joan's laugh was a happier reward than the lavish check she wrote.

Dinner had gone well, better than Joan could have hoped. There was no cocktail hour in her room this evening. She was seated in the living room wearing a simple sweater and skirt like she used to do in the evening before the accident, reading a news magazine, when Dan had come home. Fortunately there'd been few questions about Mary's departure; Joey was deep in baseball talk with his father for most of dinner, and Paige was on a blissful cloud, the result of having been informed that afternoon she would be singing a solo at her school recital on graduation day. Dan said very little about Mary. Only the reaction of the housekeeper seemed odd. Lila Franklin had said very little as they had helped Mary pack. But to Joan's surprise, Lila, generally the least demonstrative of women, had given the nurse a warm embrace before she left. And when serving dinner her eyes had been wise and, when Joan looked at her, curiously watchful.

Joan had walked carefully to her own room after dinner, giving Dan a swift kiss on the top of his head as he sat in his easy chair, using the excuse of shepherding the children to their homework to lean, just a little, on their shoulders. She did not know if Dan would come to her room that night; she guessed he would not. Being up and dressed and at the table for dinner was one thing; being his wife once more was something else. It would be up to her to make the first move. She planned to wear the new nightgown he had given her at Christmas, which she had deliberately never worn before. When the house was asleep she would make her way to his room. No. *Their* room. A couple of months can't have changed that, she'd thought as the afternoon grew dark around her. It's *our* room, and tonight I intend to share it with him, tonight and for the rest of my life.

Only first . . . he had to look at her with desire. Not as some cripple he was chained to until they both died of old age.

After she had put on her nightgown and used the perfume he had always loved, she went into her bathroom and picked up the container that held her diaphragm. Privately, after the birth of Joey, she had resolved not to have any more children. One of each should be enough, she had thought at the time, though she knew Dan would have liked a larger family. But the weeks of morning sickness, the slow loss of her figure, while it had never bothered him, had angered her. She was honest enough to know the anger was because she wanted her husband to herself. She had never had very strong maternal feelings, though of course she'd had to have . . . *wanted* to have Dan's children. Several times in the intervening years Dan had brought up the subject of another baby, but she had always put him off, reminding him it would mean delaying their first trip to Europe, their plans to redecorate the apartment, the trip to teach her how to ski. . . .

For a moment she stood there, feeling the old panic coming back. She knew her bad leg was trembling, and it wasn't from fatigue. Deliberately she put the container back on the shelf. Let what might happen, happen. It was late to have another child, risky; but it would be a perfectly logical excuse for months of awkward movements. It would be another link between them, another sign to him and to the whole world that she was a complete woman again. That her husband loved her and she loved him. That the accident was just an incident in their marriage to be laughed at in years to come, like the time in Paris he had forgotten his wallet and she had had to pay their dinner bill.

She looked at herself in the long mirror on the bathroom door. Her figure was good, maybe even a little better since she had lost some weight with her exercises and careful diet. She would hate to see it swollen and grotesque as it had been during her pregnancies, but it was a risk she was willing to take.

She started across the dark apartment carefully. There was enough light from the night sky outside to see where each chair and table in the rooms were. She moved from one to another, forcing herself to breathe easily, to rest for a second, the skirt of her long satin gown held up carefully. Her progress was slow, but she felt no pain. If only that damn nerve in her right leg would stop throbbing! But she knew she should be grateful for that; it meant it was alive, almost well. Just don't let him be asleep yet, she prayed as she moved into the corridor to their room. There was still a thin line of light under the door. She waited outside the closed door, carefully smoothing her hair over the side of her face that barely had any feeling. Let him look at me with desire, she thought. Please, God, let him want me. Don't let there be pity or shock, or the one thing she knew she could never, never bear: disgust. Pulling the top of her robe open a little, she turned the handle of the door.

"Hi, stranger," she said, leaning against the doorframe, making her voice as low and seductive as any actress propositioning her leading man. "Care for a little company?"

It's going to be all right, she told herself as he looked at her, eyes wide with surprise and already the beginnings of desire.

It's going to be all right. Forever.

In the month that followed, Mary heard nothing of the Martins and she was careful to ask no questions. At the hospital, perhaps as some sort of punishment for her extended and (everybody knew) highly paid leave of absence with the family of a member of the Board of Directors, she was assigned to the wards. Her superiors would have been surprised to know she welcomed it; she had no desire to be part of the private rooms of the twelfth floor, to be anywhere near the offices and consulting rooms she had seen so often with Joan, no wish to hear their names or any of the voices of the past months.

Coupled with her determination to put the whole family out of her mind was a sense of shame, deeper than any of her unspoken feelings about Dan, deeper than even the occasional sly questions Tim or Patsy had asked about her sudden departure from the luxurious household. A week after she came back to her own apartment she had found an envelope in her mailbox. The handwriting was vaguely familiar, the postmark California, although the name of the town was smudged. Inside was a postal money order for two hundred dollars, without any note of explanation. Jack, she knew instantly. Somehow she felt dirty. How hard it must have been for him to have saved up that much toward his debts! How many "sure things" had he turned down to collect this sum? She started up the stairs to her apartment. She wondered again if he was sleeping alone, as Dan did. But she knew he must be. It takes money to take a woman to dinner, for a drink or a dance, and on to bed: money he had saved for her. That's over, she tried to tell herself. The divorce papers were signed; he has no claims on me. Fred Reiner had never told her how he had got Jack's signature, and she had not asked. Only it hurt to look at the envelope, knowing how many quiet sacrifices Jack must have gone through to send it.

Forget me, Jack, she thought. Just let everybody forget me.

By the middle of June, Mary learned Joan was pregnant. Selena, who had commanded the nurses' station on Twelve for as long as Mary had been at the hospital, passed the news on to her in the hospital cafeteria. "That must have been some job of therapy you did for her, kid," she said when she had finished describing Joan's exit from her gynecologist's office, radiant and cool and obviously happy. "She had this parasol and I could see she was leaning on it, but I don't think anybody who didn't know her history would realize she still has a limp."

Mary tried to look politely interested. Of course Joan had gone back to bed with Dan. He was her husband. What better way to prove it than this . . . not knowing there was anyone who would want proof? Mary told herself it didn't hurt, it really didn't; but that night when she was home she tore up the card she had addressed to Paige wishing her luck in her school recital. No reminders, she told herself firmly. For anybody.

Shouts. Screaming. A woman's voice high and shrill, yelling out unbelievable obscenities, a blur of interns rushing a gurney cart along the hall toward the operating room, blood smears on their usually clean uniforms, darker in color under the hospital's fluorescent lights. The woman kept shouting over and over, "You want me dead, you've always wanted me dead!" A cluster of doctors. The operating room doors held open to admit the patient. The noise ripped through the night sleep of the other patients on the floor. You never get used to emergencies, Mary thought as she moved forward to see if she was needed.

There was one person in the crowd who was not part of the medical staff. It was Dan, eyes wild, unfocused, his face white as if there were no blood in him and never would be again.

It was after two in the morning before Joan was finally placed in her room, sedated, her face clean and calm, her eyes closed, her hair damp and lank on the starched pillow. The baby, or what would have been her baby, had been lost before she was brought to the hospital. The room she was taken to was not the one she had had before, and no one asked Mary to attend her as nurse. Mary had seen Evan Paige deep in conversation with a group of doctors, but she knew he had not recognized her. Only Dr. MacCauley had, moving rapidly down the hall toward the recovery room where they had placed Joan after the operation to stop the hemorrhaging.

"Damn it," he had growled as he passed her, speaking almost to himself rather than to her. "Trying for a child at this stage of her recovery." He stopped short and looked at Mary as if recognizing her for the first time. "I should have warned her, shouldn't I?" For once the long, plain features of his face were twisted with concern. "Only I thought her own gynecologist—that a grown woman would have enough sense . . ."

"I don't think anyone could have stopped her, Doctor."

"I suppose you're right, Mary." It was the first time he had used her name; she had not been sure he had even recognized her, although she had spent enough hours sitting in his waiting room while he examined Joan during this past half year. "Only this is about the worst thing that could have happened to her, physically and psychologically."

"She's going to live?"

"If she wants to." His voice was curt. "At the moment she's half out of her mind; we had to give her three times the usual amount of sedation. The husband's around someplace. You'd better find him, let me know if he needs anything." With that he strode down the corridor toward the elevator.

He needs a wife, Mary thought, the only thing Joan wanted to be.

She went to the nurses' station, hoping to find Dan there, and when she didn't she went down the long corridor to the darkened solarium. Technically she was off duty, had been for hours, but she could no more have left the hospital than Dan could. She found him, as she expected, sitting in a chair staring out the window at the night sky.

"Dan? Can I get you anything?"

He made no answer, although she knew he must have recognized her.

"Dan? I've talked to Dr. MacCauley. Joan's going to be all right."

"No, she isn't." His voice was tired but firm, as if he had been sitting there making some terrible decision that could never be unmade. "She hates me. You heard her."

"Dan, women in pain, women suffering a loss like this . . . they say things they don't know they're saying." She pulled a chair up to sit beside him. She could barely see his face in the darkness, but she knew his eyes were dry. There'd be no tears. "That's one of the reasons some of us are not so happy about the new practice: letting a husband in a delivery room to 'share the experience' of birth the way a few hospitals are starting to do. No one, not even a mother, can tell how she will react under those circumstances. That's a place for professionals, and the woman herself. Some of the things I've heard . . . they could rip a marriage apart if the husband heard them too."

"Only this husband did hear them." His voice was so cold, so matter-of-fact. Mary didn't dare reach out to him. "There won't be any baby to heal the wounds. Not now. Not ever."

"Did the doctor say . . . ?"

He looked at her, his eyes cold and cruel. "Anatomically? I guess it would be still possible. Mentally? No. Not for either one of us."

"Dan, you're upset, you've been through a terrible evening."

"Don't make excuses, Mary Conroy. I've had enough of that from everybody." He leaned forward, taking her hands, his grip so hard it hurt, but she made no move to show the pain. "She never told me she wasn't taking precautions. She never told me she wanted a child. Maybe I should have guessed. Maybe I should have . . . explored . . ." Even with a nurse he couldn't talk about the intimate side of his married life.

"I'm sure she wanted it to be a surprise, a sign she was well again."

"And what about me? Yeah, me. Sounds selfish, doesn't it? My wife's the one who lost the baby, my wife's the one who's been ripped apart and sewn back together again. My wife's the one in pain, half out of her mind. Let's have lots of sympathy for Joan. I'm not supposed to feel anything. Except guilt. Well, I've had a hell of a lot of that these last six months, and I'm tired of it. Guilty for taking her skiing, guilty for not stopping her from taking that slope, guilty for acting like an animal the first night she's well enough to put on her clothes. Oh, yes, I got that one from Evan. And I saw it in the doctors' faces. Heard Joan shouting it to the whole damn world." He released Mary's hands and sat back in his chair, stiff and remote. "Well, I'm sick of feeling guilty, Mary. I'm sick of discovering she's hated me all this time."

"She doesn't hate you."

"Don't lie! I'm sick of that too. She hates me. She must have hated me all these months." The intensity in his stare made Mary wonder if she should go for help, call MacCauley. Joan wasn't the only one close to madness tonight. "You know something, Mary? I think I hate her too. I mean that. My lovely Joan." His voice was soft as a whisper, as if he didn't trust himself to speak. "All I ever wanted to do was hold and protect her. And now I think I can't stand the sight of her."

"Tonight, maybe. Not tomorrow. A couple of hours doesn't change what you two have had, what you've shared, the world you've made for yourself."

"Is that how you felt when you got a divorce?"

"That's not fair." She couldn't bear to sit next to him any longer. He was saying things she had never wanted to hear, asking a question she had never wanted to face. She went to the window. "My husband and I . . . we never had the closeness you've shared with Joan." She went on quickly, before he could interrupt. "My fault, Dan, all my fault. Anyway, you can't be talking about divorce."

"Because it might kill her? Or drive her really insane? Damn guilt again." Slowly he crossed the space between them. He watched her face, gentle in the half-light. Not really beautiful. Not desirable and enchanting the way Joan could look . . . had looked at times before this God-awful night of rage and anger. But Mary's face held something he had never seen in his wife's: a concern, a gentleness that gave him comfort. It was part of what he had seen that last night they had talked together in the kitchen. Just for a moment she had shown her feelings, or part of them, and he had seen the love in her eyes when she had looked at him, not saying a word. He hadn't forgotten that look and he had tried. "Mary," he said at last. "It's been a long six weeks. I've . . . I've thought of you often."

Almost automatically, as if she had prepared not to let the conversation take this turn, she asked, "How are the children?"

"All right. They miss you. Mary? The doctors said tonight that Joan's going to need care, a lot of care, for maybe a very long time. I'd like you to come back. Permanently." Silently, she shook her head. "Mary, we need you; I need you."

"I can't, Dan. You know why as well as I do."

"I'd never do or say anything you didn't want."

She faced him with sad, thoughtful eyes. "And suppose someday I wanted it . . . the love and affection of the children? And yours? I don't have the right to them." She stepped back, almost as if she were afraid to be near him. "You'll work it out, if there's nobody in the way. I've seen it happen in a lot of marriages."

"You've made your bed, now lie in it?" His voice was dry, cold. "Only I'll be lying in it alone . . . I can't imagine Joan and me . . ."

"I can't help you, Dan. I wouldn't dare try." She knew her next words would be cruel, but she had to say them. "And don't pull any strings, get me reassigned or something. I'd just have to quit and go to another hospital."

She could see a bitter little twist of his mouth. He *had* thought of that! She could almost feel as Joan did, hating his strength and power.

"You forget I love Joan too. I won't do anything to make her unhappy."

"And me? Do you feel nothing for me?"

There was no answer she could make, none he could or should expect. She left him standing in the darkness, making herself walk deliberately down the lighted corridor until she knew she was out of sight.

Seven

"Mary?"

For a moment she didn't recognize the young, tentative voice. She had been trying to sleep that Sunday afternoon, using a headache as an excuse to get out of the family meal with Tim and Patsy. Tim was nearing the end of another job and in consequence was more difficult than usual. Mary knew Patsy hoped she would join them as buffer between his irritation and the children, but for once she had not been able to summon up the patience and the strength. She had been resting until the phone rang. Almost at once she knew the caller.

"Paige? Is that you?"

"Yes. I hope you don't mind my calling. I got your number from Mrs. Franklin."

"No, of course not. Is . . . anything wrong?"

There was a hard, brittle laugh from the other end of the phone, edging very close to tears. "What could be wrong? Mom's crazy in the hospital, Dad won't speak to anybody, and Joey's threatening to run away. Just your normal American family."

"Paige, please take it easy. Your mother will get well."

"You told me that all last winter." The old sullenness was in her voice, something Mary had not heard for a long time. "Sorry I bothered you."

"Paige! Don't hang up!" She tried to think of something that would distract the girl. "I've . . . I've been thinking about you. Your school recital's this week, isn't it? I wanted to send a card—"

"You remembered? Mary, I thought when you went away and nobody heard from you or anything that you didn't really care about us."

A lonely girl, barely thirteen. Joan and Dan hadn't thought about what her departure would mean. Mary had, but she knew there was nothing she could do about it. Only now Paige was reaching out to her. This has nothing to do with Dan, Mary told herself as she moved the phone nearer. I'm not doing anything wrong, anything that could hurt you or Joan. "Of course I care about you, Paige!" Tactfully, she added, "You and Joey both."

"Then will you help? Could you? Do you have time? See, I'm singing a solo, and I've got to have a white dress, and I'm too big for anything I had last summer. And Mrs. Franklin wouldn't know about the stores and credit cards and all that stuff, and when I ask Daddy he doesn't seem to hear me . . . and everybody else is going to be wearing white—"

"Calm down, Paige. Do you want me to go shopping with you?"

"Could you, Mary? Could you *please?* There's another reason, but I don't want to talk about it on the phone. . . ."

By Tuesday, when they met in the Young Misses' section of Marshall Field's department store, Mary had a shrewd idea of what the "other reason" was. Paige pulled her aside before they started looking for dresses.

"It started two months ago. It wasn't painful or anything. I mean, we had it all in biology and they give you books and the school nurse saw each of us individually. It was just—ugh, *messy.* You know what I mean?"

Mary nodded. Welcome to the world of women, she thought. You'll never be my little girl again.

Paige went on, a swift nervous whisper. "Only, Mary, I have a feeling it might happen the next time on the day of the concert. I've been counting. And if I'm standing up there in a white dress and it happened and everybody saw, I'd die! I'd just die!"

By the end of the afternoon Mary had convinced Paige such an accident couldn't happen, but to increase her confidence they picked a full-skirted dress lined with three layers of stiffened tulle petticoats. The saleswoman was understanding. Fortunately for both Mary and Paige, she recognized the girl so there was no problem about charging the dress to Joan's store account. After a trip to a drugstore, Paige had enough of what the druggist euphemistically called "personal equipment" to last her a year.

"Oh, Mary, I can't thank you enough." Paige looked so young and happy as they waited for her northbound bus. "You will come, won't you? It's Thursday, Thursday afternoon, and I get to sing just before they give out the diplomas!"

All afternoon Mary had been preparing herself for the request, knowing that once Paige was over her immediate worries she would think to extend an invitation. How very like your mother you are, Mary had thought, and she had her answer ready.

"I don't think I can, Paige. I'll be working that afternoon."

The girl's face went suddenly sad; not like her mother, more the look of unhappiness Mary had seen Dan wear far too often.

"But I'm counting on you! There'll be nobody there otherwise."

"Your family: Joey, Mrs. Franklin . . ." Mary knew she was being evasive, but she hated saying Dan's name to his daughter. "I'm sure your father will come."

"No." A bus pulled up, but Paige made no effort to get on. She stepped back, arms full of her packages, her face once more frozen, withdrawn. "Thursday they're taking Mother to some hospital in the East." It was the first time that afternoon she had spoken of Joan, although Mary had been waiting for some comment, even a harsh one. She knew from other nurses at the hospital that Joan was recovering physically, but her rage and depression had not changed since the night they had brought her in.

"Hospital? Which one?"

"Some funny farm in New York. The doctors think she ought be away from all of us."

Mary could hear behind the girl's words the unspoken "and good riddance, too." Joan, she thought, you're missing such an important time in your daughter's life. An afternoon like this could have done so much to ease the rivalry between them for Dan's affections.

"Dad and Granddad are going on the plane with her. She can't even do that by herself."

"She's been very sick, Paige."

"I know." The girl sighed theatrically. "Isn't it ever going to end?" The same words, the same feelings her father had. You're selfish people sometimes, you Martins, Mary thought. The girl burst into a radiant smile. "Oh, please, Mary, you won't say no to me, I know you won't. That old hospital can do without you for an hour. Just an hour? Three o'clock? I'll leave a ticket for you." Without waiting for an answer, she jumped on the next bus that pulled up. Looking back over her bundles, she managed to throw Mary a kiss.

All the following day Mary told herself she would not attend the program, knowing as she did she was already planning her schedule to fit it in, deciding as she went about her duties what she would wear if the mild June weather suddenly turned hot. It would be safe. Dan wouldn't be there; he'd be on a plane with Joan and Evan Paige. By discreet inquiries, Mary knew the patient was being released at two o'clock that afternoon. It couldn't do any harm to anyone to see the girl, hear her sing once more the soft Schubert *Lied* she'd been practicing all spring. It couldn't hurt, just for once, to pretend she had a right to be part of the girl's life.

The hall was full by the time Mary arrived, crowded with proud, perspiring parents and relatives. The principal was just finishing her address and Mary was content to stand in the darkness at the back of the auditorium with a crowd of others. Paige would be next. The accompanist came out and settled herself at the piano, and Paige made her way slowly down from the back row where the choral group had been positioned to the floor of the stage. She looked beautiful, and Mary knew even before she smiled she had persuaded the dentist to remove the hated braces just for this day. She clutched the small bouquet of roses Mary had sent. Mary had called Lila at her home the night before, suspecting that in the rush of taking Joan east nobody would remember. Lila's voice was warm on the phone. Mary could almost see the smile on her face. "Glad you called about that, Mary. I was going to do it myself, if no one else volunteered."

They talked for a few moments more, both being careful with their words. Of course Lila knew of the ties growing between her and Dan but she would never intrude on such a personal area in anyone's life without being asked. Still, on her own, Lila volunteered that "Mr. Dan," as she called him, was in "a bad way. None of the old problems, Mary," she added delicately, each of them knowing she meant the heavy drinking that had occurred the first weeks after the accident. "Sometimes I wish he were back to that. That I know he can handle."

There was nothing Mary could say, and they knew it. After promising to look for each other at the graduation, Lila hung up.

Paige stood before the whole auditorium, poised and tall, as Mary had tried to teach her. Mary was no music critic, so she had been careful not to allow her affection for the girl lull her into making more of Paige's talent than there was. It was a sweet voice, clear and accurate, not the material of which great careers are made, but touchingly effective in this gentle song. To her surprise Mary found there were tears in her eyes when Paige had finished, nor was she the only one; all through the auditorium handkerchiefs were being pulled out of purses. The applause was strong and solid, and as it went on Paige dropped her careful pose and simply grinned back at the crowd like the happy child she was.

"Did you send the flowers?" The voice was directly behind her. She didn't need to look to know it was Dan. He was carrying a bouquet in his hands, larger than Mary's.

"You're supposed to be on a plane." She kept her voice low although she knew no one around them could hear them. Everybody else was pressing forward to the railing as the graduates received their diplomas, one by one.

"Joan didn't want me." He glanced around; reassured that no one was watching them, he moved closer. "Mary, I've got to talk to you."

"No, Dan. Believe me, I wouldn't be here if I'd thought—"

"That I would show up? I rather figured that. Joan practically had hysterics when she saw me at the hospital. Even MacCauley thought it would be better if I left her with her father. Now, when can we meet? I *have* to talk to you."

"Dan, there isn't anything we have to say to each other."

"I don't mean about us. It's Paige . . . and Joey. I've got to have somebody sensible to talk to." He took a deep breath and forced his voice to be less urgent. "Look, I'll meet you in the middle of the Michigan Avenue bridge at high noon if you're worried about my intentions."

Before she could think, she found herself saying, "It wouldn't be your intentions I'd worry about."

She started to blush. For the first time in weeks, as they stood there in the shadows, she saw Dan's old confident smile. She tried to think of something to cover what she had admitted, but he broke in quickly. "Lunch Saturday, one o'clock. And don't tell me you're on duty because I know you're not. I checked." He mentioned the name of the dining room. It was in one of the few hotels in the downtown Loop that had retained its pride and grandeur, keeping level with the newer, more fashionable hotels that had moved north, toward the glittering new apartments and carefully restored old mansions that were becoming the special area of the rich of Chicago. Before she could protest, he took her elbow and began to move them through the people coming up the aisles from the ceremony. "Come on. I want to be the first to tell Paige she's going to be the next Maria Callas."

That night and the next Mary barely slept. She tossed and turned in the bed she had shared with Jack . . . how long ago that seemed! She would get up, walking quietly in her bare feet through the dark rooms, although she knew she could have stamped on the floor and it would not have awakened her brother and his family below. She warmed milk and drank it, standing by the window looking out at the back yard, knowing if she met Dan on Saturday it would be a turning point in her life, one that she could never change.

Not that it necessarily meant an affair or, if that happened that the affair would last or hurt anyone. The physical part of what might happen seemed the least important part of her decision. The strictures of her religion, she had realized through the two long nights, had never really bound her, not as they did Patsy and the girls she had grown up with. Perhaps too much had been made of the sexual act, in or out of a Catholic marriage. The threats of hellfire from the pulpit, the sober admonitions of the nuns, always seemed to be about the sins of the flesh. She remembered with a certain unhappy humor being taught that if a man were starving, he might steal up to five dollars a day to feed himself and his family and it would not be considered a sin. She wondered idly who had set that figure and if it had changed in the intervening years. However, if you went to bed with that same man, starving for love and comfort, for warmth and kindness and affection, that automatically sent you to hell forever.

In her heart Mary was honest enough to admit it wasn't the shakiness of that rationale which freed her. Since she had known she could never have children—and children, to the Catholic Church, were the whole purpose of marriage—she had felt separate from the other young women she knew.

A good thing the local boys had never discovered that, she thought. They might have thought her "easy," the worst that could be said of any girl in a neighborhood like hers. Not that she ever would have been. It had been no burden to keep her virginity until her wedding day with Jack, nor to resume the pattern of it since. No, she thought as she stood at the window, the air fresh before dawn, stirring the curtains gently, it wasn't to keep from going to bed with Dan that would make her fail to meet him on Saturday. Not that that would stop him; it would only postpone their meeting. She knew him well enough for that. What he wanted, he got.

Only what *did* he want from her?

There were other women who would share any bed he was in gladly. Kay Wallis would, she knew. And younger women, prettier than either his secretary or his wife's nurse (for that was all she really was). Dan was handsome, rich, vital, far younger-looking than his years. Ruthless in getting what he wanted; add that too, Mary thought, for she knew it could be a powerful aphrodisiac for many women. Not to her, she could say in all honesty. It was never that side of him that made her want to reach out and hold him. It was the other side she had seen so many nights when they had sat at the kitchen table and talked. The lost side, quiet, still a little unsure of himself as a boy "from back of the yards" (although the stockyards were already fast disappearing from Chicago), married to the Golden Princess of the suburbs, a princess who had turned on him.

That was what moved her, touched some part of herself she hadn't experienced since her mother had died. Jack had loved her, needed her, but she realized as the night hours ticked slowly by that she had never loved him, never given him what a wife should give. She had nothing to give, not at that time. It had been too soon, she realized. She had been like a child hurt in a game . . . the game of loving and caring for someone. Because she had lost her mother when she did, Mary as good as said to life, I'm not playing any more. I won't be hurt again.

As if caring for people were something you could cut out of your life permanently. She remembered what her mother had said so often: "You have so much to give, Mary, so much love and warmth and happiness." Now, at last, somebody wanted it, needed it, and she wanted to try once more.

Only, of course she couldn't.

Why not? It almost seemed as if her mother sat with her in that empty kitchen, talking her good dry hard common sense. You'll be taking nothing from Joan. Nothing she really wants, nothing she can manage at the moment. Still, that was the problem. This time wouldn't always last. Someday Joan would come back, Mary knew that. Would want her marriage and her family to be where she had left them. And they might be there, if Mary stayed out of their lives. For meeting Dan for lunch wasn't just the possible beginning of an adulterous relationship, a married man temporarily without a wife, and a divorced woman. He wanted to see her, talk to her, because of the children, whatever else he might desire. And whether he was being skillful in his approach to her through them, or honest, it was the one thing both of them knew she would find the hardest to refuse.

Take the chance, Mary. She could almost hear her mother whisper to her. Don't be a coward. If something good comes out of this, let it happen. If it turns out bad and painful, let that happen too. At least you'll be part of living, you'll have had *something*.

Mary dressed with care Saturday morning, knowing her own pride could not let her appearance embarrass Dan. There were neighbors watching as she walked down the street, eyes behind thin curtains, women gathering to shop for their heavy Sunday dinners. They would wonder where she was going all dressed up. That would be the phrase they would use when they told Patsy about it, as undoubtedly at least three of them would before she reached the hotel downtown. Mary held her head high. There was no money owing in the neighborhood; Dan's handsome checks had seen to that. The firms she still had to apportion payments to were not part of this community, so nobody who saw her could begrudge her the new summer suit and shoes. No one on the street would be able to tell she was planning to go to bed with a married man that afternoon, if he asked her. The sin was already committed, she thought as she walked toward the el station. The Church taught you that. Once you made up your mind carefully and the matter was serious and you were deliberately planning to do it anyway, the sin was already on your soul. It didn't frighten her, she found to her surprise. For once in her life she was going to do what *she* wanted, not what was expected of her, or owed to others, or would relieve the pain of someone else's illness or errors. She found herself smiling as she went into the station. A couple of the women on the corner stopped their gossiping and looked at her curiously; she knew them from church. She smiled and waved gaily as she started up the stairs to the platform.

Mary didn't go to bed with Dan that afternoon, and after the first few minutes, when she realized it wasn't going to happen, she relaxed and allowed herself to enjoy the luncheon. He could not have picked a more public place for their first meeting. The word *date* seemed hardly suitable, Mary thought to herself, for a man in his forties and a woman in her middle thirties. Dating was something that brought to mind acne and cherry sodas and desperately trying to think of things to say. Still, she couldn't think of the proper word for their luncheon, and it made her smile.

"What's that for? The smile, I mean?"

"Nothing. I was just thinking of something."

"It must have been pleasant." He put down his menu and looked at her soberly. "I'm glad you came, Mary. I was afraid maybe you wouldn't."

That much she knew was true. He had a copy of the afternoon paper next to his plate for company if he ended up having lunch alone. She decided not to answer, asking instead what he planned to order. By the time that was finished and they were sipping their drinks, there was no need to worry about conversation, or whether she would be invited to his bed that day. (What bed? she thought as they continued their talking. Where would he have planned to take her? You didn't consider that in your long nights of the soul, Mary Scanlon Conroy. Which shows how dumb you can be.)

". . . so according to Evan—oh, yes, we're back to talking to each other again," Dan went on, not noticing her thoughts had strayed "—they're going to want her to stay there at least through the summer."

"What sort of place is it?"

"Hard to describe. I've seen the brochures. Not a mental home, or anything like that. No bars or snakepits. Cottages for each patient, a main house, lots of lawns, a pool. Evan says a terrific view of the Sound. Walls, of course. But they're very far away from the buildings, and covered with ivy. He makes it sound like a country club. I gather that's part of the treatment."

"What kind of patients do they have?"

"Rich ones," he said dryly. "I don't think Evan realized how much we were saving by having you on hand all these past months." He went on more seriously. "I gather it's generally for patients who've had some sort of mental breakdown, although they're equipped to handle any physical problems, too: alcohol, I guess, is a big one. But they have other patients who've suffered physical injuries, and they've got a large and well-trained staff.

"Evan and Dr. MacCauley say it's set up to get the patients interested in wanting to live. That seems to be the main goal."

"Joan will want to live, Dan. Just give her a little time, a lot of patience and encouragement."

"Those aren't exactly the qualities I'm famous for, are they?" He had made no move to touch her since she had entered the large dining room, except to stand when she reached his table and shake her hand formally. Now he put his hand out, almost as if to cover hers, but Mary could see in his face that he instantly thought better of it and covered the move by lighting still one more cigarette.

"Actually, it isn't Joan I'm so worried about. Maybe time away from each other is what we need. I've got several projects I've been delaying work on, things that could be big, that need my attention." Mary knew he was already back in his office, planning the work that was the real love of his life. "I've been treading water these last months. It's time I got back to business."

What he meant was what he would call "real life," a life that had nothing to do with ailing wives or children or even the passing desires of the body. How very little any of us know you, Mary thought.

"The basic problem seems to be this summer and the kids." He ran a hand impatiently through his thick hair. "Mary, I don't know what the hell to do about Paige and Joey. Lila's got her own family to worry about, she can't live in, and I'm not sure that would be a good idea, even if she could arrange it. Not to mention she's due a vacation. The kids should be outside, not cooped up in an apartment. I'd thought of sending them to camp, but I'm not sure I know where to start. You have any ideas?"

"Paige talked to me one night about a music camp. She's quite serious about her singing."

"I know." He grinned. "She's been leaving the folders on my bed every night. Also in the den and on the breakfast table. Okay. That takes care of Paige." The smile disappeared. "Or does it? A girl like Paige? Will this just encourage this music thing? I think she's got a nice voice, but to try for a career . . . ?"

"It might be the best thing in the world, Dan." How easy it was to say his name now! To sit at the table with him, finishing her salad, two people no longer young: respectable, proper. "She'd be with other girls interested in the same things. She'll learn for herself just how good she is, and in a way that won't make you have to be the heavy disapproving father."

"You make good sense." He smiled again briefly. "Now about Joey. Evan wants him up in his place in Lake Forest—wants them both, actually. They'd have other kids to play with; the country club's not far. Joey could improve his swimming."

"You don't think it's a good idea?"

"I don't want him hanging around with a lot of rich kids. He gets enough of that in school. Plus the fact Evan will spoil him rotten." He picked up a folder that had been lying under his newspaper. "Kay suggested camp for him, too . . . even sent away for some folders."

Kay. Of course she would want to free Dan of parental responsibilities this summer, but was it only because it would be good for the children after the traumas of the past winter? So many women revolving around Dan Martin, wanting to be part of his life, wanting him to need them: Joan . . . Kay. Now it was Mary's turn.

"Mary? Would you look at the folders?" He was staring at her, a little puzzled by her silence. "I want Joey to be happy, but he's only ten. Isn't that a little young?"

"I wouldn't think so, not if he wanted to go. He's good at sports— someplace with an emphasis on baseball maybe? Not too far away? So if he did get lonesome you could visit him. Is there a camp like that?" She touched the folders, not looking at them, wanting him to make the decision.

"One in Eagle River, Wisconsin, sounds like what you're talking about."

"Why not find out how he feels? The Cubs are playing tomorrow afternoon. Why not take him to the game, talk it over?" She smiled. "It's Sunday. Even the real estate world must be quiet on a Sunday afternoon in June."

"Good idea. I haven't spent much time with him; not enough, at least." He frowned. "But Paige'll feel left out if I don't ask her too, and she hates baseball."

"Tell Paige to call me. We'll have a nice long talk about what she'll need for camp. I'll try and arrange some free time this week to take her shopping."

"The way you did for her concert dress? Oh, yes, I heard about that." He was looking at her as if he were seeing her as a person, for the first time since they had started their lunch, a woman he liked and was attracted to, not just a sensible friend. There was a flash of desire in his eyes, desire mixed with a memory of how she had looked at him that last night at the apartment, the careful words she had chosen in the hospital. "Mary . . ."

Whatever he had started to say, he obviously decided against it. He stood and held out his hands to pull back her chair. Lunch was over.

"There'll be time for you and me," he said quietly. "I don't think either of us wants to rush things."

She stood as well, with a sense of relief. Whatever was to happen, there would be no games or tricks, no obvious attempts at seduction. So much for sins, Mary thought, finding herself smiling again. Do they still count if your virtue wasn't even in danger? Dan introduced her by name to several people as they made their way through the tables. No explanations, no "my wife's nurse" or "somebody from the hospital," although she recognized one of the men as a fellow member of the Board of Directors. Just "Mary Conroy." And when they reached the stairs to the lobby he took her arm automatically, unself-consciously.

She liked him for that.

Eight

When it did happen, it was so easy, so natural, that whatever insecurities each of them may have had before never had time to enter their minds. The weeks after their lunch had been full of telephone conversations. She and Paige had joined Dan for dinner a couple of times downtown after one of their shopping excursions. Once Joey had called her, very solemnly, to say he had an extra ticket to his grandfather's box at the ball park and would she like to go? The two of them had enjoyed themselves enormously, eating popcorn and hot dogs as relaxed as if they had been in the bleachers. Nobody seemed to notice them at all.

It wasn't until after the children left for camp that anything happened that even the biggest gossips of the parish or the coolly efficient Miss Wallis could describe as "wrong." Dan had given Lila a vacation to visit her sister after the children had left. The next week, during one of those long scorching heat waves that hit Chicago at least twice every summer, he had come home one evening to find the central air conditioning of the apartment not working. It had been put in at great expense when he and Joan had taken the two top apartments and merged them into one, and Dan, in addition to being hot and sweaty, was furious.

"It'll probably take a lawsuit to get them to repair the damn thing," he said on the phone to Mary the next day. He had learned her schedule and had grown into the habit of calling her when he knew she was free or taking a break. So far no one at the hospital had recognized his voice, although Mary found to her surprise she wouldn't very much care if they did. She had grown used to his daily calls, the sound of his voice, rapid and eager, with a dozen different things he had thought about since they had last talked.

"Anyway, I moved into a suite at the hotel." It was the same one where they had lunched. "Looks like I might be there most of the summer." Mary felt a quick sense of relief. It was not the hotel where she and Jack had spent their wedding night, although that hotel would have been closer to his office. Had she mentioned it to him? They had talked of so many things in the past weeks and, before that, in the apartment.

"It's got a small kitchen, so I don't have to wait for a room-service breakfast," he went on, desire clearly the last thing on his mind. "If I offer you a grand dinner out would you do some basic shopping for me?"

As she went back to work, she found herself domestically making a list of things he would need. When she finished work it was still blindingly hot, and she hated to leave the cool of the hospital for the streets. It would be worse at home that night, she knew; the one air conditioner in her apartment, placed in the bedroom, had been behaving erratically. She had hoped she might get through the summer without having to spend the money for a new one. There were still debts to be paid, although a week ago another envelope had arrived from California with a second money order from Jack. Again there was no note, and the amount this time was only seventy-five dollars. He must be working, she thought. She'd scrupulously used the money, as she had the first order, toward their debts.

By the time she reached Dan's hotel it was nearly seven. He had told her to go right up, and when she stepped off the elevator she could hardly wait to put down her packages. A shower would be wonderful, she thought, but knew she would never have the courage to ask for it; it would seem too much like an invitation. Dan obviously had wanted the same thing, for when he finally opened the door there was only a towel hastily wrapped around his waist and his body was wet. There was even shampoo still in his thick hair, she noticed with some amusement.

"You're early," he said as he took her bundles, not as embarrassed as she would have been.

"You're late," she said. "And you're going to get soap in your eyes."

He rubbed his face absently and stepped closer. With one free hand he closed the door to the hall. Before she could step away, he was holding her, his mouth on hers. She could feel his body quickening under the towel. He tasted clean and fresh, and before she gave herself to him she had a moment to wish she were not still soaked with the heat of the July evening outside.

Only later, when they were lying together in bed, their urgent responses, so strong and passionate, briefly satisfied, could they at last talk together quietly.

"You're beautiful, Mary. Do you know that?" He ran his fingers over her breast, touching the nipple gently as if to make up for the wildness of his first assault. Without bidding, her nipple hardened.

"There should be a word for men like 'beautiful,'" she murmured. Handsome wasn't enough, she thought. Oh, my dear love, there aren't any words that are enough for you.

"Mary? I mean it. I don't mean just the things about you I knew before . . . your kindness and sweetness, the happiness you bring. I mean your body." He sat up, the inevitable cigarette for once forgotten in his hand. "Who would believe that under all those starched uniforms and high-necked little blouses was a raving, tearing beauty?"

There were so many things she should have said: that it had been a long time since he had been with a woman, that they both knew Joan, damaged or not, was more attractive, always would be. But she would not destroy this moment. Let him think me beautiful, she thought, leaning back against his naked chest. Just this time, or a little longer. It would give her comfort the rest of her life.

They made love again, easier this time, and slower, each of them exploring the other's body with curiosity and growing desire, both of them holding off their ultimate response until the tension could be borne no longer and they gave each other what neither had known before.

"You still have soap in your hair," she said at last. The suds had dried, turning his normally smooth head into a cap of stiff curls. Like a Greek god, she thought as she lay beside him, the room dark now. Not one of those slim androgynous statues of Apollo or some other golden youth. More like Jove or Neptune, a god of maturity and strength. She, who had (she realized now) always been the primmest of women, shy of her own body and certainly of the one other man she had shared a bed with, could understand finally the physical lust she had heard and read so much about. If before she had been content to want to touch his hand or the soft hair on his arms, now she wanted to feel all of him, to love him, to allow the desires she had never known she possessed a chance to emerge at last.

She sent him off to finish his shower, almost frightened of her feelings. While the water ran she put away the groceries lying neglected on the floor. Her dress was rumpled, and when she picked it up to place it on a chair she could see there were still damp spots where he had embraced her with his wet body. They would dry before they needed to go out, she thought.

Whether this lasts or not, she thought to herself, I'm glad it happened. No matter what the world says, or morality or my conscience, if I still have one, I'll never be sorry this happened.

Later they did go out, to a dark, cool restaurant where there was music. She would never remember what they had to eat, although both of them were ravenously hungry. He didn't have to ask her if she would go back to the hotel with him; it seemed so natural it never occurred to either of them for her to go to her own home. They made love again before they slept, and this time, too, it was different, neither of them actively trying for a sexual release but content to stroke and touch each other until somehow they both knew the moment had come when they were ready.

They spent the whole weekend together, Mary making breakfast in the small kitchenette wearing Dan's robe. They read the papers, contented with silence, sharing a second pot of coffee. For once the hotel maids respected the Do Not Disturb sign hung on their door. There was nowhere they had to be, no one with a problem so urgent that they had to call Dan in his suite. Tim and Patsy might wonder, she thought idly as they slowly dressed to go out for dinner, but she could make up some story—staying with another nurse, for example, after working an extra shift. That would satisfy them.

It would mean building a world of lies, she realized, for by Sunday she knew what had begun between them would continue. Exactly how long it would last she refused to allow herself to consider. All her life she had planned her days, her duties, her responsibilities. That, too, was over. Whenever he wanted her, she would go to him. Oh, Joan, Joan, she thought, I understand you so much better now; why you fought so hard to keep him, why it meant your whole life to you.

Dan was combing his hair in the bathroom. Mary could see him from where she sat. She didn't want to think about Joan or the children; that would be for later. All she could beg for was just this little time to be with him. She would train herself to make that enough.

I won't hurt you, Joan, she vowed to herself. Or your family. Just let me have this little part of his life. I promise not to want more.

Monday morning they parted almost solemnly. Breakfast, and most of dinner the night before, had been the opposite of romantic, an exchange of schedules of two busy people: when they could meet and what time, when he should call her and where. He protested slightly at her decision to return to her own apartment that night, but they both knew after the intensity of the weekend they each needed time to themselves. Monday evening when she came home Patsy met her excitedly with a long white box containing a dozen long-stemmed red roses. There was no note, nor did she expect one. There would never be a note between them, she realized; there was too much to protect to put their feelings on papers or cards that someone might see.

The flowers were a distraction Mary welcomed, for it swept away any curiosity her sister-in-law might have had of her whereabouts. Mary simply said they were probably from the family of the grateful patient she had nursed at the hospital over the weekend. An emergency, she explained to Patsy, surprised at how quickly she was learning to lie. Upstairs as she searched for a vase she realized these were the first flowers in the apartment since Jack had stopped bringing them. She thought of him briefly, without anger or bitterness, hoping, wherever he was, that he was not alone any longer, that he was finding some sort of happiness. The phone interrupted her thoughts and she hurried to-ward it, knowing it would be Dan.

The following weeks, Dan realized later, were the happiest he had known in his life. Before his marriage there had been only the grindingly hard days of trying on the G.I. Bill to finish his education with honors, as well as working to support himself. He had always worked, since he had started grade school, either on a paper route or, later, in his grand-parents' bakery, knowing whatever he could do to help was small return for the effort it had cost them to raise him after his parents had died together in an auto accident. The army—well, nobody could expect that to be enjoyable.

His times with Joan. Alone at night in his bed at the hotel he thought about them. He would not make the mistake of forgetting their plea-sures now that he had found Mary. But he'd been younger then, a wild Petruchio who could take on any strong-willed Katharina in the world. He grinned a little as he lay there in the cool darkness. Hardly fair to make his marriage to Joan a modern version of *Taming of the Shrew*. Joan was far from that, always had been. But there had been a constant sense of competition between them from the beginning.

No, competition was the wrong word. A need to be at one's best: as a lover, a husband, a companion, a host. Part of this had been his fault, maybe a large part, for he was honest enough to admit Joan had never sought such a rivalry. If he had wanted to chuck it all and move to a jungle wilderness and live on berries, she would have gone with him.

Well, at least in the early years. He doubted if she would after the children were born. But in the beginning she would have been eager, or at least pretended to be. She would have also gone out and bought every book she could find on how to live in a jungle, and when the time had come to leave (to carry the image to its extreme) she would have known more about where they were going and how to survive than he would.

Hell, he couldn't fault her for that, he thought, his cigarette the only light in the room. She'd given everything she had to him, until the damn accident. He could examine that cold afternoon finally, examine it clearly, without excuses. He couldn't have stopped her taking that slope if he had wanted to, but he knew he hadn't wanted to stop her. Not to hurt her, never that, just for the small triumph of seeing her flop in the snow ungracefully while he sped past. A little boy's trick, he thought. Make her a little more admiring of him that night at the lodge. Did his ego need that much reassurance? He considered that carefully.

It wasn't ego exactly, he decided at last. It was the fact that sometimes it was dangerous to be vulnerable with Joan. In their fights, and they had had their fights, even in the good years, she would remember every error on his part, reaching all the way back to their courtship days sometimes. And she was not above pulling the "grand lady" routine on him, sometimes subtly and sometimes not so subtly, reminding him that "nice people" (meaning the ones she had always known) didn't do certain things, say certain words, wear one of the new red blazers to the country club.

Silly things, he knew. Now he, too, was dredging up the past to justify the present. Only it wasn't just that. He felt no guilt with Mary, certainly never during the long evenings when they had talked in the kitchen of the apartment. Or rather, he realized, he had talked and she had listened. Certainly he felt no guilt over going to bed with her. Maybe in the back of his mind he had always thought of that happening someday. But it was not the prime reason for his interest in her.

The hotel bed seemed so large, lying in it alone. He had forgotten how good it was to sleep next to a woman, to feel a body alive and close to you in the darkness. All his life he'd had trouble turning his mind off enough to achieve the placidity needed for sleep. That was why he had had to turn to liquor those first awful weeks after Joan's accident. Before that there had been his wife beside him and, if not always the actuality of the relief of sex, the ever-present possibility of it. With Mary, it was different. He felt safe and calm, as if some of her serenity surrounded him softly, securely, as he lay next to her.

But you don't fall in love because you sleep well, he thought wryly, and realized at last he was going to have to face that word. He had not said it to Mary and she had not, unlike what he imagined most women in the same situation might do, asked him to say it. Was he in love with her? Certainly it was not the wild, tempestuous feelings he'd shared with Joan both before and for so very long a time after their marriage. Mary had never once, even in this bed, looked at him with that calculated smile of seduction that Joan had often used, knowing it aroused him almost instantly. The look he had seen on Joan's face that first night when she had come to their room, the night Mary had left. Thank God, he had thought the next day, that science hadn't yet come up with a way to read other people's thoughts. For when the door had opened he'd been thinking of Mary, and for a moment he had almost thought it was she who leaned against the door. Only for a moment, of course. Joan was too strong a presence for the memory of any other woman to be able to share a bed with her.

He wondered if he would share a bed with Joan again. He could still hear her crazed shouts that night. He'd been asleep when the bleeding had begun, and so it was all jumbled together, half reality and half nightmare. Joan would come back someday, and he supposed they would manage to patch together some kind of a life. Unless she wanted a divorce.

He considered that briefly, knowing he was still avoiding the question of whether or not he was in love with Mary. It was only a short diversion. He knew no matter what Joan had screamed that terrible night she would never leave him. Not just from love. She was proud of his success, had imagined all sorts of heights to which he could rise, with her standing by his side. And there were the children. If he tried, or even wanted, to be free, he knew Joan would be vindictive, using Paige and Joey as ruthlessly as a tigress protecting her cave. Not that she loved them as much as Dan did, he knew that, and also knew he had not been the father to either of the children he had intended to be. He'd not been the game-playing, thoughtful dad pictured in advertisements and in movies. But hell, there'd been so little time! Trying to keep Paige Properties ahead of the competition, trying to make the fortune he needed to prove finally and forever to Evan and Joan and, he had to admit, to himself that he was a success, not just a man who had married the boss's daughter. And there was always Joan, who could occupy all the time any other human being might have, not just the tired hours at the end of the day. She had so much energy, so many ideas. She should have been born poor, he thought. Like Mary. By now Joan would have been the head of a corporation, not a quiet nurse content with a modest salary and a lifetime of taking care of other people.

He knew, as he thought it, he was deceiving himself, or at least shading the actual truth. Joan wasn't a heartless, ambitious Lady Macbeth, and Mary was no shy, hidden violet. They were strong women, both of them, with the angers and weaknesses everyone had.

Only Joan was what you fell in love with at twenty. And Mary was what you wanted at forty.

Not every man. I must be some kind of freak, he realized. The men he knew who had affairs outside their marriages almost inevitably picked someone much younger. The most conventional reason for infidelity was the easiest to understand: a desire to recapture or prolong their own youth through a new and inexperienced mistress. He'd always rather despised such men, sweating out last night's alcohol with fierce squash games at the club, going to ever more expensive barbers as their hair thinned, buying more new clothes than some of their wives. Dan had no desire to go back for even one moment to youth, had never wanted that. He had worked too long and too hard to have any sentimental yearnings to be young again. Maybe only the men who had played through those golden, irresponsible years could want to hang on to the memories. For him being young had meant hard work, frustrations at having to give way to older bosses, constant reminders he was an unproven quantity from the rough side of the city.

Well, he had proved himself now. Even Evan admitted—in fact, did so frequently and without prompting, that Dan had turned the company around, had made a success of something that had slowly, under his father-in-law's management, been turning into a stagnant holding company. If he could just get Evan to see what he planned for the future: the land to be acquired out by the fast-growing O'Hare Airport, land that would double, triple in price in the future. Dan had forgotten it was Joan who had first suggested this.

He sighed. All that was for tomorrow. Tonight he was in bed trying to figure out which of two women he loved. Both, he realized, knowing he was dodging the question. Joan was bright and radiant and would be again. Vital, challenging, and, to be quite honest about it, far more versatile and experimental in bed than Mary. Of course, he thought with some humor, they'd had nearly fifteen years to perfect that. Mary was different.

He wondered idly what his life might have been if he had met Mary in his twenties instead of Joan. He probably wouldn't have been attracted to her. Her charm, her gentleness, her quiet humor: those weren't the things he had been looking for then. Even if by some magic it had worked, it would have doomed him forever to a secondary level in his world. He was not foolish enough to think that on his own, minus the strong social and financial backing of his father-in-law, he could have reached where he was today. He and Mary would have settled on one of those side streets, like the one she still lived on. He would be fixing things around the house, because it would be too expensive to bring in a repairman. There would have been no children; she had mentioned that cautiously during their first weekend, knowing he would want to know if it was up to him to take precautions. Would he have resented her for that? He thought for the first time of the husband who had left her, the husband who had piled up debts in a frenzy to move out of that narrow, constricted life. He might have been like that too, he thought.

It was late, and he was tired of trying to puzzle his way through the maze of his feelings. He was happy; there was a woman who loved him without demands, that he wanted to be with as often as he could. That was enough for tonight. Take each day as it comes, he thought, as he put out his last cigarette. Enjoy this time, however long it lasts. He'd be seeing Mary Saturday night. If the heat wave broke, maybe they would drive out to the country. Certainly he wanted to take a look at that property beyond the airport. They were putting up a whole section of new houses there, one-story but attractive, with front and back yards. He had tried to get Evan interested in doing that before, but Evan, bound by his narrow view of the city—Michigan Avenue turning into the Outer Drive and then up Sheridan Road, all on the lakefront—hadn't been able to see the possibilities of anything to the west. He'd have to try again. He made a mental note to have Kay check the ownership of vacant lots when he got to the office in the morning.

Kay knew almost at once when Mary became part of Dan's life. At first she'd tried to pretend Mary was just being helpful, taking Paige shopping, going to a ball game with Joey; but when the question of the summer camps had been decisively settled after one lunch with Mrs. Conroy, Kay faced the fact that Dan was as interested in Mary as Evan was in any of his Wilson Avenue ladies. Had they been to bed together? It would be so easy, with Dan in the anonymity of a hotel suite for the summer. No elevator men who knew the family to gossip. No one to observe the hours he came in in the evening. She had made oblique inquiries at the hospital about the nurse's schedule, mentioning the possibility that when Mrs. Martin "returned from the East," as she tactfully put it, the family might be considering hiring her back. The hospital had not been very cooperative, and she had not pursued the matter again. Still, she would have to have been an idiot not to know how often Dan called Mary, and while she scrupulously made a point not to listen in, she could tell that talking to her changed Dan's whole mood, just as it had in the early years with Joan.

Since the children had gone to camp, the phone calls seemed to have increased, and once, when Kay had a legitimate reason to call Dan at his hotel suite over the weekend, he had been abrupt and curt, as if there was someone with him. He had been lying in bed when he had taken the call. She had known that as clearly as if she were standing in the room with him; his voice was always different when he was sitting or standing or, in this case at four o'clock in the afternoon, lying down. Dan Martin, who had never been known to take a nap in his life!

It wasn't until the bills came the first of August that she was certain he was having an affair with the nurse. She had started to open the first one, from a flower shop, and had seen where the flowers had been delivered. Dan had come into the office at that moment, and she saw an anger in his eyes she had not seen since the first impossible days when he had returned with his wife from the ski lodge. He controlled it at once, but she *had* seen it. He simply said he would handle the payment of his personal bills from then on and had taken the ones on her desk into his office and closed the door.

Throughout the rest of that summer Kay felt lonelier than she had been in her whole life. She made no attempt to see people or to find a man to distract her, as she had when she first met Joan. She was past that now. She would sit in her coolly perfect apartment evening after evening, carefully stretching her one gin and tonic to make it last, knowing she dared not lose any of the control she had fought so hard to attain.

She wanted to hate Mary. She knew it, felt it all the way into her bones, but the cool, disciplined part of her would not let the anger master her. Mary was doing no more than she, Kay, would have done, given the opportunity, and she was honest enough to admit it. You've lost, she told herself rationally. Whatever it was that you might have once dreamed about. Of course, there were ways of revenge, and sometimes, on weekends, when she allowed herself a second drink, she would consider them with relish. A letter to Joan would be the swiftest. Either anonymous or simply an innocent inquiry as to Dan's wife's health . . . with the subtle mention of how relaxed he was and wasn't Joan's former nurse a darling to keep him company these lonely days? Mental breakdown or not, Joan would know what she meant and would be back in Chicago within hours, if she had to kill every doctor in her way. But neither of the Martins was a fool, and Kay would have been fired the next day. She couldn't bear that, and she knew it.

Of course there was Evan. It would be so easy to drop a careful hint. "I'm afraid I can't connect you with Dan at the moment, he's on the phone." And when Evan asked, as he inevitably would, who was so important that Dan couldn't break off to speak to his father-in-law, to add, oh so casually, "It's that Mary Conroy. Again." She wouldn't even have to emphasize the last word. Evan was enough of a man of the world to get the picture at once. He would do something about it, too. Dan may have built the firm up to its present success, but Evan was still Joan's father and a powerful man in every area that affected Dan's business life.

Yes, it would be easy. She could uncover the relationship and, by uncovering it before it had time to take a lasting hold, probably end it. Only she knew she wouldn't. If this was what he wanted, she could no more take it away from him, or try to, than she could have left his office for good.

Besides, Chicago wasn't that huge a city. Dan liked to live well and eat well; he wouldn't be changing his habits at his age. Somebody would see him with this Mrs. Conroy sooner or later. See them once and a second time. Kay wouldn't have to do a thing. Maybe when it was all over he would come to her. . . .

It was just a summer fling, she told herself, as she emptied her almost full glass in the drain of her spotless sink. She could wait.

They would all get through the summer, somehow.

Nine ❧

D r. Edith Keinser stood looking out the window of her office at the sunny October afternoon that stretched before her. It must have been just such a day that inspired the first settlers to call the place Golden Shores. The trees across the lawn rising from the Sound were still rich and full but had changed their summer green to the wilder colors of autumn. The name had been kept when the sanatorium had purchased the property, a turn-of-the-century tycoon's estate, nearly fifty years before. By now it was known to every reputable psychiatrist in America. Even Edith had heard of it when she was studying in Europe. Just Golden Shores. Never to be referred to as a mental hospital or an asylum, although she was sure it was probably called that and worse by the people in the nearby small town. But since much of the town's enduring prosperity had come from the existence of Golden Shores, the natives were careful of their remarks, especially when they encountered a doctor or one of the staff.

When Edith had first heard of the place, all those long years ago when Europe was only vaguely awakening to the possibility of another war, it had been the dream of every doctor, whether of the mind or the body, to work there. At that time it had been a daring experiment, to bring sick and unhappy people back, not only to life but to making something useful of whatever they had in themselves, no matter how badly they were injured. That was before the war and the remarkable (and sometimes terrifying) developments of modern science that had changed the world she had originally known. Now there were prescriptions for hundreds of tranquilizers, mood stabilizers, sleep inducers. Pills to cheer you up or calm you down, pills to stop your hunger or increase it, pills to make the drinking of alcohol a stomach-churning experience designed to assist your resolve never to repeat it. There were also new medicines that induced an almost hypnotic effect in which you would speak truthfully of your most carefully hidden sexual problems.

Dr. Keinser sighed. It would be foolish, of course, to regret the advances that had been made, foolish and old-fashioned. And at sixty-three, she had no intention of letting herself become that. Just as she kept her appearance severely trim and saw to it that her expensive and dignified wardrobe was replenished annually, so she intended to keep her mind alert with all sentiments for the past carefully under control. If occasionally she wished the rooms she worked and lived in at Golden Shores were furnished in the cozy *gemütlich* style of her childhood in Vienna, she kept her opinions strictly to herself. She could live with lean modern furniture as she had trained herself to live with impatient modern people. Only at her sister's apartment on the West Side of Manhattan would she allow herself a faint sigh of relief as she leaned against plump velvet pillows and put her feet up on a needlepoint footstool.

No, she had made her peace with this terrible century, grateful she had received a fellowship to England before Hitler had absorbed her lovely homeland; satisfied with the love she had known from Heinrich, already an elderly widower when they wed, and silently accepting his decision not to raise another family; understanding of his fear of change when finally they had come to America; and, in the long years since his death, proud of the career she had carved for herself in a field where women originally had been nonexistent.

She was good with patients; she could listen with interest, and more than anyone else on the staff she sensed the words of pain that were not being said long before others had guessed their existence. If sometimes she wished, as she did on this peaceful afternoon in October, that her work was not always with the wealthy, she was sensible enough to realize mental disorders were the most democratic of illnesses. The Park Avenue matron and the wife of the shoeshine man could both know deep suffering, and since life was longer now and the world in constant upheaval, it was probable that both of them would. Of course, the wife of the shoeshine man would not come to Golden Shores. There were no foundation grants to change that, nor would there be. There was not even time to get to the real roots of the problems that brought the wealthy here. They would have a good rest in cheerful cottages; they would exercise; they would be exposed to arts and crafts in the hopes of engaging their interests. Their bodies would be graded carefully and a suitable diet ordained and, finally, with their suitcases packed and with a collection of the pills needed to keep them on an emotional level that would not embarrass them in polite society, they would be sent on their way, back to their worlds and to the problems that had caused them to come here in the first place. One third would probably return within the year and then return a third time or a fourth, but never was a patient allowed to stay longer than six months. The Board of Directors was very firm about that. It was useless for Edith or any of her associates to try to countermand this rule. The patient would simply be sent to another institution to start another adjustment to life, Golden Shores' work forgotten.

The turnover was necessary for several reasons, some spoken, some not. Golden Shores had carefully built a reputation of repairing a patient within half a year; this made the families of the patients less critical of the enormous fees they had to pay. Since the time limit had been well publicized, and the fees exorbitant, it simply freed the lovely cottages for more patients, newer money. If the pills and the rest had no permanent effect—well, the patient would come back. But Golden Shores' reputation would still be secure.

"They did everything they could," relatives would say comfortably in their boardrooms or limousines. "You could see how improved dear Cecily (or George or Rita) was when she first came back. But you know her." Voices lowered with patronizing sympathy. "She just wouldn't *try.*"

Dr. Keinser moved back to her desk. Her next patient was not like that. Mrs. Daniel Martin. Edith had quite a folder on her by now. She was different from most of Edith's patients, although the doctor had never allowed any of the people she treated to blend together, with a pat label covering their problems: this group alcoholics, this group with sexual problems, and so forth. But Joan Martin was a special case, had been from the beginning. Both her body and her mind had needed mending, something that had not happened more than once or twice since Golden Shores had discharged the last of its war veterans.

She wished she could have more time with Joan. She had come to Golden Shores at the beginning of summer, quiet, withdrawn, her father hovering over her protectively. Now it was October and soon it would be time for her to leave. With nothing really changed.

Not that she had been difficult. Joan had learned the few rules quickly and followed them meticulously. If she was not outgoing with the staff and the other patients, neither was she sullen or defensive. It was simply a time to endure and she had accepted it all, politely and obediently, the exercises and the games of golf (accompanied by a nurse), the craft shop, and the physical examinations. It made life for everyone at Golden Shores much easier, for everyone but her psychiatrist. If there had once been rage, such as her father had described she experienced the night of her miscarriage, or even a grim determination to get well, like Edith had learned from the Chicago medical staff that she had shown a year ago, there might have been some tiny crack in her personality that would have allowed her doctor to reach her. Instead, there was only polite manners: a prisoner on good behavior, hoping for an early parole.

Edith went to the door. She had wasted two minutes of Joan's appointment hour in wishful thinking, and that did neither of them any good. Joan, she knew, would be waiting patiently outside, and there would be no complaint.

"But you do . . . occasionally . . . allow patients to leave the sanatorium for brief periods?"

Edith leaned back in her chair. Joan had chosen the chair opposite the doctor today instead of stretching out on the couch. She was, as always, neatly dressed, her manner calm and rational.

"Of course. When they feel they're ready to make a small excursion off the grounds."

"It's usually the first step toward being allowed to go home, isn't it?" Joan had obviously been well briefed before making her request this afternoon.

"Yes." Why did Edith feel so reluctant to discuss the proposed trip? She knew as well as Joan that an interest in the outside world was one of the best signs of recovery; so small a thing as asking to see the newspapers was often the first flowering of a patient's improvement.

"Are you so anxious to return home?"

"I have a husband, Doctor, as you know. And two children. I think it's time that I . . ." Joan hesitated. Edith knew she was rejecting her first choice of words and was searching for a better, more persuasive phrase. "I must start thinking of how I will manage in the real world again." Obviously concerned Edith would pounce on the word *real*, Joan went on quickly. "After all, I've been here for over four months now. I couldn't stay beyond Christmas in any event, could I?"

Both women knew Joan was using the rules to get her own way and that there was no argument Edith could give her. "It is . . . customary," the doctor replied slowly, "that the first step outside be a small walk to the village."

"With one of the nurses?" Joan allowed herself a little crooked smile, as if trying to get Edith to join her in a conspiracy. "That might be necessary for someone tempted to lift something from the dime store or head for the nearest bar, but I think you'll agree those are hardly my problems."

"And how would you describe your problems?"

Joan sat a little straighter. She had clearly rehearsed herself for this question. You carefully controlled lady, thought Edith. How much is going on behind that mask that you will not let me see?

"Physically, the nervous system on the right side of my body was badly injured nearly a year ago. I think you'll agree with the medical reports in my folder"—she pointed at the papers on Dr. Keinser's desk—"that I am almost ninety percent recovered."

"I would not put it so high," replied Edith calmly.

"Admittedly I have a slight limp, probably always will have. My right arm gets tired, and some of the muscles are still weak. But I can play almost nine holes of golf and walk a mile without a cane, and I have made a dozen ceramic pots." She smiled at the doctor almost impishly. "If they're not very good pots, Doctor, it's not because of my physical condition but simply that I'm not very artistic. I can sometimes even manage to thread a needle—if it's a large darning needle."

"And your mental condition?"

Joan hesitated. Edith, watching her, had a feeling the pause was deliberate, planned, as if she had spent hours thinking, When they ask that question you enter a dangerous minefield. For as both women knew, to say one was well would have been a clear sign of self-delusion, and to say one was not would endanger the favor Joan so very clearly wanted: a weekend by herself in New York.

"I suppose it harms my chances if I say I never thought I had a mental condition. Rage and anger at the loss of my child, knowing it would be my last; I think that was rather natural under the circumstances, don't you?" Looking directly at the doctor she added, "But I don't know . . . have you ever had children, Doctor?"

The small stiletto, Edith thought. Of course you've found out somehow, from someone, that I haven't, so you can talk about an area of a woman's life where you know I can't contradict you. The anger that brought you here is still inside, after all. Well, perhaps, that's all to the good.

Ignoring Joan's question deliberately, Edith leaned forward, returning the younger woman's level gaze. "To be alone in a modern city is not easy for any woman," she began slowly. "Even such a simple thing as getting a train, transportation to a hotel, registering . . . all these things can be annoying experiences, sometimes more than annoying—"

"But I told you," Joan broke in. "I won't be alone. I'll be going to the wedding of the daughter of a friend of mine, a woman I went to school with. I showed you the invitation. I'm sure she'll make all the arrangements."

"She will be busy with her daughter, don't you agree? You will have two nights by yourself. I think, Joan, it would put too much of a strain on you at this stage of your development."

Edith had hoped for a flare-up of rage, something to crack the smooth facade. That could bring progress, and as Joan had so carefully pointed out, time was running short. Joan did not react as she had expected; instead she leaned back in her chair, her right hand limp in her lap.

"So the first time I leave here," Joan said at last, "will be to go back to Chicago." Her eyes were thoughtful. "That rather worries me, Doctor."

Verdammt! Edith thought. I have allowed myself to walk right into her trap. The way a patient would react when released was one of the most pressing concerns of the staff and, for different, less altruistic reasons, of the Board of Directors of Golden Shores. On leaving, the patient could be sedated for the journey home, but when that sedation wore off? Once or twice there had been ugly scenes in train stations and airports with threats of lawsuits from the families involved. That, Edith knew, and she suspected Joan knew as well, was something to be avoided at all costs.

She began to reexamine the request in her hand. There was no technical reason she could cite for refusing Joan Martin's request. Independence, self-reliance, a desire to stand alone without the supporting hands of the carefully trained staff: these were all essential elements of the Golden Shores therapy. Edith knew any other doctor on the staff would have been pleased and elated if one of their patients had made such a sensible request, especially after four months of perfect behavior. Joan would not be alone, after all. There was this school friend and a genuine invitation, forwarded on from Joan's home in Chicago.

Ah. Now Edith could focus her worries. In all their sessions Joan had never talked about women friends, except the nurse who had attended her for most of the past year. Joan had apparently liked this Mrs. Conroy, and certainly the nurse had cared for her patient. Through the summer and early fall Mrs. Conroy had sent light, attractive summer dresses for Joan to wear, cheerful comments about the scorching Chicago heat that Joan was escaping, postcards that she had received from Joan's children at their camps. Those postcards had a strange reaction from Joan. She read them carefully, over and over again, her cottage nurse reported, whereas the ones the children had sent directly to their mother Joan barely glanced at.

"This friend of yours, the one whose daughter is to be married. Is she a good friend of yours?"

Oddly, Joan seemed to relax. Why is she pleased that I asked that question? Edith wondered. And what answer has she prepared to calm my fears?

"No, actually she isn't. That's one of the good things about this invitation. I haven't seen Eleanor . . . oh, for maybe ten years, not since the last time my husband and I sailed for Europe from New York. I don't think I'm quite ready for close friends to see me yet. They'd be . . . delicate about the changes. But in ten years—well, Eleanor will expect me to be changed. She knows about the accident. We'll just be two middle-aged women together. I won't feel I'm being . . . examined every minute."

So you are clever enough and strong enough to have trapped me, Edith thought. Maybe you can manage. She stood. "Perhaps it would be a good idea, Joan. I can arrange for our limousine service to take you into town Friday afternoon and bring you back again Sunday; that will solve a few of your problems. Miss Hastings can make both trips as well; she'll help you register and help check you out when you leave." She expected Joan to rebel at that, but she made no move. There was not even an expression of satisfaction on her face. "Of course if there are any . . . problems, you can call us at any hour. We have doctors who have worked here who are now practicing in the city; they can be with you any time you need them."

"That's good to know." Joan stood up as well, although she knew her hour was far from over. "But I don't think I'll need them."

When she was alone again, Edith went back to the chair behind her desk. She didn't feel good about having given in to Mrs. Martin's request. It was too soon, the excuse for the weekend too carefully planned. She had been outmaneuvered and she knew it, the worst thing that a patient can do to a doctor. Maybe I'm getting too old for this work, she thought wearily. She forced that thought away. She was making an even worse mistake, allowing herself to become emotionally involved in the life of a patient.

Only she couldn't help wondering why Joan Martin really wanted to go to New York for a weekend by herself.

Joan had planned it all carefully. The idea had been in her head since August, when she had at last realized she was getting better and that her time at the sanatorium was limited. Thank God for Eleanor's invitation! She had been spending nights lying in bed trying to invent some excuse to be in New York alone. A visit to the nearby town would be no good; what she planned had to be a secret from everyone, a secret she promised herself she would forget forever if it was successful. And it had to be successful if she was ever to go back to Dan.

She had behaved beautifully on the trip into town, discussing with the cheerful Miss Hastings current fashions and the theater, pulling back a little when she realized she was making the girl wistful about not sharing the experience. It would ruin everything if the nurse decided to stay on with her. The hotel was large and the lobby crowded, but the registering was something Joan handled with ease, her companion obviously slightly awestruck by the appearance of the place. Once she was in her room, having tipped the bellboy generously, she said goodbye to Miss Hastings.

Joan had considered every detail carefully. Nothing could happen tonight; not only was she tired, but she knew she did not look the way she wanted. Fortunately, the wedding was to be in the late afternoon so she would have most of Saturday to prepare herself. There was a beauty salon in the hotel; before retiring she had the operator make an appointment for her. She had chosen this hotel deliberately, explaining to Dr. Keinser it was near her friend's apartment. It was a commercial hotel, for all its appearance of luxury and worldwide reputation. There were arcades of shops, and she still had most of the two thousand dollars in traveler's checks that Evan had insisted on leaving with her when they had taken her to Golden Shores. She would need new clothes, something suitable for the wedding and something else for afterward. Luckily she had gained no weight during the long summer; she should be able to find what she wanted fairly easy.

That first night she looked at herself carefully in the hotel room mirror. She could see the changes that had taken place in the past year. There was gray in her hair now—not much, but several strands. She debated having it colored the following day but almost instantly decided against it. A clever hairdresser could make it look as if it had been deliberately streaked. A facial would take some of the lines away from her face, and careful makeup could camouflage most of the rest. She slept soundly, not even taking one of the pills Dr. Keinser had insisted she carry with her. First thing in the morning she'd cash her traveler's checks.

The following day went swiftly. Joan was pleased with the results of her shopping and the work of the beauty salon. A manicure, a pedicure, the facial, a new cut to her hair, and a full and professional makeup job left her feeling better than she had in over a year. The wedding was pleasant and easy. Since the groom had been married before, it was only a small gathering. Eleanor was surprised to see her arrive. There had been no time to write a note, and Joan had to explain that she had delayed sending a wedding present until she met the couple and knew what they wanted. She knew her excuses were accepted. Eleanor, totally absorbed in the ceremony, didn't even question why Joan was in the East or what she was doing walking with a cane. One or two of the guests did, later, during the reception, but Joan carried it off lightly, explaining the skiing accident. This made her seem even less of a contemporary of Eleanor's than usual. Always on the plump side, even in college, Eleanor had clearly resigned herself to the status of middle-aged matron. The idea of her venturing on a ski slope seemed ludicrous.

Some of the men at the reception gravitated toward Joan, and she debated briefly with herself if she would change her plans. But she had learned long ago that on this level of society everybody knew everybody else, even in different cities. And if they didn't know someone in Chicago, they would know someone who did. Joan had no intention of what she was planning to be discovered. It would be something that Dan would never forgive and that she could never truly explain. So she smiled agreeably and put off invitations for a late supper and, when there was a crush around the bride and groom, said a quiet goodbye to her hostess. A couple was leaving at the same time, and they gave her a ride back to the hotel. She was grateful for that; trying to hail a cab was always hell on a Saturday night in any city, and since she didn't know the hours bars and restaurants closed in New York, she was afraid she might be too late.

Ten

By the time she came down from her room she knew she had timed it right. During her day in the shopping arcades she had checked out the various lounges and dining rooms that the hotel contained. Her first choice was the Grill Room on the ground floor, decorated in a style the backers of the hotel had hoped grandly and inaccurately would make it look like an English pub. Actually, it was more of a restaurant than a bar, although during the day only the bar area was crowded. This would be where she should start. It was more brightly lit than the other lounges, but she had freshened her makeup, and in her second new dress she felt confident she could convey the impression she wanted. She hoped there would be time later, if it was necessary, for the other places. One of them, the darkest, had attracted her, but it had a minute dance floor and she wasn't sure she could handle that. She would have no real excuse, as she had carefully hidden her cane behind her night clothes in the closet of her room. There was also something called the Leopard Room, but it had low chairs and she felt it would be the wrong place for a single woman, especially one who still found it awkward to rise. No, the Grill Room was her best choice.

She had thought about going to another hotel for this—there were two across the street, not as grand and not as expensive—but she would have looked obvious without a coat and she wanted to telegraph subtly that she was a guest in this particular hotel. That would be necessary to calm any suspicions a maitre d' or waiter might have about her being by herself, attractively made up and wearing a low-cut black dress. She had brought some imitation pearls that afternoon, knowing she would need them for the wedding; the pearls and her platinum wedding band were her only jewelry. She wondered wistfully for a moment, as she took the menu the captain handed her, where the earrings and clips that Dan had given her over the years were. Probably in a safety deposit box, she thought. Carefully put away until her return.

She ordered a light sandwich and a split of champagne. She would have loved to order a real drink just to give her courage, but it had been too long since she had tasted alcohol and with the medications they had been giving her she was afraid anything stronger than wine might affect her badly. Joan was no fool, and she had read and heard enough of the dangers she was inviting to be as careful as possible.

There were several men standing at the bar, but most of them were talking to each other, obviously friends or business acquaintances. It had to be a single man, one with no friends to inhibit him from approaching. That was another reason she had delayed the experiment until Saturday night. Even on a Friday the man she chose might be a businessman from out-of-town, maybe even Chicago, and she couldn't risk that. But any man alone in New York on a Saturday night would almost certainly live here, and that reduced the chances of anyone's ever knowing what she had done.

If she could do it. . . .

By the time she had finished half her champagne she knew she had found him. He was clearly American, which in a way she felt was unfortunate. With the city full of UN diplomats, she had hoped whoever she attracted would not only never appear in Chicago but would tactfully go back to some far corner of the earth forever. But there was only one man who stared at her consistently, who signaled by his careful smile in her direction that he was lonely, bored, and, most important of all, attracted to her. She wondered how he would make his initial move: some bad opening line like "You look lovely" or "Aren't you Mary Smith?"—any of the approaches she had heard about. But while the hotel was large and commercial, it was also clearly careful of what happened inside its doors, and it was unlikely that this man would risk being stopped by the headwaiter and asked to leave.

As the waiter put down her check, she caught the stranger's eye again. He was attractive, she supposed, although that wasn't really the point. Neatly dressed, nearly tall, with dark hair. Not a well-bred face such as she had seen at the wedding; he looked as if he had not always worn good clothes or drunk expensive Scotch at important hotels. After she signed the bill, putting her signature and room number on the check, she glanced at the man at the bar once more. Almost imperceptibly he nodded toward the lobby outside and made a clear point of finishing his glass. She lowered her head slightly. It could be taken for a nod of acceptance or not. She would leave herself that much of an out if he was impossible.

He left before her, for which she gave a sigh of relief. She could control her walking for a short distance, so that the limp was hardly noticeable. Once they met, presumably he would be looking at her face, probably never seeing the effort it cost her to walk smoothly and evenly.

He was waiting outside, as she knew he would be, pretending to look in a display case of jewelry. As she approached he looked directly at her and smiled. He had obviously been told by other women it made him attractive, but to Joan it seemed to emphasize his thin lips. Still, he had good if slightly uneven teeth.

"I have a feeling you're a lady who could use a drink," he said. His manner was polite and his voice just low enough that no one passing by could have heard him. "Am I wrong?"

"No," she heard herself saying, and as he offered his arm she took it.

He didn't make any secret of his intentions, which, under any other circumstances, would have filled Joan with repugnance. But she was as anxious as he to get the whole situation over with as quickly as possible. She decided to turn down an offer of a drink in any of the other bars and suggested he join her in her room. She had already ordered room service to bring up Scotch and mixers, as well as two more splits of champagne. He accepted her invitation as eagerly as she had hoped.

The rest of the evening should have been burned in her mind forever, but parts of it were never to come back. She knew they each had two drinks sitting in the part of her room that was designed to seem like a living area, although Joan knew they were both continually conscious of the large double bed in the corner. She had arranged the lights as skillfully as she could before going down to the lobby and had already put the Do Not Disturb sign on the outside of the door. He made no move toward her while they were drinking, although he asked questions about her own life with interest. She had already arranged that part of the story: the wedding of the daughter of a school friend, and being "separated from her husband." All still within the boundaries of truth. Stumped for a last name that might match the initials of her suitcase in case he looked, she called herself Joan Michaels.

After the second drink, almost abruptly, he said, "Shall we get started?" She excused herself and slipped into the bathroom. She had a new thin nightgown and a matching robe. When she reappeared he was already stretched out on the bed in his undershorts and socks. Most of the lights in the room were off now, but she could see his body was scrawnier than she had thought and his shorts looked none too clean. He had kept his watch on as well, and as he handed her a fresh glass of champagne she noticed in the half-light it was only a cheap copy of a more expensive model. She was starting to feel a little dizzy from the liquor, and if she could have done it without causing a scene she would have asked him to leave. But before she could think of the words, he had pulled her over on top of him, pushing her head not very gently toward the other hand that fondled his crotch.

"Let's start here, baby," he said.

It became a sick blur. No matter what she tried, doing things she had done only rarely with Dan, nothing seemed to excite him. Somehow she seemed to be unable to control her body. When he suggested they sleep for a while she turned over gratefully.

Whether she slept for an hour or only a few minutes she would never know. But something woke her, forcing her to open her eyes. There was a light on in the closet of the room. He stood there, completely dressed, trying to force open her locked suitcase. He looked over at her as she tried to sit up in bed.

"Keep your mouth shut," he said quietly.

"What . . . what are you doing?"

"What does it look like? Getting money for my evening. What's the combination? Or do you want me to have to break this thing open?"

She gave it to him, remembering how proud Dan had been when he had found this new luggage. "You'll never have to look for a key again," he had said. "There's nothing in the suitcase," she added dully.

"What do you take me for? A rich broad like you—you don't travel with nothing more than a string of cheap pearls and a wedding ring." He opened the suitcase; finding it as empty as she had said, he flung it down on the floor. "Let's have that ring, while we're at it."

"No!" She could see Dan's face now, the way he had looked on their wedding day, his eyes full of love and pride, reaching out to slip the platinum band on her finger as they stood at the altar. "I'll scream!"

"You do and you'll get scarred up worse than you are already. Besides, a nice respectable lady like Mrs. Dan Martin—yeah, I got your name from your wallet—wouldn't want any scandal, would you?"

His face is like a ferret's, she thought as he took the ring off her finger. Thin and evil. How could I have thought even for a second I could make love to him? Even to prove that I was still a woman, that I'm attractive? The doctors at the sanatorium are right, she thought as the haze swept around her again. I must be crazy.

The next thing she remembered he was standing at the door. She could see her purse had been emptied, the contents scattered all over the carpet. She had had nearly a thousand dollars before she had left the room, but obviously it was not enough for him. He looked at her with contempt, as if that could make up for the thinness of his haul.

"Imagine a cripple like you thinking anyone would want to go to bed with her." He opened the door and was gone.

He left so fast he never heard her sharp shrill cry of pain.

By ten in the morning, only two hours before the limousine would come to get her, she was at last awake and able to stand and, worse, to think. Obviously he had put something in her champagne. She found the bottles empty and washed out, as were both glasses. No fingerprints, even if she had been tempted to try and have him found. Her money was gone, all of it, even her change purse, but not her credit cards. She'd be able to pay the hotel. Her face looked worse than usual, but most of that was because she had left on her makeup and it was smeared and ugly now, her eyes puffy from the tears she had shed since she had awakened and realized it was not all some kind of horrible nightmare.

The ring. That was what hurt the most. He probably wouldn't even be able to pawn it. Dan had had it engraved with their initials and their wedding date. Maybe he'd just melt it down, once he realized it was platinum. She'd insisted on that, although she would have settled for silver or white gold. Joan had been raised in the era where, as her aunts told her, "a lady didn't travel wearing gold." Which meant you carefully put your good jewelry in the bank before you took a trip (including your wedding ring) and traveled with something simpler, less gaudy, less likely to attract attention. But Joan had determined she was never going to take her wedding ring off, ever. And so Dan had bought her one in platinum.

Dan. What could she tell him? Some lie, of course. That she'd lost it either in the Chicago hospital or at Golden Shores. It was so easy to lie when people believed you. And he would buy her another one, or she might even order an exact duplicate, down to the inscription from Tiffany's, and have it sent to Golden Shores. Then he would never know.

Only of course she would know. Forever.

The cripple.

She decided to say nothing to Dr. Keinser when she returned, but Edith, after the first session, knowing something terribly wrong had occurred, was even more determined to find out what it was. Joan realized something drastic had happened to her when she found she could not win the battle of wills with the doctor. By the end of the week, it had all poured out, mixed with tears and anger and hurt pride. She wasn't calm, controlled Joan Martin any more; the weekend had provided the breakthrough for which Edith had been waiting. When the story was finally done and her patient had dried her eyes and lain back on the couch exhausted, Edith had time to choose her approach.

"All right, Joan. You made a disastrous mistake. Not just in the choice of the man; these things are not unknown to either analysts or the police. But in your decision to do this, to make love with a man other than your husband. What did you expect to prove?"

"That I was attractive. That I wasn't a cripple." The damp handkerchief held to her lips muffled her voice. "I didn't want to make love to him, I wanted him to make love to *me*. That's the difference. I felt if some man—any man, a stranger who knew nothing about me, nothing about what I had been, what I had looked like—could find me desirable . . . just as I am . . . I could go back to Dan with some pride left."

"Pride." The doctor considered the word carefully. "Is that the most important part of your relationship with your husband? Your pride?"

"Not mine! His!" Joan half sat up on the couch. "You've never met my husband; you don't know what he's like."

"He's a man. Who apparently loves you very much. And whom you love."

"What 'me' does he love? He fell in love with a girl, pretty, intelligent, or at least I thought I was. . . ." Joan seemed ready to dissolve into tears again.

"No self-pity! Go on."

"That was the girl—the woman he married. That was the person he loved. And what am I now? A twisted, semi-paralyzed cripple in the middle of a nervous breakdown who picks up a crazy pervert because she's afraid she's too ugly to please anybody. And finds out she's right."

"Suppose you let me do the analysis. That's my job." Edith sat very still. She knew at this moment any movement would distract her patient and instantly be translated into some further rejection, a signal that the doctor was bored or disgusted or impatient. "One part of what you have said is definitely accurate. The man is a pervert and probably a very sick one. He was obviously in that bar to prey on someone. If not you, it could have been a man with homosexual tendencies; it wouldn't have mattered to him."

"You mean he wasn't even a real man?" Joan's voice was quiet in its bitterness.

"What do you consider a 'real man'? Probably no one could satisfy this person sexually. But he is not the point. Suppose all had gone as you planned it. Suppose he had been a nice, harmless man of your own world, such as the men you mentioned noticing you at the party. And you had gone to bed with one of them and had sexual relations and he or both of you had achieved a satisfying climax. What would you have proved?"

"I told you. That I wasn't . . . repulsive."

"Is that how you think of yourself?"

Joan moved so she could face the doctor directly. "What else can I think?" She touched her hair. "Gray hair. Lines on my face. A middle-aged woman who can no longer carry a child. Who wants to be married to *that?*"

"There are many women with gray hair, many who are older than you are, whose husbands love them. Or if they are alone, there are men who seek them out deliberately to marry."

"Sure. Because they're lonely or need someone to keep house or are looking for some kind of mother figure."

"*Ach!* You Americans!" It was rare that Edith allowed her European birth to break through the years of citizenship in her adopted country, but she knew she would do Joan no good by speaking impersonal words to her. "You put such emphasis on youth. On being pretty. On having the perfect figure. As if God has made us to be like that. He didn't. Nor does Nature design us to stay that way!"

"I know." There was a great loneliness in Joan's voice as well as bitterness. "Whoever invented the phrase Mother Nature couldn't have picked worse. No woman could have designed a fate where men get more attractive as they grow older and women don't."

"That is nonsense and you know it! Men lose their hair, their teeth, the bodies they were so proud of in their youth, their ability to perform—"

"Not my husband." Joan's face was set stubbornly.

"It will happen," Edith replied calmly. "He is a human being. Joan, that is the lesson you must learn . . . if not from me, and not here, then during the course of your life. It is the one lesson every human being must learn, male and female, and if they do not, their lives will be twisted and miserable and they will spread unhappiness to everyone they meet."

"That we all grow older?" Joan's face twisted in a bitter grin. "Shall I embroider that on a pillow in my next needlepoint class?"

"Don't mock what I am trying to say. That only closes your mind to the truth." The room was growing darker in the late afternoon, but Edith made no move to turn on a light. "It is not just the facts of age. It is the fact that our lives are constantly changing. *That* is Nature."

"Changing for the worse."

"No! Changing. That is all that happens. Whether it is for the better or the worse is up to us and the choices we make. What are you, Joan? A face? A slender, seductive body? Pretty hair? Is that all there is to you?" The doctor's voice grew stronger. "That is only the envelope! The outside of you. The person your husband fell in love with, whom he loves now, is inside. That is Joan Paige Martin. Not makeup and clothes and a sexually attractive figure lying in bed. A plastic doll could be that. Not a human being."

"I suppose at this point you intend to tell me about all the ladies who charmed men when they were old and hunchbacked and ugly?"

"I could tell you about human beings, men and women who have done that, continue to do that even in this world that sets such artificial standards. But words are not going to help you, unless you listen with an open mind and an open heart."

"What will? Some strange new pill? Let's see, I have them in red and white and brown—"

"You are being sarcastic because you are hurt and angry and you have allowed yourself to be vulnerable with me, another human being, perhaps for the first time in your life by telling me of this bad experience. Don't start putting up defenses again, Joan. That will not change anything, and it will not help you." Edith leaned forward and deliberately switched on the lamp on her desk. Confession was over; it was time her patient faced as simple a reality as this room. "Do you know, in all of this talk, all of our previous talks, you have never discussed your children? Your father? Your friends? Even your husband: the words you use make him seem some sort of mythic figure. However, they are all part of you as much as your face and your body. And you are part of them. What do you feel for them? What can you give them that will have nothing to do with your 'envelope,' whether it is young or pretty or not?"

"I . . . I don't know."

"Good. We are making progress. At least you are acknowledging the problem. Now we must look for the answers, and we have only a few weeks left. We must make up for the wasted time."

"I . . . I just want to be the way I was."

"We can never be that. Not you, not I. We cannot be what we were yesterday or last month or last year. All we can do is find out what we can be tomorrow. I shall see you then at the usual time."

Eleven

When she looked back afterward at her first summer and fall with Dan, Mary was always surprised that she did not remember it as "romantic." It should have seemed that way to her, certainly while she was living through it, for Dan with all his usual determination and thoroughness made every meeting special and exciting, and the days when they did not see each other were incredibly dull. And yet, Mary realized, during the nights she was alone, it did not seem, at least to her, as if they were involved in some grand love affair. Obviously Dan desired her as she did him. Certainly he would have provided all the customary touches of romance if she had wanted them: flowers and gifts and expensive dinners. Luckily she didn't need those things, for they both knew it would almost certainly destroy the private life they had begun to build between them. One box of long-stemmed roses could be explained away as a gift "from a grateful patient," as Mary had told Patsy, but a box arriving every day would have been a clear scandal through the neighborhood in less than a week. One lunch in a public place was understandable and innocent, something the world could see and swiftly forget. Dinner ever night in the restaurants Dan liked would have sent a swift alert to the world of Dan's business friends and their wives. Three meals in public with a woman not his wife would have branded Dan in Chicago as conclusively involved in an

affair as if the two of them had been photographed naked in bed. Presents and gift certificates, even checks (if Dan had thought in terms like
that) would have been a slower but still more open confession of their
affair. Each, in one of the few secrets that they kept from each other, was
secretly relieved their relationship did not need externals as a proof of
love, and relieved the other felt the same.

So if Mary had been questioned, as the fall of the year drew near to an
end, about what word she would use to describe the precious weeks
they shared together, she would have been puzzled at having to retreat
to saying simply she was happy.

It seemed such a bland word for the way Mary felt, but because there
had not been all that much happiness in her life, it was as if she had at
last come out of a long dark tunnel into sunlight. She didn't need to
emerge onto a spectacular view of the Mediterranean or the garden of a
palace; just the sunlight was enough. Besides, she noticed, Chicago was
growing beautiful, a word she never would have thought to apply to it
when her life consisted of simply going to the hospital and back to the
West Side.

That was the start of the first problem between her and Dan—the
West Side. With the children back from their summer camps and the
apartment air conditioning fixed, there was no longer any excuse for
Dan to keep the hotel suite. Stubbornly he rented it for several more
weeks, but neither he nor Mary had the time to visit it as often as they
wished. She was still subject to arbitrary changes in her schedule, working all nights one week, every other day the next. With Joan still in the
East, Dan knew his children needed him at home. If only there were
someplace where he and Mary could meet, quietly and privately, where
he could see her to her door and inside, without the whole outside
world gossiping! That began to be an obsession with him, so, using
every bit of his influence and knowledge of the Chicago real estate
market, he set about solving it.

For by October there was no doubt that whatever happened when
Joan returned, if she did return, he could not give up seeing Mary. How
he would manage to keep both sides of his life from conflicting with
each other he had no idea; he would handle that when it became necessary. The first thing was for him to find a place for them.

He was careful not to mention the subject until he had succeeded.
There was a section not too far from the fashionable lakefront that
had long been known as Old Town. It had been built originally by
comfortably-off middle-class families, not of the grand world of the
Potter Palmers and Armours who in the booming years after the Chicago fire erected imitation castles on what would become Lake Shore

Drive. It had been at that time the city swerved from the fashionable South Side of the city north to begin a continuous building up along the edge of Lake Michigan to Highland Park, a process that did not end until the Depression. The real center of Chicago, as always, remained in the famous Loop of the elevated that contained the offices and banks that were making this city and, in turn, the rest of the country rich.

Old Town had fallen on hard times in the Depression, continuing its downward slide through World War II and afterward. The comfortably off began to want to live in the suburbs, or in one of the newly rising apartment towers by the lake. So, three or four short blocks to the west of the lake's sandy beaches, the solidly built homes were cut up into rooming houses and shabby apartments, with cheap paint slapped over fine wood paneling and an ugly network of the required fire escapes blotting out what little sunlight could pry its way between the buildings.

With the 1960s a resurgence began, like that taking place in the Castro Street section of San Francisco and on the edges of New York's Greenwich Village. Artists were beginning to find their way back to Chicago, a city that had been world famous in the Twenties as much for its writers and painters as for its gangsters. As always the new artists were young, energetic, imaginative, and severely limited financially. Looking for inexpensive space, they quickly found Old Town, and to the amusement of the staid of the city, the area began to become popular. Little restaurants sprouted like weeds next to small stores that dared to call themselves "boutiques." The solid German and Irish saloons were crowded again, but instead of surly, middle-aged drunks, the voices were high and shrill and the customers part of every aspect of the fashion field. Brass lamps were discovered in basements and brought up to be polished, woodwork that would have been dismissed as hideous by the previous generation sparkled with fresh paint. Old Town was becoming chic and, as was happening in similar areas in cities across the country, the young rich and those on their way to becoming rich started finding it "fun" to move in among the artists. There were still a few grim rooming houses when Dan started his search, but next to them one might look through tall parlor-floor windows at glittering chandeliers and velvet-covered walls.

What had first begun as a search for a home for Mary changed swiftly as Dan, with the practiced eye of a man who had spent most of his life concerned with the real estate of this city, realized the area had very definite business possibilities. This was one project, however, he determined would be separate from Paige Properties. He had no intention of letting Evan know of his interest in the section. As a man nearing fifty, he reasoned to himself that it was time he had something totally his own. He hired an outside lawyer and set up a new corporation, and with that he bought the first of what would become a row of houses. Nowhere on the public papers did his name appear. Best of all, the first house he bought was little more than three blocks from his own apartment. In fact, when he inspected the empty second floor that he had decided would be for Mary, he could see the windows of his bedroom high above the low rooftops.

And the building was within walking distance of the hospital where Mary worked.

The house fortunately was delivered vacant. After a hasty job to make the apartments presentable, discreet ads were placed for other tenants. The lawyer, somewhat puzzled by Dan's secrecy but newly admitted to the bar and not anxious to lose his first important client, kept his questions to himself. Still, he could not conceal his surprise at the way Dan chose the new tenants. First, he gave preference to people who had arrived from somewhere else, which made the lawyer's job of checking their credit references more difficult. And all the tenants he picked seemed to be single, although a man with Dan's real estate background would have to know that married couples were always more desirable, more stable, more interested in keeping a place in good repair. But on this Dan was inflexible.

The night he told Mary of his plans they were having dinner at one of their favorite restaurants, an elegant one newly opened in the middle of O'Hare Airport. The food was elaborately presented and generally good, the maitre d' discreet, and the chances of other Chicagoans having dinner there minimal. It was for travelers: the ever-increasing crowds streaming through Chicago that would make this the busiest airport in the world in a few years.

Dan had carefully waited until they had ordered and half their first drink was consumed before starting to talk of what he had done. Mary was silent at first, watching him with a soft smile on her face. It was the way he liked her best. He knew by proposing his plan he stood not only a very good chance of ruining their evening but of never seeing her again. Women like Mary could not be "kept," and there had been more than enough remakes of the movie *Back Street* to condemn his plans to any decent woman before he had the chance to present them. But Mary made no comment or interruption as he listed the advantages of a move.

". . . since we don't know how long Joan's going to be away. And you'd be near the kids if anything happened. They're old enough to be alone without a sitter now, after Mrs. Franklin leaves in the evenings, but I'm sure it would make them both feel easier if they knew you could be reached if they needed you." He was intelligent enough to realize the mention of Joey and Paige might well be the deciding factor, much more than the proximity it would give Mary to him. "And it's not some kind of favor, Mary. I'll be charging rent, but the way the building's been laid out, I know it would be well within your budget."

"When did you buy the building?" Her expression had not changed; still, it was not quite the answer he had expected.

"When? Well, I thought about it in September, but we only closed the deal a few weeks ago."

He went on talking, but Mary barely heard the words. He'd known in September it wouldn't end between them! Almost two months. All this time she had been thinking that when Joan came back it would all be over, a small interruption in her life and nothing more. Meanwhile he'd been planning for a future for them. Oh, Dan, Dan, she thought to herself, I wish you had told me. I could have enjoyed these weeks so much more, knowing that they weren't going to come to an end the first time Joan beckoned. You love me. And, as they sat there, she had never loved him more than at that moment.

"Mary, you've got the damnedest look on your face. Are you angry?"

She shook her head, afraid to speak. He noticed tears had formed in her eyes. Anxious, he leaned forward, putting his hand on hers.

"Mary, what is it? Are you going to cry?"

She laughed, the deep infectious laugh he so loved to hear. "Daniel Martin." The way she said his name was like a caress. "All these weeks, and you don't know me at all. The Irish save their tears for when they're happy. You'll have to remember that in the future."

He pulled his hand back uneasily as the waiter brought their first course. When he left, Dan seemed almost hesitant. "I thought maybe . . . well, you know, an apartment . . ."

"I live in an apartment now. A very inconvenient one." She leaned forward and smiled. "I know what's going on in your head, Dan. Probably has been from the beginning of all this: 'Mary will never go for some sort of *Back Street* romance.' Old Town is hardly that, not to mention that it's very convenient to the hospital." She looked at him with a certain amusement. "I imagine that was one of your considerations?"

He grinned a little sheepishly. "It . . . crossed my mind."

Her face grew thoughtful. "Actually, I can afford more rent than you're asking. I mean it. I can rent out Mother's apartment. Patsy's got a cousin who's getting married. The boy's got a steady job, and I know they've been looking. And with Tim out of work again . . . even so, I could pay more than you're asking and still keep up the taxes and mortgage on the West Side."

"You'll take this place at my price or . . ." Realizing he had no alternative to offer, he started to stammer the way Joey sometimes did until he saw Mary laughing. He found himself joining her, although, he had to admit, somewhat reluctantly. Dan still had not learned the pleasure of being with a woman as frank as he was.

"I can't wait to see it," Mary said finally.

The maitre d' was surprised by how quickly Mr. Martin and Mrs. Conroy finished their meal. Usually they lingered until midnight.

I don't care if it's a garage, Mary thought as they drove back into the city. I don't care if it's an attic or if the bathtub's in the hall; I won't care about anything if Dan's picked it for me. But the empty house was neat and attractive, even at night. Only a block from Lincoln Avenue, she thought practically; good for shopping. I can catch the bus there for the hospital on rainy days.

They went up to the second floor, Dan rather self-consciously fumbling with a large bundle of keys. "I didn't do anything with it, except give it a quick slap of paint. I thought you'd want to choose your own things."

Or leave it presentable for another tenant, Mary thought, if she had turned him down. He probably expected that, at least at first, giving him time to persuade her gradually to acceptance. Joan wouldn't have accepted right away, Mary knew, if the situations had been reversed. She would have required weeks of courtship and persuasion, if indeed she ever agreed to the idea as set up by Dan. But the Joans of the world can afford that, Mary knew. They were the beautiful, the unattainable. She was simply Mary Scanlon Conroy, a hard-working woman in her late thirties who had never expected to find herself in love and loved in return.

The apartment was smaller than the one on the West Side. There was a cozy living room and a slightly larger-than-usual kitchen. The two bedrooms were oddly shaped: one was hardly more than a closet, but it would take an overnight guest if Joey or Paige needed to stay. The other was as large as the living room, facing east. Like Dan, she realized almost immediately she could see his windows in the high-rise building by the lake. It should have given her a feeling of being spied upon, but it didn't. It would be good to know he had returned home safely. That had been one of their problems in his taking her back to the West Side the nights they had together: having to stop the car a few blocks away so they wouldn't be seen, not daring to kiss good night for fear someone might still be awake and watching.

They wandered through the apartment like young lovers that night,

Dan pleased and proud and more than a little surprised he had actually persuaded her to take it.

For Mary, it was an evening in which two emotions battled for control of her mind. One was the immense happiness she felt would burst inside her, a happiness that came not just from the excitement of being with the man she loved but of a sudden security she had never dreamed could be hers. Somehow, they were going to make some kind of a life together. If one day, sooner or later, it ended quietly or abruptly, she would worry about that when the time came. At the moment she had everything she wanted and more.

For weeks she had been noticing things about Dan, things that no hotel suite could provide and that she knew only too well were not part of the decor of the elegantly designed apartment where he lived. He would need a comfortable chair and a hassock where he could put his feet up. Large ashtrays, of course, in every room. Nothing modern. Comfortable furniture, the walls and carpets in cheerful but restful colors. Extra shelves in the bathroom for his things, and a closet of his own. No coasters; if he wanted to put a drink down on the table, let the wood be scarred; she would enjoy every mark he made. Although during this past hot summer they had both taken to drinking cold beer rather than hard liquor. Luckily there was a large refrigerator.

She talked of this to Dan, allowing herself the pleasure, for the first time in her life, of having the luxury of a home she could make into whatever she chose, in contrast to the dark reminders of her family life that had bound her all these years to the apartment on the West Side. But another thought kept creeping in, one that could not be spoken to Dan tonight or any other night, and she could not dislodge it, no matter how brightly she chattered.

Would her marriage to Jack have been different if they could have started fresh as she would be doing here? If they had been in another neighborhood, away from people who knew them, whose opinions had done so much to shape their lives—would she have made a success of her marriage? Jack had had so little chance; even such an important domestic decision as their marriage bed she had made herself. The rest of the apartment was left as it had been furnished by her mother and father. No wonder Jack had wanted to assert himself, even in such a destructive way as gambling.

Maybe that had been his only key to let them out of a life closing in around them like a wall, a life with no children but with the questioning looks that childlessness would provoke in time, a life of dreary jobs and two-week vacations and endless Sunday dinners with Tim and his family. A life of acceptance, of not raising your head above your neighbors, a life controlled by more unspoken taboos than the Vatican court. This is what Jack had tried to rebel against. Would he have been happier, Mary thought that first night when Dan showed her the new apartment, if they could have started their marriage here, in another community, where no one knew them and consequently no one could judge them?

After all, it was not as if Jack had been some wild young man, only someone embittered by his limited chances in life. There was a steadiness in him, something Mary had not realized, or at least had refused to acknowledge after the first disclosures of his gambling. The steadiness had surfaced since he had been away; twice a month now a postal order for a hundred dollars came from California, signs that he had found and kept a job, was budgeting himself, and intended to keep the promise in the letter he had left for her. How he must hate parceling out money every other week!

He was so much like Dan in that respect. Dan would have gone to the far ends of the earth and she would have heard nothing from him until he could come back and pour all he owed and more into her lap, all in one large magnificent gesture. That's what Jack would have wanted, Mary knew, although none of the envelopes he sent contained a single word for her. But far across the country he was forcing himself to think the way she did, or rather the way she had been raised to think.

But she hadn't been raised to be a married man's mistress. Such an old-fashioned word, but that was what she was becoming. Before tonight, she could think herself Dan's equal, loving him freely, expecting and asking nothing in return. After tonight it would be different. No matter how many balance sheets he showed her for the building, or how often he talked of Paige and Joey coming to see her, needing her, she knew she had somehow changed their relationship. It should have frightened her, but somehow it only seemed a sensible, practical step forward. The time for any other decision, she thought, as she talked and listened to Dan that evening, disappeared during the two nights she had spent alone in that other kitchen, almost willing her dead mother to give her permission to go to that first lunch, knowing each meeting with Dan would bring her further from the narrow life she had been trained so long and carefully to accept.

"Second thoughts?" Dan was looking at her questioningly. How quickly they had grown to know each other's minds and moods!

"No, Dan. I want to be here."

Later he dropped her off a block from the two-story house on the West Side. Tim would have a hundred arguments against her move, but in the end he would know all he was saying was useless. She owned the building, and if she wanted to move closer to work and rent out the top floor, that was her business. With the extra pay she had earned taking care of Joan and the twice-monthly money orders Jack was sending, there was no one in the neighborhood who could say she and Jack had cheated them. Most likely the parish would consider she had left at last because her shame of being the divorced wife of a runaway gambler had finally made it too uncomfortable for her to remain in their smugly respectable midst.

Her confrontation with Tim was different from what she expected. Their apartment was blazing with lights when she arrived home; clearly a party was in progress, something so unlikely, with Tim out of work, that Mary could not resist walking through their open door. Neighbors from both sides were there, and Maggie Feeney and her sisters, and even Fred Reiner, the lawyer. Patsy, flushed of face, a glass of rye and ginger ale in her hand, pushed through the happy crowd.

"Mary, love, you'll never guess what's happened! Tim's got a grand new job, the highest pay ever! And he's not going to be working with his hands any more; he'll be a supervisor, telling other people what to do." She beamed proudly at Mary. "I know! It's like some kind of a crazy miracle; I wasn't planning on starting a novena for him until next week. And now right this afternoon, five o'clock, no less, Paige Properties calls and offers him this. There's even a contract so they can't just fire him."

Dan. He did this. Mary knew instantly. Don't let me give anything away in front of all these people!

Patsy turned aside to greet another of her friends, her sister-in-law forgotten. Mary went back out into the hall, knowing she would not be missed until the next day. She tried to sort out her thoughts as she climbed the stairs to her own apartment. Dan must have arranged it. In case she turned him down about the new place? Blackmail, that would be the ugly word for it. Or, to put it as kindly as possible, a generous pressure on her to make her change her mind.

Dan, you don't know me at all, she thought as she unlocked her door. From downstairs she could still hear the noise of the party. You didn't need to bribe me. I love you. Under his obvious strength could he be so unsure of himself that he had taken the steps to locate her brother, track down his record, and find a job that Tim could and would want to do, just to make sure that Mary would be permanently part of his life? That would be a cold, ruthless thing to do, Mary realized. The side of Dan she seldom saw but always knew was there. Not that he would have said or done anything if she had refused him this evening; giving Tim a contract proved that. Oh, Dan, she thought, for the first time allowing herself to question him, what kind of man are you? Stubborn, arrogant, determined to get what you want one way or the other . . . or frightened, unsure, simply trying to help the person you love?

She didn't want to think about it any more. She would have long nights ahead of her, nights alone, to do that. Meanwhile, perhaps she'd better go back down to the party. Patsy's cousin Maureen would be there, she knew. It would be a good time to tell the bride-to-be she had an apartment.

No, she realized later, those first months with Dan were not a time to be remembered as "romantic."

Twelve

Joan came home in the middle of December. She traveled alone at her own insistence, but the family gathered to meet her at the airport, Dan and her father apparently calm, clearly determined to accept whatever changes they found, her children nervous and unable to hide their anxiety.

Kay had made the travel arrangements through the office. She would not be included as part of the family gathering, but her curiosity was so strong she got to her desk the following morning half an hour before she could reasonably expect anyone else to arrive. To her surprise Dan was already there, quietly going through the deeds of the land he was collecting for development near the airport. People were getting smarter about real estate values, and it was costing the new corporation more than he had expected to put together the large parcel of acreage needed for his proposed development.

Kay had a feeling, however, Dan was in the office early not because of business but because he did not wish to be at home. Or perhaps he had wanted to talk in the privacy of his office to Mrs. Conroy, if that affair was still continuing. Kay didn't know, and no matter how carefully she went over the office records and checkbooks, she could find no sign that Dan was still seeing "the nurse," as she always thought of Mary. Not that Kay didn't know that Dan was involved with *someone;* that had been clear since the summer. There had been too many phone calls from behind closed doors, too many evenings when he couldn't be reached. There was also a separate bank account in a bank that neither the Paiges nor the Martins had ever used before. This Kay knew as a fact; she had signed for the new checks when they arrived at the office. She had also supervised the transfer of a considerable sum of Dan's private funds to this new account. But what he used the money for, or for whom, remained his secret.

It was not a totally unusual procedure in the real estate field. Corporations were often set up solely for the purchase of one piece of property and dissolved again after that property changed hands. Still, there must have been someone in Dan's life these past months; the short temper and impatience of the previous winter had completely disappeared. Kay had heard no gossip, but that meant nothing. If Dan was not going to places where he was likely to be seen and talked about, it did not mean he had not found others.

There must be a woman somewhere, if not the quiet nurse, then someone else. Clearly not a Wilson Avenue lady; that type would want to be seen at the best and most expensive restaurants, go dancing at the big hotels in the evenings and gambling at the Arlington track in the afternoons. Obviously Dan had found somebody different and, by breaking the usual pattern of infidelity, either by his own desires or cautions, had managed to keep his affair secret.

Whoever you are, Kay thought that morning, I wonder if you know how much your life is going to change with his wife back?

Or will it? Surely it was perfectly natural for Kay to ask Dan about Joan; indeed, it would have been bizarre if she hadn't.

"Everything go all right yesterday, Dan?"

"What? Oh, yes, thanks, Kay." She put down the fresh cup of coffee she had made on the office machine and stood waiting. It was irritating, but it was only human that after all these years she would be curious about Joan.

"How *is* Joan?"

"Fine. A little too thin, in my opinion, but apparently the rest did wonders for her."

The rest. So that was how his wife's six-month stay at Golden Shores was to be described. "Is she feeling all right? Physically, I mean?" Kay persisted.

"I think so. There's barely any trace of the ski accident. She has the cane, but she seems to manage fairly well without it most of the time. Of course, she's got a long list of things she's supposed to do, and another of what she isn't supposed to do, and what looks like a whole shopping bag full of medicines."

Do you love her? Does the list say you can't sleep together? Will Joan still be able to twist you around her little finger anytime she wants? Kay had to clamp her lips tight to keep from shouting out the questions she would cheerfully have given a year of her life to have answered. But Dan made no move to continue the conversation, merely adding, "She's cut her hair. Looks kind of cute."

And what is that supposed to tell me? Kay fumed through the morning as she worked. But she knew very well the remark was deliberately made to tell her—and, through her, their business world—exactly nothing.

It was well into January before Mary saw Joan again. The holidays for once had passed peacefully. Tim was stiff with pride at his new job, very much a man of business affairs and, in consequence, more benign in his dealings with his family and Mary. The move had released her from many family obligations, but Christmas dinner was not one of them.

Traditionally she knew as the Other Woman she should have been sitting all alone with a meager meal and one lonely candle on the table in her new kitchen, mourning the fact that the man she loved was with his family. But by now Mary had realized she was no more the traditional Other Woman in Dan's marriage than his secretary or even Joan herself. After having been contented as a husband for so many years, Dan seemed to enjoy a new freedom now that his world had changed so drastically.

To be honest, Mary knew it was not just being with her. He was allowing himself to think his own thoughts, make his own decisions, plan his own dreams for his future career. It would have come about eventually, Mary realized during the evenings when he leaned back in his easy chair, shoes off, a beer at his side, and talked of the development he planned for the area near the airport. Dan would never have gone on indefinitely paying even token respect to Joan's father as the head of the firm. Evan was too old, too conservative for the world Dan wanted to build. Sooner or later he would have broken free, if not from the bonds of his marriage, at least from the conservative thinking of the Evan Paiges of his world. Mary had done nothing to encourage him, content to listen to him in the time they had together, relaxed and comfortable in bed, or fixing him a sandwich before he left on late nights. She knew she could lighten his spirits if he arrived discouraged, or fill the silences with a funny story of something at the hospital on the evenings when Evan's pronouncements had been more than Dan could stand.

Whether Mary's coming into his life had made Dan more rebellious she could not know; perhaps it was the times they lived in, the world changing so rapidly around them. People, especially the young, were actually protesting in the streets about the government sending troops to someplace called Vietnam. Even the Church was changing, something Tim fulminated against at great length during most of the holidays. The mass was being spoken in English, the priest facing the congregation instead of leaving the people assembled with nothing but a view of his back for most of the service. Confession was no longer in privileged private darkness (a mistake, Mary thought to herself, although she had no intention of going) but was to be held in lighted rooms, like a psychiatrist's office. Only, of course, psychiatrists didn't make judgments, or pronounce you guilty, and priests could and did. There was talk now of individual rights for women. This Tim dismissed as "a bunch of crazy lesbians," but Mary noticed Patsy's face was thoughtful, and if she did not openly disagree with Mary's brother, at least his wife did not just sit there and nod obediently as she always had.

Christmas Day and New Year's Day did not find Mary alone or feeling sorry for herself; she was only too happy to have them past so that she could have time for her own life. Her life with Dan.

Joan's return had changed very little of the pattern they had established. Dan could not stop by every evening after the office, but he had never been able to do that. Mary was not even free most of the time. He had a key to her apartment, and on nights when she was forced to work to midnight or beyond she often came home to find signs that he had been there. Sometimes there was a bunch of fresh flowers, sometimes there was just a neatly washed dish and glass in the sink and a full ashtray on the kitchen table, signs he had spread out his work for the evening. Mary had been as curious as Kay about Joan and what it would mean to Dan to have her home again, but she was determined not only not to question him but to put the questions out of her mind. That was a separate part of Dan's life, and she should have no desire to know about it. Except, of course, he talked to her about Joan, openly and often.

The Martins' Christmas had been happy, at least Dan felt it had been. The presents Mary had chosen for him to give had been successful. The buying of the presents had been another problem in their lives. Mary, remembering only too clearly the bills Jack had run up, was reluctant to start new charge accounts in various stores, but Dan insisted, and when she tried to explain and itemize the bills for the gifts when they came in, he simply swept them into his pocket and changed the subject. She bought nothing for herself. The burnished mahogany humidor for the table by his chair (he had grown to like an occasional cigar) she had purchased with her own money, paying cash.

Like any woman in love, she would have liked to have given him something to wear when he was away from her, a robe, a shirt, or a tie. She knew all his suits by now. It had been almost sensual to wander past a tie counter, touching the different materials and thinking how well this one would go with his gray flannel and that another was perfect for his brown tweed. But she could not buy them. For someone like Dan to wear something new would be impossible to explain. For years Joan or, if necessary, his secretary had arranged for a selection to be prepared for him, and he would make his choices rapidly and think no more about it until something wore out. The buying of clothes and ties was for wives, not for her.

They had almost quarreled over his gift to her. He wanted her to have a fur coat, but the thought of a coat brought Mary back to that first Christmas with Jack and the unhappiness that purchase had caused. Dan at last gave in, presenting her Christmas Eve with a beautiful and obviously very expensive emerald pin and earrings. "For the Irish," he said. Mary had been appropriately grateful, but after Christmas she had made him take them back. Expensive jewelry did not suit her, and she knew it. She also knew that for all the rising quality of the neighborhood, if the apartment was broken into and the jewels stolen she would never forgive herself. Finally, feigning impatience, he insisted she take shares in the new company he was forming, the one that would handle the hoped-for development in the suburbs. These, he said smugly, knowing it was a sure way of bringing on her exasperated laughter, were made out in her name, and there was nothing she could do about it. Giving in, she rented a safety deposit box for the first time in her life and put the stock away.

It was Joan who changed both their holidays. They were not sleeping together, Dan informed Mary. The night of her return she had shown him the report of her doctor, a woman named Keinser, to be presented to Osborne and MacCauley at Midwestern Hospital. It suggested that Joan still needed rest and that any return to the "physical side of Mrs. Martin's marital duties," as Dr. Keinser phrased it tactfully, should be delayed indefinitely. Dan felt nothing but relief at this, and he was wise enough to suspect that Joan did too; perhaps she had even persuaded her doctor to include it in the report. He knew if he and Joan resumed sharing the same bed in the same room, eventually their sexual life would resume. Someday, of course, it probably would, but not now, not when he was so in love with Mary. Not that Mary wouldn't have understood, she was too damn understanding sometimes. He could have done with a little more self-interest, the kind he had become accustomed to in the years with Joan.

The Martins resumed their life as before, Joan turning the guest room she had occupied after her first return from the hospital into a charming boudoir and bedroom, actively enjoying combining the rooms she and Mary had had, bringing in decorators all through the holiday season. When her "suite," as Dan called it privately, was finished she started on the bedroom they had shared for so many years, making it more masculine, more comfortable for Dan. From having no bedroom of his own, Dan thought with some dryness that January, he now had two—his own and the room he thought of as his at Mary's. This was a thought he knew he would have to keep to himself. Mary was no plaster saint; the stubbornness she had shown over his Christmas gifts had proved that.

Probably it was Kay who first realized how drastic and permanent the changes were in the Martins' marriage. There had been a Christmas party for friends and relatives, and Joan had called her personally to invite her. It was the first big party Joan had given since her ski accident, and it seemed she was determined to face all the people she had known in Chicago, face them and end the gossip and speculation she knew had been going on about her for over a year.

It was a huge party. For once the enormous apartment was filled. Joan, in flowing red chiffon, looked beautiful, with a better figure than any other woman there her age or younger. Her hair had indeed been cut short, but "cute" would not have been the word Kay would have used to describe it. What Dan had not mentioned was that Joan's hair was now almost completely silver. The short hair made a cap of gleaming curls, short enough so no spiteful friend could imagine a telltale line that meant surgery had been done to improve her face. In a strange way that she could not understand, either at the party or thinking it over later in her solitary bed, it made Kay happy to see Joan so beautiful, so radiantly charming, so clearly her old self again.

And yet . . . she was *different*.

Kay puzzled about it as she pushed through the crowds, nodding to the businessmen she knew and being introduced to their wives. She made conversation, but her thoughts were centered on Joan. Whatever pain Dan's wife had gone through had done something to her, something Kay was hard pressed to define. Joan had always been able to be the center of attention, to say the things that made people laugh, to include any stranger on the outskirts of the group around her so that no one was ignored. That had been part of her personality. Only sometimes in the past Kay had thought she had detected a superficial glitter to the charm. Or had she just been jealous?

Tonight Joan seemed to be making a special effort to be friendly to her, not friendly as to someone who works in the family office and that you've known for years, but as if she really wanted to know more about Kay herself. It made the usually imperturbable Kay a little flustered. She preferred a society where everyone knew exactly where they stood. There was no way she and Joan could be close personal friends, and surely Dan's wife must have known that. Yet here she was, not only asking questions that would make even the shyest person talk but seeming, in the middle of this large party, to be interested in Kay's answers.

It was only when Kay was leaving she found the reason for Joan's interest. They had a quiet moment alone in Joan's room while Kay was putting on her coat. The room, Kay noticed, had been strikingly redecorated, but it hardly seemed a bedroom that a husband and wife could share. It was clearly for Joan alone, and Kay was trying to decide whether the thought made her happy or not when Joan came in.

"Kay, not leaving already?"

Kay made the usual excuses, but for once that evening Joan did not appear to be listening. "Kay, there's something I've wanted to tell you since I came back. I'm so very grateful for all you've done for Dan and the children."

Kay stared at her. What on earth could she be talking about? Or was this some kind of fishing expedition?

"I've done very little, Joan," she said. You'll not find out from me who's helped your husband and children, she thought. Even if I knew, I wouldn't tell you.

Joan sat down on the bed, and for a moment Kay saw how much this evening had cost her mentally and physically. "I haven't been any use to this family for a long time, and I don't know how much longer it'll be before I can take on my full share again." She moved her hand through her crisp curls, her platinum wedding band twinkling like a new gift in the lights of the dressing table. "I just want you to know I'm grateful for everything you've done. For all of us." She looked up at Kay, tall above her. "I do mean everything," Joan added simply.

She thinks I'm Dan's mistress, Kay thought, and for a wild second she wanted to roar with laughter. But that would have hurt the woman in front of her, and Kay realized she would never do that. Instead, she did something she had never done before. She leaned forward and kissed Joan lightly on the cheek.

"Welcome home, Joan," she said. "You don't know how much we've all missed you."

When she went down in the elevator to the lobby, Kay's mind was busy. Joan could suspect she was Dan's mistress and feel no anger? No hatred? Why was she so changed? But again Kay could not put her finger on the specifics. Joan was as beautiful as ever (funny, Kay thought, how appearance was the first thing you thought of with Joan), only now she seemed both weaker and stronger. Never would Kay have dreamed of kissing the cheek of her employer's wife before. Tonight it had seemed the most natural thing in the world.

She's not secure any more, Kay realized. She's stronger—no woman could have endured what Joan had this past year and emerged from it in one piece without gaining strength—but she's also more vulnerable. Before, you felt a sharp wisecrack at Joan's expense would have been answered by an even sharper retort. Now you felt she might crumple under attack.

And she thinks I'm Dan's mistress and doesn't care, thought Kay once more as she went out into the windswept streets. The whole world is going crazy!

Mary was not invited to the party. She and Dan had discussed it, he pressing her, saying it would be perfectly natural and the kids would love to see her, Mary stubbornly refusing. The large apartment was Joan's terrain, and she had no intention of invading it. So it was at the hospital that she first saw Dan's wife.

"Mary! Mary Conroy! Are you just going to walk past me?"

"Joan, I . . . I must have been a million miles away! I'm late getting down to the wards." She made a move as if to continue down the hall. "You look gorgeous!"

"No, you don't!" Joan put out her good hand with a little of her former mock imperiousness. "I don't care if there are twenty-seven stretcher cases down there all calling for you by name, I'm not letting you go." She looked around. "Is there any place where we can have a cup of coffee? Sit down for a second?"

"I *am* on duty, Joan. Honest."

"I'm not having you disappear like that." She gestured toward a bench by the elevators. "We'll sit over here." She managed to make it to the bench without limping, but Mary noticed she was carrying a sturdy umbrella. "See? No dragging feet. Both arms move."

"An Olympic swimmer if ever I saw one. I've wondered how you were."

"Better than can be expected after six months at the funny farm." Joan made a small grimace. "For everybody else, I was having a 'rest,' but I can tell you the truth." Her face wasn't smiling. "I was in a pretty bad way for a time, Mary. I could have wished I'd had you around, to beat some sense into me."

"Nurses are not allowed to beat patients," Mary answered primly. "Only doctors can do that." They laughed together companionably. "Speaking of doctors, why are you here?"

"Just a checkup with Dr. Osborne." Joan leaned forward, her eyes narrowing. "And why are you going down to the wards? You're a private-floor nurse."

"Oh, we get shifted around," Mary said evasively. The last thing she needed was another problem at the hospital. She had tried to tell herself she was only getting her share of routine assignments, but there was a nagging feeling in the back of her head that Osborne had never forgiven her for taking Joan's case to Dr. MacCauley. Anyway, there was nothing she could do about it, or wanted to do.

Joan said nothing, but Mary had the uneasy feeling Dan's wife was making up her own mind about her situation. She went on hastily, "How are Paige and Joey? And Lila?"

"Lila's running the house perfectly as always. The kids have each grown six inches and are holy terrors." She stretched her hand out to Mary's arm. "Paige told me how you picked her dress for the concert. Not to mention the cards and letters and clothes you sent me all last summer. I wanted to thank you, but I'm a terrible letter writer. And when I got back home, I called you at the old number and got no answer."

"I've . . . moved. The new tenants probably hadn't settled in yet."

"Dan and I were giving a party. I wanted you to come, but nobody seemed to know how to locate you." Luckily Joan wasn't watching Mary's face any longer.

"I've been kind of busy with my new apartment." She stood. "Joan, I really do have to run."

"Not until we've set a date when we can have lunch." Joan's face was thoughtful. "I don't seem to . . . connect any more with the people I thought were my friends. I'm not having you walk out of my life just because I'm no longer battered and bruised." How she would have liked to tell Mary of that terrible night in New York! She would be a friend, a friend who had seen and heard everything, not like that European doctor at the Shores who gave not an ounce of sympathy. Only, of course, she couldn't tell anybody who knew her and Dan. "Lunch," Joan said firmly. "We'll have lunch next week, a long talky lunch, and I'll show you what I've done to the apartment, and the kids'll come home from school. They'll be wild to see you. Maybe you can lure Joey back to doing homework again; Dan and I are getting nowhere. Now . . . what's a good day?"

"I . . . I think I'm on night shift again next week."

"Night shift? I thought they only gave that to juniors."

"You know hospitals, always changing the routine. It gives the front office the chance to show they're working."

"I want your new phone number and your address. We're going to get together, Mary Scanlon Conroy, whether you and the hospital like it or not."

There was no way Mary could evade Joan, and she found she didn't want to. As she worked through the rest of the afternoon she realized how much she had missed her. It was strange; she should have been covered with guilt talking to the wife of the man she not only loved but knew loved her in return, the man who had taught her physical love, the man who had moved into her life and turned it completely around. Only her relationship with Joan seemed separate from that, as if Dan were married to some stranger and Joan to someone she had never met. Like they were two halves of two different couples.

Of course, they needn't meet again. Mary would be careful not to pass Osborne's office during the hours he saw patients. In time, for all her talk of not "connecting" with her friends, Joan would probably forget about her. Still, it would have been nice to see the children once more. And Lila.

Stop lying, Mary Conroy. You want to talk to Joan. You want to find out if it's her wish to live apart from Dan, if she chose this herself, if she's happy with the way life has changed for her.

You want to find out if your being with him is hurting her.

"Dan, how important is Osborne at the hospital?"

They were sitting in the living room that evening. The children were supposedly in their rooms doing homework, although Joan doubted it. They had drawn away from her in the past year, and her tentative attempts to establish a family relationship again had not been success-ful. It was probably time for boarding schools, but she would think about that later. Right now something more important was on her mind. She hadn't left the hospital after Mary had gone back to work. Instead she had gone to Dr. MacCauley's office, and while he had given what seemed at the time to be perfectly adequate answers to her questions, she had remained unsatisfied all afternoon.

"Dr. Osborne? Well, he's been on the staff a long time. He's supposed to be an excellent doctor, although after last year I'm not so sure." That was as close as Dan had come to discussing the skiing accident since her return from the East; it obviously made him uneasy.

But Joan was not going to worry about tact, not this evening. She swirled the brandy in the large snifter Dan had given her. "I think he's got it in for Mary."

Dan sat absolutely still. This was the moment he knew would happen sometime, a moment he had thought about and tried to program his reactions to: the first mention Joan would make of Mary. But it was nothing like what he had expected. He was not facing an angry, suspicious wife, ready to explode into hysterics or tears. This was Joan as she had been in the old days, cool, thoughtful, and very perceptive.

"Mary? Mary Conroy?"

"How many Marys do we know?" Joan tossed aside the interruption briskly. "I talked to MacCauley this afternoon. They really stick together, those doctors. But what it adds up to is that either Osborne or somebody in charge of the nurses at the hospital is out to give her a hard time. She's being switched from one rotten job to another; she couldn't even make a date for lunch next week." She took a small swallow from her glass. "Has Osborne enough power to do that?"

"I . . . I suppose he could have. Although doctors don't usually interfere with the schedules for nurses."

"I'll bet you a hundred dollars this one is."

"Why?"

"Because Mary went over his head about me and brought in MacCauley." Joan stood, managing it almost gracefully and made her way to the large windows overlooking the lake, her back to her husband. "And if she hadn't done that, God knows how I'd be today. But that made Osborne look bad, and he's too stuffy a man to take that, not without getting revenge."

"Joan, you don't *know* that."

"I'm not a fool, Dan." She looked at him, her eyes steady. "And I'm not going to have Mary punished because she helped me. Not to mention taking a leave of absence to stay here night and day when I needed her. And look what's happened. Mary could be doing a lot of things in that hospital that would give her a decent schedule, time to herself, time to have her own life. Instead, she's on the night shift, carrying bedpans for ward patients!"

"Did . . . Mary say anything about this to you?" No, of course you didn't, my lovely Mary, you never even hinted it to me. All these months I've been so wrapped up in myself I never gave your real life a thought. But in five minutes, Joan saw it. God, what a bastard I've been!

"Of course Mary wouldn't say anything. But that doesn't mean it isn't happening and that we can't do something about it."

"'We'?"

"You're on the Board of Directors," Joan said practically. "And Daddy's the former Chairman of the Board. You can't tell me you don't outrank that little tyrant Osborne."

"Joan, wait a minute." He thought what it would mean if he tried to pull strings to get Mary a better job. They'd been so careful in their private lives, so conscious of how easily gossip could start about them. Perhaps that was why Mary had never complained about what had been happening, but he knew as he thought it that it wasn't the whole truth. Mary wouldn't have complained because she would have thought it one more burden on his shoulders he didn't need.

Only now Joan was asking him to step in!

"Joan, I don't think we can interfere with hospital procedures. That's not what the Board of Directors of a hospital is supposed to do."

"Nonsense. If Osborne can use his power to make Mary's life miserable, I don't see why we can't use ours to make her happy." She came closer to Dan, her long robe soft, clinging. "Please, Dan? Do it for me? Mary's my good friend; I owe her this." With the contented sigh of a woman who knows she's going to get what she wants, if not right away, surely soon, Joan nestled into his arms.

See, Dr. Keinser, she thought. I *can* think of someone besides myself. I can be of help. And I will be.

Thirteen

April 8

Dear Dr. MacCauley:

I strongly suspect my husband, not to mention the rest of the Board of Directors, would not approve of my writing you (which is why I'm sending this to your apartment). By now you must know how Dan feels about any "outsider" interfering with Midwestern Hospital. (Although I hardly feel like an outsider!) But I have to thank you for your help in getting Mrs. Conroy transferred to her new job. When we had our little talks in your office these past weeks (and please, regard them as confidential conferences between doctor and patient; I don't want either Dan or Mary to know about them), I could tell you were sympathetic, and you really have been wonderful in helping. Dan stubbornly kept saying he had to stay out of the matter, but with Daddy and you on my side he never had a chance.

Actually, all the credit should go to *you*, mentioning at the last Board meeting that the hospital really needed somebody with, as you put it, "good common sense" (oh, yes, I read the minutes!) to help in the laboratory file section at the hospital. I know that made all the difference. It's a job for which Mary Conroy is totally qualified. If she hadn't checked up on my own file last year I don't like to think how long the seriousness of my condition would have gone undiscovered. While I know you cannot openly agree with me (you doctors do stick together!), I'm sure it's Osborne's being shown up as an incompetent idiot that has led to her being shoved into all sorts of unpleasant jobs at the hospital after she returned from taking care of me. Mary's been a darling, a true friend. I owe her a great debt. I like to think that in some small way, with your help, I've been able to pay some of it back.

Mary has been totally surprised about her new job, but I know she'll be brilliant at it, not to mention that at last she'll be able to live a nine-to-five existence like real people.

The raise in salary will be a great help, too. She seems to have a horde of relatives who never seem to stop leaning on her, plus I believe she still has some debts of her ex-husband to pay off. On the personal side it's good to see her without that awful nurse's uniform.

You asked at our last meeting how I was feeling. Very much improved, although I am continuing the rather restrictive regime they prescribed for me last year at Golden Shores. And, of course, like the rest of the world, I'm getting older. So when I get a slight twinge these days I don't really know if it's from the accident or just middle age.

Before I close this, I must apologize for not having written you a letter of condolence last year on the death of your wife. I'm afraid I wasn't very good about considering the rest of the world during that time. I only met Alice once or twice, but she seemed a kind and serene lady and I know you must miss her a great deal. Please accept my belated sympathy, and again, thank you for helping Mary.

Sincerely,
Joan Paige Martin

June 12

Dear Paige:

I sent your guitar up to you at camp last week as soon as I got your letter. If it hasn't arrived by now, please let me know and I'll go down and light a fire under all the clerks at the store. I light a terrific fire, I'll have you know, and without rubbing two sticks together. I'm also returning your money order; please think of the guitar as a birthday gift. With my wonderful new job I feel absolutely rich! I hope you enjoy the instrument. I was never able to learn anything musically beyond "Chopsticks." I also sent along a book of folksongs. I hope you won't think them too juvenile, but some of them are really lovely, and I could hear your voice singing some of my old favorites.

One thing I do want to mention about your letter. I think you're being a little harsh when you write that your mother and father don't "care" about you or your music. I know that isn't true. With my new regular hours I've been able to have lunch with your mother several times, and she speaks of you and Joey both so proudly. Your father may not say as much, but that doesn't mean he doesn't love you both deeply. You mustn't think they wouldn't have been overjoyed to help you in any way, even if people our age don't always seem to "understand modern music," as you put it. Remember, Paige, I'm just about your parents' age myself!

Of course you can write to me any time you want to. I love getting your letters, and as I told Joey before he went to his camp, don't worry about the spelling. I was never very good at that either. (If your father sends back your letter with the misspelled words circled in red, remember he's only trying to help you.) With me, I won't know whether you spell things correctly or not! I'm also happy that you are looking forward to going to Fairlawn in the fall. From what I hear it's a wonderful school, and I think at your age it'll be a terrific adventure to leave Chicago for a while and see something of the rest of the country. Would you believe, the farthest I've been is about a hundred miles? I'll count on you writing me all about New England. The colors are supposed to be spectacular (spel?) in the fall, and I'd love to see the crisp snow and the lovely old colonial villages. I've read about them, of course, but I'll expect lots of postcards (and letters too) if you have time.

I'm afraid September won't be so much fun for Joey. Even with the tutor this spring he didn't quite make the progress both of your parents had hoped for. (That's terrible grammar, isn't it? You're not supposed to end sentences with things dangling, but you know what I mean.) I'm afraid your father is going to be firm about sending him off to military school this fall. Please *don't* mention this to Joey if you write to him. Let's let him have the summer to relax and enjoy being outdoors with the other boys. Maybe you and I can persuade him before he leaves for school that it will be something like an extension of summer camp. At least I hope so.

May I nag you again? Please don't think because your parents haven't been writing that they don't love and care for you. That just isn't true, Paige. Your mother still has physical problems, many more than we know, because, as always, she doesn't complain. And I gather your father is very involved in this new real estate venture (the one near the airport). He's working hard for the future of you and your brother, so keep on loving him. I know he needs that very much.

It's pouring buckets of rain here in Chicago, I hope your tent is warm and dry—better still, that the whole summer is full of sunshine and happy times. After all, how do we know what can happen to guitar strings in damp weather?

Much love,
Mary

Dear Joey:

Columbus Day and the file section has a holiday! Hope you're getting one at school. The courses you're taking (I got your schedule yesterday) look awfully tough. Simple math we could figure out from using the baseball scores, but algebra! However, I know how bright you are, much more than those other guys! Our team may not have done so well this year on the baseball field, but we'll show those Easterners yet!

Your Sergeant-Major sounds, as you put it, like a real stinker. I had a head nurse like that once at the hospital. I used to think of mugging her in a dark alley, but since she seemed to have eyes in the back of her head, I figured she'd know it was me and then where would I be? They don't just give demerits at hospitals. So I decided to kill her with kindness, volunteering for all the dirty jobs I knew she was going to give me anyway, smiling cheerfully, making a point of complimenting her if she looked well. (I wouldn't recommend that with the Sgt.-Major!) Anyway, it worked like a charm, because it drove her crazy trying to figure out what I was up to.

Cookies are enclosed, not homemade, I'm afraid. There's a limit to my skills! The smaller box is just for you, the other one is for the rest of the guys, including the Sgt.-Major! And it probably wouldn't hurt to share your box with your roommate; if he's that good at Latin, maybe he can help with the translations. Don't think I'm forgetting about your promise to send me a picture of yourself in full uniform. If I don't have it by Christmas vacation, I'll photograph you myself and I'm a *terrible* photographer. Which means there will be an awful picture of you in my possession for the rest of your life, which could lead to thoughts of blackmail.

I know these first weeks have been hard, Joey dear, but believe it or not, nothing lasts forever. (Even if it seems to.)

Much love,
Mary

June 12

Dear Paige:

(Or should I address you as Honor Student Paige Martin? Just "Dear Paige" doesn't sound grand enough!) Many, many congratulations! Your mother and father had me over for dinner last night (Lila sends her love . . . or would if she knew I was writing today), and I saw the school report. I'm so proud of you! I know I had nothing to do with it, but I'm still proud.

Strictly between us, I think your father is coming around to another summer at music camp. He's talking of a fast business trip to Europe with your mother; would you believe they both asked me to come with them? I guess I could afford it, now that everything's paid off, although they were kind enough to say they would pay my way, but I haven't been at the new job long enough to get a whole month, which is what they plan. Or I gather your father does; he has some business contacts he wants to meet in Italy. What Italy has to do with Chicago real estate I'm not quite sure. You'll have to ask your Dad when you see him. Your mother will probably only go along for the Paris part of the trip. She thinks Italy might be too hot in July.

As you may have heard by now, Joey didn't do as well as you his first year away from home. I'm afraid he'll have to take summer courses to make up, which seems awfully hard on him. Both your mother and I feel he'd be happier and make more progress in a less rigid school here in Chicago, but your father can be very strong-minded when he wants to be. If you use your charm on him when you come home, and your mother does the same in Europe, maybe he'll change his mind. Joey really is unhappy.

Of course I'll be free to go shopping with you when you arrive. We'll have to find a special present for your birthday. I still can't get over how you found out about mine. The tape with the folksongs was beautiful. My brother got me a tape machine and showed me how to work it, and I listen to your lovely voice over and over again.

Love,
Mary

June 15

Dear Dr. MacCauley:

Thank you very much for your offer to intervene with the Board of Directors regarding my taking a month's vacation. While it was very kind of Mr. and Mrs. Martin to ask for this favor, I could not accept it even if the hospital agreed. Quite frankly, I do not have that much vacation time coming to me, and I have no wish to cause problems with the other hardworking members of the staff of the file laboratory. I still have a great deal to learn, and my two weeks in August will be all the time I feel I should or really want to take. It's a very happy place to work, under Mrs. Denning's management, and I've enjoyed this change a great deal, making many new friends.

Thank you again, but let's leave everything as it is.

Mary Conroy

July 10

Dear Mary:

I hope I've got your new address right! I simply had to write and thank you for what you did for my niece Moira. I know, I know, you said when I saw you at the hospital that you used no influence on the staff to handle the operation, but I know better. My sister tried over and over to reach a good surgeon there, and at other hospitals, but the prices quoted were way beyond Bridget and Jerry's means. Not to mention that all the doctors in the Chicago area who could do the kidney operation seemed booked months in advance. So don't tell me it wasn't you that put in the good word for Moira. I know better.

Today the bill came, and Jerry and Bridget couldn't believe their eyes. (Neither could I. I know what Mr. Reiner charges for special work, and he's just a West Side lawyer.) The bill wasn't even two hundred dollars! There was something about a Paige-Martin Foundation that picked up the rest of the amount. I've never heard of it, but I'll bet you had something to do with that too.

Anyway, bless you, Mary, for all your help. Moira's going to be able to go to school this September for the first time ever. She's so wild and happy and excited to be free of pain and be like other kids it would do your heart wonders to see her. Bridget and I wanted to make a special novena for you and your intentions, and of course the Paige-Martin Foundation, but that new young pastor doesn't seem to hold with the old customs. So we're lighting a candle the next nine First Fridays and saying a rosary instead.

God bless you.
Maggie Feeney

P.S. I heard from a friend in California your ex (Jack Conroy) is doing well out there—has his own carpentry shop, no less! I know how you struggled to pay his bills. I hope you're getting some of it back.

Royal Danieli Hotel
Venice, Italy

July 11

Dear Sirs:

I enclose my check as deposit of the two-bedroom suite facing the Grand Canal I wrote to you about this spring. I shall be arriving with my cousin, Mrs. Mary Conroy, the afternoon of August 10th. Please have several arrangements of roses in the rooms. At the moment our plans are still tentative, but we still be staying at least one week at your hotel. Please send confirmation of this reservation directly to Mrs. Conroy at the address listed below.

Sincerely,
Daniel Martin

August 14

Dear Tim and Patsy and kids:

Don't know how to write "Having a wonderful time" in Italian, but I am! And no, I don't miss not being part of a tour, everybody is very friendly, so don't worry about my being alone. Tell Maggie Feeney her prayers were answered. I've got everything and more that I dreamed of!

Love,
Mary

February 6

Dear Mary:

Having a glorious time down here in Tucson. The weather is heaven after the Chicago snow, and the resort is splendid (it should be at these prices). Haven't told Dan yet, but I'm going to stay on another couple of weeks. This is a BIG secret, so no fair telling anyone. I want to see if they'll notice the improvement when I get back.

I had a little "tuck" taken while I was here, and I want to be sure all the marks have disappeared before I return north. Nothing major, I promise you, Nurse Conroy! Just a little lift at the jaw and around the eyes. After all, when a woman gets to forty it's time she helped Nature a bit. I even think it's helped the "bad" side of my face; I seem to have more mobility there than before. Anyway, for the present let this be our secret.

Dan sounds very grumpy when I talk to him on the phone. Would you do me a big favor and make him take you out for dinner? He always seems to be in a better mood when you're around. You should have come to Europe with us last year, he was an absolute grouch all the time we were in Paris. I was almost relieved to fly home without him. Anyway, try to cheer him up if you can. It can't be much fun for either him or poor Joey to have to glower at each other every night over dinner. Dan just won't get over Joey's flunking out of that awful military school. With the arguments that went on all through Christmas I was ready for another nervous breakdown. (See, Nurse Conroy? I can talk about it honestly now!)

Paige writes that Fairlawn has a program for its third-year students (hard to think that she'll be that next year!) which makes them exchange students, spending two semesters in Europe. I don't know what to think about it. Dan will probably hit the ceiling. Ever since last summer's business trip to Venice he seems to think European men have nothing better to do than pinch American girls. But from the stories I'm hearing from other women down here about their so-called "clean-cut" sons and daughters, Europe sounds a lot safer for a girl Paige's age than America. You wouldn't believe what I've heard. Drugs are the least of it! And I can remember when if you so much as kissed a boy you weren't engaged to, you were considered "fast." Ah, well, as they say, "the times, they are a-changing."

Please do what you can for Joey and Dan and give Lila a big hug for me. And remember, not a word about the "tuck." Let's see if Dan notices!

Love,
Joan

January 7

Dear Martha:

Thank you for your Christmas box and letter. Of course I'm worried about Vietnam, too. Orin Junior is nineteen now and Henry almost seventeen. Their father and I have put so much love and care into raising them all these years, I think it would about break my heart if they had to go into the army and be sent someplace where they could be killed or hurt. Henry's doing so well in school, even with skipping a year, the principal is sure he can get a college scholarship. Orin Junior's growing so tall and strong, you wouldn't recognize him! He's not as good with the books as Henry, but there are such things as athletic scholarships, and he's pinning his hopes on getting one for his basketball. I don't hope, I just keep saying my prayers.

And that brings me to another point in your letter. I know you are my elder and you feel you must speak out, but I feel it is very unfair and un-Christian of you to write so sharply about the situation I told you about in confidence concerning the Martins and Mrs. Conroy. I hope after all of Mama and Papa's training I have as much sense of good and evil, as you put it, as you do. I don't have to be told adultery is a sin, but by continuing to work for the Martins I do not feel I am condoning wrongdoing. This is a situation that is far more tangled up than any "scarlet woman" in the Bible.

Mrs. Conroy is a decent, respectable woman who has done a great deal for this family. I'm here and I've seen it. You haven't, Martha. And surely what Mama and Papa taught us also was understanding and forgiveness. I know Mary would do nothing to hurt Mrs. Martin and I don't feel that she has or is. Miss Joan has never been the same person since her accident, and Mr. Dan is a man who isn't as patient perhaps as he should be with a semi-invalid. If Mary can be a good friend to both of them, I don't think it's anything that should concern you or me one way or the other. Mr. Dan certainly came back home from his week in Italy with her in a more tolerant way of mind.

If Miss Joan could get out of herself more she might see what's happening (although I pray she never guesses that it's Mary Mr. Dan's involved with) and try to be more of a real wife. At the moment she's still on her side of the apartment and he's on his. Everybody's always very polite and kind and I know in their hearts they still love each other, but not in the same way as before. Love between people changes over the years, Martha. We're both old enough and experienced enough to know that.

If people choose to live their lives this way, I don't think I'm being hypocritical to keep my mouth shut and say nothing. Certainly Mary is the only one Joey Martin seems able to talk to. He and his father get into an argument every dinnertime, either over politics or the kids' music or how long Joey can grow his hair. Miss Joan tries to keep peace but it doesn't work. However, I notice the evenings Mr. Dan goes "out for a walk," as he puts it, the next few days are usually a bit more peaceful. Some sins just aren't as bad as they may look to outsiders.

My best to your family,
Your sister Lila (Mrs. Orin Franklin)

May 20

Dear Kay:

Dan very kindly volunteered the services of the office (I'm sure you must *love* that!) to help with the arrangements for Paige's debut in July. Please get an assistant to the regular staff to help with the addresses. I know Dan's kicking about the expense, but it's not fair to put all the burden on you and the other girls in addition to their regular work. Needless to say, you are invited as well, although I didn't put your name on the list; by this time you're certainly *family*. The printers promise to deliver the invitations to the office by the first of June (that doesn't give us much time as the party will be July 1st). I've included the number to call if they don't arrive on time (the invitations, I mean).

Much of this I've tried to handle before I left. The country club is set, and the orchestra. Joey tells me there should be a "backup" group that doesn't just play "the businessman's bounce" as he calls it. Mary (Conroy) has promised to confer with him about that. I'd rather he made the choice. Tell Mr. Martin I said Joey was to do it. Maybe that will calm things while I'm away, I certainly hope so, this past winter has been hell. Without you on the business front and Mary, I think Joey and his father would have killed each other about his wanting to go to public high school.

Which reminds me—can you *please* see Joey gets a tuxedo for the party? He's still kicking about it, but I think it's just for show. Call Mary. Maybe with the two of you working on him he'll go to Dan's tailor like a good boy. And my father is going to need new tails. I know he'll moan, but tell him these should last him long enough that he can be buried in them! On second thought, don't tell him anything; just have the tailor make them up. Same measurements, but maybe let the waistline be an inch or two looser. I'll take care of the bill myself when I get home.

I'm hoping all of this is going to go smoothly. Paige in her letters doesn't sound exactly enthusiastic about a coming-out party, which is one of the reasons I'm flying east tonight. It seems the year she spent in Europe brought out all the rebellion in her. Even last Christmas I couldn't get her to wear anything but those awful blue jeans. Not to mention her marks are way down since her return. However, I'm hoping the sight of some really pretty dresses in the Boston shops will change her mind.

Oh—one thing more. I can't seem to find the address for that nice Mickey Harris who used to follow her around like a puppy when she was a kid. Can you locate him? His family's still in Chicago, but they've moved to the suburbs and I can't seem to locate them. Perhaps their old school would have it. I'd like to have him there for Paige. And please hold Dr. MacCauley's invitation until I get back. I want to put a personal note on it. I'll pull him out of his shell by force if I have to. There aren't that many attractive widowers in Chicago to let one escape.

Again my thanks, Kay. I do hope all this won't be too much of a problem. Will call you next week when I get back.

Best,
Joan Paige Martin

September 3

Dear Joey:

Now don't drop your teeth hearing from me, nobody else in the family knows your address. I had to pry it out of Mary. I knew she'd been writing you, and she thought maybe if I tried I might make some kind of dent in that thick skull of yours. Sorry. I know that's not the right way to start with you.

Joey, will you just keep reading this without making up your mind about anything first? Please? I know the debut thing was a God-awful mess. I never wanted it. I told Dad and Mom that in my letters all winter long. They must have thought I was being stubborn or something, or maybe they just don't like to hear anything that doesn't agree with what they want. I only went through with it because Mary said it was giving Mother something to be excited about, and boy, we all know how long it's been since that happened! Anyway, *I* don't blame you for being sore that night. With guys our age getting killed in a country we have no business being in, I felt like a real jerk standing there in a white dress, pretending to be some sweet young innocent virgin going to her first grown-up ball. You know I'm not like that. Certainly not since I met Phil in Europe. (And thanks for keeping your mouth shut about him. Mary knows, but nobody else.)

Your leaving home is what I'm really writing about. Sure, Granddad was furious about the drinking, and some of your weird friends didn't help any. Luckily I don't think any of the "older generation" guessed what they were smoking, although I saw old Kay giving a couple of them a funny look once or twice during the evening.

Joey, I know when you got furious with Dad you didn't mean all of what you said. Sure, he still thinks the atom bomb was the miracle for America in World War II, but you don't run away from home over that! I know he was sorry the next day, but you'd gone by then. Joey, won't you come back? Please? Not for my sake or theirs, but you've got to be at least a high school graduate to get into the Peace Corps, if you still want to do that.

And—I can see your face when you read this, but I'm being practical now—you don't get the money from the trust funds Grandma Paige set up when we were born until you're eighteen, and that's over a year away. Sneer if you want to, or laugh, but money is important. I got *my* first check last week and boy, the feeling of freedom it gave me! I'm going to salt it away and go off to college like a good little girl. Well, at least for a year. Then we'll see.

Where did Mickey Harris drag you when you left the dance floor? He's been around a couple of times since, but he won't say a word about that night. He's sure gotten big. Remember what a drag he used to be?

Anyway, Joey, think about what I've written and please come back. Even if you don't believe me, listen to Mary.

All my love,
Your sister Paige

September 6

Dear Joey:

I'm enclosing a check (not very much, but I hope you'll only need it for a few days). Your plane ticket is at the American Airlines counter of the main San Francisco office. Don't worry about repaying me, we'll work that out. I'm just happy you're coming back. I don't think we have to plan anything about your return. Just go to the apartment looking well and not hurt or bitter or anything, and I know they'll be so happy no one will ask any questions. I'll be home that night if you want to call me, but your first evening should be with your parents. They love you very much, Joey, as do I.

Mary

Fourteen

It was on a Saturday afternoon the following spring that Dan asked Mary to marry him.

They'd planned a lazy weekend in her apartment. Joan had gone east the previous Wednesday to visit Paige at college and to spend some days shopping in New York. Joey was in Florida for spring vacation with a carful of other students. It had been a reluctant gift, that vacation. Dan didn't approve of the annual southern migration of unsupervised high school and college students racing off to lie for a week on the beaches, but Mary had persuaded him to let Joey go if his marks held up. Somewhat to Dan's surprise, they had.

Joey had been different since the previous summer, Dan thought as he lay on Mary's bed. More subdued, quieter, more adult. A lot of that, Dan suspected, he owed to Mary. Or maybe the boy had had some unexpected experiences in the weeks after he had run off to San Francisco. Probably a little of both, he concluded. In any case, Joey had gone back to school and surprisingly quickly moved to the head of his class; he'd have no trouble making college in the fall. They still did not agree on most of the things happening in the world, but, Dan thought as he lit another cigarette, most fathers and sons their age probably didn't agree either, no matter what country they were in, or what language they spoke. At least Joey had become polite and was growing into a handsome young man.

Dan leaned back on the pillows, watching Mary brush her hair. He felt completely at peace with everything and everybody. Serenity: he found that here in Mary's apartment. His business was doing well; if he could hold on for another year, the airport property would sell at a huge profit. Paige was safe in a good college, not boy-crazy like so many of the daughters of his friends were. Joey was shaping up; he still talked about going off to the Peace Corps, but lately he was showing an interest in medicine. Mary would persuade him he would be able to offer more as a full doctor than if he went straight out of high school. With college and medical school, Joey would be deep in his twenties when he finished, and Dan suspected he'd have other things on his mind by then besides saving the world.

Later Dan was to wonder whether it was thinking about the children and their futures that made him propose. He was in his fifties. Time had gone by so quickly and he knew it would move even faster in the future. Or was it the sight of Mary sitting there by the window that made him say what he did? He had seen her so often, in other bedrooms and other cities when they could arrange a few quiet days together, doing the same simple activities—brushing her hair, fastening her dress, checking her lipstick—all quiet, natural, normal things, nothing that by itself was erotic, and yet they could cause a sudden quickening of desire in him— or even when desire was satisfied, as it was now, a great wave of longing to hold her again and to be held and never let go.

"Will you marry me?"

He said it so softly that for a moment Mary thought she imagined it. She looked at him through a tangle of hair, sweeping it back instantly with her brush. He was sitting up in bed, the sheet covering his naked body to the waist. Her beautiful Dan. All this time, and she still thought of him as that: when he walked into the apartment or she would see him, unexpectedly early, at their table in a restaurant. He was grayer, of course, but his body remained strong and vital, with a sexual energy that would be the envy of a man half his age. She'd never told him, knowing he would probably laugh or think her sentimental, but she would always lie on his side of the bed the nights after he had left her. It would seem some faint part of his presence was still there. Nothing so simple to explain as the scent of his aftershave lotion or the ashes of his cigarettes, but something of him stayed to give her comfort through the nights.

"Mary? Did you hear me? I want to marry you."

She put down the brush carefully. A hundred thoughts ran through her mind. They had never talked of this. She had never in their closest moments allowed herself to imagine it ever happening. When they traveled together, usually Dan insisted on the same careful reservations of their first trip for "a two-bedroom suite for Daniel Martin and his cousin." But sometimes she would persuade him to just drive through the day and settle for whatever accomodations they could find at nightfall. Then they registered as "Mr. and Mrs.," using whatever name they could think of. Even those times she had never considered the actuality of marriage. Not a public one for the world to see. Perhaps she had never felt the need because she had felt herself so committed all these years, more married than she ever had been to Jack Conroy. She had made that choice a long, long time ago, that first weekend in the hotel suite downtown.

"Aren't you forgetting? You're already married."

"To you, yes. To Joan, no." He swung out of bed, modestly pulling on the robe she had given him at Christmas. "You can't call what Joan and I have a marriage. No one could."

"She loves you."

"Maybe." He paused to think about it, the line between his eyebrows Mary had smoothed away so many times reappearing. "Yes," he said at last, "I suppose in her own way she does. And I . . . I care for her. That doesn't change." He put his hand on Mary's shoulder. She could feel the warmth of the skin through the blue silk. "Does that bother you?"

"No, Dan. That was understood from the beginning. I love Joan too. A strange thing for a woman in my position to say, but it's true. In some ways I think I understand and care for her more than you do."

She heard him sigh. "God-awful mess, isn't it?"

"No, Dan!" She said it swiftly. "It's simply our own way of living our lives. I've not regretted any of it. That's why I've never considered any changes."

"Never?" He was smiling, that faint challenging smile he had when she tried to refuse him anything.

"Truly never." She moved away, knowing from the past how hard it was to argue with him sensibly when he touched her. "I've had no dreams of anything more than what we have now. I'm with you when you want me, because I love you. I'd go on loving you if you walked out that door and I never saw you again."

"But that's not the point, Mary." The smile was gone, his voice suddenly serious. "I don't want to walk out that door, not ever. I don't want to go back to that big empty apartment or even to my very efficient, very expensive offices." He sat down on the bed. "I just want to stay here with you. And be at peace." He grinned at her, with what she thought to herself as his little-boy look. "And no light Irish humor about how long that would last."

"Until you were hungry. For something." Kneeling beside him on the bed, she smoothed the hair back from his forehead. Dan, dear Dan, she thought, this is when I love you most. When you reach out for me and don't even know you're reaching. Only, of course, this time he did. "Dan, is something wrong? Are you worried about something?"

"Nurse Conroy to the rescue? No. Just thinking about . . . time. How much more do we have left? I'm serious. Ten, fifteen years to enjoy life? To enjoy loving each other?"

"We'll always have that," she said quietly. "If you want it."

"Bits and pieces of days and nights? Arranging schedules like spies so we can be together? A quick trip someplace, both of us wondering, Suppose a crisis comes up? Oh, yes, I've seen you when the phone rings in some hotel room: Paris or New York or even Milwaukee. Has something gone wrong at home? That's what you're thinking; I see it in your eyes. And I want to be able to say, This is my home! Whatever room I'm in with you, that's my home, the only one I want."

She was crying now, not as Joan would, with wails of grief, but softly, silently. Damn it, must I always compare them? he thought. "Mary? I'm not saying this to hurt you."

"You don't learn, Danny, my boy. What you said was beautiful, and I loved hearing it and I'll remember it all my life." It was true. She wondered if other women in her position did the same thing, saving up the precious words the man they loved said to them, far more precious than any expensive gift of jewelry could ever be. "But . . . marriage? It's not possible."

Always the wrong word to use with Dan Martin. She should have remembered that. His jaw set stubbornly, and she could feel the muscles of his broad shoulders grow tense under her fingers.

"Why not? Within a year I'll have this airport deal off my back and there'll be more money than I'll know what to do with. The kids are in school; you can't say they need me. They're forming their own lives, their own world."

"And Joan?" That was always the question between them. Mary knew he'd have no new answer any more than he had in the past. But he surprised her.

"I think maybe she's beginning not to need me either." His face was serious. This was clearly not something he had just considered but something he must have been working over in his mind for a long time. "Ever since Paige's coming-out party last July, somehow Joan's become . . . I don't know . . . more social? Considering the way that evening ended, I'd have thought she would have retreated back into her shell. But she hasn't."

Mary was wise enough to say nothing. That party had been a source of disagreement between them for months. Sure, Joey shouldn't have gotten drunk, and the kids should have known better than to smoke pot, but it wasn't such an unusual occurrence these days. Most of the people at the party hadn't even heard the quarrel between Joey and his father. Only she and Joan had been present in that little room off the dance floor.

Dan was right about one thing. That evening marked a turning point for Joan. She began to do more entertaining. One could hardly open the society pages of the *Tribune* or the *Sun-Times* without seeing her picture, at least once a week. She was on the Board of Directors for Chicago's prestigious symphony, co-chairman of the Lyric Opera Ball, heading a dozen different charitable organizations.

"She's hardly ever home now," Dan said. "And if she is, it means a crowd of people are coming for drinks or dinner to talk about raising some more bucks for something cultural or worthwhile."

"It's good for her. And the city. You want her to be interested in life."

"Sure. But that's my point. She's making her own life now. That's not going to change if we get a divorce." He leaned back against her, resting his head against her breasts. "And it lets me off the merry-go-round."

"You used to love that merry-go-round."

"Once. It impressed the hell out of me. A guy from the West Side. You know what she gave me for Christmas? Seven white silk scarves . . . so I'd have a fresh one every night of the week. God!"

Not to mention a third tuxedo and a new set of tails. How handsome he looked in them! Mary could hardly blame Joan for wanting to see him like that, to be able to take his arm and enter a room, knowing what a stunning couple they made together.

"A great-looking couple, aren't we?" Once again, he had read her mind without even having to see her face. "But we're not a couple, Mary. We're just two nice polite people who live in a very large apartment, as far away from each other as we can."

Mary bit her lip to keep from speaking. Not always so far away, my Dan. He and Joan still went to bed together, not often but occasionally, when Joan had been particularly vivacious at a party or when they had opened a bottle of champagne to break the silence of the rare evening alone. The first time it had happened, after Joan came back from her winter trip to Tucson, Dan had confessed it to Mary, shamefaced, embarrassed. Mary said nothing, but the pain had been as sharp and as deep as if he had stabbed her.

They had not slept together the night he told her, and for the following week there had been no communication between them. Then Mary had come back to the apartment one afternoon to find him. Without a word, he had taken her in his arms and kissed her and, not waiting for her to take off her coat, had taken her into the bedroom and made love to her with a passion that had surprised them both.

After that, whatever happened between Dan and his wife he did not tell her. But Mary knew. Sometimes Joan would hint at it obliquely at their weekly lunch together and Mary would listen, trying to keep her face expressionless, always wondering how much Joan suspected. Surely they couldn't have been as close as they had been these past few years if Joan had guessed; no one could be that good an actress. But besides Joan's confidences and Dan's confessions, Mary knew they still went to bed together from time to time.

She never said anything about it. If sometimes she cried alone in the night, getting up at last to take an aspirin, looking at her puffed face in the mirror to wonder how Dan could love her when Joan was near, beautiful, witty, charming, she kept her thoughts to herself. She would stand at the bedroom window, looking at the lights in his apartment, wondering if this was the night there would be lights in only one bedroom. She knew it was foolish and destructive, and by the end of the year after Dan's confession she had forced herself to break the habit. She still waited for the signal they had arranged so long before on the nights when he left. He would pull the shade of his bedroom window up and then down again, meaning he was safely home.

She would pull her shade down firmly and leave it that way until morning. She would not spy on them. It was contemptible and foolish, and she was intelligent enough to know it could only make her miserable. She had no right to begrudge Joan any of Dan. She had made that promise to herself when their life together had begun, and she would not break it now.

"Sure," Dan said, that spring afternoon, breaking the silence. "Sometimes something happens. Not for nearly a year now. Not because I'm such an angel. I won't claim that. But it seems . . . wrong somehow. You're my wife, not Joan."

"Don't ever even think that, Dan."

"I want to think it! I want to say it to the whole damn world!" He took her in his arms, holding her close. "Mary, it's time I had some of my life, too! I've given as much as I can to Joan and my family, I've worked hard. Is it so wrong to want time for myself? That's time with you. Don't you think I have a right to that?" He left her, to pace back and forth. "I'm not a child. This isn't some middle-aged fling. It's been years. We know our own minds; don't we deserve some happiness together? God, it's not as if getting a divorce was some kind of scandal any more! Half the couples

Joan and I know are divorced, and for a hell of a lot weaker reasons than we have."

"And the children? If we married they'd feel betrayed . . . by both of us. They'd have a right to feel that. So would Joan."

"They'd understand. In time." She could hear the doubt in his voice.

"Would they? I don't think so."

"If they're so coldhearted, let them go." This was Dan at his worst, stubborn, cruel, selfish, determined not to be thwarted.

"You can't mean that. You couldn't, and be the man I love."

"Do you? Love me? Or have I been kidding myself?"

By now she knew the pattern of his anger so well she should have anticipated this. They would meet. Something would have gone wrong with his day and he would be irritable, with a waiter or a captain if they were in a restaurant, or something about the upkeep of her building if they were here. After the initial outburst he would calm down, and in less than ten minutes she could usually get him to tell her what had gone wrong that day. If it was something for which there was no immediate solution—the bank refusing to lend him more money to cover the airport property, or Joan's father being difficult about Dan's plans for expansion—eventually the anger would reemerge, turned on her. That was always the last of it, for they both knew she was not the cause of how he felt and he would almost instantly apologize.

The storm would be over.

Only this was different. He had asked her to marry him, she had given him the same sensible objections she had worked out for herself over the years, and it had brought doubt to him, doubt of her love, something she knew had never occurred to him before. They were older. The years they had shared should have brought them so close there could never be any doubt, but the separate lives they led had brought insecurity instead of comfort. At least to him, it seemed. Not to her.

She could and did see other people from time to time, at parties that Tim and Patsy gave or at the ones she was always invited to by Maggie Feeney's forever grateful sister. Almost always there was an "extra" man for her, a widower or (rarely) a divorced man her own age. If later they asked her to dinner or a concert, she might go once, if she knew Dan would be busy that night. Never, however, did she see them again and, of course, never would she invite them to her apartment. One glimpse of these rooms and they would know the truth, that there was a man in her life, a permanent man. She had long ago established rules for visitors, especially for Joan and Paige and Joey. Not just a phone call before they dropped in, but at least a day of warning, a day to hide things in locked closets, a day of open windows to rid the room of the smell of his cigarettes, to conceal the humidor and his toilet articles in the bathroom, to drape a softly colored cashmere shawl over his very masculine easy chair. Gradually the requests to visit her apartment had dwindled. It was always so much easier (especially for Joan, with the limp she had never lost) not to climb the two flights of steps to Mary's apartment but to meet elsewhere.

The one person who should have been asked up was Dr. MacCauley. He had been her partner more than once when Joan was hostess, her escort to an opera benefit (which they both loved), seated at her right at the formal dinner parties in the large lakefront apartment. He was not by nature a talkative man, and she, conscious of the difference in their status at the hospital, had often found it hard to make conversation with him until she realized he was perfectly at ease sitting with her in silence. Once she learned that, she became more comfortable with him. Dan had teased her about Joan's matchmaking, but the idea had merely seemed funny to both of them. Or so she had thought at the time.

This past winter, since Paige's debut when she had been with Dr. MacCauley and the Martins, it had seemed to her occasionally Dan would stare at them, and the expression of his face might almost have been possessive. That, and jealous. Which was ridiculous, Mary thought. A man couldn't be jealous of a middle-aged . . . well, *mistress* was the word she would have to use, she supposed. Not after all this time.

Still, MacCauley was the only other man she had seen more than once. In December Mrs. Denning had retired and Mary had been promoted to her position as supervisor of the laboratory files. This was a post Mary knew she had earned; it was not some hidden favor from either Dan or Joan. Dr. MacCauley had almost made a point of that and then, rather brusquely, asked her out for dinner. She could think of no reason for refusing, although she dreaded the silences that were bound to occur. That evening, to her surprise, there were no silences. Alone with Mary, he allowed himself to relax. Mary found in the three hours they spent together she had barely gone through more than two of the topics she had privately prepared to help the evening's conversation.

He had politely seen her home, making no effort to invite himself inside. After that Mary allowed herself to enjoy his company, his excellent taste in food and art, his often sharply acerbic comments about the other doctors and nurses at the hospital. His farewells at the end of the evening were polite, but there was no hint of making their relationship more intimate.

Part of this may have come from an accident that occurred the second evening they had dinner. In getting up from the restaurant table, Mary had dropped her purse and they had both knelt to pick up the contents. Most of what was on the floor could have been found in any woman's handbag, but earlier that day Mary had bought a pair of cuff links for Dan's coming birthday. They had been made from antique coins and were both expensive and unique. As her purse fell, the box the links were in came open. MacCauley closed the box without comment and handed it to her. She knew she would never be able to lie convincingly to him, saying it was a gift for her brother or a friend. She found herself blushing furiously and, grabbing up the rest of the articles, disappeared into the ladies' room.

MacCauley never asked about the box. If he saw Dan wearing the cuff links at the Martins' next dinner and made the obvious connection, it appeared to make no difference to him, either at the hospital or when they met socially.

"Well? Are you in love with me? Or is MacCauley stealing some of my time?"

"Dan, don't be ridiculous." It was another inflammatory word to use, but the idea was so preposterous she could think of no other. "Mac's a very nice lonely gentleman who enjoys talking about opera and Europe, and I like to listen."

"You've been to the opera. And to Europe."

He was turning sullen, one of his worst traits. However, it also meant the anger was disappearing and he was beginning to realize how foolish his accusations were. The quarrel would soon be over.

"Yes, Dan. I've been to Europe. And the opera. With many thanks to you." She went on, adding the next two words carefully. "And Joan."

That had begun when the Martins had wanted to see how Paige was progressing during her year abroad. Dan had talked about it to her here in the apartment. Why didn't she fly over and meet them "by accident"? That she refused to do; it was simply too risky. But at the next dinner party Joan had again brought up the subject of all of them traveling together, pursuing it after the rest of the guests had left. Dan swore solemnly he had not put the idea in his wife's head, and as Joan persisted in her campaign, reluctantly Mary had to believe him. It was almost as if Joan didn't want to be alone with her husband, that Mary acting as a shield was as necessary to Joan if she were to make the trip as it was for Dan because he wanted her. After her attempt to refuse Dan the first trip had failed so miserably, she had ceased to resist his wishes. She knew out of his own strong pride he would never bring up the fact he had helped that child to an almost free operation in order to make her change her mind. Mary had gone to Italy willingly, out of love and her own very real gratitude for the kindness he could show the helpless.

The week in Venice had been the first of their secret vacations. There had been others, and Mary no longer made an attempt to avoid them. If Dan wanted to spend time with her, how much more did she want it? But only want it, she had told herself firmly as she had flown back from Italy on a separate plane. Never let yourself grow to need it, or to ask for it.

"Dan, don't you see how impossible any change would be?" she said, breaking the long silence that had grown ominously in the room. "Dearest, I would marry you in ten minutes, if it were possible."

"You'd make me wait that long?" He was beginning to smile. The conversation was back on safer grounds.

"I think it might look a little strange, both of us at City Hall in our bathrobes," she said dryly. He laughed, but only briefly.

"I'm not giving up, Mary," he said quietly. "I want my life to be with you. And I'm not going to let it be kept from me. Once all the airport property is purchased and the city meets my price—and they will, they have to—I'm going to get a divorce. If you want to wait a decent respectable time after that"—he smiled his challenging smile—"I'll give you just ten minutes."

"Wouldn't it be wonderful?"

Don't, Mary! Don't even think about it. Don't open that little door you've always kept so carefully closed and bolted. So many years of being happy with what they had and now this, puncturing all her strength and security. One simple question from a middle-aged lover on a sunny spring afternoon and all her strong defenses, her iron promises, were starting to melt away.

"I may not even have to wait a year. I'm serious, Mary. Joan's no fool. She must know by now there's someone. And since she hasn't tried any of her usual tricks—a last glass of champagne, a new negligee, a subtle hint the door to her bedroom might just possibly be open tonight for the first time in a year—maybe she's beginning not to care any more either."

The phone rang. As Mary went to answer it, she called back over her shoulder. "I wouldn't count on that."

"If that's MacCauley, tell him you've already got a date."

It wasn't the doctor. It was Joan.

"Mary? It's Joan. Where *is* everybody?"

"Joan? First of all, where are you?" She knew Dan had moved to the doorway behind her and was listening, making no movement that could betray over the phone Mary was not alone.

"At the apartment. I decided I didn't want to face being in New York by myself, just for shopping, so I came back this afternoon. And nobody's here. I can't get Dan at the office, even at his private line. It's Lila's weekend off, and apparently she's gone down to her sister's. Even Kay doesn't answer. I feel like I'm in a ghost town." The tone was lighthearted, but Mary could sense a sliver of panic under it. "I was just wondering if you might be free. We could have a good gossip."

"Of course, Joan."

She knew Dan was frowning and shaking his head behind her, that he had guessed what his wife was asking. It meant the end of their weekend, but that was shattered now anyway, with Joan back in Chicago. "I can be over in—" she had been about to say "ten minutes," but she realized those two words would have been too cruel to both of them. "I'll be over in . . . a little while. As for Dan, he's probably out checking that airport property again. He wouldn't very well have left a note; you weren't due back until next week."

"I wonder."

After she hung up, Joan moved through the large empty apartment again. She'd done that as soon as she arrived, happy to be back. Back and safe. She'd meant to go to New York alone; she'd even promised Dr. Keinser. Just to prove she could finally face it again. Her appointment with the doctor had been her real reason for going east; she'd barely spent an afternoon with Paige at school. Joan told no one, not even Mary, that she still saw the doctor at Golden Shores from time to time. It was her secret. She had known other women who had been to sanatoriums and continued seeing psychiatrists after their return, and she had seen how their families and friends treated them, constantly watchful, careful of their words. She had no intention of living the rest of her life like that. But she knew sometimes she needed help, needed someone she could talk to even more honestly than she could to Mary. Someone who was as impersonal as a stranger. That was how she had made herself think of Edith, like a dentist or an eye doctor, to be seen when it was necessary but not to be discussed as part of her life.

After Paige's disastrous party, she had made a trip east last fall, hoping for sympathy from the doctor, and had received instead the astringent advice to continue a career in society instead of hiding in her room. The world was full of a great many things more grim than young people getting drunk, and while her money protected her from much that was harsh in life, no fortune was big enough to hide away from today's reality. Joan had taken the doctor's advice and found to her surprise she had flourished with it through the winter. Now she had a new idea, and while she knew seeing the doctor again was a little like running to Mother for approval, she rationalized it was simply an opportunity to discuss a future plan before presenting it to her immediate family. The doctor had agreed with her but had also suggested, as a test of Joan's growing strength, that she spend the time she had planned in New York.

That Joan couldn't do. She had been to New York a few times since that awful weekend, but always with Dan or Mary or her father. Never alone. And nothing would ever persuade her to walk into that particular hotel again. Fortunately, each year New York seemed to have a new, more fashionable hotel. By expressing curiosity to see them, she had never had to return to the place that had scarred her far more than her ski accident.

So after leaving Golden Shores, she directed the driver of her hired limousine to take her to the airport and had flown home. She had looked forward to it, using the time of the flight to marshal the answers to the arguments Dan might make. Only he wouldn't. She had known for a long time this was something he wanted, more now that this enormous airport real estate venture seemed destined for total success. He would be restless when it was finally over. He would be ready for change.

She had walked through the apartment confidently, happy as always to see it in shining order. To others it might seem impersonal and cold unless it was filled with people, but to Joan it had always been a symbol of the grace and symmetry she so seldom found in the world below. It was only when she was unpacking her suitcase that she realized something was bothering her. She went back to the living room and paced it slowly, carefully, wondering if something had been broken in her absence, aware something was missing. She went into the kitchen and even to Dan's room. But everything was in its place. As always, Lila had left everything neat and shining before she had left the previous day.

Slowly Joan realized what she was seeing . . . or not seeing. No one had been in the apartment at all since Lila had left, "no one" meaning Dan. All the ashtrays were empty and clean and in their proper places, including the one in his bathroom. She went back through the rooms carefully, even checking the garbage can in the kitchen. That, too, was as Lila had left it, empty and lined with a fresh bag.

Joan's bad leg began to hurt, for the first time since winter had ended. She sat down at the kitchen table. For a moment she was afraid she was going to be sick. Wherever Dan had slept last night, it hadn't been here. Poor Dan, who couldn't be in a room for five minutes without having used every ashtray in sight! Trapped, she thought, like in a bad detective story. She was surprised she could find a certain amusement in the thought. Trapped not by any telltale clue, but by what was *not* there.

She tried to tell herself perhaps he had simply been uncharacteristically tidy that morning. She knew she was lying. In all the years of their marriage Dan had never emptied an ashtray or washed a dish or made his own bed. No. He had not slept here last night. And probably he was not planning to sleep here tonight, or any of the nights until her return.

She went to the telephone, calling Lila's home first, in the one last thin hope that maybe she had come that morning and straightened up the apartment after Dan had left. But Mr. Franklin explained that Lila had taken the plane the night before to her sister Martha in Georgia. Did Mrs. Martin want the number there? Joan said politely it wasn't necessary, and after inquiring about their sons, remembering which one was in Vietnam, she had hung up.

The next call, to Dan's office, would be harder. She knew if he answered she would be unable to keep from questioning him. He was always such a bad liar she would know the truth instantly, and it was something she didn't want to know, at least not yet, not until she had made up her mind what she would do. The first years after her accident and the loss of her baby she had wondered about his sexual life, always being careful never to question him. Probably there had been girls, or women. She had blocked out the image of him in bed with someone else. It should mean no more than the girls he had known before they were married. And when she had resumed going to bed with him, wanting to enjoy the triumph of her fresh appearance after the Tucson surgery, it had seemed much as it always had been. He had not slept that first night with her, and she had been grateful. She needed to be alone in the morning to prepare her body and her face for the world outside her bedroom. Since then—well, it hadn't happened often, and sometimes when his attempts were unsuccessful she knew it was because he was tired and worried about the office. And they were older; sex could not and should not be as important as it had been at the beginning. He seemed happy with their arrangement. Content. The way a marriage should be.

And all that time she had been telling herself a lie, telling it so often she had finally believed it, until this moment when she sat in her spotless kitchen and knew there was someone else in his life. Not just a casual affair. She would have liked to believe that, but coming so soon from the clear realism of Dr. Keinser, she could not fool herself. Dan was not the kind of man to sleep beside a stranger. Sex, yes: some willing girl, a brief hour in a different bed. But not to stay the night. Dan was a man of order, of habit; he would have returned to his own home afterward.

Finally she forced herself to phone the office, trying his private number first. There was no answer, and while it increased her worries, she felt oddly relieved. She was intelligent enough to know she would prefer word of her return to reach him from some other source so he would have time to construct a reasonable explanation.

She debated calling her father but rejected that almost instantly. Evan and Dan had quarreled more than once recently. Evan was disturbed that his son-in-law was pouring so much company money into the corporation, buying the tracts of land surrounding the airport. No, her father was the wrong person to approach. If he did know where Dan was, perfectly legitimately, he would be angry that Dan had not let her know. Evan would have to be a last resort.

She called the Van Buren Club. As she expected, Dan was not there. Her mind was working a little frantically now, trying to consider possibilities. A few years before she might have suspected Dan of having a liaison with Kay Wallis, or rather that Kay had trapped him into it. She had never doubted Kay was in love with Dan, but it had seemed so unlikely that anything would ever occur between them that could threaten their marriage, she had not been concerned. Lately the chances were even less. Kay was not aging well. Whereas before she had often appeared to take special care of her appearance, changing her hairstyle and buying expensive clothes, these past few years she had seemed to have given up the attempt. Her hair was pulled back tightly, her suits grew more mannish in their tailoring, and Joan had privately decided there was no point in including her in anything but the largest of the Martin parties. Kay had simply become too grim to foist on any man at a dinner table. Respectable available men were hard enough to find without subjecting them to such an evening.

Still, she called Kay. Getting no answer, for the first time she felt frightened. New, unwelcome thoughts came into her mind, thoughts that made the question of Dan being unfaithful less important. He might be sick, might have been taken to a hospital. On impulse she called Mary, and while she couldn't explain her fears over the phone, Mary had been sensitive enough to know she needed her. Thank God for Mary! Although the suggestion of Dan looking at land was ridiculous. Perhaps when Mary knew the truth she would have another, more plausible explanation.

"Now, Joan, calm down. Drink your tea. It'll be good for you."

Joan did as she was told. She had not moved from the kitchen since she had phoned Mary, except to let her in. While Mary had no immediate answers for why Dan had not slept in the apartment, it was comforting to have her company.

"He's with a woman somewhere."

Mary had never seen Joan look so bleak, so stricken, not even in the terrible weeks after the accident or when she had gone off to Golden Shores. She's not young any more, Mary found herself thinking, with sudden surprise. It seemed incomprehensible that Joan could have aged so quickly. The cap of silver curls that seemed to make her look like an elegant duchess out of another period was, in this late-afternoon sunlight, the hair of a woman who was old, or soon would be. Oh, Dan, Dan, Mary thought, how could we have done this to her?

"There could be a million other reasons why he wasn't here last night." She had carefully rehearsed his story with Dan before leaving the apartment: a sudden call that had taken him to Springfield to meet with some downstate bankers, not very likely on a Saturday, but Joan would accept any story that had to do with Dan's trying to raise the funds necessary to keep his real estate empire afloat.

Dan would tell Joan he had rented a car and driven downstate, met his business associates, and, starting to drive back, had felt too tired to make the trip twice in one day. He would explain he had pulled off the road and slept in a motel. It was a logical story, hard to disprove. He'd left his own car in the apartment building garage because he had planned to fly back, but he had missed the last plane. So many lies, for so many years, but they had never come this close to Joan discovering the truth.

She mustn't suspect, Mary realized, looking at the fragile woman opposite her.

"A million reasons? Name one, Mary."

This was going to be harder than Mary had thought. Obviously she couldn't hint at the story Dan would tell when he arrived in the next hour; even the blindest faith would not be able to accept that.

"Perhaps he wanted to get in some golf early this morning? There are rooms out at the country club, aren't there? He might have gone out for dinner and just stayed."

"He didn't. I already checked." Joan's voice was bleak.

"Joan, you're making too much of this. We know he's not sick or been in an accident; he would have gone to Midwestern. I'm sure there's some simple explanation."

"Mary, don't try to lie. You do it almost as badly as Dan does. He's with someone, someone he cares about." Joan forced herself to stand, using the table to brace her bad leg. "I should have guessed a long time ago there'd be someone. My wonderful Dan. . . ."

Don't let her see what I feel when she talks of him, Mary prayed to herself. Don't let that happen.

Only Joan wasn't looking at her; she was staring out the window at the glowing sunset. "I've been such a fool," she said quietly. "How could I think such a vital, handsome man would settle at any age for the tiny bits of ice I've allowed him in my cold bed? An idiot would have known better." She looked at Mary, her eyes wet. Mary reached out and took her hand. "Mary, what should I do? Should I go back to Golden Shores? I went there this trip. I never meant to tell anybody; I've been ashamed of having to need that place, a doctor's help. But I can trust you. I've gone several times. Is that weak of me?"

She's so thin, Mary thought, as she put her arms around her. Not just elegantly thin, a figure to be proud of, but the scrawniness that sometimes comes as the first sign of age. And she's only a few years older than I am! Time, Dan had said that afternoon, it goes so fast. "Why would you want to go back to Golden Shores?" she asked.

"To let whoever it is have time with him," Joan said simply. "There isn't much I can give Dan. I could give him that. Time to be with whom he wants. Maybe he'll tire of her, the way he has of me."

"Dan's not tired of you! He couldn't be! Joan, you're letting one unexplained evening become a whole fantasy. It's not like that, I know it isn't."

"You don't know Dan, not the way I do."

Mary realized it was true. Carefully as she had kept the part of Dan she knew and loved to herself, certainly Joan had done the same thing, far longer and with far more intensity.

"Dan loves you, Joan. I know that. Even supposing—just supposing—there could be some girl . . . some woman he might have . . . met, she could never take your place. Not ever. She'd be a fool even to try. You'll always be Dan's beautiful princess. You must know that."

"I'm old, Mary. Maybe not really old in years, but old. And sick and dead in some kind of awful way I can't seem to change. Dan's been patient. And we both know he's not a patient man. If it isn't this girl . . . or even if by some wild chance there wasn't anyone last night, or any of the other nights I've been away, there will be."

"I've tried to prepare myself for it." She pulled away from Mary's embrace and crossed the kitchen toward the long expensive living room beyond. "To keep him amused. As if he were some sort of child I could outthink. Only he isn't a child. He's a grown man."

Her leg was hurting, Mary saw. Without the cane to lean on, Joan had to move slowly, her injured leg dragging a little. There was a scuffing on the thick carpet as she walked.

"You know what I'd thought of doing?" Joan settled herself on one of the sleek modern couches, hands on her knees, spreading the skirt of her dress carefully. "I'd thought of getting him interested in politics. It seems so silly now. But he has so many ideas, so many plans. I talked to the doctor about it. People like him. There'll be more than enough money after this airport thing goes through. The children have their own. I could make Dan a public figure. Can't you see him as governor? He could do it, I know he could. And I could help there. I wouldn't just be someone ugly and old he was saddled with. All the people I know, that Daddy knows . . . I'd be important to Dan again. We'd be partners. The way it was in the beginning." She rubbed her forehead wearily. "Maybe I can't give him what he needs sexually, but power can be a wonderful substitute. Dan likes power, Mary."

"Whatever he may like, it's you he loves."

"Don't say that! Please! I'm trying to face realities I should have been honest enough to have faced years ago!" Joan stared out the window at the long lakefront below and the endless stream of cars moving north. "Or maybe I have faced reality. A man in politics can't very well divorce his wife. Not yet anyway. All the rumors we've heard about politicians, all the secret love affairs that come out after they're dead; none of those men dared ask for a divorce. Not if they wanted a public career. Wives still have that protection. And Dan will want a public career. I think he's been wanting it for years."

"Which means you're upsetting yourself for nothing."

"No, Mary. Because I think he's found something else. Something of his own, that's gentle and private and means more to him than any ambition." Joan was quiet, the panic and fears gone back to the secret places where she had kept them hidden for so long. "Someone he loves."

Mary stayed silent. There were no new arguments to use. How well Joan knew her husband, better than Mary did! Joan had guessed the truth. Dan Martin at forty would have sacrificed everything for his own ambitions; Mary had known and accepted that. Dan in his fifties, with a fortune within reach, children grown, and a sudden awareness of time passing, was a different man. This afternoon and his unexpected proposal had proven that. Only it would destroy the woman he had married.

"There's one thing that's not more important to him, Joan," she said, choosing her words carefully. "Power, ambition, I don't know about that. But nothing—no one—can take your place. No one ever will."

"Don't be sentimental, Mary," Joan said with unexpected crispness. "Husbands . . . and wives . . . are walking out on each other every minute of the day, all over the world. You're not going to pretend Dan is an exception, are you?"

"He'll be whispering your name on his deathbed." Don't let me cry, Mary prayed to herself. Please God, not now, don't let me be any different than I've been all these years. Don't let me think of what he said, barely an hour ago.

"And the years between now and then?" Joan seemed curiously more fragile as she pulled her shell of control around herself. Her cool armor was so thin, so transparently weak, the harshest word could destroy it instantly. I should be worrying about Dan, Mary thought. I should be thinking of myself. Dan's my lover, Joan's my friend. He's just offered me the possibility of something I never dared dream about . . . and in some strange way I'm refusing it just by sitting here. Whatever he wants to offer, I can't take it at this price. As Mary struggled for an answer, Joan went on, almost as if her thoughts were speaking without any will or wish of her own.

"I could understand his going to bed with someone. Probably it would be better if it is some one person, rather than a string of silly bitches. Each new girl would be just one more possible scandal for the papers to track down—if I can make him try for what he wants. One woman, one quiet complacent cow. . . ."

Mary could feel it coming, the anger Joan had kept in so long, the anger so like Dan's. Mary recognized it instantly. So much alike, she thought. Lake Shore and West Side, arrogant and determined and so easily crushed. Not like the people I've always known: Jack and Tim and my mother and, yes, me. We can be hurt, but somehow some central part of us remains undiminished. We may be more wary in our next encounters, less easy in our friendships and our loves, but we're like stone. You aren't, you and Dan. You're pieces of paper, Mary thought. If you're crumpled, even if you're smoothed out and pressed clean and flat again, the little creases stay forever, never to be forgiven or forgotten.

A cow. That's what Joan had called her, not knowing it was her—or perhaps she did. Mary was in a subtler world than she had ever known, she who had been considered so cool and separate from her own people.

She could end it all this afternoon. Dan had given her permission, almost in so many words. She could destroy Joan's smug world, with its tricks of trapping Dan, moving him carefully but firmly into the public spotlight where Joan would have him forever. Not in bed, perhaps; Joan was prepared to throw that as a sop to the "cow," whoever she might be.

Mary could save him from that this afternoon. She watched Dan's wife move away from her to stand like an elegant statue, staring out the windows at the world below. You love Dan! Fight for him! It was as if her mother were speaking again, as she had seemed so many years ago over that lonely kitchen table when Mary had debated taking the chance that had changed her life.

It's my turn. Finally. It was no subconscious voice speaking that made her stand, no echoes of borrowed common sense, no memories of Dan's body or the knowledge of his need for her, but Mary's need to ask just once for what she wanted in her life, ask for it, knowing if she did she might never have it and perhaps might lose forever what little she did have. Jack Conroy, she thought as she walked toward Joan, I finally understand you, daring to put everything on one gamble, the winning or the losing not so important as finally doing something for *yourself.*

Only, by her standing, the figure in front of her had changed. Just the slight raising of Mary's body put Joan in a different perspective. Mary could see the curve of her cheek, instead of just her slender back. For once Joan made no sound as she cried. The tears slipping down the frozen side of her face needed no sound to express their pain. Her shoulders remained rigid; she had not moved; this was no bid for sympathy. She was simply crying, knowing she was lonely and loved her husband and, for all her brave words, had not kept his love and could never have it back, not as it had been. For all her elegance and silver curls and clever plans, she would never be that young woman Dan Martin had loved so deeply and fully two decades before. And so she cried silently.

It was growing dark outside. Mary could see her own reflection in the glass of the long picture windows, twisting her fingers together. Luckily Joan had lowered her head and couldn't see how silly Mary looked. For of course Mary would say nothing. She could see by the modern crystal clock on the coffee table that Dan would be here in ten minutes, the time they had agreed on, his story carefully prepared, Mary ready to change the subject or distract Joan's attention if Dan failed to remember some important detail. He would take them both out to dinner that evening and there would be a great deal to drink and perhaps some talk—led by Mary, she realized—of his entering politics, and tonight when they had left her at the front door of her building, she would not have to look for Dan's signal. There would be a light on in his bedroom, but he would not be sleeping there; he would be with Joan.

"He'll never leave you, Joan. You know that. You'll always be his wife." Gently, she led her back to the sofa. In a minute or two Mary would turn on the lights, carefully arranged to present the perfect room at its best. Joan would go and fix her makeup. Mary would hear the elevator as it brought Dan up to the floor, and his wife would be ready for him, bright and charming as always, her face perfect once more, ready to accept his explanations.

And Mary knew she would never let Dan talk of marriage again.

Fifteen

For all their discretion, Mary and Dan should have known the life they settled for was based on too many uncertainties to last. Joan's plans were more successful than either Dan or Mary could have imagined. Mary saw much less of Dan in the year that followed. From two or three times a week, with daily phone calls in between, his visits grew fewer and shorter. A week would go by, sometimes two, and Mary would not have seen or spoken to him.

Dan began to appear in the public areas of Chicago life. Articulate and intelligent, he was interviewed on everything from the potential growth of the city to plans for raising funds for municipal housing. He and Joan were seated on the dais of most political banquets. If a new building was opened, he would be photographed near the mayor. If a panel was needed for a television program on any aspect of Chicago urban life, he would be one of the first asked to appear. He was old enough now to represent a combination of common sense ("political maturity" it would be called in the newspapers the next day) and a practical idealism Chicagoans had not seen in a semi-public figure for years.

"It's all hogwash, of course," he told Mary that winter. He had stopped in for a half hour on his way home to change into formal clothes for yet another public dinner. "Joan's going overboard on this political thing. She's even hired a public relations firm to see I get 'exposure,' as she calls it."

"She knows you're ambitious."

"Am I? Maybe." There had been no further talk of getting off the merry-go-round he had professed to hate the previous spring. "God knows there's a lot that could be done with this city. Meanwhile it makes my position that much stronger when the city gets around to buying the airport land."

"Anything new about that?" It had been over a week since she had seen him, and she desperately wanted this brief time to be just for them, but she knew him well enough not to hope for anything romantic when he was concerned about business and already late in returning to Joan and her plans for the evening.

"They've got to buy us out by the end of the year. We've got them practically surrounded at the airport. It'll make you a rich woman."

This was still a source of argument between them. Mary had consistently refused his offers of expensive presents and, tired of her stubbornness, Dan had solved the situation his own way. The year before, he had deeded over the building she lived in to her. For birthdays and Christmases he had added to the rents of the other tenants more stock in the airport venture. Frustrated at his generosity, she had placed the shares and the deed to the building in her safety deposit box and tried to forget about them.

"I never wanted to be rich, Dan." All I want is time with you, the time we used to have. But of course she could never say that. Neither of them had any liking or respect for self-pity.

"Well, you're going to be rich. The price we're asking is fair; they know it and I know it. But I think they've got some idea I can't hold on to the property, that I'm overextended, that I won't be able to keep up the payments on the bank loans I've taken to buy the land, so they're stalling, hoping I'll cave in." He put his arms around her, holding her gently. "That's the only reason I'm going along with all of Joan's plans, Mary. Honest. Every one of these damn functions she drags me to, when they hit the papers . . . it makes me seem even more financially secure. And I need that just at the moment."

Gamblers, she thought, as he held her. Jack on racehorses. Dan on acres of land. Is it any different if one was involved with millions of dollars and the other with hundreds? She had heard from Patsy that Jack was back in Chicago and had opened a small carpentry shop out near Skokie. Although she felt no anger toward him and never had, even before he completely repaid all he owed her, she hoped they wouldn't meet. Dan was the man she wanted. Only she didn't have him, less now than before.

"Mary, I've got to go," he said, releasing her. "I'll call you tomorrow evening. Will you be here?"

"I'll be here." That was all she would allow herself to say. She'd taught herself a long time ago not to ask when they would meet again; that would be nagging and she was determined never to do that. But something in the way she said it must have sounded different. He came back from the open door.

"Look, maybe I can get away this weekend." He frowned, "No, I've got that damn municipal tax conference. Well, the weekend after that. We'll work something out."

Only the following weekend there was a statewide convention in Springfield with a reception given by the governor to which Dan and Joan were formally invited. And the week after that he had to fly to New York to raise more money from his eastern bankers.

Their times together were so infrequent and hasty each one stood out individually. One weekend the following March Joan had gone east. She told Dan it was to see friends, but to Mary she had confided she needed to see her doctor at Golden Shores again.

Joan could no longer use the excuse of traveling to see the children. Paige had dropped out of college to return to Chicago. She was living not too far from Mary with two other girls, studying music and refusing to join the social world her mother had planned so carefully. Joey had finished high school and had started at the University of Chicago. That pleased Dan. He had worried the boy might become spoiled now he had the money from his grandmother's trust. Dan hated the sight of the aimless young men he saw hanging around Old Town, clad in faded jeans. "Bums," he called them. At least Joey wasn't that. He'd continued to live at home, keeping separate hours from his parents, but still he was there. Paige's rebellion had struck her father harder, and in one of their infrequent meetings Dan had appealed to Mary for help.

"Why can't he understand I simply want to make my own life?" Paige had complained when she had Mary over for dinner. Ex-debutante or not, Paige and her roommates lived exactly the way young people always seemed to live these days: travel posters on cracked walls, surviving on spaghetti and chili, collecting pennies in a jar, despising everything elegant or comfortable they could not yet afford as hopelessly middle class. Though Dan had asked Mary to check out Paige's apartment, she had carefully waited to be asked.

"Because he'd like to feel you won't have to go through what he went through," Mary answered calmly. Paige didn't look well. Her skin was sallow, and she trembled as if she were cold.

"And do what instead?" Paige demanded. Her roommates had retired tactfully to the other room. Nice girls, Mary thought, with sense enough to know that while Mary had come as a representative of the adult world, she was sympathetic to their ambitions. "Mary, does Dad really think the sole purpose of my life is to dabble in Junior League projects until some guy marries me?"

"There's nothing wrong with the Junior League. They do a lot of valuable work."

"And my singing has no value?"

"I didn't say that. By the way, how's it going?"

Instantly Paige became defensive, tightening her mouth into a thin sullen line just as she had when she wore the hated braces. "I'm . . . trying various things. There's a little place off Clark Street, the Funky Tree. It just serves coffee, so it's not like being a real waitress or anything. I sing a couple of times an evening; we all do. They may put on a revue, come summer."

This was news to Mary, news she instantly suspected Paige would not want told to either of her parents. "Could I come and hear you?"

Paige's brief defiance disappeared. She looked confused, the way she had as a young girl when something frightened her. "I'd . . . rather you didn't, Mary. Not just yet. Not until I'm really singing steadily." She reached out to touch Mary's arm. "You won't tell Dad and Mom, will you? They'd hit the ceiling."

"If you don't want me to. What are you singing? Rock music?"

"No, folk ballads mostly. Remember that old Schubert *Lied*? Phil— he's the guy who runs the place—he's put some new words to it, a new beat. He's very talented. He and this girl he lives with run the Tree."

Phil. Paige may have thought Mary would not remember the name of the American she had fallen in love with the year she spent in France. And she's still in love with him! Poor Paige, Mary thought. So young and already fallen into the trap of loving the wrong man.

"I'd still like to hear you," Mary said. "Or don't they allow anybody in the place over twenty-five?"

"Sure. But—well, it's kind of a dump. And I'm not really working there, I don't get paid or anything. There'll be other places, when I have more experience. Then you can come."

"All right, Paige." She put her coat on. It was clearly time to go. "You know where I am. Call me any time."

Walking home that night, Mary knew she'd have to be careful in her report to Dan. Studying music was one thing, working in a "bohemian" (as he would think it) coffeehouse was another. For once Mary was almost glad she was seeing less of Dan these days. Perhaps he would have forgotten his request the next time they saw each other. She couldn't lie to him, if he asked her directly. But that would mean betraying Paige's confidence.

On impulse, she changed her direction and walked north toward the Clark Street section where she imagined the coffeehouse to be located. It was still early in the evening, and the young people on the streets didn't disturb her. Like most everyone her age, she wished young people could look happier about their lives. They all seemed so glum. And would it really mean a betrayal of their dedication to freedom and social justice if they washed their hair occasionally?

That's a very middle-aged thought, Mary Conroy, she told herself, but went on with it with some amusement. Think how the girls could progress into good looks: shoes instead of sandals at twenty-two, perhaps a touch of lipstick at twenty-four, some eyeshadow at thirty—why, they could get better looking all their lives!

Only she knew this period of rebellion was never lasting. The free lifestyles around her would end as abruptly as they had begun. One day that young man in a poncho standing at the corner arguing with the girl in the long batik skirt would be told he was about to become a father and the free spirit who had been saving her money for a trip to India expected him to marry her. And there would be babies and strollers and children in backpacks and the mustaches and beards would be trimmed and the thin waistlines of their youth would grow thicker as their hair grew thin.

And they'll be my age, Mary thought, as she moved through the crowds of the loitering young. May you all be safely on the inside of life by then, she thought. Not outside, looking in.

The thought came so unbidden, so suddenly, she had to stop for a moment, unable to move forward. She had never allowed herself to indulge in wishful thinking, never considered herself to have been cheated in life.

Why, then, had this thought come to her, and why now? Practically, she knew it was the evening with Paige and her friends, all of them just starting in life. And she, at almost . . . well, life was hardly over, yet in some strange way on this March evening she felt the best of it was. She would have liked to pretend only part of her feeling was because of Dan, but she couldn't. For the first time in their years together, she knew she was becoming unnecessary to him.

You've won, Joan, she thought, as she moved up the street again.

That word coming into her mind shocked her as well. She had never thought of herself in rivalry with Dan's wife; she had seen herself as filling a part of his world Joan no longer needed or cared about. There should never have been a question of thinking who had won or lost. But there was, and Mary was too honest not to face it.

It was Dan, as always. Whether or not Joan's ambitions were successful—to make him a congressman or even governor—he was beginning not to need Mary. The sexual side was still there, but that had never been what had kept them together, any more than it had been what had brought them together in the first place. Maybe he had wanted a refuge at one time, quiet and peace and serenity, but now he was in the center of the world he had admired for a long time, there on his own passport, without the identification of his father-in-law's firm or his wife's social position. It was his last opportunity to achieve all his goals, and whether he realized it or not, he would not be happy until he had tried.

Not that what was between them would ever be completely over. There had been too much time together, too many confidences shared and too much love exchanged, to sever them completely. But gradually Mary would become less important. They would still be friends, of course, she and Dan and Joan. The children too, she hoped. But she would not be needed the way she had been in the past. And that need had been a major part of her happiness.

You always knew someday it would end, she told herself as she pushed through the street people enjoying the first warm spring night. If not over exactly, at least different, changed. You promised yourself to accept that years ago and to shed no tears when it came. You have a good job, security, and friends, and if the love you hoped would last forever is slipping through your fingers, it has meant more and lasted longer than you ever dreamed it could.

She forced herself to think of other things, staring at the street, as foreign to her as if she were in Peking. Only a few blocks to the east were elegant townhouses and lavish apartments on the lake. To the west were the rows upon rows of straight-lined blocks filled with solid buildings such as her parents had bought. Only here was there a rip in the fabric of Chicago. Mary could have wished it was more vibrant and cheerful, the way the flower people almost a decade before had made certain areas of other cities come to lighthearted life. But those days, too, had passed and there was an irritation, almost an edge of anger, in the people passing her. It goes so swiftly, being young, she thought. Enjoy it! Please have fun while you can!

That was sentimental and she knew it. Apparently she had been on the right street, for ahead of her she could see the crudely hand-painted sign of the place Paige had mentioned. She didn't quite dare go in, although it was so crowded probably no one would have noticed. But from the street she could sniff the sour smell of marijuana, see the heavy black leather motorcycle jackets of the young men and the bored, slightly glazed eyes of the girls with them.

God, she thought, what has Paige got herself into? She knew there was nothing she could do, but the coffeehouse hounded her mercilessly as she turned into the next quiet side street, making her way back to her solitary home.

There *was* something that only she could do, and thinking back on it later, she realized it would have happened eventually knowing when it did it meant the end of the world she had built so lovingly and secretly with Dan.

It was in the last week of June. Dan and Joan had left for Washington the previous week and were not expected back for several days. Mary had trained herself to fill the time when they were gone. She went to a party given by one of the girls in her section at the hospital. Saturday was spent doing all the chores she never seemed to have time for, culminating in Sunday dinner with Tim and Patsy. Only their youngest still lived at home, and he disappeared before the meal. Tim watched him go in silence. Her brother had changed, Mary noticed. The anger and rigidity with which he used to rule his family seemed to have burned itself out these past years. Patsy, on the contrary, had gained in strength. She was thinner now, thinner and brisker, with interests and opinions she didn't hesitate to bring up, even if they contradicted those of her husband. She had started working part-time, something that was still obviously an unresolved battle between them. But with Mary as the third at the table also a working woman, Tim could only retreat into silence, knowing he was outnumbered.

"And that nice Dr. MacCauley? Are you still seeing him?" Patsy had asked as they cleared the table.

"Yes," Mary answered.

There was still nothing that could possibly be described as romantic between them, but at least once a month MacCauley phoned her at her office in the hospital and asked her out for dinner. It was always for an evening when Dan would be out of town, though it took Mary a while to make that connection. Whether he did it deliberately or not she never dared to inquire, or even to wonder how he could know Dan's schedule. They would have a pleasant dinner, stopping later at an art gallery or to see a foreign film, the type Dan hated. And always he would shake her hand when he had seen her to her front door and walk back to his car, never suggesting that the relationship progress any further.

She had been with MacCauley that June evening when her world was to fall apart. After she went up the stairs, she started to get ready for bed, although it was barely eleven and another empty weekend was all that lay before her. She had just put on her robe when the phone rang.

"Yes?"

"Mary?" She recognized Joey's voice instantly, deep as Dan's and with the same ring of authority. Just by the one word, though, she knew something was wrong.

"Joey. What is it?"

"I've got to see you. Tonight. Mary, can we come up? It's kind of an emergency."

" 'We'?"

"I'll explain when I get there. Mickey's got his car; it shouldn't take us more than five minutes. Geez, I'm glad I finally got you, I've been calling since nine." With that he hung up, not that she could have refused him even if he hadn't.

She hadn't seen as much of Joey as she would have liked this past year. He was busy at college, their hours were different, and as a young man he would naturally seek out people his own age. Still, she missed him. There was no question in her mind that something was seriously wrong tonight. She moved quickly around the apartment, putting away the more obvious signs of Dan's presence. Fortunately he hadn't been here for over a week. There were no telltale cigarette or cigar butts in the ashtrays, no lingering aroma of tobacco. The bathroom was quickly emptied; she suspected whatever was wrong might be medical, something Joey would be reluctant, as son of one of the Directors to take to the emergency room of Midwestern Hospital. But whoever Joey was bringing would be unlikely to need something from Dan's closet, so she simply closed the door.

By the time the downstairs doorbell rang she was ready. She had not had time to change out of her robe, but it was nighttime and the robe was long and high-necked and perfectly respectable. She was glad Joey had mentioned Mickey would be with him. That would be young Mickey Harris. Mary had always liked him from way back when he and Paige were still in grammar school. He had grown into a sturdy young man, serious perhaps beyond his years but reliable, as witness the way he had spirited Joey away from the argument with Dan the night of Paige's debut.

Paige. Of course it would be Paige that was the problem. Mary should have guessed even before she saw the two young men bringing the limp girl up the stairs. Silently she stood aside to let them in, and the boys placed their burden on the couch.

"What is it? What's happened? Is it some kind of drug?" This is what she had been fearing since the night she had seen the crowded coffee-house two months before.

"No." Joey leaned over and pulled back the blanket they had put over the unconscious girl. There were thick towels wrapped around both of her arms. The towels were dark blue, but at their thickest, Mary could see another, darker color forming.

"She slit her wrists," Mickey said quietly. "One of her roommates came home early and called Joey. I . . . I happened to be with him."

"Why?" Mary knelt beside the girl, carefully unwrapping the make-shift bandages. The blood was still seeping from the deep cuts in Paige's wrists, but the amateur tourniquets the boys had devised had halted the first terrible spurts that must have poured from her veins.

Mary had seen patients who had slit their wrists before, depressed and lonely people who could find no other way to handle the long terrible shadows of their lives. It was not an uncommon incident in the emergency ward, on a hot Saturday night or when the moon was full. But never had she seen such a determined bid for death. Mostly the patients she had seen had been drinking or else had never truly in-tended to die; it had been a protest to the world, to their lovers, to their families, a visible shout that they were in pain and needed love and were not beyond using this to demand and receive it.

But Paige had been serious about it. Oh, my beautiful girl, Mary mourned as she examined the long open wounds. How could anything be so awful that you could want to die this early in your life? But as she thought it, she knew age had nothing to do with despair.

"Is she going to die?" Mickey's face was expressionless, but Mary could see the anxiety in his eyes.

"I don't think so. She's lost a lot of blood, but you seem to have reached her in time."

"There was about an inch of blood in the bathtub. She had her arms over the edge," Joey said.

Paige's sweater was damp and sticky. Mary could feel the blood on her hands where she touched her. "She needs a doctor . . . and a hospital. She'll have to have transfusions. And the wounds must be sewn up."

"She can't go to a hospital!" Mickey's voice was serious. "I'm not talking about Midwestern, I mean any of them. Attempted suicide's a crime. Sure, they won't send her to prison, a first offense and every-thing, but it'll be in all the papers."

"You know how Dad and Mom will feel about that." Joey leaned over where Mary knelt beside his sister. "Mary? Can't you do something? Do the stitches or something? I mean, one look at that and any doctor would know what happened."

"I'll call Dr. MacCauley." She rose and went to the phone. "He should be home by now. You can trust him." As she dialed his number, she looked at the two frightened young men. "Get some antiseptic from the bathroom and some fresh towels. And something to make stronger tourniquets for her arms."

Joey, she noticed as she waited for the doctor to answer, had gone to the bathroom. She thanked God she'd had time to clear out anything that might be a sign of his father's presence in her life. Mickey went to the hall closet. There was nothing but linens there; she could tear them into strips for the bandages.

"Dr. Mac? It's Mary. Look, I hate to ask this, but could you come back here? Yes, I'm home. Paige Martin's . . . had an accident. She may need an ambulance, but I think you ought to see her first."

In the next half hour as they waited for Dr. MacCauley they managed to stop the blood, although Paige still remained unconscious. Gradually Mary heard the whole story. Apparently Joey had been in closer contact with his sister than anyone else in the family. He knew about the proprietor of the Funky Tree, even filling in the details of Paige's involvement with him in Paris. It seemed to be no great surprise to Mickey, although Mary could see his jaw set grimly. The affair had resumed once Phil had come back to America. That had been the real reason for Paige's dropping out of college and returning to Chicago. Phil had apparently played Paige and the girl he lived with against each other through the winter, but today he had told Paige he didn't want to see her again. He was marrying the other girl.

"She called me around eight. . . . God, Mary, she was so hysterical I could hardly understand her. It was like she was some kind of stranger. You know Paige, she always keeps everything locked up inside. Here she was spilling everything out to me, how he had treated her, what they'd done in bed together, everything . . . all over the phone. I offered to come over, but she didn't want that. Finally, I thought I had her calmed down, at least enough to go to bed, and she hung up. But I called Mickey. I guess I must have known Paige wouldn't let go that easy. Then when Nancy—that's one of her roommates—called, I didn't know what to do. I had to call you."

"It's all right." The buzzer for the front door sounded, and Mary went to let the doctor in. MacCauley ran up the stairs two at a time, faster than Mary imagined the thin, middle-aged man had ever moved. He took in the scene at a glance and went instantly over to where Paige was lying. Carefully he examined the makeshift bandages on her wrists before he said a single word to any of them.

"You did a good job," he said to the room at large. "But she's got to go to the hospital." He strode across the room to the telephone.

"But—but there'll have to be a report . . . the publicity—" Joey stammered.

"If she doesn't get to the hospital she might die, and you'd have a lot more than publicity to worry about," the doctor answered curtly. He turned back to the phone to order an ambulance. "Make it snappy," he added before hanging up.

Only then did MacCauley seem to see the two young men and Mary, her robe clutched to her throat, all staring at him. "Don't get too upset," he went on in a more reasonable voice. "I've got a certain amount of influence at the hospital. I'll try to have this listed as an accident. Trying to open a window or something, the glass broke and so forth. I don't think they'll buy it, but it should keep the police out. At least for tonight. Maybe your father can use some of his influence to see it doesn't get into the papers. . . . Where is he, by the way?"

"Washington." Joey was worried; this would be a phone call he had no desire to make.

Only Dan wasn't in Washington. For as they stood there in that silent room staring at the motionless girl on the couch, Mary heard the sound of his key in the door.

"Idiot! *Idiot!*"

Joey's mother pushed her hands against her ears, as if she could force his words out of her head, out of her life, by sheer physical strength. He had told her minutes before, storming into the apartment, angry and fierce and full of his hateful discovery, so strong, so contemptuous.

"He's not even an idiot!" Joey paced the long living room, unable to stand still. He could still see the look on his father's face, hear the stupid lies and phony explanations, interrupted by the arrival of the ambulance and the attendants hurrying up the stairs.

And Mary . . .

Mary, who had been his friend, who he had thought loved him and Paige. Mary, the first one he had turned to in this trouble. All these years she had been deceiving them, using them to get closer to his father. He hated them both, would always hate them. At least she had not tried to lie. She had said nothing, merely moving swiftly to help Paige onto the stretcher, her robe clinging to her breasts, the way *he* had probably seen her a thousand times. . . .

"He's not an idiot! He's a damn hypocrite!"

"Not your father, you fool! *You!*"

He stepped back, stunned by the hatred in his mother's face. She, too, had changed for bed, all floating silks and laces, but there was a viciousness in her eyes as she screamed at him what no elegant gown could soften. "Why did you have to put it into words? *Why?* Why did you have to come racing home with your dirty little secret?"

He'd be stuttering soon, if he didn't get control, that awful stutter he'd had as a child that only Mary never commented on. He wouldn't think about her now. He had to break through the angry tirade of this wild virago in front of him.

"They're cheating you! They have for years! I'm to keep my mouth shut about that?"

"It has nothing to do with you!"

"He's my father!"

"And I'm his wife! And I say whatever there is between him and Mary is none of your business! But no, you had to come here, so full of virtue and anger . . ." She stopped long enough to take a deep breath. When she spoke again, the anger was stronger, cold and hard. "I could kill you for what you've done."

"Me?"

He couldn't believe what he was hearing. His own mother, standing there, rage moving through her so powerfully it seemed to shake her whole body. She was blaming *him?*

"You're so wonderfully tolerant of the sins of your own generation! But God help us if someone older commits them!" She brushed off the tears she would not let him see in a swift gesture. "How could you be such a stupid, clumsy *fool* as to tell me this?"

"I—I thought—"

"That I'd want to know? Maybe I *did* know! Maybe all these years I've . . ." She couldn't make herself say she suspected it, not to her son, not here in her perfect apartment. It meant tearing up all the kindness she'd had from Mary, all the long hours of confidences. It would mean starting to wonder how much had gone back to Dan, how much it had changed their lives. She couldn't face that, not tonight. She had trusted Mary, and she had been right to trust her. She thought suddenly of that afternoon last year when she had panicked and called Mary's apartment. Had Dan been there? Had that story been as false as all the others she had made herself believe through the years? Mary had comforted her, had said Dan would never leave her, and somehow, even on this awful night, Joan knew she had told the truth. And now this stupid child had ruined all their lives!

"Go downstairs! Get a taxi!" Joan said brusquely. "I'll have to change if I'm going to the hospital." She started for her bedroom, stopped, and looked back at him. He knew he would never forget the disgust on her face, never forget it and never forgive her. "Then I want you to come back here and get your things. I don't want you in this apartment for a very long time. If ever."

Joan went quickly into her room. But not so quickly that Joey didn't notice that, for the first time in years, for the first time since the ski accident, she moved easily, using both arms, not favoring one side or the other; and both sides of her face, strident with fury, had been alive in a way Joey had not seen since he was a child.

Sixteen

Paige was still unconscious when Joan arrived at the hospital. There was no sign of either Dan or Mary. She talked to Dr. MacCauley, quietly and with a control she would not have thought possible half an hour before. Paige was out of danger, but it had taken several blood transfusions and three doctors in the operating room to sew up the long open scars.

MacCauley had stared at Joan curiously as she outlined her hastily arranged plans. She would fly Paige to Golden Shores as soon as possible for further physical and mental treatment. It might bypass any police inquiries and stop newspaper publicity. She supposed the look on the doctor's face came from the fact she was not hysterical and was able to function logically. It was only after he had agreed to her arrangements and she had gone back to Paige's room that she caught sight of her face in the mirror. It looked altered somehow. After she had checked Paige's motionless body in the bed, she found herself pulled back to the mirror. Slowly she examined herself, moving her face deliberately from a frown to a forced smile . . . and the muscles of both sides of her face responded.

Deliberately, she raised her right arm, the injured arm she had protected so carefully, for so long. It moved easily, as did her right leg. There was no pain when she walked, no weariness in her muscles as there should have been at this hour of the night and after all she had been through. She sat down deliberately in the chair by the bed and instantly rose again. It took no effort, there was no strain, none of the dizziness she had felt before when she had to change her position.

It's over, she thought. Years wasted, my husband in love with another woman, but I'm well again. She started to cry, all by herself in that quiet room, barely hearing the sedated breathing of her daughter in the bed behind her. All the hopes, the dreams she had begged for, and cursed when they had not come true, that had forced her to twist her life and the lives of everyone around her had finally been granted. Paige, lonely and lost, had walked toward death, and now her mother was free of all that had warped their lives. Like some pagan sacrifice, Joan thought.

For, unwelcome as the conclusion was, tonight's discovery had been Joan's fault. Washington had been crowded, there had been no suite available, and she and Dan had had to share a room. The enforced closeness had made her nervous, so she had persuaded Dan to fly home with her as soon as his business was finished, not wanting to spend another night where he could see her as she really looked, see her and turn away coldly.

She smoothed the sheet over Paige's thin shoulders. I'll make it up to you somehow, baby, she promised. To all of you.

A nurse came in, but Joan sent her away. She would sit here until morning, she decided. She had no desire to go back to the apartment. Joey would be gone by now, and Dan would be with Mary. It didn't really matter. She had a lot to think about. In the morning Lila would be there, someone for company in the large empty rooms. She wondered if Lila knew about Dan and Mary but then realized she would have been the first to guess. So many people to think about, so many feelings to sort out, so many emotions to choose from. . . .

She was healed. Had it all been some sort of psychosomatic trauma these long years? Or was the shock of Joey's revelation the final stimulus her injured nerves needed to react once more? She doubted if she would ever know. It didn't really matter.

She was well. She could make no more mistakes. She had no more excuses for the narrowness of her life, no more flattering screens to shield her from the realities she had avoided for so many years.

Quite literally, she thought with sour humor, she could stand on her own two feet, just as Dr. Keinser had warned her she would have to one day. Joan decided she would stay with Paige at Golden Shores. It would do them both good. It would also give her time to learn what to do with the rest of her life.

Of all the things Joan said and did that night, sending Joey away was the worst and was to cause the most harm. When she returned in the morning, Lila greeted her silently. She could smell coffee in the kitchen, and as they went back through the apartment, they passed the open door to Joey's room. It was as he had left it, torn apart in his anger and haste to leave. She hoped he'd gone to his friend Mickey's, but it was unlikely. She knew where he would go, full of anger at his parents and Mary. He would go to someone who would respond as he had, who would be as furious and as ready for revenge.

He would go to his grandfather.

Within weeks, the gossip started.

Strong as MacCauley's influence was in the hospital, too many people had been involved that night to keep the attempted suicide a secret. None of it reached the newspapers, except for an obscure item in one of the columns hinting that a post-debutante daughter of a prominent man had chosen a rough way to end a love affair, but there were no names mentioned and the police never appeared.

By the end of the first week, Joan left with Paige for Golden Shores. Joan had seen Dan only twice during that week, both times at the hospital where they could only talk politely and impersonally. Mary she did not see at all, and for that she was grateful. Joan had no idea what, if anything, she could say to her. She had no word from Joey, although she knew Paige had spoken to him on the phone. How Paige was reacting to what he must have told her of that night her mother had no way of knowing. Paige was still weak and retreated into sleep whenever the conversation became too personal. Dr. Keinser would have her hands full with her daughter, Joan thought, and was grateful she had someone to turn to at this difficult time.

It was Kay who heard the first results of Joey's discovery. Evan talked to Kay the following Monday, coldly and impersonally, about the incident. While the older man had never been as easy in his conversation with Kay and the other office workers as Dan had been, this time he was rigidly formal, dictating the arrangements to be made for Joan and Paige's trip, going down a list he had obviously worked on over the weekend: a mover to pack what remained of Joey's belongings at the apartment and transport them to his own house in Lake Forest, a search through the deeds of record as to the ownership of Mary's apartment house, and the request that all financial reports of Paige Properties be brought up to date and delivered to his desk by lunchtime. It was to be a longer and harder day's work than Evan had put in for some time.

Evan Paige was not given to self-analysis. He'd always had a comfortable life, with sufficient money and close friends of both sexes. His memories of his dead wife were few, and they had faded over the years. Joan's accident, unfortunate as it was, had not disturbed too greatly the smoothness of his life. There was more than enough money for doctors and nurses, and very little that he personally could do. So in his seventies he was badly prepared for the rage he felt, not just at Dan and the woman he described in his mind as having trapped him, but at the world that had given him so much ease and pleasure all his life. He had been betrayed. People had not behaved as they were supposed to; they had not followed the rules he had been raised to believe society had created for its own protection. Ambitious young men who married into wealth should have the decency to remain faithful, or at least to hide their indiscretions well enough not to be caught. Young girls who had been given the best of educations and every advantage should not try to kill themselves over a sleazy saloonkeeper. (Of course, he added to himself with disgust, Paige had Dan's blood in her.) Nurses he regarded as women who, at least subconsciously, had taken the same high moral oaths as doctors. Now none of this was true.

After Joey had arrived that night and told his story, his anger still blazing, his grandfather had sent him to bed. Alone, Evan had poured himself a strong brandy and tried to sort out the facts in his own mind. The first and only thought that lasted through the rest of the weekend was that he would crush Dan. If he had been more given to introspection or had someone he knew and trusted to confide in, perhaps he could have been made to see what became obvious to the rest of his small world during the following weeks.

He had always hated Dan. Kay had known it from her years of working wth both men, but soon it became obvious to all the select circle of his part of Chicago's business world. Underneath all the compliments Evan had lavished on his son-in-law through the years there must always have been a bitter envy. Dan was the man who had turned the company around; Dan was the man who had made Paige Properties grow; Dan was responsible for increasing the family fortune, even if it meant taking wild chances such as acquiring the land near the airport. Evan had never approved of that; it was not the way a gentleman did business, trying to outguess the city and making it pay his price. Hustlers did that—boisterous upstarts whose offices were generally in their hats, vulgarians who would never be admitted even as working staff to the Van Buren Club. Men from the West Side of Chicago.

Evan did not realize in his reaction to the news of Dan's long-standing relationship with Mary that his real anger came from the years of resentment of his son-in-law that were seething inside him. He thought he was merely doing what any honorable man would do under the circumstances: avenging his daughter. Whether Joan wanted this was not important, certainly not important enough to discuss with her as she prepared to take his granddaughter east. Women didn't understand such things. And so, carefully, methodically, he went over the office books.

He would destroy Dan if it was the last thing he did.

Dan came into the office late that Monday morning. One look at Kay's sympathetic face, and he knew he would not have to explain anything to her. His first shock came when he asked for one of the company's checkbooks and was told they were all in Evan's office. He had not been prepared for this, but he was intelligent enough not to make an issue of it. The books were returned to him later that afternoon when Evan left for the day.

"He'll be having dinner with some friends at the club," Kay said, looking at him pointedly.

Obviously she knew who the friends were, and if Dan had been paying attention he would have asked for their names. But he was in no position to think. Too much had happened, and for once in his life he had no clear idea of what he should do or even what he should be feeling.

He spent the weekend with Mary, a strange time for both of them. They hadn't talked much, and neither of them had wanted to leave the apartment. They had been like mourners returning from a funeral. His instinct had been to call Lila to pack up all his belongings and have someone deliver them to Mary's apartment. Mary had persuaded him not to do this, and for the first time they had a violent argument, with him accusing her of no longer wanting him. It had taken most of Sunday afternoon, that quarrel, and she had shown endless patience in calming him down. It could only hurt Joan further, she kept repeating, making the break so decisive, so final. Mary checked the hospital and learned of Joan's plans to take Paige east. It would give all of them time to think and plan for the future. When they left, Dan should go back to the apartment.

In the end Dan agreed, and allowed her to comfort him when he woke through the nights of that week. For the first time he could remember, he had nightmares, calling out in his sleep, thrashing around restlessly, finally forcing Mary to make up another bed on the living-room couch. It had been new, that couch, when she first came to this apartment. Its slipcover was at the cleaners, to remove the bloodstains Paige had made, and Mary could see how threadbare the sofa had become. Has it been so many years? she thought wearily as as she got up early to fix Dan's breakfast. Neither of them discussed their future that week; whenever Dan would try, Mary always stopped him. It was too soon; they were still sliding on slippery ice, knowing their world had changed and not yet knowing how much.

Although Dan had always shared the business problems of his life with Mary, he was strangely quiet about them in the month that followed, so the first obvious changes came in her own life. She had trained herself in the weeks after Paige's suicide attempt to react as she always did at the hospital office where she worked. Being in charge of the laboratory files, she had a small office to herself, and by closing the door she could make herself concentrate on her job. She was determined not to let the thought that people might be whispering about her become some kind of obsession. If two nurses suddenly stopped talking when she walked past them in the cafeteria, she would not allow herself to think she might be the subject of their conversation. If doctors, especially the young interns, looked at her in a special way, it was just her imagination; perhaps her lipstick had smeared or the hem of her skirt was uneven. There are millions of people in Chicago, Mary Conroy, she told herself over and over again, who know nothing about the Martins or Paige or you and care even less. Let's not make too much of this.

So the neatly handwritten note from Dr. MacCauley that lay on her desk one afternoon came as a double surprise. It was friendly but formal, even for MacCauley, explaining he had left the hospital to transfer to a research job at a prestigious medical center in the East. There was no mention of the last time they had seen each other, of either Paige or the Martins. He thanked her for the pleasant times they had together but made no mention of a farewell meeting. The letter ended, *Sincerely yours.*

This was the first time Mary had to realize there was a difference between self-centered suspicions of gossip about her and the reality of the situation. Certainly there had never been anything in the least romantic between her and the doctor, but she had enjoyed his company and considered him a good friend. Had he resigned because he couldn't bear the sight of her any longer? That seemed ridiculous; she could hardly consider herself so attractive to the proper physician. Was it some kind of jealous maneuver on the part of Dan? He had been capable of that and more before, but surely not now?

She confronted him with it that night at dinner, and she could see by his surprise that, whatever had made MacCauley leave Chicago, Dan was not part of it. They were having dinner in one of Dan's favorite restaurants, an elegantly converted townhouse off Michigan Boulevard. Mary had dined there before, but only when Joan was also present. But since his wife had gone east, Dan had ceased the cautious discretion they had always observed in the past, and they dined out every night in the superb restaurants that had begun sprouting up on the near North Side. It was as if he was determined to let people gossip if they wanted. If someone he knew was dining there as well, he made a point of stopping and chatting as they left, introducing Mary as he had done at their first lunch just by her name.

"Mary, I had nothing to do with this," he said as he handed her MacCauley's letter back. "He's been such an institution here in Chicago, I'd never thought of him leaving. I've never heard him mention being interested in research before."

"I suppose I'm just being silly. Why wouldn't he make a move if an opportunity is offered?"

"Only who offered it?" Dan ordered another pot of coffee and leaned forward, his face grave. "There've been a couple of other things happening lately I don't understand either. Somebody's been selling stock in the corporation I formed for the airport land. Selling a lot of it."

"Why?"

"I don't know. Since it'll only be a couple of months before it goes through and the real profits come in, it doesn't make sense."

"Does it affect you?"

"Badly." He turned around to see if anyone was near enough to hear them and then, reassured, leaned forward again. "A lot of my shares— well, I had to borrow from the banks to buy them. There's never been any problem; the banks were getting their interest and they could see the future as well as I did.

"Only, if somebody starts dumping stock on the market and nobody buys it, the banks are going to get nervous. They're starting already. Just yesterday one of the bankers I've been dealing with didn't return my calls . . . and I made three of them. I need an extension on my loans. There's never been any problem before, I just put up my shares in the corporation for security."

"But if somebody's selling the stock . . ."

"I've got to buy it. At the market price. To keep up the value of what I already own . . . and borrowed on."

She tried to sort it out, to come up with some solution. "The eastern bankers who helped before . . . ?"

"I've just about exhausted them. If I only knew who was dumping the stock! And why?"

It was Kay who told Mary. Over the years she had often called Mary at the hospital, usually with a message from Dan or Joan, always something perfectly proper. Nothing to hint of knowledge of Dan's relationship with Mary. They had been at the Martin dinner parties together and had established a friendly relationship, at least on the surface. This time, however, Kay called to ask Mary to meet her at her apartment. Mary, somewhat puzzled, agreed. Dan had flown to the West Coast to try and raise money to buy the corporation shares suddenly flooding the market.

It was the first time Mary had seen Kay's apartment, and she was impressed by the building and the quiet elegance of her home. Over the years Kay had moved twice, always to larger apartments. She had also taught herself many things about taste, and though hardly three people a year saw her home besides herself, it gave her a secret pleasure to know it existed, that it had been created by her with her own money. She had graceful French antiques and glittering chandeliers and the rooms were alive with bursts of fresh flowers, one of the few perishable extravagances she allowed herself.

She mixed Mary a drink, contenting herself with icewater. The glass was expensive and beautiful; the bar behind her glistened with rows and rows of crystal goblets. It was early evening, and the room was bright with the last of the summer sun. Kay wasted no time in getting down to her reason for calling Mary.

"Somebody's dumping the stock of Dan's corporation on the open market."

"Dan told me. That's why he's flown to San Francisco. To raise more money."

"He won't get it." Kay settled herself against the comfortable pillows of her sofa. She had gained weight in the past few years, the flesh she had fought so hard when she was younger, having seen it settle on her mother and older sisters, a peasant inheritance she had been determined to fight. Only lately it hadn't seemed worth the bother. She was still neatly dressed and kept her nails polished and her hair carefully colored. But there was no mistaking she was a plain woman, solidly settled into middle age.

"Why do you say that?"

"Because Evan's out to destroy him."

To Kay's surprise, this did not come as a shock to Mary. She had suspected Joan's father was behind the attempt to ruin Dan and had even tentatively broached the idea. Dan had dismissed it as insane. Evan had as much to gain by the sale going through as Dan did.

"He'll do it, too."

"Even if it means he'll lose a fortune as well?" Mary knew Kay was correct in her suspicions, but she had to mention the objection Dan had made.

"He's not going to lose a penny. After all, he and Dan bought that property when the land was cheap. Evan may not make the fortune there'd be if he held on until the city buys it, but he'll still come out ahead." She ran her hand through her hair restlessly. "No, he's determined to destroy Dan. I . . . I don't think I have to tell you why."

"You've always known, haven't you? About us?"

Kay nodded.

"And never said anything?"

"I thought about it. I'm sure you can guess the reason."

"You love him too."

Kay made no answer. She took Mary's glass and went over to the bar to put in more ice cubes. She needed time to pick the right words. "Yes, I love Dan," she said finally. "Or I did. I don't know what I feel now."

"How you must have hated me all these years."

Kay handed her glass back to Mary and settled once more on the comfortable sofa. "I think I did at first. At least I tried. But gradually . . . I don't know." She smiled briefly at the woman opposite her. "I won't say I gradually came to recognize your sterling qualities." Mary had the grace to blush at that, she noticed. "But I could see you were good for Dan, good in a way I don't think I could ever be. That maybe I didn't even want to be."

"Kay, what can I do? You must have some idea; you wouldn't have asked me here otherwise."

"I acted on impulse. Maybe I had the idea that if you left Chicago— but, hell, that wouldn't work. This thing between Dan and Evan is much deeper than just finding out about you."

"How badly is Dan in debt?" Mary was surprised at the control in her voice. For the first time in all these years she was talking about her relationship with an outsider, and instead of feeling embarrassed or apologetic all she could think of was that there had to be a solution and Kay was the only one who could help her find it.

"Don't you know?"

"I know he's got a lot tied up in this airport business. He's even given me stock in it."

"You've obviously not interested in the financial page, are you? It went down five points yesterday. If Evan keeps selling—and he will—it will go down farther."

"And the bank will call in Dan's loans." Mary got up, walking to the bar to get rid of her drink, pacing across the room, not really looking at Kay any longer. "Dan will be broke, won't he?"

"Everything he's got is tied up in this. Plus a good chunk of the company's funds. He won't go bankrupt; Evan will see to that. He'll buy what little Dan has left that he owns outright. That'll leave Dan something, just enough to stay out of bankruptcy." She moved her hand and turned on the light beside her. It was getting dark. "I'm sure he'll find a small desk for Dan somewhere and a modest salary. Just enough to keep him under his thumb for the rest of his life. He won't let his son-in-law starve—*if* he remains his son-in-law."

"Is that what you wanted to tell me?" Mary faced Kay directly. But there was no malice in the older woman's eyes, no long-held resentment. Instead Kay looked at her almost pityingly.

"No, Mary. I honestly didn't say that as some kind of threat to your happiness."

"How much would Dan need? I mean, to buy up the stock on the market?" She could call Fred Reiner this evening. The building where she had her apartment: that was free and clear; the deed was in her safety deposit box. The two-story building on the West Side: that was hers too, finally mortgage-free after all these years. The lawyer would know how to get money for both buildings, and fast.

"At least a hundred thousand." Something in Mary's face frightened her. "What are you planning."

"I could probably raise that. If I placed a bid for the stock on the market, would I have to pay for all of it at once, or would they wait? At least a couple of days?" She didn't mind admitting her ignorance. "I don't know how long it takes to get mortgages."

"You'd do that?" Kay stared at her. "To bail Dan out?"

"Of course. Wouldn't you?"

Kay looked as if she had slapped her. Her heavy face sagged, and she put her arms around herself as if she needed to warm her body. "No," she said at last, knowing she could not lie to Mary or to herself. "No," she said again, in almost a whisper. "And I guess that's why he's been in love with you all these years, instead of me."

"It's not a question of love!" Mary brushed the word aside impatiently. "This is Dan's life, his past, his future. We can't let it be destroyed."

"You're a goddamn fool, Mary Conroy."

"Don't talk nonsense! Will a hundred thousand dollars be enough?"

"Temporarily, yes. By next week, no."

The words were said so flatly, so calmly, Mary had no answer. She sat down, afraid her legs wouldn't hold her.

"Even if I were . . . foolhardy enough to join you, we couldn't save Dan. We might be able to buy up Evan's shares, although I don't think we could even do that. But you can bet Joan's father hasn't just decided to do this on his own. He's probably alerted all his cronies at that damn Van Buren Club." Kay smiled cynically. "It'll be a great coup for them. Drive Dan to have to sell what he has to pay the banks they control; then, when the stock is down, pick up all the shares they were too narrow-minded to buy years ago."

"Help him, Kay!" Mary leaned forward and took the other woman's hand. "Please! Help Dan!"

"There's nothing I can do." Kay pulled her hands back. This meeting hadn't gone as she had thought. She hadn't prepared herself; it was the one time in her careful life she had not planned ahead. She had thought she had simply wanted to alert Mary and Dan. Now it had become a tangled mixture of emotions and memories, things she wanted to forget, to put behind her.

"Mary." She started again, choosing her words slowly, for they were coming to her mind slowly, revelations she had never let herself face in all the years she had known the Martins.

"Mary, maybe I asked you here to warn you." She gave a small shrug. "I don't know why I should care whether you're hurt or not. God knows nobody ever cared that much about me. But they can hurt you, people like the Martins." She went on quickly, though she noticed Mary had made no move to interrupt. "They're alike, Dan and Joan. Evan as well. Oh, one half may be Lake Forest and the other West Side, but they're alike. Just as their children are. They're takers. They'll take your time and your love and your life and your devotion, take it all as if it were nothing more than their due, take it and give nothing back."

"Dan's not like that." But Mary's voice was tired, the words automatic.

"You know he is. They all are. And you're a giver. I guess that's what divides the world." Kay pulled herself out of the couch and moved to the bar. "I think I'll have a real drink now." As she fixed it, she went on. "I thought I was a giver too. Noble, self-sacrificing . . . God, the lies women tell themselves! Well, I'm not a giver. Not any more, at least, if I ever was. I'm not giving up everything I've worked for and saved over the years, not even if Dan Martin ends up in the gutter. I don't think any other woman would either." Although, as she spoke, she knew of one other who would: Joan. Joan and Mary. Dan had been lucky in the women he chose.

"I'd better go." Mary had to be alone, to have space and time to think. It couldn't be as hopeless as Kay made it out to be. The lawyer would think of something. For the first time she regretted turning down the expensive jewelry Dan had offered over the years. She could have pawned it; pawnshops were not alien to the Scanlons and the Conroys of this world. But stock markets and shares—Kay was right, she'd never looked at a financial page in her life.

"Did you ever think Dan would marry you?"

Kay's question stopped her. "No," she answered. "He talked of it once, but . . . it was too unreal!" There was no pain in her eyes, Kay noticed, no years of broken or postponed hopes. She clearly meant every word she was saying without self-pity or sentiment. "I could never have replaced Joan as his wife. I never really wanted to. . . . You see, I always knew he loved her as much as he loved me. No . . . more. And I love her too. If I'd ever thought I would hurt her, that she would find out, I think I could have had the strength to end it. But we were always so careful, I thought it would never happen."

"Only it has." Kay put her glass down abruptly. No liquid in the world could help her do what she knew she would have to do tonight. "That's the trouble with takers, Mary. They never stop . . . until they've taken everything you've got."

She didn't hear Mary leave. By the time she moved to the telephone she was not surprised to find herself alone again. She dialed the long-distance number fast, knowing if she waited to consider what she was doing she probably would not have the courage to make the call. As she stood there waiting for a nurse a thousand miles away to call Joan to the phone, she allowed herself to consider her future.

Joan would come back, of course. Joan would fight her father, protect Dan somehow. Whatever anger she felt for Mary or her husband, she would never let her father destroy him. But Evan would know who had alerted her; it would come out once the battle between them began. And that would be the end of Kay at Paige Properties. Joan might defeat her father, but she would not protest if Evan fired Kay. Joan would let him have that last revenge.

Takers, Kay thought, knowing it meant the end of the sensible life she had built over the years. She could still change her mind. She had given no name to the nurse. She could hang up before Joan came on the line. No one need ever know she lacked the courage to do the one thing that would help the man she had loved for so long. She could go on until she retired, seeing him each day, taking what scraps of comfort she could salvage from that.

But she knew she couldn't. The future she had described to Mary of Dan's life if he lost this battle was only too accurate. As she heard the voice on the other end she made herself speak clearly, carefully.

"Joan? It's Kay."

Seventeen

As Kay knew she would, Joan flew back to Chicago the following day. Dan was still in San Francisco, and the other secretaries were at lunch when she arrived, so the two of them had a moment alone together in the outer office. Kay had spent the morning clearing her desk of her current assignments. She kept few personal things at the office; these she had put in a large shopping bag by her side. If the other girls were curious, they had too much respect and awe of her position to ask questions.

Joan looked rested and tanned. It may have been a long flight, but her summer suit was still crisp and unwrinkled. There was no cane, Kay noticed, and though her attitude was, as always, calmly polite, her face seemed different somehow, more natural than a month's rest could have achieved. Silently Kay handed Joan the two envelopes she had prepared. Joan looked at her questioningly.

"It's a copy of the bylaws of Paige Properties. The breakdown of ownership of all the shares is on page twelve. I've marked it."

"And this?" Joan held out the thin envelope Kay had placed on top of the folder.

"My resignation."

"Kay, there's no need for that."

"Joan, let's not kid ourselves. Your father's going to consider my calling you an act of betrayal. He may be right. In any case, it's time for me to move onward."

"Where will you go?"

"I'm not sure yet. First I have to close my apartment, store my things. After that, I suppose I should visit what's left of my family, only usually I can stand them for just two days. Then . . . well, who knows? I haven't had a real vacation for year. And an old friend of mine, Kitty Sedgewick—she used to work in this building—she moved out to Denver a couple of years ago. She writes real estate is booming out there. Maybe I'll start my own firm."

"Dan'll miss you."

"Not as much as I'd like to think." She nodded toward the closed door to Evan's office. "You'd better go in. He's not going to like what you're going to say. He'll like it even less if he thinks the rest of the office is outside listening."

"You should have some sort of settlement, a pension . . . I mean, after all these years . . ."

"Don't bother. I've got some of that airport stock too."

Joan nodded and knocked on the door of her father's office.

"You must be out of your mind!"

"No, Dad. You're the one who seems to have gone crazy."

"He's cheated you, he's lied to you, he's betrayed you . . . and you'd go against your own father to try and save him?"

"What's happened between Dan and me is for us to decide. Not you. I won't let you destroy him. If you'll add up the breakdown of shares in this company—it's right there on page twelve—you'll see Dan's got twenty-five percent, I've got twenty—remember all the money you saved on income taxes by deeding that to me?—and the children have ten percent each. That adds up to sixty-five percent of the control of this company. You're outvoted."

"Paige . . . Joey . . . I'll bet they don't know about this. Once they do, they'll be on my side."

"I doubt that. Paige already signed her proxy to me this morning."

"A girl in a madhouse!"

"Do you want to make an issue of that in court?" She leaned back and lit a cigarette. "As for Joey, I vote his stock until he's twenty-one, and that won't be for another year. The city will have made its bid by then."

"You think you've won?"

"Dad, I never thought of this as winning or losing. Dan's worked on this project for years. It's been the dream of his life. I won't have it destroyed"—she tapped her cigarette in the ashtray on her father's desk, careful not to meet his eyes—"just because he's slept in a bed more hospitable than mine."

"She was supposed to be your friend."

"We won't talk about that, if you don't mind. Now, I want you to buy back all the shares you can on the airport deal. Today. I'm not returning to Golden Shores until I've seen that stock go back up to its real value. I also want you to call your friends at the bank and tell them Dan's credit is to be extended, that you'll support it personally if necessary."

"And if I say no?"

This was the side of her father that had always frightened Joan. She had seen it so rarely, the cold, cruel anger of a man who could literally destroy an enemy and think nothing of it. His first rage she had always been able to handle, but this icy hatred left him white-faced and motionless. His skin was stretched so tight over his forehead, it was as if she were seeing the skull beneath it. He would never forgive her, she knew, just as she'd always known someday there would be a clash between the two men in her life and she would have to choose one and lose the other.

"I'll wire Dan to come back tonight. As the listed vice-president of Paige Properties I have the right to call a Board of Directors meeting whenever I deem it necessary."

"A technicality—"

"One I'll use. The meeting will be here. Tomorrow. And we'll have our own lawyers. Together we have enough votes to put you out as president of this firm."

"You'd do all this for him?"

"This, and a great deal more."

Suddenly she was weary, tired of the anger and the battling, tired of trying to break this cold, implacable man opposite her. "Dad, listen to me! I owe this to Dan! All these years . . . what kind of a wife have I been? How could I expect him not to find someone else?"

"I don't want to hear such talk."

She reached across the desk as if to touch him, but he drew his folded hands back. "Please, Father. Do this easily, do it gracefully, don't destroy us as a family."

"It seems we've never been that." It was as final a pronouncement as if he were a judge sentencing her to death. "Just animals, grabbing for whatever we can get."

She felt her temper rising, the temper she had inherited from him, the wild fury that had driven Dan away forever that terrible night she had lost the baby. She had kept it controlled until now, knowing if she let it loose, whatever was finally decided she would have lost. Only now she didn't care. If he wanted to be ruthless, she could beat him at that as well.

"Did you think you were any better? All these years you've let Dan do the work, while you sat back and played gentleman. Well, now it's his turn. And he's not going to be cheated of it."

"And *your* turn?" His eyes were cold, hard. "Aren't you cheating yourself out of that?" She had not expected this, a personal attack; she stared at him, puzzled. "You've had your plans too, haven't you? Oh, yes, I've watched you these past few years. You've been trying to get Dan to be a public figure, to go into politics. The public relations firm, all the pictures, the interviews . . ."

"He's ambitious. He has a right to be ambitious."

"Don't lie to me, Joan. You wanted Dan in public life not because it's what he wants—although I'm quite sure that upstart is convinced he can run the world as well as a good part of Chicago. But the only reason you've encouraged him was because you thought it would save your marriage."

Her hands were shaking; she gripped them together tightly, but she knew her father could see he had broken her defenses.

"A man in public office—well, he can't very well divorce his lovely injured wife . . . injured initially by him and his carelessness; all that will come out, of course. And his two betrayed children: I'm sure Paige, when she's better, will have a lot to say about that. I've already heard what Joey will say—probably *is* saying at the moment to anyone who will listen."

Abruptly he turned his back to her, to stare at the city below his office windows. He's old, Joan realized. A bitter, impotent old man, but the lion still had claws and she knew as she sat there he would not hesitate to use them.

"Yes, Dan in politics would have stayed married to you. But Dan independently wealthy, which I grant he'll be when this airport deal goes through—what will he do then? I gather this affair has been going on for a number of years. The woman must have some hold on him that goes beyond youth and good looks. What will happen when he's rich enough to be able to go to her?"

"I . . . I . . . don't know."

"I do. He'll leave. Because there's going to be no political career."

Evan looked at his daughter. She was close to tears; he could push her to them easily, but he had no desire for that. He had never liked sniveling women. Sooner or later she would have to leave the office, and he could imagine the gossip if she left with red eyes and a tear-stained face. So he went on, more quietly.

"Dan will not have a political career, Joan. I may not be able to stop you from outmaneuvering me on the corporation. Anybody who has ever read *King Lear* should have known it's not very intelligent for a father to be too generous with his legacies. So I'll let Dan have his airport deal. And his fortune. But I'll see to it there'll be nothing more. The people who run this city and this state are family men, my dear. They don't like philanderers. A word here, a word there . . . you'll have no voting power to stop that. Dan is through. He'll go no higher."

He had beaten her, he could see that. It was a minor triumph, compared to defeating his son-in-law, but it might have to satisfy. "He may not even choose to be your husband any more. Now . . . do you still want to outvote me?"

She should have known it would come to this. She should have thought of some other way of handling the matter. But there had been so little time! Ever since Kay's phone call the night before, all she had been able to think about was Dan, how to save him, how to help him outwit her father. But Evan had turned everything around, leaving the final irrevocable choice to her.

"I'll take my chances," she said with dignity.

"Perhaps you're planning another solution?" He said it so coolly, dispassionately, Joan should have been on guard. "A little careful blackmail? A signed paper saying that in return for your surprising interference in the family business he will give up any plans for a divorce in the future? I could have a paper drawn up quite privately. The Board of Directors meeting could come after that." He smiled slightly.

Nothing her father had ever said had shocked her so much. The carefully tailored gentleman, the man of such strong principles, the arbiter of good behavior . . . to suggest this!

"Thank you," she managed, and with a quick thrust added, "but we're not all animals. I'll stick to my original plan." She stood. The meeting was over. She'd saved Dan. Only her father was right: the price might be to lose everything that had ever mattered to her. Still, she wouldn't turn back now, or stoop to such a low trick. Years before she had told Mary she had never felt worthy of her husband. At least this afternoon she had equaled him in strength and generosity. She would have that to comfort her, whatever lay ahead.

Dan came back to Chicago two days later. He was in Mary's apartment when she returned from work, a mass of newspapers around him, a cigarette still burning in the ashtray at his side and another in his hand. He wasted no time on greetings but pointed to the litter of papers.

"What the hell's been going on?"

"What do you mean? When did you get back? How long have you been here?"

He brushed aside the questions impatiently. "The airport stock: it's up four points. And yesterday the bankers in San Francisco very politely but very firmly turned me down. It doesn't make sense."

She made no answer, just handed him the thick manila envelope Fred Reiner had given her an hour before. He'd managed the mortgages easily at a suburban savings and loan. The interest rates were higher than seemed prudent, but she had insisted on doing it her way and at last Fred had agreed, buying all the shares he could that morning and delivering them to her at the hospital.

"What's this?" He opened the folder curiously, taking out the stiff paper of the stocks Fred had bought.

For a long moment there was silence between them. "You mortgaged the buildings," he said at last, his voice flat, no suggestion of doubt in his mind.

"I . . . I had to."

"Mary . . . oh, my God, Mary!"

Suddenly he was crying, this man she had never seen weakened before. It was as if some wall he had built firmly around his heart all these years had at last collapsed, leaving him frightened and vulnerable, younger than he had ever seemed in all the time she had known him. She cradled him in her arms, soothing him gently, letting him sob, knowing if she had to starve the rest of her life, this moment was worth it.

"I can't let you," he said at last, clinging to her, resting his head on her breast. "They're every damn thing you've got in the world."

No, my beautiful Dan, she thought. Everything I've got in the world that matters is right here in my arms. "They were never mine, Dan," she said softly. "They were things you gave me. I'm simply giving them back."

Later, when he had regained control of himself, he tried to talk to her sensibly about what was happening. The shares she had bought alone could not have accounted for the sudden rise in the stock. There had to be something else. He filled in page after page with figures, growing more and more mystified as he wrote. Although she had suggested dinner several times, he didn't seem to hear her. Stymied, he finally decided to call Kay.

"Kay? I'm at Mary's. What's happened?"

Mary sat watching him, wondering how a man could change so quickly. Less than an hour before she had held him, they had been closer than they had ever been, and now she might have been nothing more than another piece of furniture in the room.

"She did? She's still here?" This was the first he had spoken after listening to his secretary for what seemed to Mary an eternity. "Yes. Yes, I'll tell her. . . ."

He hung up and looked across the room at Mary. She had never seemed so beautiful. She had given him everything: all her love, the rich and fruitful years of her life, even the small financial security she had. She had never asked anything of him and he knew she never would. The one thing he had wanted to give her, his name and a share in the full public part of his life, was now no longer his to give. What Kay had told him of Joan's meeting with her father had convinced him of that.

"Kay wondered if you might be free for dinner. I . . . I have to go to the apartment. Joan's there."

"Of course." Dan put his arms around her, holding her fiercely. Joan wouldn't destroy them, not completely. She was too much of a lady for that. But he could never ask for a divorce, not that Joan would have considered that for a minute as a condition for her help. She had given, as Mary had, with all her heart and mind and love, and he could never desert her. At least Mary would be secure. Joan had seen to that. Financially, Mary would be safe for the rest of her life.

Only, as he held her, he knew that had never been what she wanted. Perhaps marriage had not been either. Just his love. He had given as much as he could. A more honorable man, he knew, would have refused Joan's offer. Would have taken his stand by himself and asked for a divorce and, if it meant shattering his career and his life, faced it honestly. Already the two women he loved had done as much for him. Only he did not have the courage. That was something he would remember with shame for the rest of his life.

"He went back to her?"

"He never left her, Kay. I never expected he would."

"And where does that leave you?"

"I don't know."

Kay had prepared a light meal, something simple for the hot night outside her cool apartment. Mary, she realized, was the first guest who had sat at her dining-room table, the first and the last. "She'll go back to Golden Shores after this. You'll be able to see him, at least through the summer."

"I suppose so. And you?"

"I'll be leaving Chicago in a few weeks." She had already told Mary of her resignation. It didn't seem to hurt. Maybe later, when she had time to think. She looked across the table at Mary, wondering, as she had so often, what it was that Dan had found in her so compelling that the affair had lasted all these years. She was attractive, of course, but not what anyone would call beautiful. Middle-aged by now, Kay figured, and not making that much effort to hide it. Her figure was good, and she dressed well, but there was gray in her hair and the inevitable signs of age in her face that women can see in each other long before men do. Perhaps it was her sense of dignity that made her distinctive, but from what Kay knew of men, that was hardly a quality that kept them in your bed.

"He should have left Joan years ago," Kay said abruptly, almost angrily. "He should have married you."

"I never expected that."

"What did you expect? Just a quiet romance? God knows Dan's attractive enough to make any woman want that."

"No, it's more complicated, Kay." For the first time Mary had someone she could speak to honestly. She hoped she would find the right words. "I . . . I suppose before I met Dan, I only felt half alive," she started, haltingly. "My mother had worried about that, and that's one of the reasons I married too soon, too impulsively." She laughed a little. "Hard to think of me as impulsive, isn't it? But there seemed so much of the world, of life, that I was never going to see, never going to experience. Jack came along, and he was decent; he tried to make our lives better. Tried in a way not very much different from the way Dan has. And then there was Joan . . . and the children. I guess I felt . . . sort of frozen after my mother died. It was so wonderful to feel needed."

"We always fall for that, don't we?" Kay smoothed out the napkin in her lap. It was Irish linen and beautiful. She hated to pack it away, but it would only be for a little while. She'd find another place, another city, another life. "I was so sure all these years that the office needed me, that it would collapse if I left, Dan included. Within a month they won't even remember I was there."

"He'll miss you." Mary smiled gently. "I'll miss you. I've never had anyone I could talk about Dan to before. Now everything's changed, ripped up. I don't even know what pieces are left. It would have been nice to have you as a friend."

Charm, Kay thought. That's what she has. Dan Martin, what a fool you are!

"Maybe you should count yourself lucky he didn't marry you," Kay said brusquely. "My friend Kitty, she went with a married man for years. Tried everything to get him to leave his wife and marry her. Tears, scenes, seductions, threats to tell his wife; I think once she even claimed she was pregnant. Nothing worked. Until one day his wife said she was tired of him. Just like that. There wasn't even another man. She just wanted out. He gave her a good chunk of money and she bought a condo in Hawaii, took up ceramics. I hear she's never been happier.

"And Kitty got what she wanted. He married her, practically at once. Hurt pride, I guess. That's why she moved to Denver. Only half a year later she divorced him. It seems once he married her, he wasn't any better in bed than he'd been with his wife. An affair? That was naughty, that was fun. But marriage?" Kay snorted and stood up from the table. "Men!" she added, almost with disgust.

"Dan wouldn't have been like that," Mary said quietly.

"No," Kay admitted grudgingly. "He wouldn't. Still . . . we'll never know, will we?"

Together they went back to the living room.

Eighteen

Kay had been right: Mary and Dan had the summer together. When Joan came back in the fall, escorting "a
very subdued Paige," as Dan described her, their lives did not become
that much different. There was never any confrontation, Dan reported.
No setting of rules, no scenes, no demands. Partly that was because
Paige moved back into the family apartment. She had her own room
again, and Joan set about making it as attractive as possible.

They each had their own rooms, Dan and Joan and Paige, and when
they met for meals, which was not all that often, the conversation was
polite and impersonal. There were no undertones of malice or resentment. The conversation was as general and civilized as if they were
strangers meeting on board a ship—attractive, pleasant people, but no
one to whom you would confide the secrets of your life.

Because there could be no sudden withdrawal from the committees
and boards Joan had arranged to participate in with her husband in
earlier years, they were still seen in public, at least once or twice a week.
The public relations firm was terminated by Joan. Dan did not need to
ask why; he knew the answer. Gradually, any talk among his business
contemporaries about a political career began to fade from his obvious
lack of enthusiasm. He found it no great sacrifice. He hadn't been feeling well the past months, and the thought of new challenges was no
longer attractive.

The airport land was finally bought at the price he had expected in September of that year. While it was a fair price for the expansion necessary to the growth of the city, there was still sufficient outcry in the media because the majority of the shares were owned by one firm, so clearly controlled by Dan, that any hopes of a political career would have been ruined anyway. Dan also suspected the public outcry had been, at least in part, arranged by his father-in-law. Dan had no illusions Evan had forgiven him. The few times they were forced to be in the same room together, they both tried to arrange for someone else to be present, a young assistant or one of the new secretaries. When the last of the company shares had been turned over to the city's purchasers, Evan abruptly announced his retirement and within a week had left Chicago for Palm Beach. It was a relief to them all.

Paige had come back not only subdued but far more open to suggestion than at any other time in her life. Almost gratefully she followed her mother's ideas as how to occupy her time. A part-time job was found for her at the Chicago Historical Society, thanks to a generous contribution from Joan, and she seemed happy to indulge in the activities of a post-debutante that previously she had dismissed. There was no more talk of a singing career. She and Joan spent long hours shopping for the attractive clothes that once seemed to her a sign of foolish upper-class extravagance. One afternoon, when Mickey Harris was driving her out to his country club, they passed the site of the Funky Tree. It was closed, the windows boarded up. She found she wasn't even interested in finding out what had happened to the owner. That was all part of the past. It was far more important to remember that Mickey, now in law school, hated his childhood nickname and preferred to be called either Michael or Mike.

Joey had gone back to school in September, arranging it himself and picking a college in the East. During the weeks of that summer he had made no attempt to contact either his mother or his father. He'd had one dinner alone with Paige, but she had so obviously accepted their parents' standards they found they had little to talk about.

Mary was never mentioned by any of them. Once Lila brought up her name when Paige was alone, but the girl had left her at once, going into her room and closing the door. Lila did not try again. Still, Mary was a presence in the Martin household, as the housekeeper knew by the careful conversations between Dan and Joan.

"I'll be going with the Andersons to Chez Paul tonight," Joan would say casually at breakfast, mentioning one of Dan's favorite restaurants. "Will you be free to join us?"

"No, I'm afraid I'll be busy." That was the warning Joan gave to tell him where he should not take Mary that evening.

If they had a dinner party at home, Joan would make no comment when Dan left ten minutes after the last guests. Whether or not he stayed the night at Mary's was none of her business. She would close the door to her room and settle in with a new book, only turning out the light when she heard the elevator coming up to their floor. She would not have either Dan or Paige thinking she was spying on them.

It was, Joan realized, probably the most peaceful, civilized time in her entire marriage. They each had what they wanted. She was well again, although she was still surprised to find how few people noticed the difference. Dr. Keinser had warned her that summer that much of what she had thought of as "being crippled" during the past years had been all but invisible to others. She'd argued with the doctor about that vehemently, the memory of the night in the New York hotel room still a vivid scar, but gradually on her return to Chicago it seemed perhaps the doctor had been right. It made no difference now, of course. Dan had not come to her bed since she had learned of his relationship with Mary, and she found, to her relief, she had no wish for that intimacy ever again. She had the facade of a happy marriage and a very successful, still very handsome man to escort her where she wanted to go when she needed an escort, and that was quite enough for her as she moved through her late forties. She need make no effort to charm Dan now and, relieved of that, she found she could gather her own circle of friends around her whenever she wanted company. She wrote to Joey dutifully once every two weeks, although he never replied, keeping the letters full of inconsequential news of friends and the state of world affairs.

Renewing her friendship with the network of girls with whom she had gone to school, now women her own age, she discovered which ones had daughters in schools near Joey's. By announcing his nearness and availability, she would hear reports of girls he dated and parties he had attended. It was not much that she could do for him, but at least she felt she had tried.

It was Mary who felt the change in their situations the most. The money she had received from her airport stock was enormous, or so it seemed to her, more than enough to pay off both mortgages and to leave her financially free for the rest of her life. It was an incredible, almost frightening sum, but with Dan's advice she invested it wisely. She made up her mind it was not going to change her life.

But her life had changed, and she knew it. Gradually the gossip at the hospital had stopped or, if not quite stopped, had ceased to cause much interest; too many other people there were involved with their own lives and love affairs to care about hers. What she *did* miss were Joan and the children. Half a dozen times she would start to dial Joan's number for a chance to talk, only to remember before she finished that it was now impossible. She would have loved Joan's expert advice on how to spend her new income, which clothes to buy and how to redecorate the apartment. After putting down the phone just in time one autumn afternoon she found herself smiling almost ruefully. Even in the most sophisticated of societies, she realized, one did not call the wife of one's lover to help shop for clothes to make yourself more attractive.

But it wasn't just that, had never been that, really. Joan had been her best friend, she realized with some astonishment. She wasn't close to Patsy, and the disappearance of Dr. MacCauley so suddenly and the subsequent rumors stopped her from feeling free to talk about her life with the other women in the office. They were friendly, but they were also aware Dan was still on the Board of Directors. The women she had grown up with on the West Side had their own concerns, husbands and children and in some cases even grandchildren.

Dan, of course, had always seemed to her not only her lover but her friend. But since the night he had walked into her apartment unannounced, somehow, subtly, that had changed. He still enjoyed her company, she could still make him laugh, and while their sexual relations were not as frequent as before, they remained satisfying to both of them. Only now there seemed, sometimes, a distance between them. So much of their closeness had come from the fact that he could speak honestly to her of his business and family worries. She had listened, tried to make suggestions, shared the problems. Only now the problems were over and there was nothing to replace them to bind them together. Mary found to her surprise she would plan things to talk about before they went out to dinner, just as she had done with the taciturn MacCauley.

They were just getting older, she comforted herself. These things happen. But sometimes during one of their elegant dinners she found herself wishing Joan was there as well. It would have been more fun.

Paige and Joey, she realized, were cut out of her life forever. There was no point in trying to discuss his son's future with Dan; he had turned his back ruthlessly on the boy, and any mention of his name would merely start an argument. Information about Paige was easier to get. Dan, who had always been so proud of his daughter, had changed since that awful night when the girl had been brought to Mary's apartment. Joan's attempts to move Paige into the social life of Chicago were commented on caustically by her father. As he grew older and was finally a complete financial success in his own right, he seemed to be revealing all the resentment he had kept in since he had started his business career.

He's getting to be like Evan, Mary thought one evening. Just as rigid and narrow-minded. It was an appalling thought, and she tried to explain it away in her own mind. He'd fought hard for his success; why shouldn't he have opinions . . . even if they disagreed with her own? But she had used the excuse years ago to explain her brother's narrowness, and it was no more successful in convincing her this time than it had been before.

Dan was talking more and more of their traveling. She knew this was his way of making up for the fact that he could never divorce Joan, could never marry her. He had time now, and money, and his ambitions were ended. A winter someplace warm, he suggested. She could take a leave of absence from the hospital; he could arrange that. Although he had resigned from several business and social boards, he clung stubbornly to his position as one of the hospital directors. There was no need for them to discuss why; he was protecting her. They both knew that, just as they both knew Joan would not go with them for a winter vacation and that, for however long they could manage to be away, they would be registered as "Mr. and Mrs. Martin." It was all he could give her now.

Happy he had this new interest, Mary encouraged him, although she doubted if it would ever happen. It was true he could plead ill health for an extended trip away from the cold of the Chicago winter. He didn't look well. His hair was still thick, but it was mostly gray. Like Joan's, Mary thought, and that night after he had left her to go back to the apartment on the lakefront she wondered for the thousandth time what the Martins' lives might have been if she had never met them.

She never wondered until Thanksgiving of that year what her life might have been without Dan. She had seen it all so clearly years ago, indeed, had it spelled out by her mother before she died. Only as she took the elevated train west to share the meal with Patsy and Tim as she always did, she found herself looking at the passing houses with a fresh eye. Along the lakefront the city had grown steadily more beautiful. That was to be expected as builders erected huge new apartments and families with two incomes found they could afford them. There was no stigma to a wife working today. It was to be expected and, if a couple wanted to live well, necessary.

But Mary found the streets behind the glittering row of modern buildings had been improved as well. They were clean, and a clear sense of pride surrounded each house. Even the alleys, Chicago being one of the few great cities designed with that needed addition in mind, seemed neat and orderly. It's become a beautiful city, she thought. Not romantic like Venice or Paris, but beautiful in its own way. Each house seemed to have its own personality, to have been designed as a nest of domestic security, each family safely inside behind the carefully draped curtains and the inevitable expensive lamp that stood on the table at the living room window.

Surprised at her reaction, she found herself looking forward to seeing Patsy and Tim. There would only be the three of them at the holiday meal, unless the cousins from upstairs dropped in. That was hardly likely; they had their own large, growing family. Her brother's children would not be there today either. Tim Jr., the oldest and wildest, had, to everyone's surprise except his pastor's, gone into the seminary. Ellen was working in a bank in California, and Kevin, the youngest, had been married the spring before and was already the somewhat embarrassed father of a son. Still, it would not be a lonely meal, Mary thought as she walked down the street from the station. These were her family, and whatever had happened in her life, this was still where she would always be welcome. Dan and Joan had been invited with Paige to young Michael Harris's family for the holiday dinner, and she wouldn't see Dan at her apartment until the weekend. By then, she knew he would have expected her to make some decision about the winter.

It will solve itself somehow, she thought as she started up the stone steps. Things always do. She had firmly kept Dan and his place in her life separate from Patsy and Tim, confident that whatever gossip might be spreading among the friends of the Martins and the hospital staff, it could never reach her brother and sister-in-law.

"Good! You're early," said Patsy as she opened the door. She had changed over the years. All of them had, but Mary was looking around her today in a more observant way. Patsy seemed taller, almost thin. The dress she wore came from a Michigan Avenue store; in fact, Mary had almost bought it the week before. Patsy had clearly been to a beauty parlor, and she looked remarkably handsome. Mama, Mary thought with some admiration, you should have lived to see how Patsy turned out.

Tim was in the living room. He, too, was thinner, but it was more the wizening of oncoming age than the trim figure that had always given him so much pride.

"Well," he said, getting slowly to his feet. "So you can leave the grand folks for one day after all?"

"We'll have none of that, Timothy Scanlon," said Patsy in a firm voice, as she shepherded Mary past him. "Today's a day for thanks and for families. If you can't stay civil, you can get your own dinner."

To Mary's surprise, Tim said nothing, merely grunted and slumped back to continue reading his newspaper. Mary couldn't remember Patsy ever before having the final word in any discussion with her husband.

"Don't mind him," Patsy said after she had settled Mary's coat in the bedroom and led her into the kitchen. "He gets crankier every year."

"He looks awfully frail."

"Don't mind that either. He's just getting older. After all, I've lost flesh too."

"Yes. But it looks good on you. A new diet . . . or what?"

"Just a little more pride in myself, I think." She furnished Mary with an apron, and together they went to work on the last preparations for the meal. It seemed an awful lot of food for just the three of them, but Mary could see Patsy took pride in the annual display. The silver was polished and the good cut glass was out on the table, waiting for the food bubbling away on the stove and the turkey roasting in the oven.

"I'm working full time now, you know, Mary."

She hadn't known. She blamed herself for not having kept up with the family.

"It's made all the difference. I like having an office to go to in the morning. The other girls—well, I guess you can't really call us 'girls,' but you know what I mean—they're good company. We have laughs and go out for dinner together and sometimes a show. And it turns out I'm the best typist in the bunch." She mentioned the insurance company she worked for. It had a huge office downtown, and for a moment Mary wondered if by chance any of Dan's business had come through her sister-in-law's hands. How many years had they both been so careful about little slips like that?

"Anyway, it's a relief from sitting here waiting for your brother to come home grouchy every evening. I tell you, Mary Conroy, there've been a lot of evenings when I've envied your life."

Not if you knew it all, you wouldn't, Mary thought to herself as she started peeling the steaming sweet potatoes. Almost as if Patsy had read her mind, she gave Mary a quick look. "And that includes Dan Martin as well."

If Patsy had slapped her, she couldn't have surprised Mary more. She put down the bowl in her hands and stared at her sister-in-law. "What . . . ?"

"Don't make up any fast excuses or stories," Patsy went on calmly. "We're both grown women. Anyway, I've known about it for a long time. Maybe Maggie Feeney didn't know you were working for the Martins when her niece got that free operation from the Paige-Martin Foundation. And maybe Tim out there"—she nodded toward the neat living room—"didn't make the connection when he got a good job from Dan Martin when nobody else would hire him, but I can put two and two together as well as the next one."

"You never said anything," Mary managed finally.

"What was there to say? It was your own business. You've handled it all this time with dignity and silence, with no crying on anybody's shoulder, although I'll bet you've been hurt plenty of times. I respect that. And you've helped everyone you could."

I didn't help, Mary thought to herself. That was Dan, whether because he wanted to or he wanted me, I'll never know. "You give me too much credit," she said at last.

"I don't think so," Patsy answered. "Anyway, you're free now, aren't you? If you want to be. You've got a whopping sum of money, Maggie Feeney tells me: investing in that airport business with what you got from mortgaging this place again, and the one you live in."

Maggie. Mary might have known. Time may have gone by, but the lawyer's secretary still had the biggest mouth in the parish. "That mortgage is paid off. Your house is free and clear, Patsy."

"I wasn't worried about it. That worry belonged to a dumb little dumpling of a girl who thought the world was going to come to an end every day of her life. I'm not like that anymore."

"No, you're not. I guess none of us are what we started out to be."

Her sister-in-law put down the turkey she had taken from the oven and looked at her. "I didn't bring this up today to make you unhappy, Mary. I just thought—well, maybe it was time for us to be friends, not have to lie to each other. Loving somebody the way you have all these years, I guess maybe I was afraid you were being silly, not getting anything out of it. Unless you've got racks of mink coats hidden away someplace and jewelry enough to weigh down a queen. And that didn't seem like you. I was happy to hear at least your future's taken care of."

"Does Maggie know—about . . . ?"

"Mr. Martin? No. I think she's got an idea you picked up some kind of stock-market rumor working at the hospital. Tim doesn't know either, if you're wondering, although he may be starting to guess. Working all these years for Paige Properties—well, they hear almost everything that happens in the big office downtown, and what they don't hear they make up. I think he's getting the feeling he's only held the job because your Mr. Dan got it for him. He won't quit, of course, because he knows he wouldn't get anything else, not at his age. With the kids grown and gone and me out every day, he'd have no one to take it out on any more without the job."

"I'm . . . sorry."

"Why? Tim's been a bossy little bantam all his life. It'll be good for his immortal soul to have to hold his tongue for the rest of his years. Not to mention the relief for the rest of us."

"And my 'immortal soul'?"

"I don't make judgments," Patsy said briskly. "I've seen an awful lot of people go trotting off to church for an hour every day of the year and spend the other twenty-three hours making life hell for everyone around them. There are thousands of things I can think of worse than loving a man who isn't yours."

"It isn't quite that simple, Patsy."

"No, I don't suppose it is. I've seen pictures of Mrs. Martin, you know. In the papers, the society pages. A real beauty, that one. And not putting you down, if he's been seeing you all this time when he's married to her, there's got to be a lot more between the two of you than just thumping around in a bed together."

For the first time since her sister-in-law had announced she knew about Dan, Mary laughed. Patsy was right, of course, but the image of her years with Dan being reduced to what could happen sexually was hilarious.

"Did I say something funny?"

"No, Patsy. It's just that I haven't heard anyone talk common sense about me and Dan for—well, almost never. His secretary knew; we talked once or twice before she left Chicago. It's a great relief after keeping everything wrapped up and secret for so long."

"Mary, I didn't bring all this up today just to show off what I know of your life." Patsy stopped working and sat beside Mary. "It's just . . . well, whatever's between you two doesn't seem to be getting anywhere, does it? For the future, I mean."

"We never planned on a future, Patsy. You may not believe that, but it's true."

"Sure. A lot of people don't plan for it. Only you wake up tomorrow morning and it's already there."

"You sound like my mother."

"She hated me," Patsy said cheerfully. "I can't say I blame her. A fat slob with no mind of her own, producing babies we couldn't afford and nodding my head at everything her wonderful son said. There's a lot to be said against this women's liberation business, but it's made some of us think for the first time in our lives. And in my case, it didn't come a minute too soon." She went back to the stove, moving the steaming kettles to where they could cool. "I'm just hoping it's not too late for you."

"Me?" Mary found herself laughing again. Oddly, this was turning out to be a much easier family day than any she could remember. Telling the truth to people who don't judge you can do that. "Don't you think most of the world would think me far too liberated? And far too soon?"

"Because you loved a married man? Mary, that's not liberation. That's worse than being stuck in marriage. What did you get out of it? Oh, he loved you, still does, I guess. And I gather he's been generous. All those trips and dinners out, I suppose when he can get away. But did you ever have any *choices?* That's what life's all about, liberated or not, it seems to me. Being able to choose what you want—whether it's for this evening or next week or the rest of your life. You haven't had that in years, have you? Really?"

"I haven't wanted it. I chose Dan. That was enough."

"Sounds a grand love story, Mary. But you can't tell me it's made you as happy as you could be. Looks like he's been doing all the taking and you've been doing all the giving. And don't come back with stocks and bonds and vacations and free operations for your friends. Anybody with money can do that. But does he give anything of himself? Has he ever been there when *you* needed him? I'll bet you've been there all right, for him. But has he ever slammed the door on his beautiful wife and children and his glorious business and his big successes because *you* needed him?"

Givers and takers, Kay had said. "You don't get everything in life, Patsy."

"You can try," her sister-in-law answered shortly. How like Mary's mother she'd become, Mary thought. Both practical women who knew the rules, knew the reasons for keeping them, and also knew when it was time to use their own good hard common sense. Directly above where Mary was sitting was that other kitchen where she had waited out those two long nights so many years ago listening to what she fancied was her dead mother's advice about going to her first lunch with Dan. Then, the advice had seemed to her to be to move into the world, to move into life, and now it seemed that Patsy was saying much the same, only it meant some sort of denial of Dan, and that she knew she could never do.

Before she could think of a good answer, she heard the doorbell at the front of the house ring. Patsy, busy at the stove, said, "Get that, will you, Mary? I invited one more for dinner. For company. And Tim's getting so deaf he probably didn't even hear the bell."

Obediently, Mary got up, drying her hands on the apron as she crossed through the dining room to the hall. The table was indeed set for four. Patsy had moved her through the room so fast she hadn't noticed.

Tim glanced at her so curiously as she passed him that before she opened the door she knew who had been asked for Thanksgiving.

Jack Conroy stood there, hesitant but not shy. The flowers in his hand, Mary knew, were for his hostess, not for her.

But they were roses.

Nineteen ❧

It should have been the most uncomfortable meal of her life, full of awkward silences, unanswerable questions, resentments held from the years since they had seen each other. Instead it turned out to be a happy celebration. Patsy and Tim had obviously seen Jack since his return to the Chicago area, seen him, talked with him, and solved any nagging questions they may have had from the old days. Jack of all of them had changed the least physically, and Mary was glad she was wearing a new dress and—whatever other changes had taken place—she weighed no more than she did the day he left. That Tim and Patsy had clearly designed this dinner to bring Mary and her former husband together again was obvious and should have made both Jack and Mary uncomfortable. To her surprise, it didn't. Patsy's knowing of Dan and her relationship made Mary feel a good deal more at ease than she would have been otherwise. She suspected, while Tim might not know about Dan, Patsy had probably found some subtle way of informing Jack before inviting him for the holiday dinner.

Jack was much more relaxed than Mary had remembered him. He had always had a good sense of humor, and he used it through the meal, telling stories about his life on the West Coast meant to fill Mary in while keeping all of them laughing. His carpentry shop was doing well, from what she could gather during the meal. No mention was made by any of them of the money he had gambled away or his repayment of it to Mary. That, she knew, would come up on the drive home, for she was positive he would offer to see her back to her apartment that evening. They could talk then; in the meantime she found the holiday one of the happiest she had ever spent.

"I won't ask you up."

"That's all right. I should be at the shop early tomorrow anyway."

They were seated in his car outside her apartment building. As always she glanced at her windows, knowing they would be dark with Dan out with his wife and daughter, but it was a habit she had formed when she came home at night. The ride east from her brother and sister-in-law's had been full of conversation, but none of it about the matters she knew Jack wanted to discuss. Well, that could be handled here in the car.

"I would like to talk to you for a minute though," he went on.

"Of course."

"So many things to say." For the first time that day he seemed uneasy. "I know you got the money. I . . . I kept in touch with Fred Reiner."

She thought of the postal orders that had come so regularly. Although she had paid many of their bills from what she earned as Joan's private nurse, the money continued to come until she realized everything that had been owed to her and the others, as well as a sizable sum besides, more than enough to pay the lawyer's fee for handling their problems, had been received from California. Then, abruptly, still with no personal word or message to her of any kind, the envelopes no longer came.

She had talked to the lawyer about that, but he assured her that all claims against Jack, and, conceivably, against her as well, had been settled. Yes, Reiner admitted, he knew where Jack was, but he had been instructed not to tell anyone, even her. That conversation had taken place the first summer Joan and Dan had persuaded her to go to Europe together with them. She had been rushed, trying to arrange her time for travel, and as she remembered to her shame, sitting there in the car this cold November evening, she had not really been very curious about Jack or what was happening to him.

He had gone, she had fallen in love with Dan, and, incredibly, Dan was in love with her as well. That was more than enough to occupy her mind. When she returned from Europe and the pale blue envelopes no longer appeared regularly in her mailbox, she quite honestly neither missed them nor thought about them. Occasionally, over the years, she would dream of Jack, but always his features blurred together and she could barely remember what he looked like. Once, after such a dream, she had taken down a box of photographs, searching to find one of him among them, but in the few pictures she had he seemed to be squinting into the sunlight and it was hard to connect him to the man she had slept beside for two years of her life.

"Was it very difficult?" she asked as they sat in the front seat of his car. It was a new car, she had noticed when they left Tim and Patsy's, not an expensive Cadillac such as Dan had or the foreign car Joan acquired once she could drive again. The car was like Jack today, she realized: new, American, without a history, efficient, and attractive in a way Mary could only think of as "comfortably practical." "Was it? To save up all that money? I worried about that." That much at least was true.

"At first. But I not only wanted to do it, I had to. That's when I started getting into carpentry. I'd been such an idiot before. Working with my hands wasn't good enough for Jack Conroy. Oh, no, I had to be in a store or an office, had to be in charge of things, couldn't get my hands dirty—"

"You were never like that!"

"Yes, I was. No lies now, Mary. It's all so long ago. Anyway, out in California I realized trying to step up the ladder to some kind of white-collar life wasn't for me. I'd been trained in the orphanage, and later in the army, to use wood. I found I was good at it. Not much steady work at first." He grinned at her in the darkness. "That's why the money orders were a little . . . uncertain at the beginning. But gradually I began to get a good reputation. As a solid citizen, no less. Hard to believe?"

"No," she said slowly. "I always knew you were a decent man. The gambling—well, I suppose in a way I didn't even realize I must have put some sort of pressure on you."

"You did nothing of the kind. The pressure was because I was trying to buy you."

Suddenly she felt uneasy. She knew what he meant and it was too close to the truth.

"I was. I knew you didn't love me when you married me. I guess I thought I could win you with a lot of fancy presents. Shows how little I knew you. Or myself." He sighed and leaned back, staring out at the empty street in front of them. "I was so greedy in those days. I wanted so much. To get ahead, to be a success, to have a beautiful woman like you love me. I couldn't take working one day at a time for that. I wanted to leap forward, make up for all the time I'd already lost."

"And now?"

"It's different, Mary. I think I finally grew up. Wanting to pay you back every cent I'd cost, that was a good start. Imagine me on a budget!

But you can learn anything if you want to bad enough, and I learned. And there's something good about working with your hands, something that beats adding up accounts at the end of a day in a hardware store. Or driving a truck. I did that for a while, too. But when you make something, even if it's just a cellar floor, you can see it right there . . . and if you've been sloppy or lazy or done a bad job, it's right there too."

"I doubt if you'd ever be that." And the nights? How did you spend the nights? she found herself wondering.

"I didn't become a saint, Mary," he said quietly.

It was the way he used to look at the beginning, before their marriage. She hoped she wasn't going to cry. It would make what she had to tell him so much harder.

"The gambling stopped. I wish I could make some big thing about it, like joining some kind of a group—they have them, you know—but I didn't. At first I didn't have any money to gamble, and I was new in town so I couldn't get any trusting buddies to come up with cash. Then, when I was working, I got too busy to follow all the track sheets or find a card game. And next I wanted my own shop, and tools are expensive. Gradually, the gambling just sort of slipped out of my life."

You didn't need it, Mary thought. Because I wasn't there, cold and unloving, accepting a life of failure in such a way you had to fight me back with dreams and hopes of good luck changing things.

"Fairly soon, I stopped doing cellar floors and got into fancy paneling. There are a lot of people on the West Coast with good taste and the money to pay for what they like. The shop got bigger. I had to bring in some young assistants. Before I knew it, I was in that white-collar world most of the time after all."

"Is that why you came back to Chicago? To start over again?" But she thought she knew why he had come back, and it made her uneasy.

"No. I . . . I had a good offer to sell out. I turned it down at first. Life was pleasant out there."

He thought of Vivian, the woman he had lived with those years. She had been pretty and warm and loving, at least at first. Then later, when he kept avoiding the subject of marriage, knowing he would never marry anybody again, she had turned bitter, accusing him of coldness, spending her afternoons in bars until that last day when she had been too drunk to drive a car but had tried anyway.

"There was a woman," he explained to Mary, not able to make himself look at her. "Nice. Kind. We had some good times together. But she wanted marriage and—well, I guess I couldn't think about that. She had an accident. When it was all over, I just wanted to get away. I didn't care if I ever saw the goddamn sunshine or ocean again."

"I'm sorry. I'd hoped that you might find someone, have a family. You'd have been good at that."

"She had a couple of kids," he answered, still not looking at her. "I guess I had a hand in raising them. We still keep in touch."

Just a few words, she thought, and yet she knew what his life had been like and knew his experience with her had destroyed any chance this other woman might have had for a secure world. Your sins come back to haunt you, she thought, and shivered a little in her coat.

"Cold?"

"No." Funny after all these years he could sense so slight a movement of hers as that.

"So," he went on, knowing some answer would have to be made for the question she had asked him, "I decided if I was going to start all over again, I'd better find out first where I stood with the past. That's why I came here." He looked at her directly. "It seems whatever past I have that matters is here in Chicago."

Now, she thought. I have to tell him now, make it simple and blunt and direct, not any delicate hint such as Patsy might have given him. Tell him so he can be free of me, if indeed I am the past he misses. Which is probably giving myself too much credit, she thought. After all, he'd been back several years now and had made no attempt to reach her.

"I'm involved with a man," she said abruptly. "A married man. I don't know if Tim and Patsy told you."

"I knew." He didn't want to explain to her how it had happened; he'd promised himself that day he had seen them together having lunch never to mention it.

"You did?"

"I saw you together once. He seemed like a nice guy. Good-looking. I gather a big success."

He'd been having a luncheon meeting with the owner of the restaurant, who was thinking of redecorating the place in elegant wood paneling. The shop in Skokie had just opened, and Jack was prepared to cut his price to the minimum to land the job. The owner noticed Jack's interest in the couple by the window. "That's Dan Martin. He's a big real estate guy around here. And the lady with him definitely isn't Mrs. Martin. Those two have been coming here for years. I guess they figure it's safe. We don't get much of a luncheon crowd."

Jack had moved his chair around at that, to keep his back to them, and deliberately, because his first instinct had been to punch the owner, he settled for the way respectable men fight, by doubling his price. He had no desire ever to see the restaurant again. However, the owner accepted his terms, and by establishing his work as expensive but worth it, Jack's career in Chicago had begun to flourish from then on. Dan Martin, I owe you one, he had often thought afterward.

"Yes. He's a nice guy. And a success." What more could she say? That she had loved him more than she ever loved this man next to her, who had married her and desired her and wanted to give her the world? That could only hurt him after all this time, and she had no desire to hurt anybody.

"Are you getting married?"

She knew she should give him the same answer she had given Patsy, but some part of her pride made her think of the afternoon Joan had come back to Chicago, a frightened and unhappy woman. "We talked about it," she said, hating herself for the half lie. "It's just not possible."

"I hope you don't mind my saying I'm glad."

He let her out, seeing her to the door of the building, shaking hands politely. If she had thought his last remark had been some kind of indication he intended to see her again, she was to be surprised. It was a long time before he would talk to her again privately.

Dan Martin was having a terrible Thanksgiving. He liked young Michael Harris's parents well enough, and the young man was exactly the sort he had hoped Paige would eventually choose as a husband. Still, it had come as a surprise when after dinner Mickey and his father had asked him into the den for brandy and "a little conversation on our own," as the senior Mr. Harris put it. Apparently the boy had already proposed to Paige, though he was still in school—proposed and been accepted.

"Generally, I'm not in favor of young people getting married until the husband is financially established," said Mr. Harris. "However, Mike's doing well in school, and of course he'll come into my firm as soon as he passes the bar exam. In the meantime, I'm sure we can arrange some kind of income for them."

"Paige has money from a trust fund of her grandmother's." Dan sounded surly, even to himself. He couldn't figure out why he was reacting this way. Maybe it was the heavy meal. His stomach or something was bothering him.

"That's Paige's money, sir. I want to be able to handle our household and living expenses myself." The sturdy young man seemed quite determined.

"Perhaps you will find a little something in your Christmas stocking that will help with that, Michael," his father said genially. He freshened Dan's glass. "The children would like to announce their engagement

New Year's Eve. We were thinking of giving a dance for them at the club. The wedding probably not until June, when you've finished your classes; what do you think, Michael? Then you can have the summer for the honeymoon."

New Year's Eve! Dan realized somehow he must have suspected this announcement was going to ruin his plans. Maybe that's why he had felt so uncomfortable. It meant any chance of getting away this winter with Mary was doomed. He could hardly leave before the first of the year, with the necessary celebrations that would take place between the two families for Christmas. And afterward. . . . Dan knew the level of Chicago society that the Harrises and Joan were on well enough to know there would be a series of parties through the winter, showing the two families united in their happiness at the forthcoming wedding. He could see stretching before him the long frigid months of smiling politely as the women made endless plans over weekly dinners. There would be the search he, as the real estate expert, would be expected to make for the proper home for the young couple. The business lunches he would have to have with Mr. Harris after the right property had been found about how to persuade the independent couple to accept their parents' largesse. Damn it, he thought. I've finally got more money than I dreamed possible, and I'm still not free!

She wouldn't say anything, of course, but Mary would be so disappointed.

Mary found it easier to hide her relief that their winter plans had been changed in her happiness for Paige. Barely half a year earlier, the girl had seemed determined to slide into the world of the lost and lonely, hopelessly in love with a man who would never be good enough for her, waiting on tables to try and catch his attention, trying to pretend she cared about a singing career. Now her future seemed assured, as much as it ever could be for anyone. Mary had always liked the Harris boy, and he impressed her with his strength and common sense the night Paige had tried to kill herself. Through all that time he had obviously never lost faith or stopped loving the girl. He knew her weaknesses, and it had not changed her in his eyes. How Mary wished she could talk to Paige! Just to hear in her own words she was happy, that the past was behind her, and she was really in love and counting the days until her married life began.

But she would never hear that. Paige would never talk to her. Mary knew, with a sinking feeling, there would be a warm morning the following June when she would awaken with a start, thinking, I'm late! There's someplace I must be today. Think it and sink back on her pillows, knowing it was Paige's wedding day and she could not be there. Could not see her walk proudly up the aisle to the young man waiting for her with joy and love in his eyes.

"It's all right, Dan," she said gently, the weekend after Thanksgiving. "There'll be other winters. We'll have that vacation yet."

They saw less of each other that winter, Dan and Mary. Even though Joan had placed no further restrictions, his fears of what the season would be like were only too accurate. Somehow, when the long social evenings were finally over, he seemed to lack the energy to go back out into the cold again. It was simpler to call Mary from the private line of his bedroom phone. She was the same as always, just the sound of her voice made him relaxed and comfortable, but he had the feeling sometimes he was not the person she had been expecting to call. It was a foolish thought. He knew her life as well as she knew his, and there would be no one else calling her at such a late hour. Paige, he decided. She's still hoping that Paige will call her someday, although they both knew his daughter never would.

If Dan had voiced his thoughts to Mary, she would have agreed with him, marveling, as she had so often, how well he knew her. It would have been idiotic after all this time to expect Jack to call her, especially late at night. That was a time for separated lovers, or the lonely and the unhappy or the drunk. Jack was none of those, never had been.

Though she saw less of Dan that winter, Mary found herself more at peace than she had felt for a long time. Tim and Patsy seemed to have decided with all their children out of the house that this was a year for entertaining. They had always given parties for Christmas and New Year's and the night before each of those holidays. Now they seemed to have expanded the festivities to forgotten birthdays and anniversaries. Hardly a week went by without Patsy calling Mary at the hospital with another invitation.

The reason for the parties was clear and should have made Mary uncomfortable. Jack was invited to each gathering. Patsy, at least, had made up her mind that he and Mary should become involved again. It might have been annoying to Mary if he had shown any interest in her sister-in-law's plans. But Jack, while always friendly and polite to her, never singled her out at any of the gatherings that winter. He would spend as much time talking to the other people at each party as he did with her, and after that first night he never offered to drive her home again. He was not being rude or distant, Mary realized as she thought about it. He was just not making any more of their past than she herself wanted. She wondered sometimes if it were an attempt to intrigue her, but she dismissed the thought almost instantly. She was a middle-aged woman, in love with someone else. Jack was simply showing good manners in not making life uncomfortable for her. Besides, there were other women at the parties, younger than she and better looking, who made no secret they found him attractive. He was managing his own life very well, and she was happy for him.

She told herself.

One party she knew she would not attend was the one Tim and Patsy decided to give on St. Valentine's Day. It was so unlike them to be sentimental about such an occasion, Mary would probably have declined in any case. But that had always been a very special day in her life with Dan. Generally he was the least romantic of men, but that particular day seemed to mean something special to him. No matter what plans might separate them on other holidays, that day, or rather evening, had always been just for the two of them, from the time they had first become lovers. A long box of flowers would always be waiting for her when she came home from the hospital, taken in by the two Canadian sisters who ran a dressmaking shop out of their ground-floor apartment. There would be no note, of course; that had not changed in the years they had known each other. At their last meeting they would have set the time of his arrival and where they would go for dinner, their choice limited by the necessity of picking a place where the kitchen stayed open late, for they had formed the habit that evening of going to bed together first. It was the one predictable custom of their quiet lives, and Mary, even in the lean years, would plan some special treat beforehand, caviar or imported pâté, all carefully arranged for his arrival. That was the one evening of the year she allowed herself to think of their relationship as something illicitly erotic. Almost laughing to herself, she would put on a special robe, something he would not have seen before, and indulge herself in the perfume he persisted in giving her, although it was usually much too strong for her tastes.

This Valentine's Day would be the same, she knew. He had already canceled any tentative plans for a gathering with the Harrises, stating firmly this was one evening the engaged couple didn't need older people around. He made that very clear, he told Mary the preceding Saturday night, when they planned their evening. If Joan or Paige knew why he was so firm about this, they had the good taste not to dispute him.

By seven o'clock Mary had everything ready for his arrival. The apartment was fresh and shining, the tray with the cocktail food was on the low table near his easy chair, and she had filled the silver ice bucket to the top. She had managed to leave the hospital early, so she had time to take a long bath and to soften her hair that she'd had newly styled during her lunch hour. It was snowing outside, and occasionally the small fire in the fireplace hissed when some flakes made their way down the chimney. She settled on the couch with a magazine to read while she waited.

By a quarter to eight she was beginning to be a little concerned. Dan was often late. It was one of his less attractive qualities, but at least it was consistent. She had learned over the years there was nothing she could do to change him and, considering their situation, to become upset about it was useless. She got up and went to the window. The snow was heavier now; the street below was almost completely white. She shivered a little and put another log on the fire.

By eight thirty she could no longer pretend that he had just been delayed. Before this she had never had to face one of the major problems of being involved with a married man: the broken date, the missed meeting, the waited-for phone call. During the time they had been separated in the past years, when it had been difficult because of the life Joan had planned for him and his evenings had grown increasingly occupied, he had never failed to call her either at home or at her office. If he would not be able to meet her when they had planned or one of their evenings had to be canceled, he always phoned, never leaving her to sit alone and wonder where he was or with whom. Even if he was delayed for as little as half an hour, he would try to call to let her know that a conference was running late or that he was out at the airport site and the traffic was impossible. Never had he let an hour and a half pass in which she would worry. He knew her too well and loved her too much for that. It was one of the courtesies she had not expected; she knew how busy and also how singleminded he was during his days at the office. True, he would take it for granted she would wait for him, no matter how late he might be, or be accepting if their plans had to be changed because other matters in his life came ahead of being with her. But she had known that was part of the bargain when their relationship began. She had not complained then, and she would not complain now.

Only by nine o'clock she could no longer pretend she wasn't worried, and, having faced that, she realized for the first time in the years they had been together there was literally nothing she could do. If it had been a missed luncheon date, she would have called his office; she had no hesitancy about that, even before the night Joan learned of their life together. But at nine in the evening there was no way she could reach him. It was impossible to call the apartment. It was too late for Lila to still be there, even if she dared take the chance she might answer the phone and be willing or able to talk to her. If Joan or Paige answered the phone, they would hang up as soon as they heard her voice.

Conceivably, she could dress and walk through the snowy streets to his apartment building and ask the doorman if he had come in, but if she got an answer, it would only cause more problems. His family might know of their relationship, but it had been a matter of pride to her that no one else would learn of it through her. Kay, of course, had guessed, and so had Patsy, but that had not been her doing. Even talking about Dan to Jack, she had never mentioned his name. It had meant she had never been able to talk about the happiness he had given her any more than she could seek comfort for the difficult times, but it gave her the security of knowing he could never blame her if people learned of their affair.

By ten o'clock she forced herself to make a sandwich and to eat half of it. She took off the new peignoir almost in anger, it seemed so silly and foolish to her now. She thrust it impatiently into the back of her closet and wrapped herself in the navy blue wool robe she had bought for Dan two Christmases before. It was warm and comfortable, and she tried to pretend as she hugged herself by the fire that it was Dan's arms holding her.

She allowed herself to call the hospital; if anything had happened, surely he would have been taken there. But in chatting with her friends on duty on the private floors, she could not bring herself to mention his name, only hoping that if anything had happened they would mention it first, either out of the desire to discuss any change in their routine or because they had heard the gossip of her relationship with him. But she learned nothing from her phone calls.

By eleven the fire was dead. She turned out the lights but left the chain off the door, just in case the snowstorm had delayed him in some way and he might still come.

She thought of taking a pill before she went to bed, knowing without it there was no chance of her sleeping that night, but she was afraid some emergency might come up and she didn't dare risk the chance of being too groggy to handle it. She checked the lights of his apartment from her bedroom window. The lights were on, although not in his room, and she wondered who was still up. Tonight she would not pull down the shade. From her bed she would be able to see if the lights went on in his room. It would be something to occupy the long hours ahead.

The phone rang shortly after midnight.

"Mary? It's Lila. I'm afraid I've got bad news for you."

"Dan . . . ?"

"He had a heart attack this afternoon. The whole house has been crazy. This is the first time I've had a chance to get to the phone."

"Heart attack?" Someday the irony of its happening on the special feast day for lovers would make her cry out in pain, but all she could do at the moment was to keep the panic from rising inside her. "Where is he? How . . . how did it happen?"

"They took him to the hospital." Lila mentioned the name. It was not Midwestern. While it had an excellent cardiac care unit, it was no better than the hospital where Mary worked and where Dan was still a member of the Board of Directors. "Miss Joan was very insistent on where they take him," Lila went on. "He came home after lunch complaining he wasn't feeling well, that he wanted a nap."

Dan? A nap? Never would he have thought of such a thing if he were well. In fact, when they had a day together "nap" had been one of their code words for going to bed in the afternoon—and not to sleep.

"They got an ambulance. I think he was trying to tell me to call you, but they were all around him, and Miss Joan, she was close to hysterics, and the doctor made me go out there with them to look after her. I just got home now."

"Lila, how bad is it? Did they say?"

"Mary, I honestly don't know. They gave him something to make him rest, but he was all pale and drawn-out looking. I know they've sent for Joey. I just hope that boy has enough love in his heart to come." Lila waited for Mary to speak, but when the silence on the other end of the line continued she said finally, "Mary? Are you still there?"

"I'm here."

"I'll try to call you every day. If I hear anything."

"Thank you. I . . . I'd appreciate that."

"Mary, you sound . . . are you all right?"

No, of course I'm not all right, she wanted to scream. Part of me is dying and I can't do anything about it! I can't hold him or comfort him or touch him; I may never be able to do that again. Because *they* surround him and they'll never forgive me, or him.

"It's . . . all right, Lila," she managed at last. "Thank you for calling." Very gently, as if she were holding something fragile, she put down the phone.

After a long while she stood and pulled down the shade at the bedroom window.

Twenty

I f Mary had ever believed loving Daniel Martin was something that deserved punishment, she received it during the next weeks. It took all her strength to go to work each day, to appear calm, to keep her section of the hospital functioning efficiently, to force herself not to jump every time the phone rang. It rang often, but seldom with news of Dan. Lila tried to keep her informed, but there were few developments. She had not actually seen Dan since the day they had taken him to the hospital, and the conversations she heard at the apartment gave her little to report to Mary.

"He just seems to be holding his own," she would report to Mary when she did call. "They've brought in specialists and they keep taking tests and there's some talk of putting in a pacemaker."

"Is it that bad?" It still seemed a weird new invention to Mary, even though it had been in use for several years. The thought of something foreign placed under his skin . . .

"They haven't made a decision about it yet. Joey's still here, he goes out to the hospital, but I don't know if he goes into Mr. Dan's room or not. Paige's turned out to be a real help. She keeps her mother quiet, and she doesn't get all stiff-backed if something doesn't go her way. Not like she used to."

Mary could see Paige as Lila talked of her; she'd be someone Joan could lean on, the warmth and kindness that had always been inside her finally allowed to come out now she was safely in love.

"Thanks, Lila. Call me tomorrow? Please? Even if there isn't anything new?"

Lila would promise, and Mary would put down the phone. A dozen times she started to call the hospital herself, but she knew she would get no information. She spent one long Sunday afternoon going through the personnel files of Midwestern Hospital, checking them with a directory for the hospital where Dan was to see if there was anyone, even the slightest acquaintance, who had transfered there that she could contact. There was no one.

Often in the evening when she finished work she would be tempted to walk to the hospital itself, make up some lie, some excuse, anything so she could at least see him, but she knew it would be pointless. The small story in the newspapers of his attack had mentioned that the family had requested no visitors. It might have been printed especially for her, she thought with bitterness.

Yet she could feel no anger at Joan. Her strongest impulse besides seeing Dan was to help his wife. Joan had built so much of her world around Dan and his strength she must be more lost than Mary at this time. There was a terrible irony in the fact the decisions they had made in their lives made it impossible for the two women who loved Dan most to be unable to comfort each other when they both needed it.

The people in Mary's life who had always thought her cool and serene would never have believed the wild switches of mood she experienced these days. On impulse she would enter a church, any church, and kneel, praying fiercely, promising all sorts of impossible things to a God she knew existed but whom she couldn't seem to reach. Or she would find herself striding down a side street late at night, unable to sleep, her face contorted with anger, her lips moving wordlessly. If anyone had been tempted to harm her those lonely nights, the very fury of her walk would have turned him away. Sometimes, exhausted, she would spend hours just lying on the bed in her apartment, her arms stretched out wide as if somewhere in what had become a vast expanse of sheets and blankets she must surely be able to reach him. Two of the weekends she kept the television set on all night, hoping to find something that would distract her, only to see an actor who had hair like Dan's or another whose voice sounded like his. Once they had shown a movie filmed in a place in Europe where they had been together, and she found herself sobbing uncontrollably.

By the end of March she thought she would go mad.

It was Jack who helped her, almost by accident. She had turned down several of Tim and Patsy's invitations, not bothering to make an excuse, so she had a feeling her sister-in-law sent Jack the night she found him waiting for her outside the hospital. He denied it, saying he'd been called in on the possibility of doing some work on the rather austere front lobby. She didn't believe him, but it was good to see someone to whom she would not have to lie or pretend that everything was normal. Jack took her firmly by the arm and walked toward his car. "I think you need dinner and somebody to talk to," he said, and it was not a suggestion but a statement.

They went to a modest place on the North Side. Mary had never been there before, but the owners seemed to know Jack and with great tact seated them at a quiet table and, after taking their orders, left them alone. Jack asked no questions but led her into talking. It wasn't hard. So much had been bottled up inside her these past weeks she probably would have babbled everything to a complete stranger, if she could have found one with the patience to listen. When she finally finished and was mopping her eyes, their meal forgotten in front of them, Jack sat back silently for a moment, obviously thinking his way through what she had told him.

"His family doctor," he said at last. "You must know who his doctor is. You could make an appointment, tell him what you've told me, and he could fill you in on how bad it is."

"I thought of that." What hadn't she thought of? "Only he doesn't have a real doctor, not on a permanent basis for checkups and things. I've tried to get him to have one for years. But he's always been so healthy."

"The heart specialist. Working in a hospital you must know who the family would pick."

"Jack, I've been working in the laboratory file section for years! I don't know any more than anyone else!"

"Maybe I can find out."

"You?"

"Sure. Some of my customers are rich . . . and not any too young. One of them is bound to know the best heart specialist in town. The way you describe Dan's wife, she'd have called in the best. I know they all take that oath about secrecy, but they're human beings too, aren't they?"

That night was the first time since Valentine's Day that Mary slept without nightmares.

By the end of the week Jack had found the name of the specialist in charge of Dan's case and had made an appointment for Mary. "I gave him your maiden name," he said as he picked her up in the car to take her to the appointment. "Just in case. We don't know what the family has been telling him. No point in getting his guard up."

"Jack, how can I thank you?"

He smiled at her, somewhat enigmatically, a look rare on his face. "Maybe I didn't do it for you, Mary. Maybe I felt I owed Dan a favor." He got out and held open the car door on her side. "Take your time. I'll be here to drive you home when you come down."

He didn't have long to wait. The meeting went badly from the beginning. She recognized the doctor as soon as she was shown into his office. He often had dinner with his shrewd-eyed wife in the restaurants where Dan would take her, and while the two men would nod to each other, this was one couple to whom Dan made no effort to make introductions. They were clearly of Joan's circle of friends, although Mary could not remember meeting them with her. However, from the look on the doctor's face when she entered his office, he was all too aware of her position in Dan's life.

"I should have expected you," the doctor said, making no effort to rise. "Scanlon's not the sort of name I usually have as a patient. I suppose I should have been wondering how long it would take you to track me down."

"I want to know about Dan Martin," she said simply.

He looked at her for a long moment as if trying to decide something. Certainly she did not look like the sort of heartless homewrecker his wife claimed she must be. In fact, she had never looked that. If it weren't for the frequency with which he had seen her with Dan he would never have considered them to be involved in such a way. She was a neat, attractively dressed middle-aged woman, pleasant enough to look at but certainly no beauty. And yet "the affair," as his wife described it with a malicious bite in her voice, had apparently been going on for some years, must still be going on, or why would she have come to him? Not to mention that Martin himself had been fretting almost since his arrival in the hospital for a phone to be placed by his bed. The family, wisely, had forbidden that. Looking at Mary, he began to wonder at their wisdom.

He made up his mind abruptly. "Mr. Martin's had a major heart attack. We put in a pacemaker earlier this week. How he'll react to that, we'll have to wait and see."

So many questions she wanted to ask. She should have written them down beforehand, but she hadn't been thinking clearly. "Can I see him?"

"No." There was a stricken look on her face, and he made an effort to speak more gently. "It's not just the family's orders, although they *have* given them. At this particular time it would be bad for the patient to get upset, to be worrying—"

"He must be anyway."

How well she knows him, the doctor thought. "He has a very good chance of recovery," he added. "Basically speaking, he's in good health. Blood pressure too high, of course, but that can be brought down with a change of diet and medicine. If he agrees to a . . . calmer life, there's no reason why he shouldn't live another twenty years."

"I see." She got up to leave. "Thank you."

She had not asked the one question the doctor had been waiting for her to ask, the question he imagined any mistress would want to know about the man she claimed to love. "Aren't you going to ask me if he'll be able to resume a normal sex life?"

"No," she said quietly and left the office.

An unusual woman, he thought, but that was an opinion he decided to keep to himself.

In the end it was Lila who broke through the walls of silence the family had built around Dan. She had been to see him on her afternoon off, finding Paige in the room and, when she went outside, Joey waiting as well. Dan seemed pitifully weak in the hospital bed, and there was little she could tell him in front of his children. She simply held his hand and said, "It's going to be all right, Mr. Dan. I'm keeping everything the way you'd want it." It was the closest she could get to giving him a message, but he didn't seem to understand. His eyes were sad and puzzled, as if he had moved very far away from them all. He's bad, Lila thought. Real bad.

Paige and Joey walked with her to the elevator. They were uncharacteristically silent, and she knew they were waiting for her to speak, to tell them what to do as she had when they were children.

"Let's sit down here for a moment," she said as they reached the small lobby. "I want to know more about your father's condition."

"He doesn't seem to be getting any better," Paige said. Tears were forming in her eyes, and tears were the last thing Lila wanted to see. All they would do was make everything fuzzy and sentimental, and she needed to speak to them strongly.

"No crying, Paige. Your father's a strong man and he can be again."

"They're not so sure about that." This from Joey. He'd grown since he'd gone away to school; he had a long, lanky look that reminded Lila of her older son, safely back from war. Pray God Joey never has to go! "The hospital's calling in another expert tomorrow. And there's talk of taking him either to Johns Hopkins or the Mayo Clinic."

Out of Chicago! That would just about kill Mary, Lila thought. She'd heard the tension growing each day in the other woman's voice when they spoke. "There's something right here that'd do him more good than a lot of experts and trailing around the country." She wondered if she'd have to spell it out, but they both looked away from her steady gaze. They were embarrassed, which was a lot better, Lila thought, than tears. "You know what I'm talking about. And whatever you may think or feel has nothing to do with it, not if you care about your father. That's between the two of them, and it's nobody else's business."

"Lila." Joey straightened up and tried to stare her down, but she was too strong and knew about too much of their lives to give in.

"I mean what I say. Mr. Dan's fretting and he's not going to get any better until his mind's at rest about her. All the doctors in the world can't change that." She could see this was something they had already discussed, probably more than once. "I think it's time," Lila went on firmly, "that everybody that's healthy acted like a grown-up."

Paige didn't look at Joey. She reached for the phone on the table next to the couch where they were sitting and asked for an outside number. When the connection was made, still without glancing at the others, she said in a clear voice, "Would you connect me with Mrs. Conroy, please?"

They arranged it carefully. Lila promised to stay with Joan in case she decided to visit Dan on impulse that evening. Joey, who had not said a word during or after the phone call, disappeared, leaving Paige to wait for Mary. Paige didn't know what she would say to her. Anything that came to her mind seemed either too formal or, worse, vindictive. However, when the elevator finally opened, there was no need for words. Mary reached out for her in silence and Paige found herself embracing the older woman.

"Thank you," Mary whispered. "Oh, thank you, Paige! I've been so worried!"

Paige nodded, unable to trust her voice, and led her down the corridor to her father's room. "Don't be too long," she forced herself to say. "They'll want to give him another pill."

Mary nodded, trying to smile. "I know. Hospitals don't seem to change, do they?" She went in and closed the door behind her.

Dan was propped up in bed, although his eyes were closed and the book he had been holding had slipped from his fingers. For a moment Mary thought she had come too late, but he opened his eyes and looked directly at her. Slowly he began to smile.

"Not much of a Valentine's Day, is it?" he managed.

"We've had better." She came close to his bed and took his hand. How could he have become so thin in so short a time? Always his hands had been warm and strong, so vital and full of energy it was like feeling an electrical current all through her body when he touched her.

"I . . . I tried to call you—"

"Ssssh. Don't worry. Lila let me know. She even persuaded the kids . . . well, it's all right now."

"Mary?" Even his voice sounded different, strained and thin, like an old, old man, and yet he wasn't; he could never be that to her. "I'm scared."

"You'd be the fool of the world if you weren't," she answered, trying to keep her voice brisk and light. She'd known other patients who had lived full, active lives, never meeting illness, and when something drastic happened to them they became suddenly defeated by the realization of their own mortality. It had almost happened to Joan, and it mustn't happen to Dan. "However, if you have to have a heart attack, this is certainly the right time."

That sparked his curiosity, as she had hoped it would. "How could there be such a thing as a 'right time'?" he said, almost with a trace of his old indignation.

"With what they've been discovering the last four or five years, I'd say the time is right now." She leaned over, touching the bandage she could feel on his chest under his pajama jacket. "Does the pacemaker hurt?"

"No." He was growing surly. Obviously, during the last weeks everyone who had gathered around him had been anxious and worried, regarding him with faces that clearly spelled death. And here she was, after all this time, treating him as if he were here for nothing more than an upset stomach, something that could be cured by some new miracle antacid pill!

"Don't look so grumpy. You're going to get well."

"Maybe I don't want to." He turned his head away from her sullenly. So like a child, she thought. But she knew this time she could not comfort him as such; it could mean the fear inside would continue to grow and she must put an end to it this evening, for she doubted if she would have another chance.

"That's fine talk from a man like you," she started. She sat on the bed beside him. It was strictly against the regulations of all hospitals, but she did it anyway, touching the back of her hand to his, just as they had that night so long ago when she had first revealed her love for him. "I can't see you just quitting, now you're on top of the world."

"I'm dying," he said.

"Do you know anybody who isn't?" He smiled a little at that, and she took his hand silently, allowing herself to study him for the first time. He was pale and terribly thin, but she could feel the pulse of his blood, moving steadily through his wrist. "There can be a lot of life ahead of you, Dan. If you want it."

"With you?" His voice was harsh. "A sick old man with a heart attack? I wouldn't dare touch you."

"They say sex can be very good for heart patients," she said lightly. "Gets the heart moving." She smiled. "Besides, there's been a lot more between us than just that."

"Not enough." His voice was quiet, and she had never seen him look so sad. "I should have married you. You deserved that."

"Nobody deserves anything they get, Dan. Not the good or the bad. Haven't you learned that yet?"

"I don't learn so fast, Mary."

He sighed a little, but there was a faint color in his cheeks for the first time and she could feel that he was beginning to relax. The fear and panic were starting to leave, at least a little.

"It's not death I'm so afraid of," he went on, when he had eased himself into a more comfortable position. "It's the dying part. Tubes and medicines and this." He pointed one finger at the bandage covering the pacemaker. "All the stuff they tie you down with . . . being dependent. . . ."

"Being patient," she added, with a small smile. "Even the rich and successful have to learn that sooner or later." She'd said the same to Joan once, long ago, and the thought made her sad. Now everything was changed: it was Dan who needed her and Joan who was well. In that moment she realized again how much of her life had been devoted to them both. "You're going to get well, Dan. I know that."

"Only I still won't have what I want."

"Did you ever know what that was?" Don't let him say it was me, she thought. Don't let him torture himself with dreams of a life that never could have existed. It would only hurt him more if he still thought that was the truth.

"I guess I didn't," he said at last. He took her hand, holding it loosely in his own, not from fear or desire but just in companionship. "I thought it was all the things I've been fighting for all these years, only they don't seem to matter much any more. I guess I've never quite known where I was. You go from being broke, your knees out of your trousers, to marrying the boss's daughter, to having the freedom to think big, and then to make the big things happen—well, somehow the step between seems to get forgotten."

"The step between?" She had never heard him talk like this before. He was searching for something not realistic and down-to-earth, but something vague that he could not quite describe.

"I guess you'd call it being middle-class. Something like that. A home and someone who loves you. No big ambitions, no big thrills or triumphs, just the quiet, ordinary things that millions of people take for granted." He looked at her as if he were seeing her for the first time. "I guess in a way you were part of that. Your apartment. I could be myself there. Not having to be something I wasn't."

But that was only part of you, Dan, she thought. Like an actor coming offstage away from the spotlights and the successes that meant far more than a quiet dressing room. For in time you would have tired of it, tired of me, and would have considered yourself chained. That would have left me with nothing.

"You're thinking I don't mean it." For a moment his eyes were as wise and shrewd as they had been when he was well. Quick as always, he guessed her thoughts. "But I do. All those houses out by the airport; as I was building them, I kept thinking, This is where I could have lived with Mary. This could have been my life. Maybe that's why I cared about them so much." He smiled for the first time, remembering. "The fights I used to have with Evan because I wanted the homes to have real back yards, not just a little patch of grass. And big windows and fireplaces that worked. I was building our house, Mary, the one we'll never live in. Lying here, I think about the couples that will, and I envy them. I hope they'll be happy."

He sounded so sad she knew he would make her cry if she didn't change his mood. She wouldn't cry, not tonight, not when this might be the last time she would ever see him.

"Half the people in those houses will go to their graves wishing they had become someone like you. So don't give me any nonsense about wanting a vine-covered cottage, not at this stage of your life." She made herself smile as she said it, but she could feel the strain in the muscles of her face.

"Won't let me get away with anything, will you?"

"Six months in one of those houses, Dan Martin, and you'd be organizing the community as a separate town and suing the city. I know you."

"You do, damn it." He sighed. "But you would have been happy there."

"I'm happy right where I am, in the home you found for me." She let herself touch his brow; it was warm but not feverish. His eyelids closed for a moment, enjoying the touch of her hand soothing him as she had for so many years.

"It's strange, lying here, Mary. You think of so many things, what you did and what you didn't do." He looked at her directly. "We've had good times together, haven't we?"

"The best." He'd taken her out of her narrow life, shown her the world, loved her, and let her love him back; how could he feel she had missed anything? Only she knew it bothered him still. "I saw Paige. She's grown so beautiful, Dan."

"I think she understands now. I don't know about Joey."

"He'll grow older, the way we have. He'll learn."

"Joan . . ." The way he said the name, Mary thought for a moment he had forgotten who was touching him, and the sick feeling of the past weeks came back. "Can we talk about Joan for a moment?"

"Of course." Like old times. How many nights had he started a conversation the same way, worrying about Joan: her health, her progress, whether she could possibly guess about their relationship, all the worries that had surrounded him in the outside world.

"She'll need someone like you, Mary, if I'm not around." He reached for her hand and squeezed it tightly. "She needs you anyway. The way we all have. Maybe she won't admit it—at least, not while I'm alive—but it's true."

"Please, Dan, don't talk about death!" All her stratagems had failed. She'd not altered his mood one bit.

"I have to, Mary. It'll happen sometime. Joan'll be alone. She'll hate that. The kids will be married and leading their own lives. Evan will never forgive her. I think you could help her then."

Joan. Mary was sitting beside him, holding his hand, and with all the agony she'd been through trying to reach him, Joan was still the person he worried about the most, the one who needed to be protected. All right, God, she thought. Whatever I've done, I'm paying for it now.

"We'll help each other, Joan and I. If she'll let me."

"She will. If there's anger, it's . . . only because she loves me. I guess she always has, even when she turned away from me."

"I know." She knew she should go. He was getting tired, and the last thing she could afford was for her visit to have injured him in any way. Only they'd had so little time, in all their lives together. So very little time to themselves. I must be a monster, she thought, to begrudge his talking about Joan now. But then his hand tightened on hers once more.

"Did I ever say 'I love you'?" He was getting sleepy. His eyes were starting to close.

"Often."

"I'd like to say it again."

"I think you just did." Perhaps it wasn't much, but she could remember that, whatever happened. She leaned forward to kiss his cheek, but his eyes had closed.

Paige was not waiting for her outside. The corridor was empty, but a woman sat by the elevators staring out at the evening sky. She had her back to Dan's room, her silver head erect, her body straight. Mary knew who she was before she saw her face.

They looked at each other in silence. Finally Joan moved over on the bench and indicated to Mary to sit down. "Is he all right?"

"Just going to sleep, I think. Have you been here long?"

"Twenty minutes. Half an hour." Joan dismissed the time spent waiting. "At first I was going to call the orderlies and have you thrown out. Bodily. But after sending Paige home in tears, I . . . I calmed down a bit."

"I think I would have felt the same. In your position."

"Only you're not in my position," Joan said, biting off the words sharply. "And you never will be."

"I know that." She hesitated, but Joan made no effort to speak again. "Don't blame the children, they were trying to do what was best."

"For you? Or for Dan?" There was anger in Joan's eyes. "Certainly they weren't thinking about me, their own mother. Nor was Lila. Oh, I got it out of her easily enough. I'm surprised she didn't call here to warn you. She must have known where I was going once I guessed the truth."

"Maybe she wanted us to meet."

Joan stared at her. The fierce, hot anger disappeared and something of a puzzled look came to her face, as if she had been outwitted and was not sure yet whether she wanted to be or not. "Why would she want that?"

"Because she knows how much I care about you. Because she knows Dan loves you."

" 'Love'! The magic word that's supposed to absolve everything? He loves me, but he goes to bed with you." This was Joan at her worst—brittle, cold, the hard, edgy malice she had inherited from her father.

"Did you really care that he went to bed with me?"

As swiftly as Mary had seen Paige's moods change as a child, the spite left Joan, no trace remaining, almost as if it had never existed. "Mary," she said finally, "why must you always ask the hardest questions?" She took a deep breath. "No, I suppose I didn't care what bed he was in, at least not enough to fight to get him back to mine." She shifted so she could face Mary directly. "I just didn't want it to be yours. That was betrayal. You were my friend. Some nameless stranger, some slut, some fool that he could lie to, somebody who might believe him if he said, 'My wife doesn't understand me' . . . that I could take. But not you. Whatever else I am, you know the truth and I *do* understand him. And love him."

"He always knew that."

"Did he say so? Did you talk about me? Did you lie together in bed and pass my secrets back and forth between you in the dark?" There was a desperate edge to Joan's voice. Mary saw now how much Dan's wife had suffered these past weeks, even more perhaps than she had. "That's what I've been thinking about all these months since the night Joey told me. I think it's driven me a little mad."

This was why Dan had asked her to look after Joan if anything happened. The woman next to her was as close to a breakdown as any patient Mary had ever seen. "Dan would never say anything against you, Joan. Nor would I. You must know that. He worried about you, as I do. He's still worrying." It would be hard to say what she must. It meant facing the reality of her life with both of them, but she owed this to Joan and she could not pretend otherwise. "Just now, he asked me, if anything happened to him, to look out for you, to help you."

"He said that?"

This was the last thing Joan had expected. All the way to the hospital she had seethed with anger, her worst fantasies of the life Mary and Dan had had together crystallized into the venom of this final betrayal she had discovered this evening in the people she had felt were so securely hers. She'd imagined deathbed wills, tearfully romantic scenes of lost years, with herself as the villainess who had kept them apart, even to Dan pleading to Mary that his family—no, his *wife*—was keeping him a prisoner. She had never thought they would be talking about her, caring about her.

"He knows I love you both," Mary said quietly. "I always have."

"I hated you." But Joan said the words without anger.

"I know. I don't blame you. I've hated myself often. Joey and Paige mean so much to me, to have them think I was some kind of trickster, using them—"

"Did he ever say he loved you?" Joan broke in. "Did he ever talk about divorce?" She reached out for Mary's hands, taking them into her own with the urgency of someone drowning. "Please, Mary. I have to know!"

All right, Mary, she thought. It can't matter to tell one more lie. Dan had asked her to help Joan. "Of course not, Joan. He's married to you. He would never want to change that."

"You accepted that? All these years?" Joan released her hands and leaned against the back of the small couch. "All this time I must have known it was you. No silly girl would have put up with that." She made herself stand. Mary would notice she was using the cane again, but that was because the evening had frightened her, and no matter how much she had recovered, she would always tire easily. "I'll go and see him now. Just to say good night." She looked at Mary. "I won't make any more scenes. If you want to see him again, I'll arrange that no one will be here between six and seven each evening."

"I don't think I should come back." Mary was surprised at what she had said, but she knew it was the only thing possible. "Perhaps . . . if you'll let me talk to him on the phone? Sometimes I can get patients out of bad moods." She smiled faintly. "At least I used to be able to."

Joan looked at her for a long moment. For the first time there was compassion in her eyes as she remembered the hours she had depended on Mary herself. The two of us, Joan thought. He needed us both, and we needed her. "You might call me," she said levelly. "I have bad moods too."

"Of course." Mary reached out and took Joan's free hand. The skin was almost as cold as her large diamond ring and platinum wedding band.

"We may be leaving soon," Joan went on, not taking her hand from Mary's. "There's talk of tests at Johns Hopkins . . . and there's a clinic in Switzerland where they're doing a new kind of bypass surgery. The doctors want me to go with him." She smiled briefly. "After all, I *do* know about hospitals. And sometimes Dan isn't very patient."

"He will be now, I think. With you there."

"If there is an operation, he should have a long rest. I thought, perhaps a cruise."

"That'll be good. For both of you."

"I meant that. About you seeing him."

Mary shook her head.

"I wouldn't have meant it before. That's why I had him brought here, rather than Midwestern. I was so jealous."

"You needn't be," said Mary. "Not ever again."

Joan was looking down the long corridor toward Dan's room. "I guess not. He really needs me, doesn't he? It's been such a long time. . . ."

Without saying goodbye, Joan started slowly down the hall. She did not look back. Mary did not expect it. She sat there without moving, thinking of the evening so long ago when Joan had confided her fear of not being the woman Dan would always love.

Only he had.

Twenty-one

Paige did not marry in June but during the first week of April, quietly, in the hospital chapel. Her parents were to leave that night for a formidable series of tests for Dan in the East, and Paige was determined they would see her properly married first. Dan was allowed to be present, sitting in a wheelchair, dressed in a suit and tie from the waist up, his pajama-clad legs covered with a blanket. Joey gave his sister away and remained at the small altar to act as Michael Harris's best man. There was no satin wedding gown or veil such as Paige had dreamed of when she was a little girl, no reception at an expensive hotel with champagne and an orchestra to play the first waltz for her to dance with her father. Paige discovered all that seemed unimportant.

Joan had arranged at the office for announcements of the wedding to be sent out after they had left. Whatever dreams she'd had of her only daughter's wedding day had to be canceled; there were only Michael's parents in the chapel and Lila Franklin. Joan thought of asking Mary, as she knew Paige had, but in the end she could not. Mary would understand when she got the announcement and the set of pictures Joan had arranged for the photographer to send to her. It was all she could make herself do.

Lila came to Mary's apartment after she had seen the Martins off at the airport. She didn't know what she could say to Mary, but she sensed this was not a day to leave her alone. In the end, it was Mary who comforted her, letting the older woman sob out her unhappiness about the family she had cared for for so long.

"Don't be sad, Lila," Mary said, as she held her. "Things have worked out the way they should." It was the first time she had ever seen the housekeeper break down; always she had been the symbol of sense and security.

"Mary, I just felt so . . . lost," Lila said as she mopped her eyes. "Watching that girl marry, seeing Mr. Dan looking so weak, him going off with Miss Joan and none of us knowing if he'll come back alive or what. I try to say to myself, 'They're just people you work for,' but it isn't true. You can't spend the hours you and I have worrying about a family and just walk away from them. The heart isn't made like that."

"No, Lila. But you know from your own family, when you love someone, someday you have to let them go."

"Can you? Can you let Mr. Dan go?"

"The part of him that will be the future . . . yes, finally, I think I'll have to let that go. But the years we had, they won't ever go. They're as much a part of us as the bones in our bodies." She smoothed Lila's strong black hair. "I don't mean just memories. We're different people because of what we've all been to each other. Dan and Joan, Joey, Paige, you . . . you've all helped make me different, as we've changed them." She smiled a little. "Maybe some of it I'd like to do over. Little things. Words I didn't speak. Thoughts I shouldn't have had."

"And regrets?" Lila looked at her with sad eyes.

"No, Lila." Mary was surprised at how calm her voice sounded. "No regrets."

It was a beautiful spring, or so it seemed to Mary. She tried as the days went on to understand what she was feeling, even to wondering why the fears and panic she had known when Dan was taken to the hospital did not reappear. He was still dangerously ill, although now at least she could be sure of hearing if his condition worsened. It was true she could not see him, but that was because Joan had taken him to Switzerland after the tests in the East. There were no letters. Perhaps she felt easier because it was only distance that kept them apart, not anger or jealousy or the rules they had all been raised to live by. In some way, he seemed safe now. Paige, happily married, made no further attempt to contact her; this she understood and accepted. It probably would have happened anyway, even if she had not learned of Mary's relationship with her father. Paige was a young bride, with a home to make and a husband to love. No healthy young woman, Mary knew, would want someone older around to advise her, whether she asked for it or not. Joey had gone back to school; he would spend the summer in the East. How he felt about Mary she suspected he did not even know himself. As she had told Dan, his son would grow older. There would be a time for forgiveness. Lila, having been given a paid vacation, closed down the apartment, going there only once a week to keep the rooms in the order she had maintained for so long. There were no lights in any of the windows in the evenings, and gradually Mary found herself no longer looking for them.

It should have been a lonely time for her, because so much of her life had been arranged around Dan and his family, his world, his problems. But somehow, as the weather grew warmer and the leaves came out on the park trees, Mary found herself feeling happier than she had for a long time. The happiness had none of the wild excitement she had known with Dan, the intimacy of their evenings in elegant restaurants, the warmth of their lovemaking, the nervous uncertainties of what mood he might be in when he called or arrived unexpectedly. All that spring those emotions seemed to have belonged to another person, in another life. She felt, in a strange way, free.

Not that she loved Dan any less, but it was becoming, in a way, remembrance. She tried sometimes as she walked home from work to pin down when her feelings had changed, deciding at last it must have been the evening she had talked with Joan, talked with her honestly, with nothing hidden between them. The lie she had told, she realized, was not really a lie. Dan *had* loved her, *had* talked about a divorce, but even as he had, Mary had known it could never happen. He was married to Joan, and that marriage was safe again and would be for the rest of their lives.

None of this happened at once. It was gradual, little things like deciding to cut her hair, which Dan had always wanted her to leave long. Or buying a new dress and realizing her first thought was, did she like it, not would he. The apartment needed painting, and for the first time Mary had the pleasure of using some of the money the airport stock had brought her. When the work was finished she found Dan's big chair seemed too large for her living room, and the heavy ashtrays and sturdy furniture he had liked looked out of place. As if it were an embarrassing secret, she consigned the things she thought of as his to the back bedroom. Whatever miracles might happen to him medically, she had the feeling he would never climb the stairs to her apartment again. It should have made her sad, letting him go, to become part of her past. Only it didn't. I'm acting like a widow, she thought to herself with some surprise one afternoon when she was packing his clothes away. As if he were already dead. For a moment she was frightened. Standing there, she smoothed the tweed jacket in her arms over and over, trying to recall how he had looked when he had worn it, where they had been, what they had said, but the memories were beginning to jumble together. When she closed the door of the back bedroom behind her, she felt less a sense of loss than a feeling of quiet peace.

I still love him, she thought. I always will. That can't change, not in a couple of weeks, or even months. Only it had changed, in some subtle shifting way she couldn't describe, not even to herself.

For the first time there were new people in her life. She had always remained on friendly if slightly distant terms with the other tenants in the building. It was *her* building, Dan had constantly told her, and she had the deed in the safety deposit box at the bank to prove it, but she still felt as much a tenant as any of them. None of her neighbors knew she owned the building. All the details were handled by the lawyer Dan had first hired. So she had nodded to the other tenants and smiled politely, but with Dan as part of her life, she knew she could not allow herself the time or the openness of friendship with them.

But as the days grew warmer she grew to know the people around her better, even to being invited to some of the parties given by the three artists on the top floor. They were all younger than she, but somehow it didn't seem to make as much difference as she had thought it would. The two sisters on the ground floor shyly admired her new hairstyle, and on impulse she invited them up for tea. She couldn't remember when she'd had outside guests before, but now, with no traces of a man in occupancy to raise questions, the meeting turned out to be the start of neighborly calls among all the people in her building. She had extra days besides her vacation due to her, and she took them during the spring months, finding she did not miss the routine of the hospital office as much as she had expected. Filling out a form that June she realized that, in one capacity or another, she'd spent twenty years at Midwestern. People younger than she were leaving their jobs. It was a shock to realize she was older than Mrs. Denning, the woman who had preceded her, when she had elected to retire.

It was a surprising thought for Mary, the idea of retirement. She had naturally expected to continue working for another twelve or fifteen years at the least. But one afternoon she carefully went through the folder of the investments Dan had made for her; these plus the income she was receiving as owner of the two buildings made her realize she could live more than comfortably if she never worked again for the rest of her life. She had no intention of quitting, of course. For one thing, she had no idea what she would do with her time. But gradually that time became more fully occupied than it had at any other period of her life. Before there had only been Dan, with the unexpected changes in his schedule to which she had to adjust. Before Dan there had been marriage, and before that her parents to take care of each day before and after work.

Now there was only herself to please. If she felt like a slice of pizza and an early movie, there was no one waiting for her to object. If she wanted to meet Patsy and her friends for a Saturday of shopping, there was no phone call she would be missing. Even as a schoolgirl she had never enjoyed such freedom, she confided to Lila over dishes one Sunday when the housekeeper had her to her home for dinner.

That dinner became a permanent source of laughter to them both afterward. Mary wanted to bring something as a gift but felt any attempt to buy flowers or candy would look patronizing, and she had a strong suspicion Lila did not approve of wine. So for the first time in years she decided to bake a cake. Baking had been something that, in the past, women like her sister-in-law did; Mary, working, had fed her mother and later Jack on what she could pick up in a store on the way home. But with a huge cookbook and what seemed an enormous number of pans and dishes, she decided to try. It took three attempts before the cake even looked like a cake, and she could only hope it tasted better than the previous two failures. She transported it carefully by taxi to the South Side, and while Lila stared at her with a rather dubious look, she served it proudly. One bite and both women shot eat other a startled look. "I think a little too much salt?" Lila said, trying to keep her face expressionless, but when she saw Mary roar with laughter she let herself relax and the two of them laughed until they cried. Orin, Lila's husband, stubbornly insisted the cake was perfect and even took a second helping, which reduced the two of them again to giggling. It was so good to laugh again, Mary thought.

Somehow she had half expected to see more of Jack that spring, with the Martins away from Chicago. She accepted every invitation now from Tim and Patsy, but Jack was seldom there. Then one day he called her, inviting her to a barbecue "to celebrate his new house." That sounded ominously like a man who might be ready to announce another marriage, and Mary found herself curious as to which of the single women who hung on his every word the previous winter it was. After all, Jack was a good-looking, interesting man with a successful business. If he was contemplating marriage, any woman would be honored.

This time she persuaded Lila to help her attempt a party gift, and together the two women prepared a large basket of various homemade cookies. Mary would have been surprised if she had known what Lila was thinking, what any woman who knew her might think: that she was making a determined effort to appear domestic. She must still like that man, Lila thought to herself as she and Mary worked together, and the thought gave her happiness. Lila had few letters from the Martins, and no indication of when they might return to Chicago.

The only real news Mary had of them came from Kay Wallis. Kay had written her a long chatty letter the week before, and as they waited for the baking to cool, Mary showed it to Lila. Kay had heard from Joan; apparently Dan had survived a heart-bypass operation, and they would be vacationing the rest of the summer in Europe. It was only at the end of the letter that Kay talked of her own life. Apparently Denver had been good to her. She had her own real estate office and (as she wrote)

If you can believe it, a gentleman friend. He's older than I am, which makes him no dashing hero. Retired, and his own insurance business, wife dead and children raised and on their own. To my enormous surprise, he absolutely seems to dote on me, can't think why, as I'm no younger, thinner, or prettier than I was when I left Chicago. His kids are pushing for us to get married. I have a feeling that, with old age approaching, they're scared he might turn into an invalid and they'd have to look after him and would rather I did. Frankly, I suspect he'll bury them all; he's got more energy than even Dan had in the old days. He's got me to take up golf and is talking about our going to Palm Springs for a month this winter. As for marriage, I'm not committing myself just yet, but don't be surprised if I write someday and sign the letter "Mrs. Hubert Eldon."

"Sounds like she's happy," Lila remarked as she returned the letter. "I'm glad."

"I'm glad, too, Lila. It's nice to know you can make a new life for yourself at any age."

"Yes, it is, Mrs. Conroy," said Lila, pointedly using Mary's full name. She didn't have to look at Mary's face to know she was blushing; besides, it was time to turn off the oven.

The Sunday of the barbecue was bright and clear, cooler than usual for July in Chicago but warm enough to make an outdoor affair pleasant. Patsy and Tim picked Mary up, and they drove out to the suburb where Jack lived and worked. It was north of the part of the city where the airport land was, but Mary was constantly reminded of Dan's last talk with her. Here were the homes he had thought of as "the step between," the step he had missed in life. Peaceful, quiet streets, with small neat front lawns and large back yards; one-story houses, most of them, with flowers along the fences and carefully trimmed hedges. Over the years she had probably passed hundreds of houses like these without thinking, but today they made her unexpectedly sad. For if Dan had missed this secure, peaceful life, hadn't she?

She tried to recall the wonderful times she had had with Dan as she sat in the back seat of Tim's car, but they didn't seem to belong with this summer Sunday. She didn't want to think of Dan today, but he kept intruding in her thoughts as they passed street after street of cheerful homes. There's no reason to be sad, she told herself firmly. I've missed nothing I really wanted, or could have had. But she knew if she had been alone she would have turned around and gone back to her apartment. It was just Kay's letter, she decided, as they neared their destination. That and the fact that Jack might have found some new woman. Men who intend to stay single didn't live in suburbs and give outdoor parties. It's Kay and Jack . . . that's why I feel like I did when we were kids and played musical chairs and I got left out. I'm just feeling sorry for myself. I'm going to stop it right now. I'm healthy and financially secure and I'm making new friends, and I don't need anything else.

Only she couldn't shake off the feeling of loss.

The party turned out to be fun. She was amazed at the number of people the house held, with the yard behind it, amazed also that Jack had in the few years since his return made so many good friends. But he had always had that knack, and today there would be no uneasiness among any of them about money owed or promises broken. The house was handsome, not any larger than the others on each side, but beautifully designed and full of Jack's careful work with wood. The paneled living room might have seemed too grand for such a house, but he had done it in light shades and the room was both cool and comfortable. An extension for his shop had been added to the garage, and they toured it dutifully. It was a pleasure to see how Jack's face lit up as he touched the work he was doing, his hands strong and firm as he explained to them how a stair rail could be curved or a cabinet door made to fit imperceptibly to cover shelves.

Outside in the yard and through the house there were people Mary's age and many younger, but she noticed no special woman who seemed to be acting as hostess. She was relieved to see that young and older women had also thought as she had and brought covered dishes of their own favorite recipes, obviously not trusting any single man to feed the crowd he had invited. Their husbands were gathered around the barbecue fires and the two huge kegs of cold beer set out on the grass. Babies were crawling on blankets spread out under the three trees, and a vigorous game of tag was going on among the older children. This is what you should have, Jack, Mary thought, as she talked with the people she knew. This is what you should always have had. And she knew, even as she thought it, that serious as Dan might have been in examining his life in the hospital, he would never have been happy here.

But I could be!

The thought so stunned her, she excused herself and went into the house, hoping there might be some quiet place where she could be alone for a moment to think out what had just occurred to her. There was no way she could explain it away as a sentimental moment, tell herself that all this was just a picture used a dozen times in every American magazine to advertise some product, the romantic view of the happy modern life. It was more than that, and she would be less than honest if she didn't face it, question it, and try to understand and place it beside her own life in the proper perspective.

A friendly woman in the kitchen asked her if she knew where there were more platters. Mary stepped into what had obviously been designed as a pantry and started searching among the shelves. Keep busy, she told herself. Leave all the self-examination for when you're back in your own apartment tonight. She reached for a platter on the top shelf. As she held it, something about the pattern of the china seemed familiar. She realized suddenly it was the same design she and Jack had used during their marriage, her mother's china.

"I couldn't find a complete set," Jack said quietly. He had filled the doorway behind her before she realized she was no longer alone. "I guess they don't make it any more. But when I saw this, I had to have it." She leaned against the shelves, her shoulders shaking. "Hey! I didn't mean to make you unhappy!"

"You didn't," she managed. I won't cry. *I will not cry!*

"Mary? Do you like the house?"

This she could answer without making a fool of herself. "It's beautiful!" she enthused. "Handsome and right for you. Not to mention a wonderful showcase of your craftsmanship. There isn't anybody who wouldn't want to live in a house like this."

"Would you?" he asked bluntly. He had closed the door to the kitchen, and they were alone in the small room. He took her right hand, fingering the wedding ring she had moved there after their divorce. "I'd like to put this back on the hand where it belongs." His smile was a little tentative, but while she could see hesitancy in his eyes, fearing her answer, she saw beyond that there was still the love he had offered her so many years before. Something he saw in her kept her from having to answer, for he held her close, kissing her gently over and over again, comforting her tears as if she were a lost child.

From that day on, he saw or called her at least every other day. If he had been diffident in his courtship in the months before, he more than made up for it the rest of that summer. Never again did he bring up the subject of marriage, at least not specifically. He knew she was still torn between her feelings for Dan and her own uncertainties, and if he had shown patience in his first courtship, he seemed to redouble his efforts this time. There was no pressure, no demanding she choose between the two men she had known and loved in her life. It's because we're older, she thought. But she knew that was not the reason. He had made his love clear to her, he had offered her a chance at a new life, a new beginning, and he was content to wait until she could make her choice freely and securely by herself. *She* would have to come to him, if that was what she wanted, bringing the dowry she had not brought before, the gift of genuine love. He too had been hurt, and she knew he was too healthy in his mind and life to face having just part of her, simply because they were both lonely.

They went out together as often as he could persuade her. There were quiet evenings when they went dancing in the open-air gardens of restaurants in the older sections of town. There were parties with other couples their own age, not just Tim and Patsy. For once Tim said nothing of their new relationship; Patsy had clearly spoken firmly to him, and neither of them indulged in any heavy-handed attempts at humor about whether they were going to remarry or not. Mary still had the freedom she had just begun to enjoy, but she realized how much happier it was to have freedom and also have someone to enjoy it with.

Late in October the Martins returned.

Twenty-two

Lila had warned her first, calling to say she had heard from them and she was to make the Lake Shore Drive apartment ready for their arrival. In the week that followed, Mary grew increasingly nervous. There was nothing she needed to worry about, she told herself. There was no reason for them to call her or want to see her, and yet somehow she knew it would happen, that their lives had been too entangled for all of them just to drift apart. Lila called her the night they had returned, knowing Mary would be anxious for news.

"He looks fine, Mary," she said on the telephone. "Very tan. He's still too thin for my liking, and he doesn't move fast any more the way he did. But anybody seeing him would say he was healthy."

"Only you think he isn't?"

"I'm not sure." Lila hesitated, trying to find the right words. "Maybe it's the way Miss Joan treats him. She seems to be watching him all the time and trying not to let him know."

"How is she?"

The relief to Lila of being on safer grounds was obvious, even over the phone. "She looks just grand, Mary. Not scrawny any more like she was getting. Not embarrassed to use her cane either, if she feels tired." She paused once more. "But . . . I don't know, Mary. They're different people somehow. You know before there was always talk . . . from both of them . . . of something they would be doing tomorrow or next week or next month. Plans for some kind of party or business thing or something. They don't talk like that now. Paige and her husband came for dinner. Paige is going to have a baby—"

"She must be so happy."

"She's glowing, and that boy she married is just as pleased as can be. But Mr. Dan and Miss Joan, they just sort of smiled politely, as if it didn't have anything to do with them. Oh, they were enthusiastic about it, and they all had champagne, but it was sort of like they were just passing through here, not really settling in." She hesitated again. "Does this make any sense to you?"

"I think so. They've been through a lot, Lila, and they've been through it together. That makes for a bond. That's what we were hoping for, wasn't it?"

"I don't know, Mary." Lila sounded dubious. "Sometimes when I pray for all of you at night, I just don't know what to pray for any more."

"Maybe we should all just pray for what we need. And not be greedy for anything else," she added.

The following Friday Joan called.

"Mary, it's Joan Martin."

"Welcome back." There was a control in Joan's voice that kept Mary from letting herself be more enthusiastic.

"Thank you." She had obviously planned this telephone conversation in advance; her voice sounded stilted and her words were said in a way that made Mary realize they had been carefully rehearsed. "I . . . I was wondering if you'd care to come and see us. I mean, we were both wondering, Dan and I."

"Of course. How is he? How are you both?"

Joan's voice took on an edgy brittleness. "Oh, nothing can kill me. And Dan—well, all the doctors seem to think . . . why not let me tell you about it tomorrow? You can see for yourself. Are you free?"

Saturday Mary had planned to spend with Jack, a last picnic planned by one of their friends, and Mary was already busy fixing the food she would bring. But she knew Joan might not have the courage or kindness to ask her again if she refused. Jack would understand.

"I can be." They set a time, in the early afternoon—"before Dan's nap," Joan explained—and Mary realized the word was not said for effect, to point out how ill he had been or might still be, but simply as an accepted fact, one his wife had learned to live with during the spring and summer.

Jack listened to her vague excuses for not letting him pick her up, only breaking in at the end. "You're going to see them, aren't you?" There was no question whom he meant.

"I have to, Jack."

"All right." He sounded noncommittal. "You do what you have to, Mary. Maybe it's better this way." He gave her the address of the party and the time they were expected, not revealing any of his feelings in the rest of the conversation. Mary could not even tell if he was disappointed in her.

The following day was clear and sunny, with a crisp breeze coming off the lake. The trees had started to turn. Summer was over and autumn had begun. Mary dressed carefully for this meeting, wondering, not for the first time since the phone call, whether it was Dan's approval she sought or Joan's. It seemed strange to walk into the lobby of their apartment building again. The doorman recognized her and waved her past, not reaching for the house phone until she had entered the elevator. She found herself dreading the meeting, although she could not give herself any specific reason. They'd all known each other for such a long, long time. There would be no scenes or recriminations. The time for anger must surely be over.

It was Dan who opened the door. He was thinner, as Lila had warned her, but not with the gaunt, emaciated look he had had in the hospital. Instead, he seemed almost dapper, in a beautifully cut navy blazer and gray slacks, clothes she had never seen him wear before. But they would be new, she realized, tailored for his thinner body. His hair was now completely white, but against his tan face it made him even more handsome than she had remembered. Oh, Dan, she thought in the awkward moment as they stood in the hallway, of course I fell in love with you; what woman wouldn't?

He smiled, as if once more he had guessed what she was thinking, and stepped forward to kiss her gently on the cheek. "It's good to see you, Mary. Come in. Joan's in the living room."

He closed the door behind her and followed her into the long room that spread across the whole apartment. She hasn't changed, he thought. She was still the same tender woman he had fallen in love with years before. He wondered about their meeting today. He would not have suggested it six months before, but since Joan . . . but they were in the room now and Joan was coming forward to greet Mary.

"You look wonderful, Mary," Joan said with a genuine smile. "You've cut your hair. I like it."

"And you've let yours grow." Mary couldn't help smiling. Dan may have been ready for death, but his preference as to the appearance of the women in his life were still strong. Joan did look well, as Lila had told her. The gauntness of the past few years had disappeared. With her silver hair in a stylish twist at the back of her head and in a softly colored dress she looked ten years younger than her age, as beautiful as when Mary had first met her. "It's very becoming, your hair."

"Thank you. Dan's orders, as you've probably guessed."

"I've never ordered any woman to do anything," he protested, but with both of them smiling at him, he relaxed and grinned back. "Get you anything, Mary? A drink or a cup of tea? It's Lila's day off, but I still mix a good martini."

She caught a sudden worried look in Joan's eyes. "No, thank you. It's too early for me to drink, and I don't really feel like tea."

"Dan? Why don't you have your rest now? Mary and I have a lot to talk about."

"Being sent out of the room like a child," he grumbled, but he made no further protest, just touching Mary's shoulder lightly as he passed her. "Don't you disappear now. I'll be back in half an hour." He stopped at the doorway and looked back at Joan. "Which is it this time, the pink pill or the green one?"

"The green one."

He nodded and went down the hall to his room. Mary felt awkward, alone with Joan. She had hoped this meeting would be short and relaxed, a happily married couple, the husband recovered in health, a pleasant discussion of their travels and the news of Paige's pregnancy. She should have been prepared that it would never be that simple between them.

"He looks well," she said at last, breaking the silence.

"Does he? I can't tell sometimes." The false cheerfulness was gone from Joan's voice, and her eyes were sad.

"The operation? The bypass? Kay wrote me—"

"It was a failure." Joan said the words quietly, although they had both heard the door to Dan's room close behind him. "He survived it all right, and they managed some sort of patch-up job, but he seems to be having trouble with the implants. That's why he's not supposed to be out of bed too long. Or have more than one very mild drink a day. Or walk upstairs."

Mary wondered if Joan was thinking of her apartment three blocks away and the long flight of steps. She had been right to put away his clothes; Dan would never come to her again. "Is there anything they can do?" It was not just for him she worried. She could see the lines of tension in Joan's face under her careful makeup. "Lots of people have bad hearts; they keep discovering new techniques every day."

"They won't help Dan." Joan rubbed her forehead. "Don't you think I've tried everything? Every doctor? Every clinic? I've called or written letters to everybody I've ever heard of all the way around the world. We've tried every test, every medicine. They're going to try a heart transplant next . . . that's why we'll be leaving for Arizona in a few days. Dan has to rest first. He can't take too much traveling."

"It's that bad?"

"He's going to die, Mary." Joan said the words flatly. "There hasn't been a doctor I've talked to for the last three months who's held out any hope. It may be weeks or months or maybe even as long as a couple of years if we're lucky, but it's final."

Impulsively, Mary moved to where Joan sat on the long couch and took her hands. "Joan . . ." There was nothing else she could say. Joan sat in silence, not moving away from Mary, allowing herself to be comforted by her touch.

"It's all over, Mary," she said finally. "His life. And mine." She freed her hands. "That's why I wanted to see you, why we both did. Because it's an ending for you, too."

"I don't matter in this."

"Of course you do," Joan said calmly. "He loves you. Since he's dying, more than at any other time he needs you. That's why we both want you to come with us to Arizona. He'll need a nurse. He'll need people he loves. He's so frightened." Her eyes were suddenly shiny with tears. "Our wonderful strong Dan is frightened. I've got to help him. Any way I can. We both do."

"Joan, you can't want me with you! Not after all that's happened, all you know."

"I want what will make Dan happy!" The tears slid down her face unchecked, but her voice was strong. "If he has to die, I want to give him courage and strength and love. You can do that. Yes. Finally, I can say it. You love him as much as I do. If you can bring him peace, then I want you with us."

"Does he know about this? How you feel? That you were going to ask me?"

"We talked about it. I should tell you, he wasn't in favor of it, not at first. He has his pride. He doesn't want you seeing him grow more feeble each day. But he's thought of you. Knowing I couldn't upset him, we made ourselves talk about it calmly. I understand a lot more than I ever did before."

"Because at last he can turn to you." The words came out before Mary realized she had thought them. "You're the one who can help him now, not me."

"Both of us, Mary. Without jealousy or anger. You told me he had asked you to look after me, if anything happened to him. Well, it's happened." Her voice weakened. "Don't desert me, Mary! I don't know how much more I can take. Don't desert either of us."

Mary felt as if she couldn't breathe. It meant the end of any chance she might have of a life of her own, whether with Jack or not. He would never understand her going off with them for however little time there was. Rather, he would understand completely. But how could he forget she had put Dan once more ahead of him in their lives? There was an end even to his patience and, what was worse, an end to his belief that she could let Dan become part of her past, to make a future that would be theirs alone.

Only Joan was right, she could not desert them. She could help them, both of them. All the love she had held for Dan over the years was pulling inside her until she found herself finding it hard to think. She wanted to see Dan again, to be with him, to help him along this last corridor of life that remained for him to travel.

It was the hardest decision she would ever have to make, and she knew it. She could afford to leave her job. Dan had given her that gift by making her independent. She would probably leave it anyway, if she were to marry Jack. There were no other claims on her other than the two people who loved her. The three people, she reminded herself, for she knew the closeness she had with Joan was still there, under the tension and hurt that had brought her to making this offer.

"I don't belong with you, Joan," she said at last. "I never did. I was a small part of his life. And yours. Whatever else happened . . . was by accident. You have your marriage, your life with him. I had no right to make myself part of that. Not then. And not now."

"Suppose I'd died? Suppose he'd divorced me? You'd be his wife. You'd never leave him to face this alone."

"I'm not his wife, Joan! I'm not angry about that. Don't think that. It was never possible."

"What if it could be?" Joan sat very straight, tears gone; it was a question she had thought about all the months since that night Joey had come to her. That night she had been willing to fight, to kill for Dan. But he didn't need that, not now. "Would that make you agree? I could divorce him so the two of you could be married. You could be together at last."

"You can't mean that! Never!" Too many things were happening too fast. Mary knew she should stop and consider her words, the wrong ones could hurt so deeply, but there was no time. "Joan, I've realized something these last months. Maybe I haven't thought it out clearly before, but I'm trying now. If Dan had been totally free, I still wouldn't have married him." The other woman looked at her, eyes wide, full of questions and an almost hurt pride. "Yes, I loved Dan. I respected him, I admired him, I still do, I always will. But I could never have married him. I understand that now. For the first time, I guess. That's the reason why I never felt cheated of anything. Maybe he thought I was just being generous. Maybe that's what you thought. It isn't true. I couldn't have made a life with him, not a whole life. We're too different. That hasn't changed, no matter how badly hurt he is now. He's too powerful, too overwhelming for someone like me." She put her hand on Joan's shoulder, almost as Dan had touched her when he left the room. "He was right to marry you, Joan. You were the wife he needed, the woman he loved and admired, the only one who could be his match."

"But I wasn't."

"You became frightened. I don't think you're frightened any more. I know you're suffering, I know how deeply you love him. Any wife who could make an offer like you've just done . . . don't you see? You love him more than I do, you always have. I may have hurt you in the past, but to come with you now, to be even a small part of the last of his life, that would be the worst thing I could do to both of you. You must understand that."

"I don't know what I understand any more. Not about love or marriage. None of the old rules seem to matter. All I know is he loves you and misses you. And if I can make him happy, I'll give you to him, just as I'd give him the last drop of my blood."

"He doesn't need that, Joan. And he doesn't need me. He needs you, your strength, your courage. He needs the beautiful girl he married, who's become a strong, beautiful woman. He needs the home he makes with you, wherever you go. I've already become part of his past; didn't you feel that when he was here, in this room? We're friends now, just friends. To try and make me anything more would torture all of us. We can't let that happen."

"It sounds as if there's someone else in your life." Joan tried to say it lightly, but she couldn't hide the break in her voice. "So soon?"

"Jack," Mary said. She could see from Joan's expression the name meant nothing to her.

"The gambler?" Joan *had* remembered. "He's come back?"

"He's not a gambler; in a way he never was. Unless you'd call Dan that." Mary hesitated. The thought that had just come into her mind stunned her. "Joan, I think maybe I've only loved one man in my life. He just had two different names."

"You'll marry him again?"

"Perhaps. But even if Jack hadn't come back, I couldn't go with you." She made herself walk over to the long windows, looking at the drive and the lake below as she had so many times in the past. "It was never just Dan I loved. It was you and Joey and Paige, the family I never had. You let me move into it. I'll always be grateful for that. As I am for having had some small share in Dan's life. But not the largest share. That was always yours."

Joan came to stand beside her. Together they watched the afternoon sun shining on water below, the small boats making straight trails as they moved swiftly through the water. The trails we all leave behind our lives, Mary thought, only ours don't disappear so easily. She spoke softly now.

"Let me go, Joan. Be generous. Be kind. You've always been that to me. Let me have the rest of my life without feeling guilty. Please? Let me go."

Joan studied her. Dan would understand, she thought. She hadn't been lying about his being ashamed of being ill. He wasn't, not with her; these past months they had been through too much together for that to matter. If only she could have allowed him to share part of her pain after the accident and the miscarriage. What had Dr. Keinser said so many years before? That we cannot be what we were yesterday; all we can do is find out what we can be tomorrow. She alone would see Dan through the last of his life. She could do it with the strength and courage and peace Mary had given both of them. They were a married couple: not as she had wanted them to be in the bad years, desperately trying to stay the young bride for the handsome husband who had been so deeply in love with her; that time was gone, would have gone no matter what had happened, only she hadn't been wise enough to understand. But there were days ahead, few as they might be, and they would be just for the two of them.

"I'll call you," Joan said at last. "If there's any change. If anything . . . bad happens."

"Thank you. And come back? Please, Joan? None of us have that many friends in our lives that we can afford to lose the best."

Mary left, not waiting to see Dan again, not needing to, confident she had at last made the right choice, a choice that never should have been hers to make. The elevator stopped on a lower floor to let some people on, and she wished they would hurry.

Jack would be waiting.

Epilogue ᴈ⌾ℰ

You can see them in many places, although perhaps in a city they might be less noticeable. In cities, three people at a table is not so unusual a sight. At resorts, on cruises to the Caribbean, or hotels where it is cool in the summer, they are a bit more obvious.

They are always two women and a man, about the same age. They tend to stick together on trips, even if they are placed at a table for six or seven. It's not that they are standoffish or "grand"; it's just they seem to like each other's company. One of them will bring out a letter or a clipping from a news magazine, and they will discuss it eagerly through dinner. Even without that, they always seem to have a great deal to say to each other.

They are not distant to their fellow travelers. On the contrary, they seem to enjoy meeting new people, even to using the excuse of needing a fourth for bridge. They are not closed off on a tour or a ship, or a day excursion to a place that at least one of them has never been before. Attractive, friendly, they are almost urgent in their curiosity, exchanging guidebooks with others, anxious not to miss any point of interest. There is this feeling they will not come to these places again.

If you talk to them over a drink, you will find them, perhaps, almost boringly predictable. The man is of that age where, if he is not retired, he has enough competent assistants to run his firm without his loss being missed that much. There is the cheerful woman who makes them laugh, less attractive than the other. The beautiful woman, or at least she was once and still holds that territory as her right, is not as strong as the other two. She will use a cane sometimes, or even the portable wheelchair they take with them everywhere. She is not an invalid. With sturdy shoes and the man's arm, she can climb to any historic site the other two feel should be seen.

The first impression a stranger has is that this is a married couple and the sister of one of them. But who is married to whom, and who is the sister? Most people traveling as they do don't think of such things, for these three move in a world of people who have solved the problems of life. The men have gray hair, although some of it is barely visible. Their wives have tinted glasses for their evening gowns, the frames the exact shade of their eyeshadow. With these couples will be pictures of grandchildren and (sometimes) of disappointing daughters- and sons-in-law, but this trio reveals nothing. They smile politely and discuss the next day's excursion.

It is only when names are exchanged at the end of the voyage or on checking out of the hotel that the other people understand their relationships. The cheerful woman called Mary is married to that nice Mr. Conroy who danced with every woman at his table.

The other woman, the widow, is a Mrs. Martin, who is simply an old friend.